ALSO BY JENEANE O'RILEY

The Infatuated Fae

How Does It Feel?
What Did You Do?
Where Did You Go?
Can You Take It?

A SECRET IN THE GARDEN

JENEANE O'RILEY

Bloom books

Copyright © 2026 by Jeneane O'Riley
Cover and internal design © 2026 by Sourcebooks
Cover design by Antoaneta Lisak/Sourcebooks
Cover images © fotograzia/Getty Images, Artemisia1508/Getty Images, Volodymyr TVERDOKHLIB/Shutterstock, Abigail210986/Getty Images, Tarzhanova/Getty Images, naropano/Getty Images, Jackyenjoyphotography/Getty Images, GarryKillian/Getty Images
Internal design by Diane Cunningham/Sourcebooks
Internal image © pichet khunchiang/Getty Images

Sourcebooks, Bloom Books, and the colophon are registered trademarks of Sourcebooks.

All rights reserved. No part of this book may be reproduced in any form or by any electronic or mechanical means including information storage and retrieval systems—except in the case of brief quotations embodied in critical articles or reviews—without permission in writing from its publisher, Sourcebooks.

No part of this book may be used or reproduced in any manner for the purpose of training artificial intelligence technologies or systems.

The characters and events portrayed in this book are fictitious or are used fictitiously. Any similarity to real persons, living or dead, is purely coincidental and not intended by the author.

All brand names and product names used in this book are trademarks, registered trademarks, or trade names of their respective holders. Sourcebooks is not associated with any product or vendor in this book.

Published by Bloom Books, an imprint of Sourcebooks
1935 Brookdale RD, Naperville, IL 60563-2773
(630) 961-3900
sourcebooks.com

Cataloging-in-Publication data is on file with the Library of Congress.

The authorized representative in the EEA is Dorling Kindersley
Verlag GmbH. Arnulfstr. 124, 80636 Munich, Germany

Manufactured in the UK by Clays and distributed
by Dorling Kindersley Limited, London
001-357434-Feb/26
10 9 8 7 6 5 4 3 2 1

For those who have carried a pain no one can see, who have buried wounds in the depths of your shadows—this story is for you.

PLAYLIST

"Michelle"—Bear McCreary
"Some Dreams You Never Wake Up From"—Valerie Broussard
"Fragile Thing" (acoustic version)—Winona Oak
"Dancing with Your Ghost"—Sasha Alex Sloan
"Punish"—Ethel Cain
"his land"—Paris Paloma
"A Dangerous Thing"—AURORA
"Devil I Know"—Allie X
"Für Elise"—Faouzia
"God Needs the Devil"—Jonah Kagen
"Broken"—Jonah Kagen
"trouble"—Camylio
"over me"—Camylio
"Another Love"—Tom Odell
"I Found"—Amber Run

TRIGGER WARNING

This story, at its core, is about healing and contains themes that may be difficult for some readers, such as guns, bones, dead bodies, loss of a loved one, ghosts, blood, mental health issues, abandonment, grief, narcissistic behavior, abuse from a parent, spiders, suicidal concerns, mentions of chiseled jaw clenches, sex scenes, heights, and violence.

Help is available
- 988 Suicide and Crisis Lifeline
- National Suicide Prevention Lifeline: Call 1-800-273-TALK (8255)
- National Domestic Violence Hotline: Call 1-800-799-SAFE (7233)
- Love is Respect: Call 1-866-331-9474 or text LOVEIS to 22522
- Rape, Abuse & Incest National Network: Call 1-800-656-HOPE (4673)
- ADAA, Anxiety & Depression Association of America https://adaa.org/find-help/support/support-groups
- NAMI: National Alliance on Mental Illness https://www.nami.org/

CHAPTER 1

ELIZA

NEEDING TO BEG A MURDERER FOR A FAVOR WAS HARD enough without worrying about a lack of guardrails. No one thought about guardrails or salmonella until it was too late; they were merely an afterthought. I was thinking about them both now, mainly the guardrails, though the mystique of salmonella poisoning was never far from my thoughts as a tightly budgeted woman in STEM who liked to push the boundaries of expiration dates, and they were intermingling with thoughts of him—especially as I looked over the cliffside.

The road I had been driving coiled round the mountainside like an asphalt serpent, twisting and turning, snaking through the dark forest of looming pines, hazy with smoky-gray fog.

I shifted, my spine so rigid I feared it would slice itself from my overwhelmed skin and fall back on the charcoal gray upholstery of my Nissan Leaf. I made a mental note to write a scathing letter to the state's department of transportation about their glaring disregard for safety and lack of foresight in addressing basic infrastructure needs—such as the installation of guardrails. Better yet, I'd have my mother call them. She loved yelling at people.

As a child, I had never been allowed to go to amusement parks because of their energy consumption of nonrenewable sources and water use, so maybe it was lucky for me I was driving on what may as well have been a roller coaster. I wondered if my screams would sound the same as those from people on the big drops of Millennium Force or Steel Vengeance when I plummeted to my untimely death as I took the next curve *with no fucking guardrails*!

My stomach growled and twisted. I considered grabbing my water bottle, but my tightened fingers were currently locked onto the steering wheel in a way that caused me to believe they were now permanent fixtures.

My phone rang in the open leather fanny pack on the passenger seat, and I screamed.

A real daredevil, I risked a half-second glance at my phone, recoiling slightly when my mother's name appeared. She was probably tracking me again—or she knew I had contraband on me. I looked longingly at the bottle of Dasani water in the cupholder. If I didn't call her in the next twenty minutes, she would start calling me repeatedly. And then things would get bad—another quick glance at the phone.

You need both hands on the wheel. You can't call her right now.

My eyes snagged on the headline of the newspaper under my phone: "Hester Blackwood Spotted Alive in Florida Outside Local Psychiatrist's Office."

I shook my head; they would do anything they could to keep Hester and Darius Blackwood in the papers—tabloids, more like. But I hadn't been able to resist buying it since I was headed to see their infamous son.

The anxious thrum in my body doubled as my car crawled around the edge of another tight curve, my stomach twisting again as I looked at the clock. I had eight minutes to answer my mother's now continuous calls before she would call Andrew, the owner of my tiny apartment as well as my neighbor. He worked with my mother and was all too happy to report when I left the house outside of my normal work hours.

The urge to get off this winding mountain was outweighed for the briefest of seconds by the thought of my mom waiting at my apartment when I got home—*if* I got home. How many ridiculous things were going to ramp up my anxiety today?

As if in response, I saw that the rain from earlier in the day had dampened the asphalt, creating a slick sheen that caused my tires to slide a bit on the narrow path and make a soft whirring noise as the residual water splashed the undercarriage of my car. I cracked the window and took a deep breath as my car filled with the scent of hot asphalt, rain, and crisp mountain air. I wasn't used to this kind of driving—narrow, treacherous roads where the cliff on one side seemed to stretch down endlessly, threatening to plummet me to the bottom with a single misstep—but there was no choice now. There was no turning back.

Politics and issues over the new mayor of Pinehurst had caused several of the botanical garden's biggest benefactors to stop their donations. And being that I was the newest on the team—last one in meant first one out—I was holding on to this final thread of hope that I could save my job. I had only been there a few short years, and though I was competent and did my job well, I was far from being so good that they wouldn't let me go if push came to shove. I needed to bring something to the gardens that made it *impossible* to fire me—and hopefully make up for the funds we had lost.

The road tightened into one lane. I doubted it mattered, since no one else but the Blackwoods lived this high up, but still, it sent a current of fear through my already taut and frayed nerves. My hands shook through their death grip on the steering wheel, my onyx ring digging into my middle finger; it was supposed to bring the wearer protection. I had the feeling an onyx suit couldn't protect me from the man I was about to see.

Afraid to blink for too long, my dry eyes were locked on the road ahead in the hopes of seeing any other cars before it would be too late. Though, where was I going to go if I saw another car up here? There was no pulling over unless I planned to nosedive over the ledge and rain down on Pinehurst.

As if angry mothers, cliffs, and slick one-lane mountain roads weren't enough, the fog rolled in from the valley below, thickening the air around me like ghoulish clouds until it swallowed everything in view outside of the car windows. My fog lights barely pierced the mist, their pale beams illuminating only a few feet ahead. Seeing around the large, choppy stone wall of the mountain as the car climbed the road was difficult enough, but this fog was unforgiving and doom-laden.

Like a shadow rising from the depths of the earth, Blackwood Manor appeared. My stomach suddenly threatened to empty its contents onto my lap.

Dear God, please let my stomach settle before I have to get out of this car and act like I know what I'm doing.

The manor's silhouette loomed through the mist, a collection of towers and spires crowned with dark rooftops. It gave the appearance of another world risen from some ancient, forgotten age. And I suppose it had.

The outer walls of the giant estate stood tall, made of a dark charcoal and slate stone that shimmered lightly in the damp air as if the house were alive, pulsing with a hostile energy all its own. The wail of the wind pushed at my car like a veiled threat; the high-pitched howl was an unsettling reminder of the isolation that clung to the antiquated castle-like estate.

The manor was an architectural phenomenon built against the mountain's side, but the Gothic structure itself appeared preternatural and unyielding, as if it were usurping the mountain instead of the other way around. It was a proud beast of a mansion with its rear facade suspended over the abyss, latched onto the stone cliff like an unrelenting barnacle on a giant humpback whale. The majority of it was out of my view, shielded by the fog, but the dark, jagged outline of spires peeking through was enough to make goose bumps rise and prickle on my skin. Everything about the place felt wrong; even the air in my car seemed to turn thick, tinged in warning.

The myriad rumors about the Blackwood family echoed in my mind, each more worrisome than the last.

The phone finally stopped ringing, but my relief was short-lived. With a sinking feeling, I saw it was because I had lost service. I struggled to swallow, my throat too dry and gritty to allow the trespass of saliva. I shouldn't be here. No one from town comes here. Not to visit Jasper Blackwood—the murderer.

CHAPTER 2
ELIZA

Jasper Blackwood—the name alone sent a shiver down my arms.

The reclusive heir to Blackwood Manor was a figure of illusion and mystery in the small town of Pinehurst and everywhere that surrounded it. There were whispers of how coldhearted he was and the way he would disappear for years at a time, returning only when the house seemed to demand it, like a curse. There was something sinister beneath his surface, something dark in the way people spoke of him; though in the end, every one of them would mention his power and wealth with an admiring glint in their eye.

According to the stories, Jasper Blackwood was a heathen of a child. I suppose it was not entirely his fault initially, as he was apparently never told "no" and got anything and everything he ever wanted as the only child of Darius and Hester Blackwood, the tremendously wealthy owners of Blackwood Bladecraft—yes, *that* Bladecraft, the knife company that Jasper later grew into the huge weapons conglomerate Blackwood Industries. They said he was unruly and awful then and was now a disturbingly wealthy, cutthroat, lawless businessman. It was all well-known. A former nanny said he tried to push her over the cliff when she put her foot down and told him no to having another piece of cake. The older residents of town swore he was the devil incarnate, formed by the spirits of the people killed by the knives his father's company made. He'd gotten kicked out of private school after stabbing a kid and putting another in the hospital with a broken jaw. From the sound of it, he'd always had a dark obsession with the massive cliff drop that was his backyard. They said his parents had to build a stone wall around the drop-off after he got angry and shoved one of his father's valets over the edge. Thankfully the man clung on for dear life even as Jasper stepped on his fingers, because he held on long enough to be recovered and tell the rest of the town about it after he quit. Unfortunately, Jasper's next victims weren't quite as lucky.

Hester's and Darius's deaths were unnatural and unexplained, though many thought they knew what really happened. Their bodies were never found, likely because, like the valet, they'd been pushed over the cliffside. A fifteen-year-old furious Jasper was found by the cliff's edge, covered in his mother's blood. Some said it was an accident; most said it was murder. If someone had asked me, I thought he did it. But no one knew for sure what had happened or why, only that it was by the hand of their malicious, vile son. He never denied it, instead smirking ruthlessly at the cameras when the case was dismissed because of police misconduct and mishandling of evidence. Some believed that his overpaid lawyer made that happen, while others were convinced the Blackwoods had the cops on their payroll. I don't know if it was true back then, but I knew it was true now—it was well-known that Jasper Blackwood was untouchable.

Another chill rippled up my spine as I took another curve and the view expanded before my eyes. The houses in the distance looked deceptively small, even though most of them were mansions. It looked like a busy patchwork quilt—save for the barren, empty rectangle where the old Blackwood manufacturing facility used to be. The road curved again, and the view was replaced with a fresh patch of tiny houses.

I didn't grow up in Pinehurst and had only moved there to work; my parents still lived in our small family home a few towns over. All I knew for sure was that Jasper Blackwood was disgustingly wealthy and that the conservatory on the property—supposedly at one time, a lush, vibrant space—had essentially been abandoned and needed to be restored, and the botanical garden I worked for was on the verge of being closed. The conservatory at Blackwood Manor was my last hope. I had studied it for weeks using old photographs and news clippings, imagining what it could become once again: a sanctuary of rare plants, an oasis of life hidden within the shadows of the manor. The horticultural society at Pinehurst Botanical Gardens had been trying to get inside it for *years* with the hope of propagating some of the rare plants rumored to be inside. Even if they had been left to die, nature had a way of refusing, and that tiny, stupid little notion held every last one of my hopes.

Unfortunately, the horticultural society was overbearing and aggressive with their approach to everything, and I had no doubt that was how they'd tried to get into the conservatory. Stupidly, the idea that I could do better had crawled in my head and possessed me like a spirit one day, and I couldn't seem to shake the thought that maybe I could get him to agree to our team restoring the gardens. I was quiet and soft-spoken, the least threatening person imaginable. I had learned at a young age the skill of making myself invisible, something I hoped would be to my advantage here.

Apparently, after Jasper's mother's death, the conservatory had fallen into ruin. No one had been allowed to touch it—not even the gardeners of the estate. The garden had started when his mother, Hester, had poured all of her love into it, and eventually, her doting, besotted husband built the conservatory around it, so she could spend the entire year with the plants she held so dear.

Bringing my thoughts to the present, I swallowed hard as I approached the massive gates of the manor. They were intricately designed with dark wrought-iron posts twisted into elaborate patterns. Rich green vines of English ivy overtook the metal in spots. It was as if the house itself had grown a cage. The design was beautiful, but the sight of it was unsettling, as though the gates were not just for keeping others out but was also keeping secrets in.

My tires crunched to a halt just before the massive gates. I sat in my car for a long moment, staring up at the imposing structure. The heavy ironwork stretched high above me, and even though the gates were open, there was something about them that made me feel as though I were trespassing. Every nerve in my body screamed to turn back around before it was too late. I twisted my hands together and dug around to find the courage I knew I'd had at some point. My eyes snagged on a small green light on the code box to the left of my window. They were watching me.

I lifted my chin and tried not to pass out. So much was riding on this. I couldn't mess this up.

I reminded myself that I had come here with a goal: to convince Jasper Blackwood to donate $250,000—enough to keep our doors open another year, and to allow my team to restore the conservatory, something that could bring a large amount of publicity to Pinehurst Botanical Gardens—as well as a few tiny propagations in return. To him, it would be nothing, but to us—to me—it would be everything. Without this funding, I was going to lose my job, the one thing in this world that made me feel that I had a life of my own.

I had to make him see why donating would be beneficial to him and that this was more than just a job for us. I would guarantee our discretion and that we would be quiet and unbothersome. I collected my paperwork and quickly ran through my pitch. I took a giant gulp of air and held it at the back of my throat. *In...one...two...three...* I blew out the breath, moving the brown strands of hair that dangled in front of my face.

Sitting there, the manor looming in front of me, I couldn't shake the feeling that there was something much darker than a donation waiting for me behind the gates. It was a wonder how something so immaculate and beautiful, so opulent, reminded me of one of those spring-loaded traps used for catching raccoons. As though I would move my car another few feet, and the iron gates would slam shut behind me, trapping me here. I moved forward, wincing as I parked my car in the large roundabout surrounding a boxwood hedge enclosing a large three-tiered black fountain, pristine but empty of water.

My fingers gripped the gray plastic door handle of my car, and I froze.

What was I doing here, alone, at dusk, facing a man who was known for little more than his nefarious business dealings and probably killing his own family? What if someone else didn't handle the conservatory business and I had to actually speak to Jasper Blackwood? This whole time I'd inadvertently prepared myself to talk to an estate manager or whoever actually ran Blackwood Industries. The idea of having to talk to Jasper Blackwood in person rattled in my chest, and there weren't enough breathing exercises in the world to calm the fear it produced in my body.

There were other rumors too—stranger, more outlandish ones that he was cursed or that the manor itself was; that the tormented souls lost to the weapons his company made haunted the halls of Blackwood Manor, their voices lingering in the rooms, hoping to torture him back.

Darius Blackwood had been a greedy, money-hungry

monster who only cared about himself. Even though many of the stories had died down, the town of Pinehurst—and especially my mother, though she didn't live there—held a grudge against the Blackwoods for the incident at the plant. It had been covered up, and they'd underreported the disaster, paid off the local officials, and buried it.

Darius had had a secret division of Blackwood Bladecraft working on cutting-edge materials and tech that were biologically engineered—not for helping the people or for combat but for profit in the medical and biotech fields. My mom said the weapons plant had begun working on a new alloy that could withstand extreme conditions—ideal for both weaponry and medical tools. Darius realized that to create the alloy, the chemical process that was used could be repurposed for regenerative health treatments. I supposed that wouldn't have been so bad, but the problem was that the chemicals involved were volatile, dangerous. Creating the alloy caused chemical reactions that generated waste byproducts, some that were mishandled and couldn't be disposed of in a conventional way. The town's water supply was hit and a lot of people got sick—some even died. And the Blackwoods did nothing but save their own asses and, not long after, disappeared completely.

They say that the house was left in ruins for years after Darius and Hester died. Jasper was a teenager then but quickly poured himself into the family businesses and building an empire of his own far more powerful and lucrative than anything Darius had done. Looking at the house now, there was no sign of neglect. The front grounds were immaculate; every hedge and blade of grass was lush, though it didn't give off a serene or beautiful vibe—it felt almost like it were being threatened to remain still and green. As a botanist living in a wealthy town, I enjoyed ogling the beautiful landscapes of the mansions I frequently passed, but something about this landscape felt wrong. I realized at once what it was that stuck out to me about Blackwood Manor's immaculate landscape: There was not a single flowering species of plant to be seen, not even trimmed back and out of season—a design so blatant and odd looking, it had clearly been intentional.

Blackwood Industries, the company Jasper had turned Blackwood Bladecraft into, was not bereft of its own rumors—it was a company known for its mysterious ties to elite weaponry but now famously produced rope. Apparently, they had a contract with NASA to make ropes engineered for space missions and deep-sea exploration. The man had earned his millions making rope and weapons. Talk about fueling the rumors. Paranormal investigators from TV were always coming into town trying to get into the manor, to capture footage of ghostly victims of Blackwood Industry's weapons, after a few disgruntled household staff claimed they left after being harassed by spirits.

I knew far better than to put stock in ghost stories. I was logical-minded, rooted in science, not someone who wasted time on superstitions. Yet, as the thoughts slid across my mind, sitting there at the edge of the Blackwood estate, I felt an overwhelming sense of foreboding. I wasn't even out of my car yet, and it seemed I had already entered an entirely different world. Reasoning and rationale, two traits typically residing at the forefront of my mind, seemed unable to fight the surrealism of the spectral atmosphere before me. I could reason with myself all I wanted, but the fear inside of me wasn't listening—it was running off feelings.

What if the rumors were true? What if I *was* stepping into a place that was more dangerous than I could understand? My eyes traced the shape of its towers, the heavy windows staring down at me like dark and watchful eyes.

With a deep breath, I steadied myself. Jasper Blackwood saying no to a donation and my team being refused admittance to his private garden was the worst thing the tyrant could do to me, and no matter how harshly he delivered the answer, I'd heard worse from my own family. He couldn't hurt me with his coldness when I was already dead with frostbite.

I pushed open the car door and stepped out onto the gravel. The cold air bit into my skin, and the mist clung to the edges of my coat as I walked toward the wide steps of the stone house. I could see the faint outlines of the conservatory off in the distance, nestled to the side of the manor like a forgotten relic. Even from here, I could make out the faint outline of the glass panels that had once been clear and pristine. A few looked shattered, and all were clouded with grime, the structure sagging slightly as if the very weight of the neglect had begun to drag it down back into the earth. It felt like it was calling to me, begging me to bring it the help it needed.

I knew our team could restore it. We had to. A few rare propagations would bring light to the botanical gardens, and with it, new paying visitors. But it would take more than just expertise and time. It would take Jasper Blackwood's approval. I'd seen photos of him in the media—he wasn't horrible looking if you liked your men expressionless with an air of "I'm going to strangle you if you say anything I don't like." I personally preferred more laid-back, funny, nerdy, gamer types.

The wind picked up once more, rustling the drying leaves barely still holding on to the trees and sending a jolt down my spine. The manor seemed to grow larger as the mist drifted around me as I approached the front doors. Taking a deep breath, a sense of inevitability settled into the depths of my chest. I had come this far.

I would not be deterred. Not now. I had nothing left to lose.

I straightened the crisp white blouse I had bought yesterday and knocked on the door.

CHAPTER 3
JASPER

"YOU'RE CERTAIN YOU WANT TO MAKE THAT LOW OF AN offer? If they get offended and pull out—"

"Then they'll quickly learn they have nowhere else to go," I said, cutting off my VP's argument as my feet pounded down the hallway toward my office.

The small chime alerting me that someone was at the front door poured into the hallway from the surveillance room, grating against my already inflamed nerves like a Taser to the back of my neck. I fucking hated people at my house—hated it. I was meeting with some old fuckwad from a botanical garden or something. Sowerby had always been perturbed by the state of Mother's old conservatory and had finally nagged me enough that I'd agreed to a meeting when the garden society or whoever the fuck from town came begging to get into it again. I would take the meeting, but I wasn't allowing them in the conservatory. I'd sooner plow it under than allow anything of hers to be alive in this manor again.

"Jasper, be reasonable," Easton tried to argue.

"They are lucky I'm offering them any—" The words dropped off as my feet stilled in the hallway. My eyes were dialed in on the driveway's security camera. "Make the offer," I said before I hung up my cell phone and turned into the surveillance room.

I noticed it in her eyes instantly and it hit me…uncomfortably. She was beautiful, but that wasn't what was interesting about her. It was hidden, but once I caught sight of it, it was impossible to ignore. Only those who have felt it could pick up the deep anguish in her eyes. I'd never seen it outside of a reflection in a mirror.

What had caused it in her?

A host of emotions pressed in on me and my steady hatred for life returned. I pulled my gaze away from the camera and continued down the hallway to my office, grabbing the letter from my mother out of my pocket along with the lighter.

CHAPTER 4
ELIZA

My low heels clicked sharply against the gleaming marble floors as I followed a butler—seriously, who has a butler?!—through the expanse of Blackwood Manor. So this was how wealthy killers lived? The grandeur of the place was exquisite but suffocating—tall, darkened windows, heavy curtains that blocked out the sunlight, and portraits of what I assumed were long-dead ancestors stared down at me, judging my every move. I hadn't been expecting comfort inside, but I hadn't quite been prepared for the oppressive weight of it all either. The manor seemed to stretch on endlessly, each room more foreboding than the last. The thought of one singular man living in this massive structure was unfathomable when it could have housed two dozen comfortably.

The butler, an older, white-haired gentleman with an air of quiet authority, hadn't spoken much since he'd opened the doors and led me inside with a deep-set scowl upon his face that pulled at his marionette lines. He hadn't offered me tea or asked if I'd like to sit down, as was customary in many smaller estates that I'd been to around here.

Alfred, Batman's butler—that's who he reminded me of!

I felt an unwelcome smile pull at my mouth, amused at the comparison as my eyes watched the man leading me. He was more sinister looking than Alfred, with that expression on his face. Though he was dressed in a pressed pair of khakis and a fine wool sweater that was appropriate with the cooling weather, there was a rough-hewn air about him, like a sharp-eyed falcon dressed in a cardigan.

"Mr. Blackwood is expecting you. He saw you arrive." The words felt more like an order than an invitation.

As we passed under a stone archway that led to what appeared to be a drawing room of sorts, my mind raced. Looking at the dark, traditionally modern interior of the manor, I couldn't help but wonder how I was going to face this man the town gossips spoke of with so much fear. He had an infamous scar, and it wasn't known how he had come to own it. He had seemed handsome in the way that some serial killers were and was rumored to have dated Hollywood sweethearts and models.

I didn't care if he looked like Damon Salvatore, my focus was the donation and the conservatory.

I *had* to convince him.

I didn't realize how tightly my jaw was set until the butler stopped in front of a large shiny black door, and I caught a glimpse of my reflection before he turned the round brass handle with a soft click and our reflection disappeared. He glanced at me once, and then, with a slight bow, stepped aside.

"Mr. Blackwood will see you now."

I stood for a moment, eyeing the doorway, and then stepped forward. The atmosphere of the room was thick with expectation, like the manor itself was holding its breath, waiting to see what fury I would cause. I desperately wanted to run through a breathing exercise, but I had no time for hesitation—my career was on the line.

The door creaked as I pushed it farther open. The jarring

scent of something burning wafted from the room. A small gasp lodged in my throat, and I felt my eyes widen briefly.

Jasper Blackwood sat behind a massive wooden desk that seemed far too large for the room. The office was meticulously organized with neatly shelved books, all with the pages out so you couldn't read the spines—which seemed psychopathic enough on its own—and the smell of smoke accompanied a strange chill in the air. The chill quickly turned warm and uncomfortable as my eyes fell on the man behind the desk. He was a striking figure—tall, angular, with jet-black hair that seemed impossibly dark in the dim light of the room. His features were sharp, his jawline defined with an almost predatory elegance. He was the kind of man whose presence filled the space, whose silence seemed louder than any spoken word.

For a split second, I wondered why I was there, forgetting about the donation and who the man was entirely. I snapped my attention back to the issue at hand and fought the urge to shake my head to clear it. My eyes flickered to the scar that went from under his right eyebrow, up in a diagonal line, across to the left side and stopping before his hairline. It was thin and jagged but only added to his image. He had such a magnetic pull that it made the photographs I had seen seem almost misleading—or perhaps they weren't, and the added layer of appeal was more of an aura that seemed to roll off him. It was unfortunately quite easy to see why the man had gotten away with so much over the years; he was absurdly good-looking, and he carried himself in a confident, mysteriously alluring way.

I bristled, loathing him all the more for it—some of us didn't experience pretty privilege; some of us weren't just handed millions of dollars or mansions.

His eyes lifted from what looked like a burning envelope as I entered, and for a brief moment, they locked onto mine, at first with a tinge of surprise and then something else as a prickle of electricity danced up my arms and over my shoulders and neck while I felt the full weight of his eyes. Cold. Hard. They seemed to take in every detail of me, as though measuring my worth. Quite familiar with harsh scrutiny, though maybe not from anyone that looked like he did, I stood tall, my spine straight, my breath steady. I had come here for a purpose, and I would not be intimidated by a pair of espresso-brown eyes and whatever current momentarily zapped between us.

He casually dropped the remainder of the burning envelope into a decorative brass bowl on his desk as he held my eyes.

Out of respect I waited for him to speak first, but he merely raised a thick eyebrow, his gaze lingering on me for another beat too long before he motioned to the chair across from him. Just the way he moved, with his air of superiority and overinflated confidence, *instantly* grated against my nerves. It practically wafted off him that no one ever told him no, probably the last ones who had were his parents...

"Sit," he said, his voice low and quiet.

I hesitated only for a moment before I crossed the room and lowered myself into the shiny leather chair. His eyes never left me, and I could feel the weight of his attention, as if he were peeling back the layers of my thoughts, searching for weakness.

"Mr. Blackwood," I began, my voice steady despite the tension that coiled tight in my chest. "Thank you for meeting with me. I know you must be very busy while you are in Pinehurst."

His lips twitched slightly in a mocking manner, but the movement was so subtle, it might have been a trick of the light. "I'm not sure I'd call it busy," he said. "Though you should know I don't typically take appointments. I'm not a salon, Miss...?" His sharp words hung in the air like a challenge.

"Eliza." I felt my face pull into a scowl and I attempted to readjust, hoping to appear more friendly. I'd tell him whatever he wanted to hear to get the botanical gardens this money. "Eliza Arnold, I'm from the Pinehurst Botanical Gardens, about a two-hour drive."

"I know where Pinehurst Botanical Gardens is. You people have already come here about the conservatory, and I've already told you no. To be quite frank, Miss Arnold, I only took this meeting as a favor to my head butler, who has been nagging me *incessantly* about the state of the conservatory for years." He glanced at his watch, some shiny black, expensive-looking thing, and returned his slightly annoyed gaze back upon me, obviously expecting his rude sentence to push me back out the door.

Joke was on him. I was an overthinking, awkward woman; this wasn't even the most uncomfortable conversation I'd had this week. If he truly wanted to belittle me and break me down into tiny, minced pieces, he should take a lesson from my mother. I pushed the conversation I'd had with her as far from my mind as possible. I needed to remain put-together and strong.

"Well, sir, I'm not here to waste your time," I said, setting my bag on the floor next to me and pulling out the folder containing my proposal for the conservatory's restoration. As I stretched my arm out and leaned toward him, I struggled not to shake, almost worried he would lash out at me. "You are going to donate $250,000 to the Pinehurst Botanical Gardens and you are going to let us fix up your conservatory. You've had a rather high earning year, and as an intelligent businessman, I know that you are looking to offset your taxable income. A donation of that size would also serve well as environmental philanthropic branding geared toward your community, something that I'm certain will interest you after Blackwood Industries' former issues." I placed the folder carefully on the desk between us, watching as his eyes eventually flicked down to it after remaining on me for a surprised second.

There was no sign of interest on his face. He didn't even move to open it. Instead, he folded his hands in front of him and leaned back in his red leather chair. "It's a shame you drove all the way here when I could have easily told you no over the phone." His dark eyes lit with the same look a cat gets as it toys with a newly discovered mouse.

Fuck.

Our eyes held in silence for a moment. It felt like we were playing some sort of game, challenging each other, and we both knew it even though it was painted with common formalities. I bet no one ever pushed back against the spoiled brat. Unfortunately, I was quite possibly the worst person to do that. I had taken great pains in my twenty-five years to become malleable and quiet.

I stiffened and forced myself to remain composed. "The conservatory is in disrepair, Mr. Blackwood," I began, my voice firm. "I'm a botanist. I have a team of skilled restoration specialists who could bring it back to its former glory—bring the plants back to life, give it purpose again. It could become a valuable asset, not just for you, but also for the entire community. If you allow us to have any duplicates, it and the publicity the botanical gardens would receive could be enough to keep us open, while a donation would ensure we *remain* open and able to sing your praises." The words sounded rehearsed because they were, though the irritated glint in my eye seemed to be what he was paying attention to. As practiced as I was, I still found myself incapable of hiding all my annoyance about the fact that I was having to quite literally beg this man for money.

He watched me without speaking, his expression unreadable, and for a moment, I wondered if he was still bothering to listen.

"You seem abnormally passionate about this." His voice was barely a whisper, but there was a dangerous, amused edge to it. He was toying with me.

"I'm passionate about keeping a roof over my head," I replied, keeping my voice steady. A light pulse of anger unfurled from my stomach, surprising me. I never reacted. *Never.* "And the conservatory…it was your mother's pride and joy from what I'm told. I understand why you'd want to protect it. But surely you must see that it's beyond repair without specialized help. And I'm here to offer that help."

His eyes flicked down to the folder again, still not reaching for it. Instead, he tilted his head slightly, his dark brown, almost black eyes studying me as though I were some curious specimen. "You're begging me for money and to fix something that's been left to rot for years?" he asked, his voice as cool and detached as ever. "Let me assure you, I don't care about my environmental impact, the community…or your roofing. There are already far too many people here with an addition to the manor being constructed. You should leave before the sun goes down."

With every cocky word he spoke, I could feel an unfamiliar irritation rising, but I bit it back. This wasn't just about me and my future, my freedom; it was about the botanical garden and the horticultural society—and not letting some arrogant prick off the hook.

"I will gladly accept a donation on its own; however, regarding the abandoned conservatory, I don't see it as rotting, Mr. Blackwood," I said evenly. "I see it as an opportunity—a chance to restore something beautiful. I understand your feelings about it, but I don't think your mother would have wanted it to decay. She would have wanted it to be cared for. My team would be happy to take care of the entirety of it for you, with the agreement that if any rare specimens are found, we would propagate them, leaving the original in its place. It could be incredibly beneficial to both you and Pinehurst." I fired my last shot. "I believe it's what your mother would have wanted."

Jasper's expression remained unchanged as he glanced toward the smoking copper bowl on his desk. "You don't know anything, especially about what my mother would have wanted." His words were biting.

I felt the sting of them, but I refused to let it show. Instead, I held his gaze steadily. It wasn't hard—something about him irritated me so much, I almost hoped he'd keep saying no just so I wouldn't have to look at him for another second. If I had to bring my team here, I'd have to see his stupid, smug face all the time.

"No," I said, my voice calm but firm. "I don't. But I know what I can offer. And I think that's what matters."

Jasper's lips twisted into a faint smirk, and for the first time, I saw a flicker of something—humor? Contempt? I couldn't tell. "You think your team at the botanical gardens can fix this place, put a nice bow on it and brush away all the demons?" His voice was low, a barely restrained growl. "You don't understand anything about Blackwood Manor, Miss Arnold."

"I understand more than you think," I said, leaning forward slightly. "I understand that the conservatory has potential. And I understand that the Blackwood legacy doesn't have to be one of isolation and neglect. You don't have to carry the burden of this grand manor alone."

For a moment, his gaze softened a fraction, but it was gone in an instant and again I wondered if I'd imagined any human qualities to him. His face hardened again. "We can add my burdens and the Blackwood legacy to the list of things you don't know," he said, his voice barely above a laughing whisper.

I opened my mouth to reply, but he raised a hand, silencing me—old habits die hard—and I flinched.

"I'm afraid I don't need your help. I don't need anyone's help," he said, his voice suddenly quieter, almost like a confession. He reached into his pants pocket and removed a wad of folded bills. He pulled a hundred-dollar bill from the top layer and tossed it on the desk near me. "Take your proposal and leave."

My heart hammered in my chest, the anger rising within me. I stood up slowly, my movements deliberate. There was a weird challenge that hung between us, and I found myself unable to leave without a victory. "I need this job, Mr. Blackwood. I can handle any challenge you put forward. Name it and it's done...*please*."

CHAPTER 5

JASPER

I HAD BEEN EXPECTING HER. MY BUTLER, SOWERBY, TOLD ME he had accepted her appointment and encouraged me to agree. The botanical gardens had been hounding me for years about that damn conservatory, and now here the woman was in the flesh. I admit that her approach was different than the others. None of them had bothered to bring family sincerity into the negotiations. She thought she could walk in, fix my mother's dead and decaying monument, and somehow save the day. And she had a look in her eyes—the same look I saw in everyone who dared to step foot on my property: the belief that they could somehow change things.

They didn't know a damn thing about my family or what this place had taken from me. The conservatory was a relic—a shrine to my mother's obsession with plants, something that had outlived her and now served only as a painful reminder of everything I didn't want to remember. The last thing in the world I wanted was to bring life to it.

Something in her eyes pressed into me like a bayonet, sharp and uncomfortable. There was something familiar within the looks of despair she tried to mask.

"Mr. Blackwood," she said, her voice steady with a touch of steel to it, "I'm desperate."

I didn't need to hear more. I knew exactly what she was about. Botanists—gardeners—whatever you called them—had been sniffing around here for years, looking for ways to revive what had been dead for so long. I had no interest in any of it. Not even for oddly intriguing ones like her.

I leaned back in my chair, studying her as she stood across from me, arms crossed as if she were already claiming a victory she hadn't earned. "I have no interest in restoring that place. You can tell your team to look elsewhere."

She didn't flinch from my words, though I had noticed the slight flicker earlier when I had raised my hand to silence her. Someone had obviously been physical with her at some point. Now, her posture stiffened, and the light in her eyes grew sharper. There was something spurring her determination on that caught my attention.

The woman was, at first look, ordinary: mousy brownish-blond hair and plain, common features with a soft and short body that was as easy to overlook as an undecorated wall. But upon further inspection, it was almost as if her blandness was intentional. Behind her oddly blue eyes was an intelligent, intriguingly beautiful woman who didn't wish to be noticed. Despite my best efforts, I found myself filled with questions about this random woman and her strange determination.

"I think you'll reconsider," she said, setting another folder on the desk and sliding it toward me. "My team and I are more than capable of bringing the conservatory back to life. The plants there are rare, and it could be a valuable asset to the property."

I didn't touch the folder. Instead, I stared at her, wondering how anyone could be so damn persistent and so...so quiet all at once. Perhaps she was used to getting her way, used to having people bending to her sad eyes. But I'd had enough of people manipulating me for a lifetime. I'd had enough of people in general, in fact.

"I don't want your team or anyone else on this property," I said, my voice as sharp as the blade of a knife. "I told you. I don't care about the plants. I don't care about the conservatory. I've let it rot for a reason."

Her gaze faltered for a fraction of a second, but only for a second. I could see the calculation in her eyes, the way she assessed me, trying to figure out what I would do next. She wasn't backing down even though I could tell she was a bit uncomfortable being so tenacious. That, at least, I respected—though I found it annoying.

"You're missing the point," she pressed, her voice shaking but determined. "This isn't just about plants. It's about history, about what your mother created here, and what you've allowed to wither away. You can't just let it all rot, Mr. Blackwood."

I clenched my jaw, every mention of my mother cutting into me like nicks from a penknife. I had been very clear about my feelings on that conservatory. My mother had tended to it, yes. But that was long before everything fell apart. Before she was gone—before I was left with nothing but guilt and hatred.

"I don't care about history," I snapped. "And again, I don't need some team of strangers coming in and poking around where they don't belong."

I watched her face for a moment, seeing the way her expression hardened. Desperation of some sort had driven her to this point. It suddenly clicked. Her job at the botanical garden must be on the line. I'd seen their numbers. I was no doubt a last resort before the garden went under and they all lost their jobs.

I had no intention of giving her what she wanted. Though she had sparked some weird interest in me—I found myself wanting to push and toy with her, see how far this woman would go for a dilapidated glass building that meant nothing to me.

She opened her mouth to speak, but I raised a hand, cutting her off and moving from my desk out the door, guiding her out with me. She recoiled from my touch as if I'd tased her.

If she wanted to restore this goddamn conservatory so badly, then she should see the fucking state of it up close and personal.

"Where are we going?" she asked, following behind me as I quickly strode down the corridor until I was at the disused hallway of the manor that led to the conservatory's indoor entrance.

I remained silent until we made it to the double glass doors to the garden. Unease prickled at my nerves. I hated even being in the hallway that led to it. Pain and guilt pulled and ripped at me like a dozen wild bears ripping off my flesh. I suppose that's what I deserved.

I opened the door and was instantly hit with the scent of musty soil and humidity so strong it made my eyes water.

Her eyes were the size of plates as she stepped inside—only as far as the reaching vines and weeds would allow.

"Let me be clear," I said, my voice dropping to a low, warning tone. "You won't bring your team here. I don't want them on my property, and I won't allow it." Fascinated, I watched her chest fill with air as if she was going to argue further. My mouth quirked with an idea. "You'll do it alone."

Her eyes widened for a brief moment. I saw the flicker of surprise, but it was quickly replaced with something harder, sharper. "I'm not interested in hearing how teamwork is essential for the job," I challenged. "I don't want anyone else touching these plants or taking up space on my property." I wanted to push her over her cliff of determination and watch as she fell to the bottom. "It'll be you—only you—who works here. No one else. That's my offer." I leaned back on my heels and watched smugly as she took in the large conservatory and all its ruin, obviously far too much work for one woman.

For a moment, she was silent. I could see the frustration building in her, and I relished it, even as I fought to ignore the strange tug of something else—a tension I couldn't quite place, a spark that made my pulse quicken. It wasn't just irritation I felt but something dangerous.

She looked at me, eyes narrowing, as she weighed her options. She had none and she knew it. I'd thrown out an impossible offer, and we both knew it.

"You can't be serious," she finally said, her voice tight. "You want me to do this alone? I'm a botanist, not a landscaper. I'm not a contractor. You're asking me to rebuild an entire conservatory with no help?"

I leaned back and crossed my arms over my chest, allowing the silence to hang between us for a moment. I could feel the heat of her gaze on me. "You wanted the job," I said coolly. "This is the deal. You work alone. No one else comes near this property." She hadn't folded as quickly as I'd anticipated, so I upped the ante. "Also, you'll need to stay here. Full-time. I'm not about to have you discussing my business with people not approved to be on my property. I don't trust you won't just steal whatever plants you find. I also don't trust you to be discreet in your comings and goings. If I sign your contract, you and the botanical garden will sign an NDA, obviously."

She froze, the challenge in her eyes faltering slightly. I could see the internal conflict raging in the pale blue. She didn't like being told what to do—or maybe she just didn't like being underestimated. But she was desperate. Even had she not outright admitted it, I could smell it on her—the way her fingers tangled with each other, the slight tightening of her lips, the way she held herself back, probably from telling me to fuck off. It was admittedly the most fun I'd had in a while.

"You want me to stay *here*? At Blackwood Manor?" she

asked, the disbelief in her voice tainted with fear—so she had heard about me. I had started to wonder, what with her being so adamant about getting this job. "Stay on your property for the entire restoration?"

My brows rose and my voice filled with challenge. "Three months is more than a generous amount of time, don't you agree?"

I watched her like a hunter watches a doe, taking note of the way she resisted the impulse to snap, how she was barely holding on to her composure. I knew I had pushed her just enough that she was struggling, and god was I enjoying it—until the realization struck that I was doing something I rarely did: making myself vulnerable. If she agreed to this absurd idea, it would mean having her here for three months. I couldn't deny the unsettling tug of curiosity I felt at the thought.

Eliza Arnold seemed different. But she was still a stranger, one of *them*. I didn't want her here. I could hardly stand the thought of anyone in my space physically or any other sort of way.

But the idea of her working here alone was…different in a way I couldn't fully articulate.

"You stay. You work. You don't leave unless I say so."

She looked at me, as if trying to read something in my face. "You're out of your mind," she muttered under her breath. I could see the decision to run beginning to settle into her posture, her body tensing as if literally getting ready to flee…when her sharp eyes darted to the center of the overgrown space. She gasped. "Is that a corpse flower?"

Puzzled by every word she had just muttered, I looked at the spot that held her eyes and saw nothing but piles of green and brown madness. "How should I know?" I snapped.

"One condition," she said suddenly, shocking me that she was not only agreeing but still negotiating.

I raised an eyebrow, intrigued despite myself. "Go on."

"When the restoration is complete," she said, "you'll host a party, a grand event that I can invite anyone I want to—for my colleagues, the press, philanthropists. I want this to be more than just some quiet, private restoration. If I'm going to work here alone and complete this in that time frame, you'll give me the recognition I deserve. And you'll host it in the conservatory when it's done."

The audacity of this fucking woman. But then again, I was sure she'd quit long before the conservatory got finished—it was far too much work for one person to manage, and stubbornness only got you so far.

"Done," I said.

Her hand was outstretched before I'd even finished the single word. I took it without hesitation, feeling the faintest pulse of heat between our palms.

"We'll begin in a week," she said, her voice tight with unspoken frustration.

"Three days," I countered. "And don't be late." I pulled my hand back and retreated down the hallway, nodding when I saw Sowerby. "Sowerby will show you out and make the necessary arrangements."

The manor was so big, I probably wouldn't even know she was here.

CHAPTER 6
ELIZA

THE AIR INSIDE THE ENORMOUS CONSERVATORY WAS DIFFERent. Not fresh like the clean, crisp breeze I was used to in the gardens of Pinehurst. Here, it was thick and heavy with a weird, cloying scent, as though it had been sitting for centuries and frozen in time. I'd only been at the estate for the better part of an hour, and already I felt the weight of Blackwood Manor pressing down on me. How anyone could stay in this enormous place all alone and remain sane was beyond me.

When I ventured over the twisted, gnarled vines and the patches of bamboo so tall they had broken through the ceiling glass to stand at the far end of the Victorian structure, I could see the edges of the cliff. Half of the manor's grounds jutted out like a cape, filled with gardens, manicured hedges; it was where the conservatory was positioned. The other half of the manor's backside was seated against the large stone cliff, resting high above the nearby towns. At first glance, it appeared as though the manor and the cliff were fighting, each trying to swallow the other whole. It was beautiful and imposing at the same time, but the gravity—pun intended—of what it meant to be this high up the mountain wasn't evident until I was at the back of the property, where the dangerous beauty toyed with my senses. The angle of the property gave all the back windows of the manor a breathtaking view, making it feel as if I could reach out and touch the heavens with the distant twinkling lights of towns and the stars. But the land drop was alarming. No fences or blocks—like an infinity pool of land. Nothing to prevent someone from stumbling to their death. There was a solid-looking concrete bench twenty feet from the ledge to enjoy the view.

But I couldn't enjoy the view. Even from inside the confines of glass, I found myself unable to look out at the sea of sky.

My eyes turned back to the manor, the morning sun pressing heat against my cheek and arm while I scanned the dark balconies and windows. My room was one of those. It was as if Jasper Blackwood knew I was deathly afraid of heights and chose to get in one last shot in our—whatever it was that seemed to be brewing between us. I didn't know if it was a stand-off or a fight or what.

I didn't like him.

For the sake of pacification, I'd told my parents and colleagues that the rumors were obviously just that: rumors. But I believed them more now than I did prior to meeting him. Jasper Blackwood had the demeanor of a boa constrictor. There was a suffocating power that quietly swirled about him.

Luckily, I hadn't seen him since that first meeting. Sowerby, the older butler, and a few of the other staff members helped me with my belongings when I arrived the following day. I hadn't brought much—a basket of clothes, another of books, and random hygiene products and other things I didn't want my mother to find while she took care of my apartment: journals filled with entries about her, a bottle of purple Fabuloso, half a pack of cigarettes that I bought on my eighteenth birthday and hadn't brought myself to throw away, things like that.

The morning fog rolled around the property, obscuring

some of the view, and I was grateful for it. The drive up here had been frightening enough having to look out at the road and see nothing but empty sky in the distance. It wasn't like I could close my eyes, though several times they flinched closed. Of course, there are no guardrails on the property either. Why would there be? Much easier to kill someone when they "accidentally" fall from the edge of your property. Had he killed anyone since his parents? By now he was so powerful and wealthy, I had no doubt the Pinehurst PD was comfortably seated in his padded back pocket, so he may have gotten away with god only knew what.

I shook my head, trying to free the plaguing thoughts and turned my focus back to the chaotic, overgrown garden at my feet.

Caged within the conservatory's glass panels was a field of disarray, with wild tendrils of dead vines and creeping weeds overtaking what was once a place of beauty. The structure looked like a broken relic, a forgotten dream tangled in nature's ruthless embrace.

It was essentially what I'd expected after that first glimpse, but still, nothing could have fully prepared me for this. I wasn't someone who shied away from hard work. But this? This was something else entirely. Standing there, I felt as though I was intruding, like someone—some*thing*—was watching, waiting for me to make the wrong move before hurling me over the ledge as punishment.

The pressure of the job was suddenly overwhelming. I was far from the most skilled person for this, and the fact that it all rested in my hands made me want to cry in frustration. My boss was thrilled at the prospect of a hefty donation and the chance at the infamous Hester Blackwood's rare propagations, though he wasn't shy about vocalizing that I was undoubtedly the last employee he would have chosen for such a job. Unfortunately, I had to agree with him. I was the least skilled of our botanists, and I'd only been there for a short time. He was right to question my capabilities—*I* certainly was—but I had something in my favor that the others did not: pure desperation. I would do anything to keep this job; it was my only source of independence. As a botanist, my focus was on research and conservation, not this; this was the job of an expert gardener, someone who cultivated and cared for plants, not studied them. I'd barely helped in my family's backyard garden growing up and only had a small amount of experience in the large gardens at Pinehurst. I had no idea how I was going to do all of this.

Jasper Blackwood surely knew that as well as anyone else, and that was why he pushed for it—to go out of his way to make me feel unqualified for this while ignoring my actual expertise.

I pulled the door open to the outside in an attempt to freshen the air. The screech of metal was unsettling, like a warning, but I pushed farther. It took me fifteen minutes of cutting through warped, knobby vines and weeds before I could fully open the door, only for a gust of irritated wind to push the stale air back in my face. It smelled of rot and earth mingled with the faintest hint of mildew. It was as if the very walls were breathing, exhaling centuries of pain and memories.

I took a deep breath, but it only felt like I was swallowing the decay, becoming a part of it. I'd never been a very emotional person; I thought my friends—if I had any—would say I was detached, numb, boring, which I suppose I was and why I didn't have any. My coworker, Nick, said he was my friend, but he said that to everyone at the botanical gardens. He was happy and round, and his skin was always a shade of pink. I liked him immensely, which was why I never knew what to say to him and remained quiet most of the time we worked together.

The conservatory was far larger than I had realized. The glass was cracked, and entire panes were missing in places. The windows were stained with a thick layer of grime and dust that obscured the sunlight. Thin beams of pale light managed to filter through, casting shadows on the overgrown paver paths throughout the space. I'd have to speak with him about hiring someone to fix the windows, god forbid he expected me to do it. If I'd been able to bring my team here to work, I could have been enjoying the specimens while the horticulturists and landscape specialists did their jobs, even hired a glazier to come in and fix the windows, but no, I was somehow supposed to do it all.

The floor of the garden was cracked, uneven, with patches of moss and dampness creeping into the seams of slate-colored square pavers. One foot tiptoed in front of the other as I stepped with careful intent, trying not to disturb the plants too much just yet. I didn't want to start my cleanup until I could map everything out on paper. I needed to be precise and certain that I wasn't ripping out valuable plants. Lithgow, my boss, was nervous about my inexperience, and had told me to text or call with any questions.

My heartbeat sat in my throat as I made my way deeper into the wildly overgrown conservatory. I wasn't afraid of plants or bugs—I'd spent my life among them, studying plants, coaxing them to thrive where they would otherwise wither. As strange as it sounded, it felt like there was something different about these plants. I had no doubt the fumes of some expired fertilizer or chemical inside the greenhouse had poisoned the air and gotten to me, but it…it felt like the plants were alive, and not in the traditional sense. The possibility of squatters inhabiting the space, watching me, crossed my mind but was quickly put to rest. No one would be on the Blackwood property without Jasper knowing. I had walked past the surveillance room on my way to the conservatory that morning and caught a glimpse of Blackwood's hypervigilance. The silence of the conservatory—broken only by the sound of my soft footsteps and the occasional howl of wind—made the hair on the back of my neck rise.

One of the negatives to being alone while I worked was that being a perpetual overthinker, my mind did what it always seemed to do and started to wander, going to the thoughts and memories I didn't want to relive. This was an escape from that situation at least, as I was distracted by the sense of desolation in the place, but I was certainly overthinking that.

"Focus on the plants," I reminded myself.

Letting out a heavy sigh, I moved to where I saw the plant that had made me agree to this stupidly absurd arrangement. It was my personal *Winged Victory of Samothrace*, reminding me of the battles I had yet to fight and the victories I hadn't yet achieved—my beacon of hope.

With trembling hands, I knelt next to a patch of dead vines, brushing away the thick blanket of foliage covering the plant that used to be a focal point in this garden, if its location at the center of the conservatory was anything to go by. It was nestled against a water feature, most likely a koi pond of sorts. The tendrils of weeds, thick and twisted, clung to anything they could. I ran my fingers through them, pulling apart the layers of decay, being gentle to not break even the plants I knew were weeds. Beneath it, a faint shape emerged. A stalk. The camouflaged outline of the *Amorphophallus titanum*, the Titan arum.

Better known as the corpse flower.

I stilled, afraid to move—afraid to blink for fear the plant would disappear from where it sat in front of me. The breath caught in my throat when I reached out and touched it. A shiver rolled down my body, leaving goose bumps across my skin.

It was rare. Impossibly rare. I thought the species had been lost to time, a nearly forgotten about, borderline mythical plant only whispered about; yet here it was, hidden under layers of neglect. It was faded, not flourishing, but still alive somehow. I could almost feel its pulse of life as I gingerly touched the edges of its growing bud. There was an elongated, pointed tip emerging from the soil, surrounded by protective bracts that had already started to show signs of drying and splitting, indicating the flower was preparing to open. I'd have to check, but I'd guess it was going to be about three months before it showed its rare bloom—something that only happened every seven to ten years.

It was exciting to think that there may be corms in the soil right now that could be collected after it bloomed. This individual plant had the ability to single-handedly save Pinehurst—and my job. Which meant, I would be able to keep my apartment and not have to move back with my mother: a priceless victory.

An idea hit me like a punch to the gut. If I could restore this conservatory—if I could do it in time to showcase the corpse flower's rare bloom—I would prove myself. Not just to *the* Jasper Blackwood—and truly, did I really care about that?—but to the botanical world. To my family. To myself. I would finally be able to stand on my own two feet with confidence. Maybe other gardens, like the Kew Gardens in London, would even want to hire me then, and I could be with my sister, Lucy, again—away and safe.

But I couldn't get too excited; I needed to remain logical. The task ahead of me was monumental. This conservatory, the plants here—they needed care. They needed attention. They needed someone to love them while letting them breathe.

The thought of my mother lingered in the air like the faintest perfume. Almost reflexively, I pulled my phone out to send her photos of the garden, but I had no service. A quick tinge of panic rushed through me—only for a second. The woman was explosive when she couldn't get ahold of me. There was no doubt already ten missed calls waiting to pop up as soon as I got service. My mother would show up here before she went another two days without talking to me. No matter how much I'd like to escape her reach, it seemed I never could.

In truth, being out of reach from the world was a draw, not a setback. It was the reason I agreed so quickly to staying on site at Blackwood Manor despite living with a known murderer.

My parents met working for an environmental advocacy organization as conservation biologists. They said they fell in love at a campaign for sustainable land use practices. Romantic.

My mom was especially...let's go with *serious* about her mission to save the planet. She believed in the importance of protecting nature and had always pushed both my sister and me to follow in their footsteps, not only because it was a noble cause but because they wanted us to continue their fight for the environment. It was drilled into us that their line of work offered the opportunity to make a lasting, positive impact on the world. My mother—an intelligent, stubborn, eccentric woman—was emotionally overinvested in everything we did, be it the no-plastic rule in our house or the mandated seven a.m. green smoothie or changing every single facet of our lives to benefit her and the earth. Somehow, she had masterminded ways to maintain control over me well into my twenties. Just three weeks before, I had been called home from work for a fire in the living room of my duplex. It was small and put out quickly with no real harm.

It had started when my mother had gone through my house and gathered every nonrecyclable, polyester, nylon item of clothing and lit it on fire on the new, non-sustainable area rug I had just bought. She had called me while the firemen were still there and asked me what it felt like to live in an environmental disaster.

My father was just as set in his fierce role as environmental god as my mother but with a contrasting personality—quiet and intelligent and completely unwilling to help us for fear he would befall her scrutiny.

My younger sister, Lucy, had become a chemical-using hair stylist—just to spite my mother, I thought. She'd always been the rebel of the family in some way or another and always hated me for getting their approval and doing what they wanted. In some ways, I'd always been jealous of her for doing what she wanted. I always wondered what kind of relationship the two of us could have had if the flame of our jealousy hadn't been stoked by my mother and instead been allowed to settle into appreciation. I only realized how much I needed her in my life once she moved away.

As the oldest and the "good child," I was petrified of disappointing them, though in truth, I also tried to be what they wanted so they wouldn't yell at her when she wasn't, but it never worked out that way. She moved away and I became a botanist. I never had my own passions or interests; there wasn't enough room to. My blueprint had already been drawn up before I was born.

In the conservatory, I took another deep breath and steadied my hands, shaking off the moment of weakness. I had always refused to fail, and this time would be no different.

There were so many other plants hidden under the layers of ruin and neglect, all of them somewhat exotic-looking. Several stuck out like lights in the dark, while others were more subtle. I couldn't identify half of them; their shapes were so distorted, their once-beautiful features marred by age and decay. The lack of sunlight and proper conditions had changed the colors and shapes of some, hidden them beneath the deciduous layer, but there was more variety than I had dared hope for. The vines twisted and curled like something out of a nightmare, creeping up to the tall ceiling in some parts, enveloping everything in their dark embrace.

It was overwhelming. Every inch of this place was filled with the repercussions of abandonment, and it wasn't just the plants that were dead—it was the entire atmosphere at Blackwood Manor. It had the feel of Dracula's castle with the dressings of a luxurious hotel…and the ambiance of Alcatraz.

No one ever smiled with more than a tight-lipped formality, no doubt terrified of the head of the estate.

I glanced around, the skin on the back of my neck prickling again with the sensation that I was not alone.

I turned quickly, half expecting someone to be standing in the shadows.

Nope, no one there. It was just me in the sad ruins of the garden. My heart was racing. The silence pressed in even closer now, so loud it made me wince. I shook my head and chastised myself to pull it together. It was just the isolation of this large, lonely space—I was sure of it. Er, I was trying to be sure of it.

Still, I couldn't shake the feeling that something was lingering here. Something more than the dust and the dead vines.

There was a soft creak in the distance, then a scrape of stone.

A soft, almost imperceivable melody sounded, and I caught a few notes before I turned, adrenaline shooting through my system, but again, there was nothing. I turned back to my small section of a flower bed and squatted, careful not to crush anything. I needed to pull soil samples. Determining the soil composition as well as the nutrient and pH levels was imperative to determine which areas were more fertile or depleted. Noting the way that it looked like the plants moved toward me, I was most definitely going to have it checked for toxins and heavy metals. After letting the soil samples air-dry, I would get them mailed out to the lab tomorrow and have the results back in a few days. A chill filled the air, and I shivered when there was movement in front of me.

My head snapped up. The faintest translucent figure of a woman in a billowing scarlet red gown stood over me, looking down at the small hole I'd just dug with my trough with her hollow black eyes.

A scream ripped from my throat, but it came out airy and soundless as I launched myself backward onto the moss-covered stone path. My eyes closed from the jolt to my backside, and when they opened again, they found nothing—the misty figure was gone.

I remained still, afraid to move and unsure what to think.

But I knew what I saw...didn't I?

I wondered if there was some sort of gas in there that was causing me to hallucinate. There was no smell of gas, but suddenly there was a faint soapy scent of aldehydes in the air that blended into a familiar burst of citrus, jasmine, and rose that wasn't there before.

Chanel No.5.

My aunt Louise, my mom's wealthy older sister, used to wear it to our house, and my mom would complain about the lingering scent for days.

Mystified, I sat in terrified silence, unsure of what to do. The minutes stretched on, and I convinced myself that the sun reflecting off the glass had caught my eye in a...unique and odd way.

Albeit reluctantly, I continued working, moving from plant to plant, cataloging what was salvageable in my notebook with a loose sketch of my guess at what each area looked like in its prime. I took several soil samples and placed them in small plastic bags along the way. The sense of being watched didn't go away. It only grew stronger, creeping over my skin and into my blood. I tried to ignore it, tried to focus on the task at hand, terrified to look around too much, but the feeling didn't lessen, only making me jumpier by the hour.

I could feel time stretching before me as the sunlight outside began to turn deep orange.

I couldn't help but think of the conversation with Jasper earlier this week. His challenge. His...offer.

"You'll do it alone," he had said. "I don't want anyone else touching these plants or taking up space on my property."

At the time, his words had seemed like an insult, but now,

in the silent hours of the conservatory, I could almost understand why he said it.

This place felt cursed, like something secret was locked behind its walls.

I pushed through the thoughts and focused on what I was doing and on the corpse flower. *That* was my goal. I needed to save it. I needed to make sure it survived…that we both survived this place. As soon as I could ask about the cell service, I would send Lithgow the photos and get some help.

The more I worked, the more I realized this place was more than just a ruin. It was a labyrinth of life and death, each plant I touched able to tell a story, each vine clinging to its memories. The plants here were survivors.

I thought back to my family, to my father's bored gaze, my mother's obsession. I wasn't here to fix anything with them. But if I could make this place thrive again, if I could bring these plants back from the brink, maybe I could finally prove to myself that I didn't need their approval to survive.

A chill trickled over the back of my neck. I felt the presence of the ghost return like the weighted black shadow of an eclipse claiming the sun. My eyes immediately pinched shut and I prepared to see the woman in the red dress again, every nerve in my body screaming with fear.

A shadow moved through the far corner of the glass room, dark and tall, not a ghost, but a human.

For a flicker of a second, I was relieved to see another person—until I realized it was Jasper Blackwood. My heart pounded faster than it did at the sight of the woman. I didn't know when he entered or how long he'd been standing around, watching. He hadn't said a word. He just watched.

His eyes on me were heavy and intense. I tried not to look at him, to keep my attention on the plants, but his presence was like a physical force. And it immediately stirred a spooked irritation within me.

"Everything all right?" His voice broke the silence, but it was cold, detached.

I didn't answer right away, unsure of what to say. I wanted to appear tough and unbothered, but more than that, I wanted to ask about what I thought I'd seen, but with things already tense, I didn't. I just nodded, keeping my eyes on the plants in front of me.

Was there any possible way the rumors of victims haunting the premises were true? But that was ridiculous. Did I even believe in ghosts? I'd never had to think about it before; the beings that haunted my life were still very much alive. My good senses firmly told me: no, I didn't believe in spirits trapped on earth, mostly because I could hear my mother telling me how foolish and silly it was to believe in spirits, ghosts, whatever you wanted to call them.

I hadn't really eaten anything that day and with the stress of everything, all alone in an eerie manor, whose imagination wouldn't have bled into their reality a little?

He was still watching me. I could feel the pressure on the back of my head like a sight from one of Blackwood Industries' rifles. His presence made the shadows lurking seem darker. Suddenly every hair that brushed against my arm, every leaf that skimmed against me wound my tension even higher until I could have screamed from the weird energy passing between us.

"Are you sure you should be cutting all of that off?"

He was referring to a wild clump of climbing black velvet ivy that had gone absolutely feral, choking out everything else in the bed.

I immediately second-guessed myself before bristling in frustration at my reaction and reaffirming, "Yes, I should be." My nerves were heightened in his presence, and I was a little frightened. There was something about him that made the little muscles in my stomach jump and tighten. I wasn't even looking at him, but I could feel his volatile, coiled aura. Goose bumps took over my skin like tiny spiders crawling across the top of my forearms.

"The broken panes will be getting replaced next week. I thought you'd like to know," he said with an annoyed tone to his voice. Like I should crawl over and thank him for fixing up his own building. As if he was doing me a favor by not making me do it.

"You'll also want to get someone in to fix the water feature and check it for cracks. You should pick out and order some koi for it also," I said, turning to face him. My stomach clenched even tighter when I looked at him head-on. I had forgotten how good-looking he was. Why did that piss me off even more? Like being rich wasn't enough, the murdering prick had to be attractive too. Why were all the hot men assholes? Was it because they knew that even if we hated them, they'd still produce that carnal pull, making us want to touch them? Jasper Blackwood was that good-looking but far too intimidating to want to touch. There was something unpredictable and uninviting about him that squelched that desire, despite his modelesque features. Scary prick.

I was unsure if my irritation stemmed from the spirited environment of this space or the pressure I felt to conquer it, but something about Jasper Blackwood gave me the feeling of metal shavings crawling under my skin.

"The water feature is a part of the garden. You can fix it. Anything you need, tell Sowerby and he will procure it, within reason obviously."

My polite veneer flickered, and I scowled at the man.

There couldn't be more than twenty feet between us, but it was filled with a challenging, confusing air, a weird tension that I couldn't put my finger on. It had cracked like lightning the day we met, before either of us had spoken a word. I didn't like it—it made me off balance and uncertain.

Did he feel it too? Was he causing it on purpose, with his intimidating aura? Whatever it was, it was uncomfortable and creepy.

"Did Sour—Sour." *Sourpuss is not the butler's name. That is NOT IT. Do. Not. Say. Sourpuss.* "Sour—" I stared blankly at Jasper.

Instead of offering me any help with Evil Alfred's real name, his face hardened. "Yes?" he pushed.

I looked like a complete idiot. I needed to say something. *Don't you dare, Eliza, that's for your thoughts only. Don't say Sourpuss.* "Evil Alfred—" *OHMYGOD. Just keep talking. Don't acknowledge it.* "Is there a gas line in the conservatory by chance?" I asked, unable to believe I'd just said that out loud.

"Evil Alfred? Like Batman's Alfred?" he asked with a tone as heavy as a hammer. "Sowerby will be thrilled with the comparison, I'm sure."

My face heated. "Please don't tell him that I called him that. I have a hard time with names, and I—"

"I'm afraid that is simply out of the question now." His handsome mouth widened, and a flash of perfect white teeth showed, softening the hard lines of his face and morphing it into something different...something lethal. It came and left so fast that I wasn't sure if I'd imagined it. His face was back to looking stern and cold.

I cleared my throat and wrote off whatever had just contorted his face—he was probably reveling in my humiliation. "Do as you please, but keep in mind I still have to work with him for the next three months," I said as I returned my attention to the plants. It was much safer and less confusing on the plants.

To my surprise, he kneeled next to me and watched as I carefully checked a small patch of dandelions before pulling them from the compacted ground. My hands shook with the attention. I wanted to crawl into one of the dark corners and disappear. Why was he still here?

A fresh, aquatic cologne scent gently mingled with the earthy soil in a pleasant blend.

"I'm Batman," he stated after a few minutes of silence. Everything about him was completely unreadable. I couldn't tell if he was threatening me or telling a joke. The tension in the room had crept to a level I'd never experienced.

"Four out of ten. Michael Keaton's voice is significantly deeper. Try Affleck or Clooney," I returned stone-faced, keeping my eyes on the plants, though I caught a flash of movement in my periphery.

"If my butler is Evil Alfred, does that not make me Batman? Even *I* acknowledge we have a fair bit in common…" Was he teasing me or being serious?

"I most definitely do not call you Batman in my head. Many, many other things, but not Batman." *Ohmygod. He's going to throw me out of the conservatory right now.*

"In truth, the similarities really are uncanny, between Batman and me."

In an uncharacteristically bold move—he seemed to bring it out in me—I put my cultivator down and turned my full attention to him. "You both have a penchant for capes and tights?"

He stood and brushed the dirt from his tailored black pants. "I was thinking more along the lines of us both being wealthy orphans," he replied, raising a dark brow.

Wealthy orphans? Had it been anybody else, I probably wouldn't have hesitated to ask more questions, but I was too afraid to prod—Batman wasn't rumored to have killed his parents—and frankly, I was having a hard time figuring out what my stomach butterflies were doing.

"You think this will take three months to complete?" he asked with a hint of something in his voice that I couldn't place.

"As I'm required to do it alone, yes." I shot him a look, surprised yet again by my own brazenness. "To be honest, three months is quite a tight guess as it is, but I'm incredibly motivated by the corpse flower's state," I said, standing up, tired of feeling his presence towering over me.

"A corpse flower?" His dark brows wrinkled together.

Embarrassingly ecstatic to finally be able to talk about it, I practically skipped over to the center bed and methodically stepped in with gentle tiptoes, moving about some of the living and dead chaos that shielded the Titan arum. "This is a corpse flower. It's incredibly rare. Most of them have died off in the last decade. They used to be found more readily, but now even the most renowned botanical gardens struggle to possess one. It only blooms every seven to ten years, if you're lucky, and sometimes it goes completely dormant or goes through a leaf cycle where it produces a single, massive, umbrella-like leaf with no flower. Even in its blooming cycle, the singular, large bloom only lasts twenty-four hours," I said excitedly. I reached in my pocket for my phone to show him a picture of a bloom, but remembered it was impossible with my lack of service and pushed it back in.

Noticing the movement, he said, "I can set you up with service for the time you're here. Give your phone carrier and information to...Evil Alfred and he will sort it out for you." Light from the sunset sparkled in his dark eyes. "Why is it called a corpse flower?" he asked, deep voice rasping against me.

I watched him for a second. "Because when it does bloom, it emits a horrible odor that closely mimics the scent of dead, rotting flesh."

Jasper's mouth curved with dark amusement.

"I am going to do everything in my power to time the completion of this conservatory with the bloom, so my colleagues will get the opportunity to see and appreciate it during the grand party that was promised before I leave," I said, unable to disguise my pride at the thought.

When I glanced over at the silent man, the stiff, sharp lines of judgment and superiority were there. Before I could say anything else, he turned around and walked away.

Shaking my head, I pushed thoughts of Jasper Blackwood and the…apparition out of my head and continued my work until Sowerby came to escort me to my room. In his deep, haggard voice, he warned me not to wander about Blackwood Manor and to stay away from areas I didn't have permission to go into. When I told him I thought I remembered my way back to my room, he huffed at me coldly and told me Mr. Blackwood didn't take kindly to those wandering about his home and that it was in my best interest if I had a chaperone. I decided to take the fact that he didn't refer to Mr. Blackwood as Mr. Wayne as a good sign and followed him quietly.

The room I was staying in, like all the other things in Blackwood Manor, was opulent and beautiful with a cold, mysterious lacing to it. Long white curtains flowed down over the huge glass door of the balcony—which was seated over the cliffside, the one I refused to go near. The moment I was alone inside, I pushed a velvet green fainting couch across the room to block the balcony door, though, really it did little more than create a hazardous barrier on the way to the bathroom for myself. The view of the sky was impossible to ignore through sheer white curtains, and I found myself constantly pulled to glance warily at it.

A large bathroom was just past the balcony door, the size of it nearly as large as my living room, though it was modest with its bronze faucet, large mirror, and clawfoot tub/shower combination. I showered, hoping for the steamy relaxation I so desperately needed, but instead remained rigid and jumpy, nearly slipping and falling several times because I kept getting the sense someone was standing outside the shower curtain. Every time I ripped it back to look, the bathroom was empty except for me, and I had to scramble not to injure myself in the slick tub.

Exhausted from the long day of anxiousness and the physical work, I didn't have the energy to focus on the eerie feeling of the room or bother to go on the hunt for dinner. I ate a granola bar from my purse as I curled up in the creaky, four-poster bed. I was completely unwilling to let myself focus on or give attention to the dark mysteries that haunted this manor. It was nonsense. Myths the locals had fabricated—understandably with the way the manor felt, but I wouldn't let them sink into my brain. I knew if I did for even a moment, that kind of darkness would consume me.

Unfortunately, they were more than willing to give me all of their attention.

CHAPTER 7
ELIZA

THE NEXT MORNING, THE STILLNESS OF BLACKWOOD MANOR was loud and thick, as though the house itself were holding its breath. I lay awake in bed, staring at the dark ceiling, my thoughts tangling and sprawling like the plants that twisted through the neglected garden. There were no sounds except the occasional creak of the house settling and the rhythmic crackling of the glowing fire in the hearth I'd lit in my desire to make the space feel cozier. Even the fire seemed to be fighting a losing battle against the chill of the house. If I could have figured out how to get enough light in the conservatory at this wee morning hour, I'd have settled my anxieties and calmed my nerves with work. But it was three in the morning, and I didn't want to startle anyone else in the house, even if I could have talked myself into stepping into the creaky hallway.

The room Jasper Blackwood and Sourpuss had put me in was large and bare, with cream walls decorated with lines of wainscoting and the occasional black-framed photo. There was a window to the right of the mahogany bed and a Victorian dresser with detailed carvings, dark wood finishes, and a mirror framed with floral motifs. My eyes, heavy with sleep, took in the plasterwork ceiling, tracing the rose medallions and cornices, hoping it would lull me back to the comforts of sleep.

I hadn't noticed it before I fell asleep, but now the smell in the room was damp, moss and earth, as if the overgrown gardens had crawled their way to my room. *Maybe it's just old firewood*, I told myself. The wind outside moaned, pushing through the trees against the house. A scraggly, bare branch caught on the glass, in a sound that confirmed for me that my haggard nerves were not going to let me go back to sleep.

I pulled the crunchy duvet up over my chest as I registered the faintest scent of Chanel No. 5 clinging to the air again. I couldn't rid myself of the unease that clung to the space. I'd always been someone who craved logic, explanations. But here in this place, I couldn't seem to make sense of anything—how I felt eyes on me when I was so clearly alone, the weird scents that were so out of place, the…general *feel* of the house.

I'd spent the last two hours awake, trying to lose myself in making lists of supplies and plants for the conservatory. I hadn't been able to tell what all was there originally, but I would ask if Hester Blackwood had kept some sort of log. As of now, the plants seemed as if they grew in defiance of their long neglect and their hateful new owner who had left them to die. Maybe they were silent witnesses to the whole thing—a morbid thought that I pushed away.

The soil was rich and dark, teeming with life and decay in equal measure. The conservatory was beautiful in its ruin, and already I'd grown fond of it, though was still incredibly intimidated. I'd never done a project so complex.

The firewood popped like a gunshot, and my nerves were so tense that I nearly cried out. The manor—this sprawling, brooding fortress—felt alive with secrets that I wasn't supposed to learn, things that I'd be punished for knowing. I still couldn't figure out why he'd insisted on me living here to do this when he clearly didn't like anyone on the property.

Jasper Blackwood. It felt wrong to call him anything else—certainly not *Jasper*. His full name carried weight, like a warning shot. Omit a syllable and it was as if you'd missed the danger entirely. Like *Madonna*, but in reverse: ominous instead of iconic. It was a name you spoke whole or not at all. He was a mystery. Handsome in a way that felt almost cruel, distant in a way that made it impossible to know what was going on behind his stern, cold eyes—eyes that seemed to hate everything they landed on—except for when he had *almost* smiled yesterday. It was barely even a smile—*was* it a smile?—but it had changed his face and made me question if he truly was as terrifying as everyone thought. He was a weapons dealer who had murdered his parents and had bought off everyone of consequence. My thoughts drifted again, teasing me at the edge of sleep, when I heard it—a faint rustling, fabric brushing against something. It was so soft, I dismissed it as the wind moving through the trees outside. It had been howling steadily for at least an hour as a storm passed.

I heard the sound again, and my heart bottomed out. It was in the room with me.

Pulse racing, I sat up quickly. The firelight flickered wildly in warning as it cast long, devious-looking shadows against the walls. Instantly everything felt wrong—the air, the silence, even the dim glow from the hearth. It was tinged with something that words wouldn't let me explain. Quickly, my eyes moved across the room, searching for whatever might have disturbed the stillness, searching for the thing that didn't belong.

And then I saw it—*her*.

The figure from the conservatory was at the foot of my bed—an ethereal presence, illuminated faintly in the dim glow of the firelight.

Every muscle in my body jolted before locking up, my heart stuttering in my chest. Shock and fear stabbed through me in unsuspecting waves; the bed felt unfamiliar and damp beneath me, and I couldn't seem to find anything to ground myself. In that moment, I couldn't tell if my arms and limbs were my own or not. I trusted nothing, especially not my sight. I clamped my eyes shut hard before forcing them to open again, terrified of what they would reveal.

The ghostly woman was tall and slender, draped in a flowing red dress that pooled around her like satin splashes of blood, the fabric the same color as the vital fluid. Her skin was smooth and pale, almost fully translucent, and her hair—long and dark—flowed around her shoulders in soft, glossy waves. Her delicate hand fastened tightly around her throat as if she were being choked. The scariest part was the expression on her face. She seemed my age, maybe a few years older. It was difficult to tell, but she definitely had decades more wisdom and desolation in her eyes.

The eyes themselves were large, dark, and mysterious; shadows pooled under the lids, as though they had known nothing but tears for a long time. Her pupils were wide, glassy, and unfocused, as if she could barely see past what was in front of her, lost in the echoes of a pain that wouldn't leave. There was an unnatural stillness in them—too quiet, too empty. Still, they appeared to glimmer with the weight of memories that lingered. Even the ghost woman's lashes appeared to be damp with unshed tears, the skin beneath slightly swollen, showing a life spent in grief. The sadness that poured from her felt like it had been carried for decades—maybe more.

After a moment, when she didn't make a move to attack me, confusion pushed through the edge of fear in my veins as we continued to stare at one another.

Her expression was delicate, almost fragile—like a thread ready to snap. There was no anger or bitterness, only a soft kind of yearning, the kind of sorrow that wraps itself around one's chest and makes it difficult to breathe. It was the look of someone who felt as though they'd been hollowed out by tragedy but who still longed for something they'd never have. Her crimson lips quivered slightly, humanizing her. My eyes widened and strained with tears. It seemed as if she was trying to form a word but couldn't seem to find the strength. A single shining tear fell from her eye, down her cheek. She seemed too numb to wipe it away or too weary to care.

In some strange, aching way, I wished I could take that sorrow from her, if just to see what this enigmatic creature looked like as her eyes lit up.

For a long, breathless moment, we just stayed there, staring at each other. Her face was serene, if sad, but there was something unnerving about the way her dark eyes seemed to look through me. It was obvious she could see parts of me I didn't understand, and my insides trembled, as if they knew something I didn't. The room felt so cold, and the fire was almost out.

I wanted to scream, to call out for someone to help me, but my throat was still tight, and the words wouldn't come. It was as if my body didn't belong to me anymore in this whirlwind of heart-stopping fear. Was she making it so I couldn't cry out? What else was she going to do to me? Though her appearance was brittle, she was magnetic—even the shadows in the room lengthened toward her, either in reverence or fear. Something threateningly powerful sat beneath her translucent skin, indicating to me that she could kill me without moving if she wanted to. Would she need to?

Suddenly, she moved, and I startled, shoving myself back against the hardwood of the headboard. She glided silently across the floor, her gaze never leaving mine as she got closer. I wanted to scream until I was hoarse as I ran out of the room, but I couldn't move. When she reached the left side of my bed, a pale hand lifted, her thin fingers pointing toward the door, soft at first, then a firmer instruction.

There was a motherly quality to her sad eyes that tugged

at something deep within me, and I found myself wanting to please her. It wasn't a command, not quite. More like a gentle invitation, but one I didn't dare ignore.

Slowly I swung my legs over the side of the bed and my feet touched the cold wood of the floor, but even that did nothing to anchor me from this horror. I glanced at the door she was pointing at—open just a sliver, and beyond it lay the dark, vast hallway.

No.
This is madness.
I need to stay here.
I should shut the door and lock it.

It felt like she was going to lure me to my death. What if I was discovered wandering about the manor in the middle of the night? Would Jasper Blackwood hurt me? Probably. His smile could be nice—when it didn't seem predatory—but it didn't camouflage his cruel and callous nature. He seemed like the type who would enjoy hurting me—maybe he even wanted to. But my feet moved on their own. The pulse of the house under my skin pushed me toward her, toward the unknown, and the need to satisfy this uncontrollable curiosity. I was held in a dreamlike calm, though I knew I was awake.

My knees trembled, my breath remained shallow—I was unwilling to take up more space than I felt like I was allowed to. As always, it was safer to do whatever was wanted of me.

She didn't speak, and she didn't need to. Her presence was enough as she led the way—it was what made my body move, what forced my legs to carry me out of the room and into the hallway, plunging me into the darkness of the house…where I was not supposed to be alone.

Did Jasper Blackwood know about her? Did the staff? How could they not? The seedling of curiosity bloomed the longer I followed her. The walls were lined with old portraits, their eyes touching me with lingering judgment as I passed.

The flickering glow of the firelight from my room was gone, replaced by the eerie stillness of the manor in the depths of the night. I glanced back only once, but there was nothing there—only darkness behind me.

The woman silently led the way through the winding halls, her translucent form and billowing dress moving with an unnerving, almost-underwater grace that made my skin prickle. Every cell in my body knew this was wrong, but I was drawn toward her like a moth to a flame. She could lead me to my death—and likely was—and it didn't matter. I couldn't stop. Every instinct in my body was screaming at me to run and find help, though in truth, I didn't think anyone here would help me.

The house was a labyrinth, unfamiliar, and yet I felt as though maybe I'd been here before. I struggled to grab the thread of familiarity before it was gone, but it was untouchable and fleeting.

We reached the conservatory doors, and the ghost paused. She seemed to be waiting for something—for me to understand, for me to make the choice. She watched me and I noticed a change, a gleam of hope in her eyes.

I reached for the door, my hand trembling as I grasped the cold, stiff handle. The doors opened with an unsettling click and creak, the air inside hitting me just as it had every time I'd been there—the scent of earth and damp plants, of something secret. The glass cage of plants was strange. Half forgotten and sad, half alive and fighting, it was both beautiful and haunting in its struggle. I glanced back to see if she would follow me inside…

But she was gone, vanished into the faint white mist that filled the room.

When I turned back around and stepped deeper into the conservatory, the crunch of broken stems beneath my feet was sharp in the silence. Misty, slow-curling fog moved around my ankles, and my breath clouded in front of me, the cold pressing in on my exposed shoulders and arms as I moved toward a small patch of earth near the center.

Something is hidden there.

I didn't know how I knew it, but I did. It was like she was in my mind, pushing me. I could feel it in the trembling marrow of my bones, though I still saw nothing.

I glanced over the space in front of me, wondering what to do when a glint of golden light caught my eye. On autopilot, I moved; my fingers shivered from the cold as I knelt, pushing aside the compacted soil. The nearly black dirt pushed under my nails as I clawed through the earth. There was something metal sticking up—a thin gold chain revealed itself more as I dug. My hands came to rest on something hard and smooth.

It was small, and when I lifted it from the earth, I saw it was a delicate oval locket, tarnished by time but resplendent in its intricate design. Turning it over in my fingers, caked soil crumbled away, and I began to feel a warmth radiate from the piece, as though it were alive.

My chest strained as my breathing grew faster. This was what she wanted me to find. I opened it slowly, struggling to push my nail in past the crease of dirt, where the two sides of gold met.

The tiny hinge clicked open. Inside, a faded portrait—a woman, her features haunting and familiar, her eyes dark and knowing, stared back at me. She was wearing the same red dress, but in the photo she was holding a small toddler lovingly against her chest, the boy beamed a magical grin; her own smile and happiness rivaled his. There was a shadow from his newsboy hat, but the round brown eyes were unmistakably those of Jasper Blackwood. It hit me like a truck: Was this Jasper's mother? The one people said he strangled? The woman whose ghost now allegedly haunted the halls of Blackwood Manor—and apparently was haunting me? Could this woman be someone else important to their story? Perhaps an aunt or something?

I stood in stillness for a moment, holding the locket, the weight of it in my hands a strange comfort and a heavy burden. It felt wrong, and yet I couldn't bring myself to let go. I could put it back where I'd found it, buried in the soil.

But I knew I couldn't. The warmth of it pulsed in my palm, as if it was trying to tell me something—something I didn't yet understand.

But suddenly, it felt as if I was meant to be here, to find this locket and find out what had really happened.

I don't know how long I stood there, holding the locket, feeling the pulse of this woman's history in my veins. But I knew one thing: I wouldn't leave this mystery buried.

I didn't know why, but I felt this strange protectiveness for the garden, for the memory of the woman who used to walk these halls. Something wasn't right, and I was determined to uncover the truth. Her appearances—both in the conservatory and in my bedroom—were horrifying, jarring, but what if... what if I could help her somehow? What if that was why she sought me out and guided me? I couldn't shake the feeling that if I didn't, the consequences would be dire.

I would help her.

If Jasper Blackwood had truly murdered Hester, and Darius, then he needed to pay, and with the appearance of this woman—Hester, I was nearly sure of it—I would find the proof to make that happen. I would do whatever I could so that Hester and her husband could rest in peace—and so the woman in the red dress would leave me alone.

CHAPTER 8
JASPER

There was a reason I didn't want people swarming in my privacy. People were only worth what you could use them for—something I'd learned early on in my life.

The girl shouldn't have been here. It would ruin everything. As soon as the press heard about this, the brief, temporary calm would be over.

Why had I let Sowerby talk me into doing something with this conservatory? Why had I challenged this girl? And why had she accepted? And why, for god's sake, could I not keep my focus on these proposals?

It had been barely a week since she'd arrived, but somehow during all of my business meetings, my mind continued to drift to Eliza Arnold and me in the garden and her dubbing Sowerby "Evil Alfred." I was oddly intrigued by how reserved she pretended to be. Typically, it was the other way around, with people pretending to be humorous or outgoing when they weren't. I made her nervous—something I didn't hate. She should be nervous around me. I was still surprised she hadn't left the manor yet. She was foolish and stubborn, but I doubted she'd make it another week here.

I liked when she pushed back—I hated when people pushed back, but with her, I was so unsure of whether she'd cower or snap, I found it...interesting.

It was even a bit addicting.

I found myself constantly thinking of other ways to bring a conversation up with her before I stopped myself. I'd spent too much time in isolation, and I was bored, that was all. I knew not to trust anyone, but still, sometimes I had to remind myself why it was important to keep everyone away. It had been a long time since I'd needed a reminder and one was due, that was all. I had no interest in starting *anything* with this woman, or anyone else for that matter. I had cultivated a tight circle of people who I could predict enough to keep in my life. The fact of the matter was, Sowerby was probably the only soul on this earth I would ever trust again, and I was fine with that. I wanted nothing more than control—over my legacy, over my family's ruined name, over everything. I would never be blindsided again. Everything in my world was carried out with cold precision and she would be no exception.

People couldn't be trusted. Give them a little bit of yourself and they would plow over you, leaving every part of you torn up in their wake. Now, I did the taking. No one had cared about me before, besides Sowerby, and no one would care about me later. People only wanted me because of what I'd made myself; they wanted a piece of my money and power. They didn't care what I'd done or what kind of fucking human I was—they just wanted to use me like a fucking tool. Fuck 'em all, every single last one of them.

At least Eliza was clear about what she wanted from me. I appreciated that in a person. Perhaps that's why she ended up staying here; our paths were meant to cross. But as she so quickly reminded me, in three months, she would be gone from Blackwood Manor too.

All the better. I hated strangers lurking about. I'd already caught her wandering the halls at three thirty in the morning the first week she was here; she said she couldn't sleep and wanted to check something in the conservatory but got lost on her way back.

Walking her back to her room had felt oddly like a date. I imagined that was how it went—it's something I wasn't actually very familiar with. I intentionally dated—and I use that term quite loosely—vapid, gold-digging women for a reason. They didn't want a connection with me just as I didn't want one with them. They wanted my money, and I wanted their presence at an event, and, on occasion, I wanted their body, nothing more—never more. It was purely transactional, the only kind of relationships I allowed. I didn't like that I kept thinking about Eliza Arnold. She felt unpredictable. I wasn't an impulsive person, and it seemed, in the few times this woman had been in my presence, I didn't think the way I normally did.

There was a tightness to her, like all her corners and edges had been sharpened with experience and were ready to cut you in this polite, superior way that she carried herself. It had slipped through too.

Still, this manor had been filled with nothing but darkness for decades, and Eliza Arnold, the pretty, anguished botanist, had already brought a bit of light into its murky corners. Katya, my ornery chef, had already raved about her, and she hated everybody. Maybe the woman staying here for three months wouldn't be quite as awful as I had originally thought. Or maybe it would destroy everything, all the privacy and calm I'd worked so hard to achieve.

Another impulsive decision pressed in on me until I couldn't deny it.

"Lidia," I said into my cell phone, leaning away from my desk. "Cancel my upcoming business in London; I'll be staying at Blackwood Manor until after the holidays. If they'd like my business, arrange for them to come here. There's a project at the manor that I need to make certain is completely finished in twelve weeks." I hung up the phone with a tap and dropped it onto the desk.

"I don't like her being here," Sowerby said as he walked into my office, as if he'd been reading my thoughts. "It's one thing to have the men working outside, but it's an entirely different thing to have her inside."

"I hardly notice any of them. Evil Alfred, good to see you. Where have you been all morning? I missed you at coffee. You'll be pleased to learn I've just canceled my plans for London," I said and immediately tracked his bloodshot eyes. Aside from the occasional construction noises, I'd almost forgotten the men were still working on completing the addition. I paid them well to be as invisible as they could be, even though my men watched them so closely they knew what color their shit was.

The older man stopped in the middle of his stride from the door. "I already told you, don't call me that. You what? You're staying at Blackwood for the holidays?" His deep-set wrinkles softened temporarily around his wise eyes. He moved to sit in one of the two leather chairs in front of my desk, all the while, deep in thought. "Because of the girl?"

I could feel his knowing, familiar eyes dissecting me with curiosity.

"Yes, I suppose I ought to be here to oversee the project myself instead of dumping her off on you, since I am the one who made the arrangement," I replied nonchalantly. "What is your gripe with the woman now? Has she been playing her music too loud again?"

I didn't tell him, but seeing the crotchety old man get so riled up by her unbothersome presence had been surprisingly entertaining.

Sowerby straightened up again into his curmudgeonly old self. "I can't say I'm not pleased to hear that you will be staying at Blackwood longer." There was a twinkle in his eye that belied his bored voice, something only I would recognize from years and years of knowing him. "But if you truly wish to know why I missed coffee this morning, then I *implore* you to ask the chaos demon herself. She's a timid, frightened thing, but I daresay the woman's spell has been cast upon more than just you and the rest of the staff, as she somehow managed to talk me into crawling to the bottom of the old koi pond like a friggin' kelpie to help her with the installation of a new pump. You should see what she's done to the black velvet vines and the way she has trimmed the fiddle leaf fig," he harrumphed. "If I didn't know better, I'd think she lied about working at the gardens altogether."

"You were in the koi pond? On the cement?" Laughter boiled out of me. She truly was a sorceress if she had managed to get Sowerby to do that type of physical labor. "You, my friend, are far too old to be crawling about anywhere. Next time, have her tell me and I'll get someone younger to do it."

"I beg your pardon! I am *not* too old. Why you are set upon thinking I am some wrinkled-up old bag that does nothing but waste away in this manor is beyond me." He rolled his eyes indignantly. "And by the way, I am absolutely *insulted* by your recent deposit. I've told you to stay out of my accounts. I don't want your money," he grumbled as his bushy gray eyebrows furrowed together conspiratorially.

I felt the corners of my eyes crease. "You *are* a wrinkled-up old bag who wastes their life away in this manor. I've given you a small fortune in the hopes that you'll wise up and finally leave this hellhole. Your dues have been paid." As I said the last sentence, I flinched slightly. It was a phrase I knew would rile up the old coot, and it had slipped out before I was able stop it.

He stood up from his chair with a withering scowl that made me sink into my seat like a lad in trouble.

Sowerby was not the kind of man to be messed with. He

hadn't always been a butler—in moments like these it was apparent. He was one of the few people who still had the ability to spark any amount of fear in my system. He had earned every crease and wrinkle he wore. He and I didn't talk about the past for a reason. We were both different people now and had tried to put our mistakes behind us.

His bloodshot blue eyes pinned me to the chair, daring me to utter another disrespectful syllable. My jaw tightened, biting a bit of my cheek as it did.

I cleared my throat. "Why don't I go and see if there's anything I can help Ms. Arnold with before dinner?" I felt the man's eyes attempting to pierce through the back of my head as I scurried out of my office.

CHAPTER 9
ELIZA

AFTER SEEING THE GHOST, I FELT CHANGED—SPIRITUALLY, yes, but also in a way that was deeper...if that was even possible, deeper than the soul itself. I didn't speak of what I saw to anyone—mostly because I wasn't sure that it was in my best interest to go telling everyone that I had seen a ghost without finding out a few things first, such as: Did the rest of the house know about her? If not, would the ghost want them knowing? Something in my gut told me it would be a betrayal to the woman, like I would be doubting her. I was terrified knowing that it wasn't likely the last time that I would be seeing her, and I certainly didn't want to infuriate her by doing something she didn't want. Besides, who would I tell? I was a solitary creature, without friends, and without investigating a bit further, it wasn't something I would bring up to anyone at the manor. I wished I had someone to talk to about the experience. Keeping all the tension and fear that this manor and that interaction had created inside me was only making me more paranoid and tense. In my twenty-five years of life, my controlling mother had excelled at keeping her influence the main one in my life—the only one in my life, really. She was already furious that I'd managed to get out of her reach and into the confines of Blackwood Manor—something she would have prevented had she known before my departure.

Even in her spirit form, the ghost in the red dress radiated a gentler, more loving, maternal presence than my mother was capable of producing, though both women were terrifying—at that moment, though, I was still more afraid of *my* mother. That realization dragged my emotions down and sank into my soul like an anchor plunging to the ocean floor. The picture in the locket, the way Jasper looked up at that woman as if she hung the moon caused a whisper of jealousy to curl around my heart. I wasn't certain, but if the woman in the red dress was the ghost of Hester, how could he have killed her? What I wouldn't have given to have been hugged by my own mother like that—just once. It was infuriating to think that someone had had that and hadn't appreciated it.

I wouldn't let him get away with it. Hester Blackwood deserved better than to be murdered by her own son.

As foolish and naive as it sounded, I wasn't sure I'd ever felt so important in all of my life.

I'd been there a little over a week, and I hadn't seen the ghost since that first day…and night. The next morning, I had almost convinced myself that none of it was real…until I'd felt the foreign weight of the chain around my neck. Every time the antique locket shifted against my chest, warm from being pressed so close against my skin, I was reminded of how real that night was. I reached up and closed my hand around it.

The locket felt oddly warm in my hand, heavier than I remembered. The gold had obviously dulled with age, but it still cast a faint glow in the dim light that I couldn't quite decide whether it was my imagination or something more. I ran my fingers over the delicate engravings, tracing the soft curves of the metal. It was clearly an heirloom, the surface worn by people long before me, each one leaving their invisible imprint—though, in some strange way, I could have sworn I could feel them all with just a touch. There was something sacred about the way it rested in my palm, as though it held a secret far too precious to be spoken aloud. I marveled at it, this small object that had endured for years—maybe even centuries—and still carried generations of memories. I knew I was foolish to cherish something like this—for all I knew, the ghost could have been using it to curse me or worse, but that one look of hope I had seen in her eyes affected me more than all the fear the interactions with her had caused.

I pressed my fingernail in the crease, and the tiny latch opened with a soft click, like the heavy sigh of something hidden that had finally been allowed to stretch its wings. Inside, the picture waited, delicate next to the red velvet lining of the other side of the locket. I leaned in close, my breath slow, almost reverent. The organ in my chest squeezed and stuttered at the sight before me.

The image had changed.

It was no longer a picture of the woman in a flowing red gown—but instead, a tiny painting of a single white dove, so beautifully detailed I could nearly feel the rush of its wings as if it were poised to lift off and take flight.

The dove's feathers were delicately painted in soft, ethereal whites. I thought it might be oil paints, though I was unsure. All I knew was that every brushstroke conveyed something intangible: a quiet elegance, a sense that the artist tried to capture not just the bird, but the very essence of hope.

The bird's eyes were soft, filled with a dreamy sort of optimism. Its posture was peaceful, graceful, yet beneath it all, there was a heaviness to the image, a sadness that whispered through the delicate curves of its form. I could almost hear the soft flutter of wings, see a brief glimpse of something untouchable, something lost, like the bird was carrying a message that could never quite be spoken, though it was understood.

How had the image changed since I'd last looked at it? It was impossible—the entire thing was impossible. The stress had finally gotten to me, and I'd snapped. All rational sections of my brain urged me to gather my things and leave Blackwood Manor at once, to put all of this nonsense behind me. Ghosts? Dead mothers? Magical hidden lockets?

It was impossible to believe any part of it—the most unbelievable thing being that anyone would choose to ask for *my* help when I was incapable of even helping myself.

The very real and tangible feel of the locket spoke to me, though. I couldn't ignore what was happening. I knew this was real.

What was she trying to tell me with the locket?

I closed my eyes for a second, letting the image of the dove fill my mind. Immediately, I understood that she was putting her hope in me. I imagined her wearing the locket and wondered if she, too, felt the weight of its beauty, the sharp pang of its quiet melancholy. Or was it simply a trinket that she wore and then forgot—left behind in the garden with the other discarded things, forgotten like the flowers in the conservatory had been for so long now? I couldn't begin to count the number of times I'd absentmindedly worn a piece of jewelry to a garden, only to have it get in the way as I dug or pruned; rings and necklaces clinking against the wood, annoyingly catching in the sleeves of my work clothes. As with any gardener, I never wore them for long, taking them off quickly so they didn't distract me. How often do we carry things we forget about until they're in the way or gone missing?

The way I related to this woman, this ghost, stirred something inside of me—something that felt too raw, too deep, to be comfortable. Already, it would have been impossible for me to abandon her. My curiosity alone was too great.

I hesitated, my fingers lingering over the closed locket, the image of the dove still vivid in my mind. I sat up in my bed, eyes squinting against the bright morning light that poured through the windows. I stretched, and as I did, felt the locket against my collarbone, its weight a steady, comforting presence. Like I wasn't really alone in the manor after all. I knew there were other people here, but I seemed to feel alone wherever I went, no matter how many people were with me.

As I got dressed, I tucked it beneath my shirt. There was a part of me that felt like Gollum with the ring, hoarding something precious, something too dangerous to share. Rightfully, it belonged to Jasper—even if it wasn't his mother's, it was someone in his family; the child that looked like him in the original photo proved it hadn't just belonged to someone who worked for the Blackwoods. But what if it was evidence that could help get justice for his parents? I was certainly not going to hand it over to the man—allegedly—responsible for killing them. I didn't want to hide it, not really. It was too beautiful, too meaningful. And though I couldn't explain why, it felt like it belonged close to me—close enough that I could always feel its presence, even if I couldn't see it. I touched the oval locket through the cotton of my shirt, my fingers lightly moving the fabric over the smooth metal.

I let my fingers linger for just a moment longer, wondering what else Blackwood Manor would reveal to me. The dove, hidden now beneath my shirt, was a secret I hadn't even begun to unravel. Something told me this was only the beginning—whatever the locket held, whatever it symbolized, it would find its way to the surface in time if I let it. The ghost was no longer alone. I was here to help her.

It struck me how calm I acted after seeing a ghost—about having interacted with her. The truth was, I was still terrified. I was jumpy and filled with nervous tension. If I saw her again while fully awake instead of in the haze of exhaustion, I was sure I'd be more frightened than ever. Maybe I'd have a heart attack and join the list of manor victims. I was haunted by more than just the fear of her, though—I was tormented with empathy.

It was how wild bears got rescued when they were wounded. It was why, when people heard someone crying for help from a well, they focused on helping and didn't think of the psycho clown that could be waiting in the shadows. Our bodies buzzed with the instinct to help, to save. That's how I felt—terrified yet needed and useful.

For now, though, without answers, I let the locket rest against my heart, a silent companion, carrying with it the promise of something I couldn't yet name—perhaps my own bit of hope.

Even this late in the afternoon in the conservatory, I could still feel a mournful chill in the outside air that occasionally flowed in through the broken panels. The heavy smell of moss and the earthy scent of rot swirled together in the stagnant space. The scent seemed to be lessening the more attention I paid to it, though a layer of dust and pollen still coated everything in sight. The windows cast warm golden streams and squares of light across the garden.

I knelt by the koi pond, feeling the sharp pressure on my knees as I continued scrubbing at the moss that had choked the edges of the pond's stone perimeter. I only needed to clear it away a bit more and then I could switch positions, relieving my kneecaps. Everything seemed to ache today, forcing me to realize how little physical labor my job as a botanist actually entailed comparatively.

Sowerby was brash and grumpy, but there was a softness to his edges, even if he fought it. Still, there was something a bit off about him, something that I couldn't quite put my finger on. Likely it was just my paranoia, but I couldn't help wondering if he was simply keeping tabs on me and my activities inside the manor. There was something dark sitting beneath his surface.

Unable to stay on my knees another second, I moved to the edge of the water feature. The soil was damp from where I'd watered it, yielding beneath my fingers as I pulled up clumps of weeds and scattered them aside, making sure to leave the pretty, flowering purslane and groundsel to the side for a nightstand bouquet. The task was simple, almost meditative, but there was a pressure sitting on my chest—a weight that had nothing to do with the decayed pond or the neglect that stained every inch of this glass room. It had everything to do with the man I could feel just beyond my peripheral vision.

Jasper.

His presence lingered in the air of the conservatory like a storm waiting to break, and I couldn't escape it. I wasn't sure if I wanted to. I felt like a storm chaser on the edge of an EF5 tornado, knowing I should have left long ago but unable to stop watching the spinning cyclone.

Refusing to acknowledge him first, I tried to focus on my work, on the trowel in my hand, on the feel of the rough stone beneath my palms and the musty earth scent in my nose, but my thoughts refused to stray and kept returning to him. He was everything the house was—dark, distant, brooding, and horrifying, covered up with a beautifully expensive varnish. There was an intensity in him that I didn't fully understand, a quiet sorrow. I'd seen it in his eyes, felt it in the silence between his words. Was that what happened when you became a murderer? Or did something else happen?

I wanted to hate him. I despised him for what he'd gotten away with, but instead of hate, I found I mostly feared him and the things he was capable of. Sometimes I was reminded that I was sleeping in the tiger's cage—a tiger that was thought to have killed before and could easily kill again.

The scrape of my trowel against the stone was too sharp,

too jarring against the stillness; it felt like a cry for help. I almost expected him to say something. But there was nothing but the deep quiet stretching between us.

And then, just as the thought flickered across my mind, his voice cut through the silence, low and gravelly. It snaked through my chest like it was my own vibrating breath.

"I heard you needed help this morning."

I could feel him standing in the doorway, watching me, his eyes like a force pressing on my skin and nerves. I didn't acknowledge him. I'd been in my own head in the silence of the garden for too long, and I wasn't sure how to take his words or his presence. Had he come to fight with me for not doing the job alone and having Sowerby help? I shrank in on myself, hoping he'd just go away. I continued pulling weeds from the pond, pretending the sound of his voice didn't rattle through me like an unexpected thunderclap. My eyes suddenly caught the way my soil-streaked fingers had begun to tremble.

"I heard you needed help this morning," he repeated, as if testing my reaction, the words curling between us like smoke. His voice had a slight rasp to it now, the words too soft, too deliberate—almost…kind. It was like he was forcing himself to speak, like he didn't want to but couldn't avoid it. "I just spoke with Sowerby."

I could feel the flicker of something in his words, an undercurrent of challenge, of disapproval, but also something else— something I couldn't quite name. It frustrated me how often I felt that with the people in this house, like they were all hiding something. I'd originally assumed that all the clipped words and nervous looks from the staff were born from fear of Jasper, but after seeing the ghost in the red dress, I wondered if it was something more. I needed to say something. He wasn't going away, and I was making it awkward. As much as I hated the man, I still needed him to not fire me and throw me out of the manor.

"Yes, he was incredibly helpful," I answered with a polite, humorless smile. My eyes stayed on the pond with my focus fixed on the task at hand. Still, I felt the need to fill the silence with something—anything. "I hope that doesn't negate our deal. The filter was too heavy for me to lift, and he volunteered. I assumed it would be okay."

He stepped forward, his polished boots creaking softly against the worn stone pavers, but I still didn't look up. I could feel his presence growing larger, more imposing, like a rain cloud gathering in the distance. I curled my body in a little, trying to make myself smaller, more compact, while respectfully redirecting my focus elsewhere. If I'd gained any skills in my life, it was the art of invisibility. I'd mastered the subtle art of being forgotten.

I kept working, knowing he'd turn and leave any second. He didn't.

"Sowerby isn't as young as he thinks he is," he said, his voice dropping lower, quieter now, like he was testing the very air between us. "And I'd hate to be left without my butler."

His words hit harder than I'd expected. They were quiet, but they were laced with genuine care for his aging staff—something that irked me more than I cared to admit. I wanted them to be cold, dismissive, but they weren't. They challenged me in a way I wasn't prepared for. My hands stayed frozen on the stone, the trowel stuck halfway through its scrape. I didn't answer right away—not because I didn't know the answer, but because I was afraid of what the answer might mean. God forbid the man have any redeeming qualities to add to the mess swirling in my mind.

"I thought Sowerby had mentioned you were leaving for business," I said finally, my voice steadier than I felt. I didn't meet his gaze, but I felt it on me all the same. Instead of him growing bored and leaving, I felt him staring at me, watching me in a way that made me aware of every part of my body. It was like he was trying to look inside of me, past the surface, past my carefully constructed mask.

He didn't reply at first, just watched me with that unnerving silence of his. I wanted to break it, to fill the space with noise, anything to make the tension between us more bearable. But it lingered. Was it because he was so attractive? Was that the source of this tension? Had I created it? I hated myself for it. He was a cold, awful murderer.

Why did I have to remind myself of that so frequently?

"Katya told me you would be away on business for the next three months," I said, unable to hide the annoyance creeping into my tone.

"Something here keeps me," he muttered under his breath, almost as if speaking to himself, as though the words were too much for him to say directly.

"Is it the addition? I thought they were almost done. That's what Katya said. I never see the workers, even when I go outside."

He ignored me. "This really does seem like too much work for one person. This place isn't...what it once was."

His words were softer now as he surveyed the conservatory, but no less intense. They hung in the air between us, sharp and raw, as if they'd been waiting to be released for a long time—like he wasn't just talking about the manor, but about something else entirely.

As he spoke, there was an understanding in his tone that complicated things more than I could handle, like maybe he wasn't as cold and horrible as the rumors would have me believe. It was confounding. The nerves in my body were strung tighter than a harp. His wistful words about the state of the manor felt unrehearsed and genuine, confusing me still more.

"Being broken creates character and strength," I said slowly, my voice quiet, still trying to remain small, though I wasn't sure if the words were meant for him or for me. "In places and in people, I hope." The instant I said the words, I regretted it. They were laced with a vulnerability I wished weren't so audible, one I prayed he didn't detect.

He stepped closer, his boots scuffing softly against the stone floor. It felt like he was closing in on me, and for a moment, I wished I could retreat, put distance between us. But I didn't. I couldn't. This odd kinetic energy between us wouldn't let me.

"Most broken things can't be salvaged," he said, his voice edged with something like frustration—or maybe something else. Something more meaningful. "Sometimes places and people aren't worth the effort."

I inhaled sharply, a flicker of something—hurt, maybe—sparking in my chest, but I wouldn't let it catch. Not now, not in front of him. I didn't know why it was so hard to remain invisible around him—it was normally so easy. "Just because something requires effort, that doesn't mean it isn't deserved," I said, my voice sharper than I intended. I finally looked up at him, meeting his gaze for the first time.

His eyes were darker than I remembered; they looked like the black of a storm right before the downpour. There had been a flash of something like surprise, but it disappeared quickly, replaced by that familiar coldness—the wall he was so careful to keep up. I couldn't blame him; I had my own set of walls. I could only imagine the skeletons in the hollows of his mental structure.

I didn't know why I was so irked. I didn't know why his words bothered me so much. Everything about him—this situation—was so wildly confusing. I wished he would leave, so I could maintain the awful image of him and continue despising him. I also wished I could find out what had happened to his mother and father. I'd already heard all of the rumors. I wanted to know the truth.

Unwilling to let my broken metaphor go, he continued. "You know nothing about this garden or the things it's seen," he said, the words sharper now but still quiet. "You can't restore this place in three months, and you and I both know it. So why do you insist on putting yourself through this day after day when you know you won't make it? It's been a little over a week, just quit now. I see you wince on your knees already. What could you possibly get from this? A raise? I doubt that. I've seen their figures. My donation will only be enough to secure another year, and you won't get another of that sum. Quit and find a new place to work. You were practically offering the sale of your soul to get this job. Why, Eliza? Why are you so determined to fix this place?"

I realized it was the first time I'd heard him say my name. It made me feel the same way I imagined a lock felt as a properly fitted key was inserted with a soft and satisfying click after sitting untouched for a time. The charged air between us snapped like a taut rubber band, so tight it threatened to break. I felt the anger rise in me again, hot and uncomfortable. But underneath it, there was a flicker of vulnerability. A crack in the wall between us—something raw and fragile that we both shared, but neither of us was willing to acknowledge.

I took a deep breath and looked away, feverishly pushing the trowel deeper into the soil at the pond's edge. "Because if I can't do it alone," I muttered, though the words felt hollow as soon as they left my mouth, "then I fail, and nothing changes. I can't do anything without her." I felt the fear sliding through my chest and arms, amping up the more openly I spoke with him.

"If you fail..." He was so close now that I could feel the heat of his body, the side of his hand brushing against mine, and my breath caught in my throat. His breath was warm against my cheek, and it sent a shiver down my spine. Somehow, he understood what I was saying. I could feel it. And I hated it. I wished the pond in front of me were full so I could drown myself—or him. The rigid, prickling fear in my body swirled suddenly with something more evocative.

"I can't fail," I replied, my voice quieter this time.

We stood there for a moment, the silence thick, both of us unwilling to break it.

I stared out across the conservatory, feeling him watching me, the intensity of his gaze too much to ignore, but I didn't look up. I couldn't. If I did, I was afraid I'd see something innocent I wasn't prepared for—something I wasn't sure I wanted to see.

Jasper stepped back, breaking the moment. His presence lingered, but he was no longer so intimately positioned. He turned toward the door, his shoulders tense, and my breath finally began to slow.

"I need to go," he said, his voice almost a whisper, though I knew it wasn't meant for me. I should've felt grateful he was leaving, but I didn't. I felt something else—something caught between frustration and the unsettling sense that, somehow, I had accidentally bared the tender pieces of myself only to have them repulse him.

Why did this happen to me in his presence? This manor—this man—seemed to crawl into my veins and eject my quiet, intentional disposition, only to bring forth a confrontational, vulnerable woman. Why did I speak so much to him?

I wanted to bang my head against the large display boulder in front of me. I heard his footsteps, slow and measured, as they echoed too loudly in the stillness of the conservatory. His boots sounded angry against the uneven floor, but it was the sound of the door closing behind him that cut through the air like a sharp exhale.

This was going to be a long three months.

Silence settled back over the room. My pulse quickened, my hands still gripping the trowel, my fingers white against the worn handle. I tried to shake off the thickness in the air, but it lingered, curling like smoke in my chest.

What had that been? Why was there this...this weirdness between Jasper and me?

I breathed in slowly, trying to steady myself. The scent of

dirt filled my lungs as I inhaled. There was nothing left to do in the spot I was in. The weeds were cleared, but I didn't want to move. Not yet. Not with this strange, magnetic pull between us still humming in the air. I was ashamed of the information I had volunteered. Why would I put myself out there like that to him? We hardly knew each other, and what I did know of him should have had me running out of here. He was not a good guy.

I needed to do some digging of my own and find out everything I could. I would get online tonight and find out what I could about Hester Blackwood. I shook my head. He hated everyone. There was nothing more to him than a spoiled brat turned deranged killer…whose roof I was now trapped under. And I had an opportunity that no one else had. I was inside the manor. I could snoop around and find some answers for myself about what had happened.

Jasper Blackwood, with all his brooding silence and cold detachment, was like the storm that had been building on the horizon outside. I knew it was there. I felt it. But I didn't know if I was ready to weather it. Without a doubt, he was the most dangerous part of Blackwood Manor, but just like a raging storm, as much as I knew I needed to stay away, I couldn't help but want to watch it.

I set the trowel aside, my fingers still tingling from where his hand had brushed against mine earlier. I couldn't shake the heat of it. I couldn't stop the way I reacted to him. It was maddening. Had he hung around any longer, I probably would've had a heart attack. There was something in the way he had looked at me when he spoke about this house—about the conservatory. It was like a glimpse into a part of him he never let anyone see—or at least that was what it felt like. Perhaps it held the answers I needed.

I rose from my crouched position, dusting my hands off on the fabric of my tattered baggy jeans. My legs were stiff from kneeling so long, but I forced myself to move to the back edge of the conservatory, away from where he had been. I stepped in the bed along the back wall. My hand brushed against a shard of glass, jagged and sharp, and I gasped as it cut my skin, the thin line of blood quickly welling up. I pulled my hand away, startled by the sting, but before I could even process the pain, I heard the quick sound of boots returning.

Jasper.

Fuck.

I hesitated; the last thing I wanted was another vulnerable moment with him. I could feel him approaching, and I wanted to hurl myself through the glass wall and over the distant cliff that I was too afraid to look at.

"You're bleeding," he said, his voice quiet. There was a dusting of concern. I glanced down at my hand, the thin line of blood trailing from my palm to my wrist. It wasn't serious, but it stung.

I was about to brush him off, but the words caught in my throat in a mix of fear and intrigue as his hand gently covered mine, guiding me farther away from the broken glass as if I were a lost child. His touch was unexpected—gentle but firm. I was still in shock from the contact, the heat of his skin radiating into mine. My eyes refused to blink. It felt like everything stopped moving, or I had just started. I couldn't seem to remember anything—including why I disliked him so much.

I turned to look at him, and his eyes were dark, unreadable, but there was a flicker of tenderness there. And I was too stunned to do anything but glare at him.

"Don't," he murmured.

His hand stayed on mine, and every muscle in my body tensed, every nerve lighting up in such an intense way that it made me want to pull away, as if I'd accidentally touched a hot stove. But I didn't move, and neither did he.

"Let me help," he said after a long pause, his voice a raspy whisper.

I could feel my pulse in my throat, in my fingertips. I should have pulled away. I should have stepped back, told him to leave me alone. But the words were stuck, lodged somewhere deep in my chest. Instead, I nodded, just slightly, too stunned to speak, too intoxicated by his masculine nearness.

He reached into the pocket of his coat, pulling out a small dark cloth, and gently pressed it against the cut on my hand. I could smell his cologne or aftershave. It was dark and mysterious, like him. Oud and vetiver cloaked in rich leather coiled into my senses. His touch was careful, deliberate, and for the first time since I'd met him, I saw something not so guarded, not so distant. His fingers were cool against my skin, and my breath wouldn't seem to regulate. A thrum of fear ricocheted up my spine and lower belly, making my shoulders quake for a second. A much different sensation danced with fear and fluttered in my lower abdomen.

"You don't have to do this," I whispered, my voice rougher than I meant it to be. "I'm fine."

He didn't pull away. Instead, he looked at me with a heavy gaze, his expression unreadable. "You're not fine. Not here."

I could feel the shift between us, like something was unraveling. I was torn between feelings and logic.

"Don't worry, I don't think you'll scar," he said with a hint of humor, referencing his own scar.

"How did you get it?" I whispered, unable to stop myself. He was so close, it took everything to not reach out and touch the deep, jagged line across his forehead.

He focused on my hand, cleared his throat, and kept his eyes down, looking almost ashamed. "Bike accident when I was sixteen," he murmured.

"How did the bike fare? Matching scar?" I said in an attempt to lighten the moment.

His face grew even more stern and humorless. "Bike was fine; the scar was given to me when the man I stole it from bashed my head in with a shovel."

I tried not to visibly show how surprised I was at that.

The muscles in his jaw twitched and his brows lowered. "I know what it's like," he said, his voice quieter now, almost a murmur. "To feel...like you're alone and everyone is waiting for you to fail." His voice broke on the last word, but only for a second. Just a crack, like a faint echo of something deep inside him.

I swallowed, my throat tight, but I didn't know what to say. I didn't know what words could fix whatever it was he was feeling or if I wanted to.

I thought of the rumors, all the tales of him murdering his parents after being an evil, spoiled child and all the stories of him lashing out at them in public. The sight of Jasper's mother grasping at her throat at the foot of my bed snapped into my head. Suddenly, I was feeling a thousand different things, and I couldn't pick just one to focus on. Pure danger seemed to ooze out of his pores in a confusing, almost appealing way.

"You don't know what it's like," I said defensively. "I doubt you even loved your parents before you killed them." The words slipped out before I could stop them. I hadn't meant to say any of them, hadn't meant to go there, but the words were already out, and I was grateful. I needed the distance—but I prayed it didn't come with consequences.

His gaze shifted, a flicker of something dark crossing his features. He pulled his hand back, as if my words had physically pushed him away, and I flinched reflexively before seeing his hand was at his side. I'd never met another person that elicited such a chaotic, loose-tongued response from me. Of course it would be someone extremely dangerous to do that to.

"I'm sorry for whatever it is you've gone through." His voice was cold again. His eyes didn't meet mine anymore. They were focused on something else—something far away. "Though, contrary to what you might believe, I did very much love my parents."

Underneath his anger, I heard it—the rawness in his voice. The echo of something broken, something that spoke to a pain I knew too well. I was struck by the realization that he didn't want to be confessing his vulnerabilities to me either, but like me, he couldn't seem to stop.

"I don't need you to be sorry for me. My parents are still alive."

The words hit harder than I meant them to, but I couldn't stop them now.

He didn't speak at first, but the silence between us was no longer full of distance. There was a flicker of understanding—silent, fleeting—but there. Just for a moment. We were both thrown off with our response to one another.

It made Jasper seem…human. He wasn't the impenetrable figure I had tried to understand. He wasn't the brooding man hiding secrets in a strange, dark manor. For one moment, he was just someone who felt the same brokenness that I did.

His lips parted, but no words came out. Instead, he glanced down at my hand, the cut still there but the bleeding slowing. His eyes flickered to my face. "You shouldn't have come here," he murmured again, his thick brows pinching together.

He turned to leave again, and I didn't stop him. I watched him retreat into the shadows of the doorway, my heart still hammering in my chest.

Something was happening that I didn't fully understand. Never in my life had I experienced such dark fear from someone mixing with such a confusing whisper of attraction. There was something so oddly thrilling, intoxicating about the sensations that shot through my system when he was close to me. Danger had swirled with hunger in a very, very unsafe way. I had never been one to play with fire, and I wouldn't start now. I knew that if I wanted to leave this manor alive, I needed to stay as far away from Jasper as possible.

CHAPTER 10
ELIZA

There were muscles aching in my back that I didn't know I had. Hours spent bent over in the garden, digging and pulling weeds, had broken me. I'd never even come close to working on a garden that required this level of labor, and I wasn't even halfway through weeding. Every day seemed to get longer and harder, with the small break of sleeping never bringing enough recovery time.

My hands were stiff, stained with dirt after abandoning my gloves from friction blisters, and now carrying calluses. The exhaustion had settled deep into my bones, each movement slower than the last. God, I just wanted to fall into my bed, but I couldn't. I doubted I'd sleep anyway, not with my mind racing the way it was. My heartbeat even felt odd, irregular, with a deep thumping every few minutes that hit my chest like a timpani drum.

It had been a few days since Jasper and I fought in the garden—if "fought" was the right word—and my mood had only gone downhill since. There had been no more signs of the ghost, and every single day that passed showed me how truly incapable I really was. I'd thrown myself into the labor, avoiding the kitchen and dining spaces when I knew Jasper might be there. I was embarrassed by everything I'd said to him, even if I shouldn't have been. Everything was starting to cave in around me, and I'd never felt more alone.

Earlier, I'd called into my work to check in and see if they could help me identify a few plants. I'd flagged several specimens I was unsure of, and after my boss had easily helped me, he chuckled awkwardly and asked me if I'd spoken with my mother lately.

My stomach had bottomed out and sunk through the floorboards somewhere.

She couldn't let there be a single part of my life she didn't control, and I'd angered the beast by working at the manor. Apparently, she had called him earlier in the week to tell him that working on Blackwood Manor alone was far too advanced for me and that he should send someone else to "be safe." She also apparently told him that I wasn't all that happy at Pinehurst Botanical Gardens and that I had some more important environmental work I'd rather be doing.

I'd texted her, telling her where I was and what I was doing, but until today, I hadn't picked up a single phone call from her since arriving here—the massive iron gates giving me a false sense of distance and courage. This was my punishment for not answering her calls. It never failed. Every. Single. Time. I tried to distance myself from her in an attempt to actually look out for myself, and she would punish me somehow worse than before.

Dr. Lithgow, my boss, had been kind but understandably uncomfortable, and told me that if I'd rather not be at Blackwood Manor or Pinehurst, then he would start working on finding my replacement, and then he gently but sternly told me how much he disliked being "in the midst of family drama."

I was mortified.

Pinehurst Botanical Gardens had been the one place I had

been able to keep her away from—the one and only place I'd been able to have a normal life. The familiar feeling of being overtaken and dismantled washed over me. I didn't know why I bothered to fight back anymore.

Now more than ever, my worries about failing this project haunted me. It was an impossible task, just as Jasper had said.

My hands vibrated with fury as I tapped my password and scrolled until I found her contact in my cell phone. I was so angry I could hardly think straight. The only reason I was even at Blackwood Manor was to secure rare plant propagations and a donation for the botanical garden that would secure my job. I was exhausted and frightened every damn minute of my day, and now she was going to risk me losing my job no matter how well I did the job? Why couldn't she just for once leave me alone and torment someone else? Irritation caused my heart to race and pound in my throat. This was it, I was going to let her have it for once.

The phone rang once before she picked up.

"I hope you're having a good time." Her voice shot through the line, and I felt her irritation.

"Hello, Mother," I said. Automatically my anger went from a boil to a simmer, de-escalating at the sound of her voice. No matter how angry I was, experience had told me she could be angrier. "No, I'm not having a good time. I'm exhausted. I'm working nonstop."

"Child, do not get an attitude with me. This was all your doing. Do you know how stressful the last two weeks have been for me?"

My eyes closed as I tried to rein in my emotions.

"I just spoke with Dr. Lithgow, Mother. Why would you call my work? Why? You could have cost me my job." My voice broke as a crackle of emotion surged into it.

"Cost you your job? You should be thanking me for calling him, Eliza. Look at your judgment right now."

"My judgment?" My fingers gripped the phone so hard I thought it might snap into pieces.

"Yeah," she snapped back. "You're at Blackwood Manor, Eliza—voluntarily. Of course I'm right to question your judgment. It just proves that you have no discernment to make your own choices. How many times have I told you about how awful the Blackwoods are? Do you have any sense of self-preservation? Obviously not. Do you think they care about you? They—he doesn't. They didn't care about an entire town of people when that factory of theirs was leaking toxic waste. How many times do I have to drill into your head how horrible they are?"

I had to put my palm over my forehead before my headache caused my skull to split open and spit out my brain. I had heard the story of the toxic chemical leak that wrecked the town of Pinehurst more times than it had rained. It was horrible what had happened, the entire place was shut down after people in the town got sick from chemicals in the water supply. The Blackwoods had paid off the people that mattered and after most of the plant's workers moved away and everything was fixed, it seemed Lorreta Arnold, my mother, was the only one who hadn't seemed to move on from it.

"I know, but you don't need to invade my privacy and call my work," I said with a softer tone. As annoying as it was, in her own way, she was just worried about me.

"You should quit the botanical gardens anyway and come work with me like I've been telling you."

"I don't want to—" I tried to object carefully. This was also a discussion we had too frequently. It was probably the one thing in life she had wanted from me that I hadn't bended to her will on.

She cut me off, as usual not caring about my reasons. "Jasper Blackwood is worse than his parents were, and they were awful. The only reason that boy isn't rotting in prison for murdering them is because he got their money and has everyone in his back pocket. He was evil at fifteen and he's no better now. It's all hidden by Blackwood Industries. If you can't see the danger that you're in, then as your mother, it's my responsibility. I'm coming to get you now."

A chill ran through my body at the thought of her coming to get me. "No, Mother. I'm not leaving yet. Everything is fine. Jasper has been fine. I'm here until I finish this conservatory. You should see the corpse flow—"

"You're fucking him. I knew it. You're more like your sister than I thought." Her words cracked across my heart like a whip, and my mouth fell open.

"I'm not having sex with him, Mother!"

"You know I wondered why of all people he'd let you inside that place, and now I know. The only reason he's letting you play around in that conservatory is so he can sleep with you. He never cared about his mother or her things, and you don't know what to do with plants of any value. You're barely even a botanist," she said coldly.

I had to sit down on the stone paver path before I fell. It was hard to believe how much hope had to do with keeping you steady and upright. When I said nothing in response and she could sense that she had tamped down on any defiance I may have had at the beginning of our conversation, she continued.

"If you're going to be a slut, you should at least get some money for yourself and not just the botanical garden," she continued.

"I'm not being a slut. We are not sleeping together," I repeated quietly.

"Right," she said condescendingly. "If you take some to the nonprofit Dad and I work for, they will give you a good position. Better than what we could get you."

"I need to go."

There was a brief moment of silence.

"One day, I hope you have a daughter just like you, so you have to go through all of this stress and pain." Her breathing picked up until she was hysterically crying. "God forbid I love you and want what's best for you, what a horrible mother I must be. I'm so sorry that you have a mother who loves you so much." Her crying grew louder and more dramatic.

I was still angry, and even though I knew she was being manipulative, I still couldn't help but feel bad. I didn't want to make anyone feel bad. I didn't agree with how she loved me, but I didn't think she could help the way that she was.

My voice was soft and comforting with only a whisper of irritation. "I need to go, Mom. Don't come here. I'm fine. I'll call you later."

I hung up the phone, completely drained and defeated. After almost two weeks, it was hardly evident I'd done anything to the conservatory if you didn't know where to look, and to make matters worse, after sending pictures of the corpse flower to Dr. Lithgow, he believed I only had two months until it bloomed—I'd thought three when I first got here, which meant I had two fewer weeks than I'd originally thought.

I was defeated physically and emotionally. I had nothing left to give and I could feel myself breaking even as I stood on the stone path and looked around. My mother was right. Everyone at work was right. Jasper was right. I couldn't do this.

There was no way I'd be able to restore the entire conservatory in two months. I'd hardly begun and already I was failing. My chest thumped uncomfortably, the stress growing painful as it ate at my sore body.

I wasn't sure I'd ever felt lonelier or more defeated, which spoke volumes. I thought about trying to take the drive into town to meet with some friends from work, but the truth was, I didn't really have any friends. I had people that drained my energy and unloaded on me. People who would complain to me but never cared how I was doing or wanted to hear what was bothering me. I had no one that I could lean on. So I worked another few hours into the night, fighting away the burn of hot tears in my eyes until I knew I didn't have another hour left in my body.

Slumping down into the weeds, I let the tears fall into the soil. I had nothing and no one. What had I been thinking to even attempt something like this? Who did I think I was? Why was I even fighting for Pinehurst Botanical Gardens so hard? Things would be easier if I stopped trying to go against the grain and just worked with my mother. Maybe things wouldn't be so hard then, maybe she'd finally lighten up on me.

Even as the thought filtered through my head, I knew it wasn't true and never would be. My mother would never be nice to me and things would never change. This was just my life. Some people got families that were kind and sweet and gentle…and others didn't. A wave of guilt rippled through me, knowing I was being selfish. Things could be so much worse—things were so much worse for other people. Some people didn't have parents.

My damp face burned as I rubbed the cotton of my sleeve over it and let out a sigh. I needed to grab something to eat from the kitchen and go to bed. I didn't want to be awake for another second.

On my way to the kitchen, I tried to move as quietly as possible. But my legs were sore, the sharp kind of ache that stabbed and ripped. My back was stiff from hunching over, and my swollen, blistered fingers protested with a throb every time I flexed them. I knew I was pushing myself beyond what was reasonable, but I wasn't sure I could stop even if I wanted to.

Maybe I should quit and run off, away from everyone. It was a fun fantasy until I remembered I needed to eat, and food and housing weren't free—and I couldn't leave without helping the ghost of Blackwood Manor.

For a few seconds, though, as I walked through the dark

house, I let myself imagine what it would feel like if I did pack up and run away from everything. I wouldn't be a botanist anymore. No, I'd do something I wanted to do, something creative, like be an artist. I loved painting, even if I had only ever done it in secret. As a botanist, the book I used to sketch plants was called my botanical sketchbook or field notebook. Botanists typically used them for recording observations, drawings, and notes about plants we encountered in the field. I always chose to paint my specimens. It was the closest thing to becoming a painter I would ever get to experience, and that was okay.

It was late; the house was still and quiet; save for the faint hum of the wind outside and the occasional creak of the old timber beneath my feet and the soft sound my Vans made when they hit the marble floor of the kitchen. I thought I would be alone in the kitchen, but as I reached the threshold, I tensed and froze.

Jasper.

He stood in the doorway on the other side of the kitchen, his broad shoulders outlined by the dim light coming from under the cabinets. His eyes flickered to me, and for a second, neither of us spoke. The air between us felt like it was still holding on to the remnants of our argument from a few days ago. The disagreement that had been hanging over us, unresolved and jagged. I wondered if he even cared. Probably not.

I swallowed, trying to make the discomfort fade, but it lingered. "Didn't think anyone would still be awake," I said, my voice rougher than I expected; the words were clumsy in the quiet of the room. There was a bite to them. I was too tired to fix it. Let him fire me—at least I wouldn't have to fight staying here anymore.

His gaze ran over me, lingering as if he was making certain that I felt the trail of his brown eyes. He'd probably noticed the exhaustion on my face, the way my hair had fallen loose from the tie at my neck, the way I was carrying myself like I was about to collapse. I wished I could say I was too tired to care about how I looked or much of anything except getting some peace for a few minutes, but the truth was, I hated that he was seeing me so run-down. For some stupid reason, I found myself wishing I looked prettier, which only caused me to grow more irritated for feeling that way. I needed to keep far, far away from him while I worked to unfold what happened to the ghost or else I might join her. It was easy to see how one got tangled in his dangerous web.

"I didn't think you'd still be out there," he said, his voice quieter than usual. I could hear the hesitation in it. "With the garden."

I nodded. I didn't trust my voice enough to say anything else. I should've turned around and left.

He looked at me, and I felt the depth of it—the questions that hung between us. I knew he could tell I'd been crying. I couldn't stand for another second without leaning on something, so I moved to the kitchen sink and pressed my body against it and turned on the faucet. The cool water was a small relief to the burning ache in my hands. I rubbed my palms together, working the dirt away, but it didn't come off. Not all of it. There was something in that, I thought. The way I couldn't seem to wash it off, no matter how hard I tried to get rid of it. There were a lot of things I felt that way about, especially in this kitchen, right now.

The silence and the tension were too much, and eventually my resolve cracked.

"I've hardly made a dent in two weeks, and my boss thinks the corpse flower will bloom in two months, not three," I rambled, my quivering voice quieter than I intended, barely a whisper over the sound of water running. I didn't look at him. I couldn't look at him just yet. Not when the tension between us was still sharp, still raw. I was afraid I'd burst into tears. Had he not been standing in this kitchen, I wasn't sure I could've kept the sobs inside.

My heart thumped again, and in the stillness of the room, I realized that it wasn't my heart that beat so loudly.

The gold locket moved and twisted under my shirt, violently thudding as it landed back against my chest.

It felt like the blood in my veins stopped.

What should I do? Do I grab it? Open it?

Jasper was standing right there. What if he recognized it?

It was still for another minute and then lifted and twisted angrily under my shirt, as if something were trapped inside the brass oval.

Jasper didn't move for a long moment, and I wondered if he was going to say something else. He probably thought I was crying, hunched over like I was. But instead, he sighed—low, like he was trying to let go of something. His footsteps were slow when he finally stepped a little closer, the sound muted against the cold marble floor.

Fuck.

"I never meant to..." His voice trailed off, and I could tell he was wrestling with the words, unsure of how to finish the sentence. He exhaled deeply, like it was a struggle to get the words out at all.

I could feel him moving closer behind me. What if he saw the locket move?

"I shouldn't have said what I said about your family," I said, cutting him off nervously. "I don't know why I—You were right. It's unbelievably lonely here. I'm sorry I—" Words left my brain as the locket moved, making a sound as it rattled from under my shirt, louder this time. I needed to get him away from me before he realized I had what I suspected was his mother's locket in my hand.

Panicked, I turned to see if he noticed. Thankfully he'd turned around, facing away from me.

Keeping my back to him just in case, I hurriedly pulled the chain out from under my shirt and grasped ahold of the locket.

It rolled slightly in my palm. Something *was* inside, desperately struggling to get out. With a quick glance backward to assure myself that Jasper still wasn't looking, I opened it.

I swallowed my scream as a white dove flew out of it and whipped past my face, flapping its wings wildly as it soared directly toward Jasper. The dove painting was no longer a painting but a real-life dove, gliding through the kitchen of Blackwood Manor.

I whipped around to watch the chaos unfold, unsure of what to do.

"Holy...shit," Jasper said as he fell back away from the bird. "The fuck?" He moved the crisp button-up he wore to grab a sleek black pistol tucked in the waistband at the back of his dress pants.

A shiver ran across my skin. Did he always carry a gun in his own home, or was that just while I was here? Which of those would be the better answer?

"Don't hurt it!" I cried, and he dropped his shirt instantly and started swatting at it. It was fluttering in circles above his head, trying to land on him.

"What the fuck is a pigeon doing in my kitchen?" he said as he dodged the bird chaotically.

"Just hold still. It's a dove!" I shouted at him. "Let it land!"

"It's gonna shit on me!" he called back as he continued to flail frantically.

A snort of laughter escaped me as I watched the scary, handsome millionaire spin and twirl, trying to keep the flapping bird off him.

"Oh, you think this is funny, do you?" he said, as the corner of his mouth lifted slightly.

"Stop!" I shouted back when he moved across the kitchen, bringing the flapping bird toward where I stood.

Laughter left my throat as I tried to evade him and run into the large, open pantry, but he cut me off with the stealth of a panther, cornering me in the nook of the L-shaped counter.

"Get back over there!" I commanded through my throaty giggles and the sound of flapping wings. My hair was whipping into my eyes with the wind from the bird's chaos.

"You do think this is funny," he said with a huff. He put a muscular arm on either side of me, completely boxing me into the corner with his body, trying to transfer the bird onto me.

He was so close that I could see the loose thread on the top button of his shirt, the smattering of stubble across his tan face, the soft look in his deep brown eyes as they caught on mine.

The air shifted between us, no longer full of humor. Instead, a curious hunger filled the room.

His eyes dropped to my mouth, and I was suddenly aware of every molecule in my body. It felt as if they'd all awakened and suddenly started to reach for him. I couldn't seem to look away from his mouth, from a tiny freckle on the bottom corner that touched his lower lip. I couldn't stop no matter how hard I tried.

His breath tickled across my face. My eyes wouldn't move, my energy too focused on not leaning in any farther. *We are going to kiss*, I suddenly thought. *What do I do? Do I grab his gun? Kiss him back? Taste the small freckle on his lip?*

"Has it landed yet?" he whispered.

I continued to watch the freckle. I had no idea what he was talking about.

I stared at him for a second before realizing he was talking about the bird. My eyes moved over him before I realized that the dove had landed on his shoulder and was happily watching the two of us with a hint of mischief in its expression—could birds look mischievous?

"Don't move, it's on your shoulder," I whispered and looked around the kitchen. "Should we try to put a pot or something over it and take it outside?" I was at a complete loss for what to do when your haunted-locket dove went haywire. Was I supposed to put it back in the locket somehow? That seemed harsh. Release it? Oh my god, was it Hester? I needed to find pictures of Hester to see if she even was the ghost. It could be an aunt or someone. I looked at the bird again with more apprehension. There was most definitely a familiar twinkle in the bird's dark reddish eyes.

Was it Hester? And was she...trying to get me close to her son?

Jasper's low, raspy whisper interrupted my thoughts. "Don't move one fucking muscle, do you hear me?" I froze just as I'd lifted a pan off the drying rack on the counter. "Attagirl, now get on my fingers."

I nearly dropped the pan before I realized he was talking to the dove. A third-degree blush overtook my face and body in complete mortification. When I glanced at him, he'd managed to get the bird on his finger. His large, muscular body was rigid as he slowly moved to the door. I saw the tips of a black tattoo creeping up past the collar at the back of his neck. I wondered what it was of. My eyes scanned his back, trying to imagine if he had others. I bet he did. I swallowed a gulp of air. Oh my god. I was attracted to him—like really-fucking-physically attracted to him. *Hello, body? He's a fucking MURDERER!*

"Eliza, could you please be a lamb and follow me to open the window?" he asked calmly as he walked into a large laundry room at the back of the kitchen.

At the sound of him calling me a lamb, my mind automatically pictured a sacrificial slaughtering. Trying not to make any quick movements, I got ahead of him, flipped the latch on the window, and pushed it up. We both flinched when the window screeched, afraid that the bird would get wild again.

"No, no, don't fly off. I know you're frightened, and I know I'm scary looking, but I've got you. I won't let anyone harm you." His low, raspy voice was soft as he spoke to the bird. "I'm going to set you free, okay?"

"Okay," I whispered before snapping my head up and

sucking my lips inside of my mouth. Another blush crawled across my cheeks.

"You okay?" he asked me.

I heard the window close.

He'd already set the bird—or quite possibly his mother—free while I stood there and stared at him like a woman in heat.

"Yeah…" I answered, completely caught off guard by everything that had just happened.

"Must've gotten in through one of the broken conservatory windows and followed you in the house," he reasoned as we walked back to the kitchen together.

"Yeah…must have," I said as I tucked the locket back under my shirt carefully. "I'm sorry about what I said to you in the conservatory," I said, my voice thick with something that felt like regret but was tangled up with all my other emotions now. "I just… Everything's been so much, and I didn't know how to handle it, I guess." I could have just let things go, but I wanted things between us to be okay. Perhaps Hester *was* behind this. "What is your tattoo of?" I found my station by the counter in the kitchen again. My fingers gripped the edge of the sink to stop the slight tremor in my hands. I couldn't tell if it was from exhaustion or the weight of the conversation that hung between us or something else, but I didn't dare let go.

His eyes narrowed slightly, and a smirk touched his mouth. He took a step closer, and I could hear the soft rustle of his shirt as he moved, feel the subtle tension in his body. Another dark tattoo, this one on the inside of his palm, flashed into my focus as he hooked the back of his shirt collar and lifted it, revealing a black-and-gray photorealistic skeleton hand curled around the back of his neck. A small gasp left my mouth at the haunting realness of it—and how hot it looked on his tan skin. It made him look even scarier and more unhinged. It looked so out of place and yet oddly perfect all at the same time—though that was kind of how he looked—all scarred and muscular in his expensive suit. He looked like he should be some sort of MMA fighter or something. My feet shuffled backward, but my heels hit the cabinet, stopping me from moving back even another inch. Surprising even myself, I boldly grabbed the hand covered in tattoos and flipped it over to see what was on his palm. It was some sort of dragon-looking snake that formed a circle with its body as it swallowed its own tail. Inside was something written in Latin.

"It's an ouroboros," he said with darkening eyes. He watched me with the focus a wolf keeps on a doe that's about to run. "It symbolizes creation and destruction, war and peace."

"What does it say? Is it Latin?"

He nodded. "Ego sum finis. I am the end."

I swallowed and dropped his hand, but not before he noticed how mine trembled. He was powerfully intimidating from far away; this close, it was almost hard to breathe.

"You don't have to explain," he said, his voice quiet but insistent. "I get it. I know the rumors. This place—it gets to you over time. Believe me, I understand. I'm sorry too." He ran his hands through his hair. "I suppose I don't need to tell you, I'm not really good with people, never have been." There was a vulnerable crack in his voice before he cleared his throat. "I—I didn't kill my family, Eliza. I want you to know that. The ghosts of victims, everything, it's just lies and rumors."

There was something dark in his eyes that wouldn't let me believe his gentle tone. It felt like he was trying to trick me. Like he could snap at any second and the gentleness would be replaced with danger. My nerves tingled under my skin, waiting to see if he would pull out a gun and put it to my temple or wrap his palm around my throat and watch as he squeezed.

"No one knows what really happened—at least, not anyone outside the manor."

It seemed important to him that I know, and I didn't know

what to do with that. It wasn't what I expected from him. There was something sincere in his tone that felt genuine. He seemed so tender and human now even though I knew better than to believe it.

"Why does everyone think that?" I said, still staring at the sink, unable to meet his eyes. "How did they die?" I knew I shouldn't ask, but I couldn't seem to help myself.

The silence in the room was thick, heavier than anything I had felt in a long time, none of the secrets wanted to come to light. Anger and hurt tugged at his face. For a moment, I wondered if maybe I should tell him about the ghost visiting me. Maybe it would disturb him, and he'd tell me what had really happened. Maybe then I could find evidence or whatever it was the ghost wanted from me.

But then, his voice—soft but steady—reached me. "My parents aren't dead," he said, and something in my chest tightened, then released, like a knot slowly unraveling. "They are still very much alive."

They are still very much alive.

The words sat at the edge of my brain, refusing to sink in no matter how many times I replayed them. His parents weren't dead. His parents weren't dead?

Then how was the ghost of his dead mother haunting me? If it wasn't Hester Blackwood, then who was it?

He could have been lying to me. He had to be—which meant he really did do it. What was I talking about? Of course he did it! Was I crazy? Was something wrong with me? I knew I had seen the ghost; I knew it. Not to mention the dove flying out of the locket. What was going on in this house?

I tried to keep a neutral expression, but I couldn't slow down my breathing—I was about to have a panic attack. I looked at my palms, searching for some sort of proof that I was still here, that I was real. My shaking hand flew to my chest and felt for the locket beneath the fabric of my shirt.

The locket was there, the one the ghost led me to. The ghost was real. What was going on?

I wanted to scream and cry, but I couldn't. I couldn't let him know anything that was happening.

"Your parents are alive," I repeated in complete shock. "How—"

"Yes, but not tonight. It's late and I'll never sleep if I get into it now," he said, stopping my questions.

A few layers between us had been peeled back, and I hoped I was one step closer to helping the ghost—of his mother? Of another ancestor? Regardless, if I could get him to open up to me more, with her help, I could figure out what had really happened.

I swallowed, suddenly feeling like I was standing on the edge of something I wasn't sure I could handle. "Not tonight," I whispered. The words felt like they might break apart in the air. He wasn't telling me no—just not now. It was something.

He nodded. There was a quiet acceptance in his eyes, but also a flicker of…relief, maybe? Or perhaps just the same uncertainty I was feeling. He turned then, walking back toward the door without another word. My eyes trailed over his back as he left.

I stood for a long time after he was gone, my body aching, my mind still tangled in the conversation we had just had. I was suddenly terrified to go to my room, horrified by the thought of seeing the ghost woman again and unsure of what to believe.

If it wasn't his mother, then who was it? And if it was Hester Blackwood and he was lying, then it was safe to say Jasper and I getting closer was more dangerous than I could have imagined. For some reason, the thought of him lying to me stung. I realized I desperately didn't want him to be lying to me and didn't want to admit that I was attracted to a fucking killer.

But if his parents weren't dead, where were they?

CHAPTER 11

ELIZA

I RUBBED THE SOFT FABRIC BETWEEN MY FINGERS METHODI-cally in soothing repetition.

I sat on the edge of my bed and stared over the top of the chair, out across the endless expanse of sky, looking through the nearly translucent safety of the sheers that blurred the terrifying image. I was terrified by the lack of anything but sky when I looked out, but this morning I was too exhausted to fear it—as long as it stayed on its side of the chair.

I glanced at my laundry basket of clothes, grateful that I had never unpacked them from their makeshift suitcases. The other one, filled with books and random things, sat next to it, ready to go in a second if needed. Even in my own apartment, most of my things were kept this way—in baskets or boxes that would be easy to carry out should something happen. I didn't know why I did this, but I always had. Even in my childhood home, I had never taken up too much space, hoping I could fly under my mom's radar and leave in a flash—if I was ever allowed. It never worked, but the habit stuck.

Tears threatened the back of my eyelids as my eyes fell closed. My palms were red and swollen with blisters from the wooden handle of my hoe; it burned every time my fingers moved. The simple act of letting the weight of my head drop sent searing pain down my spine and across my back.

I hadn't even stood up yet.

If I quit and left now, I'd have nowhere to go. Not really. My mother had a key to my apartment—the apartment I would no longer be able to afford after I lost my job. And I couldn't face my mother right now. This would be my last straw—if she laid into me about how much I'd fucked everything up, if she got angry enough to get physical, my body couldn't handle it right now.

Nothing strange had happened last night—at least, not after I'd gone to bed. No see-through ladies in red had appeared, no odd creaks, not even a weird scurrying in my peripheral vision. I almost wished it had. Then maybe I could analyze it, ask her something…make sure I wasn't just seeing things. When I was a kid, I'd always thought I saw things in my room, just at the edges of my sight, where the lines of certainty blurred enough to keep me guessing.

I wasn't just going to take Jasper's word and believe his parents were still alive, but it definitely made me more nervous and opened a million more questions. The number to the Clearview Psychiatric Clinic was still on my phone's screen from when I had pulled it up last night, after briefly convincing myself that the ghost was probably a result of some sort of psychotic break I was having. But again, the locket quickly squashed that worry—she had not been a figment of my imagination.

I shouldn't have believed a word he said, but I just didn't get the feeling that Jasper was lying about his parents still being alive. Alive people couldn't appear see-through at the end of your bed and communicate with you through magical lockets, but I had no guarantee the ghost was Hester. Every time I started to think that the trauma and stress had finally gotten to me and made me snap, my logic was caught on the locket.

I was grateful for the grounding reminder, even if it was less than comforting. I'd taken it off last night, but it was still there, on my bedside table, real and tangible. I was afraid to open it, unsure of what I wanted to find inside. Even though there was this tug telling me I wasn't mentally unwell and that it was all real, the exhaustion was not making it easy to think.

The thought of going into the conservatory this morning felt like I was preparing to walk into a losing war.

The only reason I hadn't gotten in my car and driven off was the woman in red. No matter how hard I tried, I couldn't seem to get past the look in her eyes when I'd followed her and went into the conservatory to find the locket. She needed me, like her life—her death?—depended on it. I could tell, and even if it wasn't Hester, she still needed me.

I didn't know what to think about how I felt about Jasper either. Sometimes I hated him and wanted to kick him in the shin or tell him how arrogant he was, and then other times I wished he'd notice me as more than just the botanist fixing his garden—and then sometimes I thought he had, and my stomach got all tingly at the idea of it—and sometimes, that all happened in one conversation with the man.

It really did take a certain kind of man to make you blush when they talked to a bird. I couldn't deny how attracted I was to him, which made the whole situation even worse now. I was getting all hot and tingly over a fucking murderer—and not just any murderer, a millionaire, weapons-dealing murderer.

The memory of the woman as she stood at the end of my bed flashed in my head, and suddenly the blood drained from my head down to the soles of my feet.

The rumors were that Jasper had strangled his mother before shoving her over the cliffside.

The ghost had kept a hand clenched to her throat. Even as she guided me to the locket, her hand had remained around her neck.

Oh my god. He did it.

Of course he was lying. The realization sparked a new wave of determination in me, and I was up and out of bed. I needed to talk to him, interrogate him. I needed to stop being so stupid and naive just because we had some sort of chemistry and find the hole in his story.

I grabbed the locket off the antique table next to the bed and clasped it in my hands with a renewed sense of wonder. I was put here for a reason—to get to the bottom of all of this, and I wasn't leaving here until I did. But I needed to keep Jasper at a distance too. I couldn't seem to stop getting all silly around him, and the last thing I needed was to fall for a killer with an unlimited supply of money and power. If he killed me too—

The truth was, if he killed me, the thought of haunting my own mother gave me some sick sort of pleasure.

My curiosity sparked again, and I pushed my thumbnail between the locket and the clasp. As it clicked open, something fell to the floor with a clang. The inside was nothing but the red velvet lining the piece.

I looked at the floor in search of whatever it was that had fallen out of the locket. There was movement under the corner of the bed—something shiny. I dropped to the floor to get a better look. Whatever it was, it was moving, and quickly.

A glimmer, a golden gleam of something almost too bright to be real, crawled across the floor. At first, I thought it was a trick of the light, but when I looked again, there it was—a spider.

Not just any spider, mind you.

It was golden, glimmering with an antique sheen that could only be described as eerie, as though it had been crafted by someone who had forgotten the rules of nature. Unlike the ordinary spiders in the corners of the manor, this one's body was shaped like a skeleton key—long and delicate, tarnished gold that caught the faintest glimmer of light on its metallic-looking back as it moved.

The legs, long and spindly, seemed to stretch on forever as it crawled out from beneath the bed. Its movement wasn't frantic, not like a regular spider racing to hide itself. Instead, this creature moved with the calm precision of knowing exactly where it was going.

And I—well, I had to follow it. I grabbed a pair of jeans, rumpled atop the nearby laundry basket, and stuffed my sore legs into them.

I buttoned my pants and crept forward, my breath quiet. I took a few tentative steps after it, then another, a little faster this time. I found myself in the hallway, eyes fixed on the golden arachnid as it scuttled silently beneath a door. The door creaked slightly as it passed beneath, and I felt my pulse quicken. I had no idea where this path would lead, but I had already crossed the threshold. I couldn't turn back now.

In my haste, I practically fell as I turned into a new hallway just in time to see its body disappear under another door.

I reached the door and stood for a moment, listening. It was futile; all I could hear was the sound of my heart hammering in my ears. I couldn't just walk into this room—what if someone was inside? I couldn't let the key—or the spider or whatever the thing was—get too far away or I'd lose sight of it, and it would be gone forever. My fingers were already on the knob, twisting it open, and—nope. The door refused to budge.

I gave it a little more force, but still, no luck. Of course, it had to be one of those damn doors that only opened if you turned the knob just right. So, with a huff, I took a step back and stared at the door, fully prepared to hip-check it like a SWAT breacher.

Thankfully, I saw it then—the smallest latch, hidden beneath the knob—the sort of latch no one ever notices. I slid it open with a slight click, feeling a small rush of triumph—a small victory—and pushed the old, heavy door forward.

I expected to see a room, but instead, another hallway

lay stretched before me, dark and winding. The spider was nowhere to be seen...but it couldn't have gone far.

Fuck! I had to find it!

I hurried down the hall, glancing hurriedly to either side. The lure of each door I passed felt like a potential detour, a trap. I turned a corner, then another, caught in a labyrinth of my own making. The spider was clever, leading me on some sort of chase, but why? I rounded another corner. A long stretch of stone. A door. But—no. Not there. I could feel it—the certainty that this wasn't right, that this wasn't the way.

Blindly trusting my instincts, I retraced my steps. A shiver ran through me. Where had it gone? Where in the house was *I*?

I made a mental note to beg Jasper for a quick tour of the manor while I was still in his good graces and then, just as I was about to give up, I heard it. A sound so faint I almost missed the susurration—the tiniest click, the softest scrabble of tiny metal legs tinkling against wood. I spun on my heel just in time to catch a gleam of gold—it had gone down another hallway, impossibly quick.

I followed, faster now, a thrill of excitement pumping through my veins as the hallway stretched on, winding and twisting like a maze. The spider didn't slow. It seemed to be taking me on a tour of the house's most forgotten corners, past neglected cobwebbed rooms, through narrow stairwells, and across floors so old the wood creaked beneath my feet. It had a destination—I could feel it.

Finally, after an eternity of turns and near-misses, it scurried under a large, ten-foot-tall door. I came to a stop before that door, just a bit ajar; I could see where a sliver of morning light broke through. From the outside it was no different from any other door in this giant house, but the moment I saw it, I knew something important was inside. I could feel it.

I pushed the door open, my heart pounding, and stepped inside, gasping when I realized where it had led me.

Jasper's bedroom sat before me engulfed in a heavy, haunted silence. A light breeze from my opening the door swept through the room, stirring the dark curtains slightly. And then my eyes landed on it: the trunk.

It was the most peculiar thing, standing at the foot of the bed like an artifact from another world: dark, textured wood, nearly black with age, brass handles that had long since lost their gleam, the trunk looked both heavy and fragile, ancient and enduring all at once.

The skeleton-key spider scuttled toward the trunk, its long golden legs tapping like the clicking of a clock, each step deliberate, as though it had completed this task a thousand times and was simply finishing another turn. It reached the trunk, climbed up the side, and then paused at the keyhole.

I watched, breathless, as the spider crawled into the key-shaped hole—no hesitation, no struggle. It fit perfectly, as though the lock had been waiting for it, and the sound of the lock turning was as soft as a sigh. A click, and the lid of the trunk fell open.

My heart leaped in my chest. I took a step forward, though my feet felt heavy, as I was afraid of what I might see. But inside was simply a stack of letters—old, yellowed, and brittle as though they had been kept hidden from the world for centuries.

Each letter was opened; its paper was slightly curled at the edges. But it wasn't the letters themselves that made me catch my breath. It was the wax seals—dark red, almost black in the stream of sunlight that poured into the room. An intricate, sharp, but strangely beautiful symbol was stamped into the wax. A bird's wing? No. Something…other. A twist, a jagged line—was it a flower?

I stood there, rooted to the spot, my heart still racing as I peered at the stack of letters. The spider had led me here, but to what end? What did these letters hold? What was it that had been hidden away, so carefully, so purposefully, for so long?

Nervously, I glanced around the room again. The luxurious furnishings were different in here than the rest of the house. A small collection of expensive-looking watches in a case on the dresser, a sleek-looking bottle of cologne, a few books that looked to be about war, and nothing else to say for certain whose room it was, but no one else in this house would have such expensive possessions but Jasper.

Not wasting another second for fear the room's owner would return, I grabbed the letter closest to the top and began to read. It was dated only a few months ago.

Dearest Son,

I know you dislike my letters, but I can't bring myself to stop writing them.

Your father is out at the moment. He is making great strides with these foreign officials and was asked to attend an event that could change the fate of all the children in India. He really is such a wonderful man—just like you are now.

I came across a lovely family whose son is a doctor somewhere in the States. Darling, please do be certain you are getting regular checkups. Every time, have them run all the blood panels and everything offered. You never can be too careful. Also, your father mentioned something about your stocks the other day with the market's current volatility; he recommended putting 60% of your portfolio into stable, blue-chip stocks—companies and the remaining 40% into bonds or other low-risk assets for balance, ensuring you're protected should the market take a downturn. For your next move, consider buying into Aurora Solar Solutions now, while it's undervalued, but don't go above 5% of your total holdings. Watch for the next earnings report—if the numbers are strong, you can increase your position.

Now for the always somber part of my letter where I tell

you how much I love you and how horrible I feel for not being there. No part of you can fathom what I wouldn't give to be able to hug you again. Should this letter have tear stains as all my others do, then I hardly need to sign it for you to know it is from me.

As always, my darling son, know that everything I've done has been with nothing but love for you in mind. One day I pray I will rest with a heart of peace knowing you've forgiven your father and me for what we did. Please God, forgive us, Son.

With every ounce of my love,
Mom

P.S. Remember to get a checkup!

I barely had time to finish reading it before the sound of footfalls outside gave away that someone was approaching.

Just as the door creaked open, I flung the letter back into the trunk and slammed the lid shut, spinning in time to see Sowerby peeking in the door.

"Eliza. What are you doing in here?" he asked sternly. His eyes darkened as they danced about the room, looking for an answer.

I froze. I'd never been a very good liar, a fact that I'd always foolishly taken a bit of pride in until this very moment.

"I—uh—" I just stared blankly at the butler, his scowl growing more aware and concerned with every passing second. A blush at being caught heated my face.

Sowerby took another step in the room, looking quite angry now. His gaze touched the trunk behind me, and I saw something click in his eyes. He started to close the door behind him, and prickles of warning rolled over my skin. Why did he suddenly look so terrifying, like he was going to hurt me?

"I have diarrhea and Katya told me I could go to the private bathroom up here and no one would hear me." I felt my face turn a darker shade of crimson blush. "Did I go too far? Is this not the right bathroom? I'm sorry."

The muscles of his face relaxed, and I watched with unease as his shoulders let down a bit. "No, this isn't the bathroom to go in. Did you already go in there?" he asked as he scrunched his face, pointing to the giant bathroom attached to the large suite.

"I—I'd rather not say." If Sowerby didn't kill me in this room, I may die of embarrassment anyway. "Could you please show me how to get to the conservatory from here?" I rushed past him, out the door, and back into the unfamiliar hallway.

"Yes, of course." He closed the door behind him, latching it in a way that said he'd done it a thousand times in his lifetime.

I said a silent prayer and steadied myself. "Sowerby?"

He glanced at me with knowing eyes that warned me not to say another word, but I couldn't help myself, I had to ask and there never seemed to be a right time. "Are there any pictures of Hester and Darius hung up in the house? I wondered what they looked like."

He stopped abruptly as if unable to control his legs, but quickly started up again, this time at a faster pace, as if trying to get away from my question faster. "No. Master Blackwood has burned all photos of his parents. If you are interested in any further inquiries on the subject matter, I suggest you use Google and not me," he snapped gruffly. There was an edge of discomfort in his tone that made goose bumps erupt across the back of my neck. Why would he be so defensive about this? Though it did serve as a reminder to google what I could about them.

Something about the interaction felt dangerous, which struck me as odd. Sowerby had always been a grumpy, too-stern man, but he'd never really frightened me, not like Jasper did…until now. Something about the way Sowerby was acting felt like a warning. Still, I had been waiting to ask him some questions, and I needed to know the answers now.

"Did Jasper kill his parents?"

The butler turned on me so fast, I ducked with a flinch. He moved his face so close to mine, all I could see were his yellowing, bloodshot eyes. The smell of cigarettes and roasted coffee beans strangled my senses.

"Questions like that get people buried around here. You want to keep digging, be sure to bring a shovel." He gave me a cold glare.

"Lucky for me, I arrived with my own shovels," I muttered back, cowering against the hallway wall.

"Well, if you want to leave with them, I suggest you keep your nose out of places it doesn't belong," he warned, finally backing up a little.

"I'm sorry. I just—" I began to stammer, unsure of how to get myself out of this mess and back on good ground with the butler. Would he tell Jasper that I was asking? Of course he would. What was I thinking?

"I was looking for you earlier, but you weren't in the kitchen or the conservatory, the only two places besides your bedroom that I've ever seen you," he said. "Would you prefer that I clean up the deciduous piles or that I do the weeding of the south bed? I believe there are some orchids thriving under there if we can get to them. The missus loved her black orchids."

"I'm sorry, I'm not following. What do you mean would I prefer if you did the weeding?"

Sowerby had a fittingly sour expression that showed his distaste of the situation. "Mr. Blackwood has placed me at your disposal, miss. I am to be your assistant in the gardens for as long as you require it."

What?

"Jasper asked you to help me?" I muttered, hardly able to believe what I was hearing.

"Yes, miss, Mr. Blackwood did, and though I'd rather pull thorns from my skin, I will do as he asks."

I could hardly believe what I was hearing. In the kitchen last night, Jasper had heard me breaking down about the lack of progress, and now he was giving me extra hands.

The letters from his mother seemed to prove his side of the story—he didn't kill his family. What happened between them, I didn't know, but in his eyes, they were obviously still alive.

I looked down and fought the smile off my face, but it refused to leave me. Jasper's kind gesture seemed to hit more places inside me than if a firework had gone off in my stomach. It felt like maybe there was a light at the end of the tunnel, though I still needed to make sense of it.

I paused again as I looked at Sowerby's dour face. "I can't possibly ask you to do work in the weeds and dirt knowing you'll absolutely hate it. You seem like the type to wisely avoid that type of labor. Besides, you'll get your fine clothes all dirty." A nice way of saying *you're going to be a complete dick and take it out on me if you have to get dirt on your nice clothes*.

His chest puffed out a bit as we continued to walk.

"Nonsense, I'm admittedly reluctant to work in the conservatory again, but I'm not afraid of dirt," he said as if I'd truly offended him.

"Again?" I asked, a tingle of nervousness tickling at the back of my mind.

"Yes," he said as we finally got to the hallway that led to the conservatory. "Ages ago, I was the head gardener for Mrs. Blackwood before she…left us. I was the only one she trusted to work alongside her in the conservatory."

Something in his words felt eerie.

The conservatory door opened abruptly, and Jasper pushed through them, soaked from head to toe, sopping wet with streaks of water trickling down the lines of muscle that rippled over his chest and stomach, wearing nothing but a pair of thin, slate-gray shorts.

"The pond is fixed!" he declared triumphantly.

I clamped my mouth closed before too much drool fell out.

Oh my god.

Ohmigod. Look at his chest...

OHMIGOD. "Sorry? You fixed the pond? But...that was going to take me weeks. Sowerby and I couldn't quite figure it out!" I said in shock.

"Not anymore, my friend. It will be ready for fish as soon as the water parameters are in order," he said with a bright, handsome grin as he pushed the wet locks of brown hair off his forehead. It bunched up in loose curls, more unkempt than normal. He looked so rugged and undone—such a stark contrast to his normal tidy appearance.

The pond was fixed.

I wanted to lick him.

The pond was fixed. That just shaved two weeks of work off my timeline not having to send its custom pumps out for repair.

He'd called me *friend*. It felt like a good thing, so why did it twist my gut?

"You're kidding!" I screamed excitedly. I tightened my mouth to keep my untrustworthy tongue inside and moved to shake his hand or pat him on the back or... I wasn't actually sure what I was planning to do, but my body went rogue, my arms wrapped around his neck and squeezed in a loose but very friendly hug. "That is amazing! You're the best!"

Jasper's warm brown eyes softened at my words.

Before my arms had the chance to drop back down to my sides, his were around my waist, pulling me tightly against him. As if it was the most natural movement I'd ever made in all my life, my arms tightened at the back of his neck, causing the front of my body to press into his naked, wet chest. His broad shoulders and bare arms curled around the edges of my body, funneling me into a spot that felt like I'd been built to fill. Every worry and concern I'd had in the last two weeks floated out and away from my tired body, and my eyes closed of their own accord as my chin rested on the top of his (very solid) shoulder. I felt a similar heavy sigh to the one that wanted to leave me leave Jasper's chest. It was the first time I'd ever experienced a hug that seemed to actually alter the chemicals of my body. And what was even more astounding was that somehow there was nothing sexual about it.

In that hug, it was like I felt a part of my soul push against his and suddenly everything was different.

Realizing time wasn't actually standing still for us even though it felt like it, we both pulled back, our eyes locked, and our arms dropped away from the embrace. But our gazes seemed to be in their own entanglement and didn't want to break away.

Sowerby cleared his throat. Loudly.

Unfortunately, I didn't think I'd ever felt so much in my whole life as I did in that ten-second hug. I didn't want it to end.

It wasn't the type of hug you gave someone you missed or hadn't seen in a while—or the kind of hug you gave as a goodbye. It was the kind of hug that curled so tightly around your soul that it pressed the sharp edges back together again.

I knew I was supposed to talk now, to say something to break the silence, but my head was floating in the clouds.

Jasper himself seemed caught up in the same wonderment as me as we just watched one another in stupefied surprise.

"Eliza, please show me where you'd like me to start," Sowerby said, cutting the silence. He walked past us, through the doors of the conservatory.

Becoming aware of my body again, I reluctantly pulled my eyes away from Jasper's and followed Sowerby.

"Thanksgiving is next week. Will you be going home?" Jasper asked as he gently grabbed my arm, keeping me from walking away.

It felt like a swarm of bees filled my head when he touched me, like every logical thought simply melted away, replaced with warm, fuzzy feelings that I wanted more of. It was the oddest mix of sensations for someone like me. Touch always felt invasive, like a power move someone did to warn you or hurt you...but not this. I knew I'd only just experienced the very edge of this feeling, and like a drug, I couldn't help but wonder how more of it would feel. Of all the people in the world to touch me and make me feel like this, I'd have never suspected the man who secretly terrified me to be the one to cause it.

"Sowerby always stays here for the holidays. If you'd like, he can continue working, so you don't lose any progress while you are gone from the manor," he added softly.

Thinking about going home and being ripped to shreds by my mother was enough of a javelin to shoot my chariot down from the clouds. I hadn't even thought about the holidays. I didn't want to go home, but if I didn't, my mother would *definitely* show up here and cause a horrible scene that would no doubt get me fired from this job. I could go to my apartment, but what was the point? And she would find me there anyway; there was no escaping her unless I moved out of the country, like my sister, who even at those lengths wasn't free from our narcissistic mother.

"No, I will be staying here...if that's all right?" I finally said after a moment of thought.

"Of course. Chef Katya stays as well. She gets really into the themed holiday cooking, so you will be well fed," he added with a small smile that lit his face and made his brown eyes glitter.

"Eliza! Do you wish to keep the periwinkle or eradicate the plant entirely?" Sowerby shouted impatiently from inside the garden.

"I'd better go in there," I said gently, still not wanting to pop the compassionate bubble Jasper and I seemed to be inside of.

He nodded with a hint of regret in his eyes. "Look at the pond, and if you need anything adjusted, let me know. I should go change before my meeting. They will be arriving anytime now."

I gave a nod, and we both turned in opposite directions.

"I want to see you at dinner tonight," he stated at the last minute, just before the conservatory's glass door was almost closed.

I pushed it open again and let my eyes roam over his shirtless chest. "A business dinner?" I scrunched my face. "Three out of four of the outfits I brought here are overalls. No thanks. Besides, I don't really have time to not be in there," I said, tipping my head behind me.

His face hardened, losing any friendliness. "I wasn't really asking, Eliza." A cocky smirk lifted the corner of his mouth. "It will be *exponentially* more bearable if you're there, and you have to eat anyway, so you may as well join me—us."

Something in my stomach flip-flopped. I really was doing a terrible job of staying away from him, I suddenly realized. It was much, much easier when his shirt had been on. The invitation hadn't really sounded like I had too much of an option for refusal anyway.

How my body could be both terrified of the man and want him so badly was incomprehensible. There was something in the way his eyes roamed over me that made me tremble with fear *and* excitement. Maybe he wasn't as horrible of a man as everyone thought? Or worse, maybe he was, and I was being lured into his web of manipulation just like he wanted.

The truth was more time with him sounded intriguing and would give me a chance to investigate things with the ghost in the red dress a little more—ask him some questions. But I wasn't going to embarrass myself or him by showing up looking like a complete mess.

He must've picked up on my hesitation, because he said, "Katya or Leah can pick you up something. They're still in town. Leah knows your size from doing your laundry," he said with hope in his voice.

I knew this was wrong. I knew deep down I should say no and stay away from him—at least until I figured out if he actually was a murdering liar. He wasn't inviting his other staff to dinner, just me, and stupidly, I couldn't help wanting to go. If I got closer to him, it would be easier to figure out what was really going on with the locket and the ghost…at least that's what I told myself, but secretly I knew I was playing a dangerous game. He was devastatingly handsome and powerful, and like a moth, I couldn't seem to stop from being lured into the fire.

"Okay," I agreed, though deep down, I knew I never really had any options.

His eyes danced with mischief. "Great. Feel free to bring as many wild pigeons to this dinner as you like. Keep them on their toes," he said with a wink before turning the corner and disappearing.

So that was that.

I was having dinner with Jasper tonight.

CHAPTER 12

JASPER

"THEN IT'S SETTLED, I'LL HAVE THE PAPERS DRAWN UP, AND you can sign the contracts right here over dinner tonight."

I closed my leather portfolio and stood to shake the men's hands.

The two luxuriously dressed CEOs stood in unison and took turns shaking my hand.

Got 'em, I thought with a wave of excitement that left as quickly as it had come on.

Business didn't drive me anymore, not the way it used to. I had more money than I knew what to do with, and the deals didn't strike the same nerves that they once had. It used to be exciting and give me a burst of primal power when I would dominate a new field or company, but the feeling was fleeting.

It was depressing to realize you didn't care about anything.

For as far back as I could remember, Blackwood Industries fueled every angry, spiteful desire I had. Not anymore. Deals didn't give me the same boost of adrenaline they once did.

Blackwood Industries was a paradox—a company that once began with knives, then ropes used by astronauts, before quickly evolving into a weaponry empire that now had its fingers in every conceivable sector of power. The knives that started it all, the ones designed by my father, were still made today, but now, they were sold not just for personal defense but also as tools of war. High-performance rope used in space exploration now helped secure elite military units as they descended into the chaos of modern warfare.

When my father up and left the company after spending all of its funding, back when it was only knives, the company had crumbled. No one expected any different and no one cared. My father didn't care, not even when the crumbling was of the manor and his son.

I remembered speaking to Sowerby the day that everything changed—the day I changed.

I was sixteen, my head still bandaged from getting my head bashed in after I tried, unsuccessfully, to steal Callum Parks's motorcycle.

I had just returned to the manor with a pocket full of cash. I can still remember how hard it had been not to take the drugs I was running. I almost did that day. Had it been just me to watch out for and not Sowerby, I would've. I had made just enough to afford to pay the heating bill for the old gatehouse and a little bit of food. Back then, the property still had the small, sturdy structure that was built directly over the entrance gate of the property. The gatekeeper had left with all the others, and it was the only place small enough for us to keep any heat in the winter. The best thing I ever did after making my first million was demolishing that old gatehouse. My father had run the company into the ground and took with it everything but the company name—something I changed as soon as I had learned how. I couldn't have stayed at Blackwood Manor if I'd have had to look at it every day and remember all of the things I wanted to forget. I had planned on demoing the conservatory too, but I ended up being unable to destroy something she had loved so much; instead, I let her own actions be the thing that killed and ruined the conservatory as I watched. At first, I had enjoyed watching as her favorite things wilted and died, how they struggled to survive and couldn't. I had thought everything in there was dead and nothing but weeds now, but Eliza Arnold had apparently found out that parts of my mother were not only still alive, they were still thriving.

That day, so long ago, Sowerby had limped in, the heavy drag of his bad leg more noticeable than normal. He was gardening at a few houses in town for next to nothing. I couldn't remember a time when Sowerby wasn't old as dirt. I remembered watching his old ass in the conservatory as a toddler, and even back then his face was thick with lines and wear from the sun.

"You're too old to be out there gardening," I'd told him as I twirled a Blackwood knife in my hand like the douchey sixteen-year-old that I was.

"Enough with the party tricks. Put the knife down before your hand matches your face. There's no gardening this time of year. I'm shoveling driveways. And find a new fucking way to earn money. You're too young to be ruining your life doing the shit you're doing. You're going to die long before I do if you keep it up," he'd answered.

"So what? Nobody cares if I die. It'd make things easier for you anyhow," I had grumbled.

Sowerby was in my face in a second, his grip on my arm was like a vise. I'll never forget the look in his eyes.

"I do—I care, and if I have to beat it into what's left of your head, then I will! Your father is a coward and a weasel, and just because he threw his life away doesn't mean I'm going to let you. That piece of shit—instead of keeping a good thing, he changed his mind and ran. He did it with the knives when he couldn't take the world's criticism about making weapons available in markets that sold to kids, and he did it with you when he left." His eyes were full of an anger I hadn't seen from him before. "Don't let that man ruin your life any more than he already has, Jasper. For god's sake, don't you want to show him how fucking high you can fly without him?"

"That's why he left? Because he was upset about what his knives were being used for? *That's* why they left?" I'd asked. Sowerby *never* spoke about my parents; neither of us did.

His eyes widened for a second before he grumbled angrily and moved to the fire to remove his worn leather boots, wincing and struggling with each one. I remembered watching him fight against those old boots and realizing how much the old man had done for me.

"Sowerby, when I grow up, you're never going to touch a shovel or a garden again," I had said with naive bravado.

"Oh, is that so?" said the old man with a sentimental spark in his eye.

"Yeah, it is. You're going to live a life of comfort, and your feet and legs will never hurt you again," I proclaimed, and I meant every word.

I took every drop of spite, anger, and sadness and hurled it into learning everything I could about how to fix what my father had left of Blackwood Bladecraft—soon to be Blackwood Industries—and earned my first million two years later.

The rumors about my parents' disappearance only fueled me on. And somewhere along the line, I began to enjoy the way everyone startled and got nervous when I'd enter a room. It was easy being thought of as a merciless, power-hungry killer, far easier than a worthless, unlovable kid whose own parents didn't even want him. I didn't try to quiet the rumors; I used them to benefit my sales. The only problem was that along the way, I became as cold and uncaring as they all said I was the day I was born.

My parents deserved what happened to them and so did everybody else, including me. By the time I turned nineteen, Blackwood Industries had grown into a multinational corporation with sprawling R&D facilities in Europe, the United States, and even the Middle East. A subsidiary, Blackwood Defense Systems, was created to oversee government contracts, while another division, Blackwood Tactical Solutions, catered to private military companies and even wealthy individuals seeking personalized defense systems.

As Blackwood Industries expanded, its secretive nature grew even more pronounced. The company's dealings were shrouded in mystery. Rumors of illegal arms trading, covert operations, and shadowy dealings in war-torn regions became commonplace, along with word of the aggressive designs and technology. Everything about me, including my company, had become dark and lethal.

By the mid-2010s, Blackwood Industries had become a global titan, with annual revenues in the billions. Our stock price soared, and the company became a staple in the portfolios of the wealthiest investors in the world. Blackwood weapons were used by national armies, paramilitary groups, and private contractors in nearly every conflict zone across the globe, from Africa to the Middle East to South America. And to this day, every weapons deal I did, I thought of my father's face looking at a paper from wherever they were and seeing his fine Blackwood name painted across the front page in a new weapons controversy.

My life force was no longer blood at this point, only spite. When anyone heard the name *Blackwood*, it was associated with weapons and killing, and there was something deeply poetic—okay, maybe not poetic, but at least cathartic—about that.

Presently, the men across the desk from me smiled even though they continued to look around the room, a bit jumpy. It fed my soul even now, their fear. I could get the same reaction without saying a single word that someone else would only get by pulling out a pistol and aiming it between their eyes. My own custom 1911 Cabot was currently tucked behind my

Italian leather belt, the matte clip keeping the Damascus steel a shadow inside my waistband. I could feel them staring at my scar, wondering which of the various rumors were true. It was so rare that I did deals from the manor because I strongly disliked anyone being here, even for a little while. I hated their presence so much it filled my senses, and I could taste it.

Except Eliza. For some reason, it didn't feel like she took anything away from me or the manor. Instead, it felt like she was adding something to it, soothing it. She was starting to feel a little like a flashlight that brightens up the darkness a bit. Except, that was the problem when someone shined a bright light into a dark, empty hole—sometimes all they found was nothing but more darkness. It didn't matter how much brightness Eliza Arnold brought into this manor—it would always be a black hole of horrors…just like me.

From the moment she stepped into my office, I had been drawn to her in a way I couldn't explain. She had a way of challenging me that felt…fun and exciting, even when I didn't want it. She had a deep, underlying determination that was so familiar to me, I couldn't help but feel connected to her on a different level.

I shouldn't have invited her to dinner tonight. I didn't want to blur the lines between us too much; I didn't want her to develop any expectations. Even if I could have, I wouldn't have subjected myself to another person in that way, but at this point, I didn't even think I could anymore. I swore to myself long ago that I would never let another person hurt me, and I meant it—and that included pretty botanists who made me laugh.

I liked Eliza and didn't want to hurt her, but I was incapable of more. She was leaving in two months, and I needed to make sure we didn't cross any lines before then. I thought if I were able to trust people enough to have any sort of friendship, she would have made a good one. Unfortunately, I didn't trust a soul outside of Sowerby, but the thought of being friends with

Eliza felt nice. None of the other people I've been around have had that. Maybe they just hadn't been good people, but Eliza struck me as the type of person who wouldn't leave someone they loved to die in a burning building; she would die trying to pull them out. I'd probably be the one setting the place on fire. Except if Sowerby was inside; I'd tear the bricks off individually to get to Sowerby if I had to.

After dinner tonight, I vowed to keep my distance from Eliza. She was afraid of me, and she should be. I liked that I made her nerves fire. I enjoyed watching her breath catch when I towered over her—I liked it too much. I wanted to push her farther and farther into that fear until she was so riddled with tension she felt like she would explode. There was something almost parasitic about how much that feeling had burrowed inside of me. I got what I wanted, no matter what it was. I could already feel the stirrings of obsessiveness. I'd felt it after she hugged me. It couldn't go any further. I let out a heavy sigh and forced my shoulders to relax. It was a business dinner: boring and short. We'd eat and that was that. I showed the two men to the entertainment room and excused myself.

I gave Don, one of my security guards, a nod outside the door. He wouldn't let them out of there until I told him to, though, even with that in place, they would slip photos of something to news outlets; they always did. Sometimes I wished there really were ghosts here just to fuck with people, but it wouldn't matter. It never failed: a lamp got knocked over or a floor creaked wrong, and someone swore they saw something, and boom, the place was haunted. The news outlets and paranormal investigators would be hanging off the gates by tomorrow to get in. It happened every time I let anyone into this manor—except for Eliza. At least she hadn't resorted to telling ghost stories yet.

"How's it coming?" I asked Katya as I sat down at the back of the kitchen.

"Get out of my kitchen. I'll get Leah to get you when it's ready," the older woman said sternly.

"I don't want to go back," I grumbled. "Were you able to find Eliza something to wear?" I asked as I absently flipped a pen over and over on the table. When Katya didn't answer right away, I looked up only to see her smiling at me as she stirred something in a pot on the stove. "What?"

"Nothing," she said with a twinkle in her eye. "Leah is helping with her hair and makeup now."

I scowled before my forehead landed in my palm. "Her hair and makeup? Eliza is a dirt-loving, overall-wearing botanist, not your Barbie doll," I grumbled. Leave it to the only women in the house to make such a fuss. It did make me chuckle inwardly thinking about how much Eliza was probably hating this.

Katya let out a gruff laugh that I only ever heard when Sowerby flirted with her. "Mr. Blackwood, you know nothing about women. Now get out of my kitchen. Go get your business associates; dinner will be served by the time you come back."

I glared at the woman. She and Sowerby were the only, and I mean *only*, people I let talk to me like that and get away with it. Reluctantly, I left the kitchen and made my way back to the entertainment room downstairs. I *really* needed this deal with JV Plastics, so an evening of kissing their ass—especially John, the man making the bulk of their company's decisions—was in order. Millions of dollars were at stake, which was just enough to make me act friendly. It was a blessing Eliza would be there to help lighten the evening because the thought of doing it all alone made me feel like smashing my head in.

After gathering John and Omar, I showed them to the dining room. Omar sat next to me, leaving Eliza's seat next to John's. I had wanted her to sit next to me, mostly because I wanted to see if I could make her nervous, but across from me was fine—she was much more fun to look at than Omar.

Leah came into the dining room, filled our water glasses, and got drinks for everyone.

"Where is Eliza, Leah?" I asked quietly when she was next to me. Given Leah's style, I couldn't help picturing Eliza with sprayed eighties hair and a frilly tulle dress. Katya and Leah were great, but both women were in their fifties, a little eccentric, and for some reason, I pictured them both descending upon Eliza with puffy sleeves and neon makeup. This was about to be the most entertaining business dinner I'd had in a while. I fought back a grin.

Leah leaned in close, so her answer would remain private, accidentally knocking my folded napkin off the table in the process. I bent down to get it, and before Leah could answer, Eliza's voice broke out across the dining room.

"I'm sorry I'm late," she said.

The other conversation suddenly stalled. Chairs creaked as the fine-mannered men eagerly stood. An ancient tradition that would have never continued had it been up to me. Women didn't rise when men got to a table, and they were perfectly capable of sitting without assistance—I'd seen it done many times. With a gentle exhale, I grabbed the napkin from the floor and straightened myself back up to see Eliza at the other end of the room.

Holy shit. I was momentarily breathless, caught in the space between exhale and inhale.

She was mesmerizing.

She wore a simple black dress that tastefully hugged every curve of her body, stopping just above her knees with a small slit on one side that gave the slightest extra glimpse of a toned thigh. Where had she been hiding those curves? I'd never seen this much of her skin…or the shape of her body for that matter. There was also a light in her eyes and a glow to her complexion that I hadn't seen before. She looked less timid and more confident, carrying herself with an air of boldness. I felt like a starved man as my hungry eyes took in the full sight of her. The other men practically fell over themselves to greet her.

I remained seated, wondering how she got that much hair into the little frizzy ball onto her head that she wore when she worked. Now, it spilled over her shoulders in glossy brown waves that begged to be touched…and pulled.

I closed my mouth and stood. "Omar, John, this is Eliza." *My friend. My…friend.* "She is currently working to revive my conservatory." Eliza's eyes snagged mine briefly, but I couldn't read anything in them before hers were back on John, who was pulling out her chair.

"Oh, wow. You're the prettiest landscaper I've ever seen." The men laughed at John's stupid remark as he pushed her chair in and sat next to her. "I should hire you to work at my house."

Eliza opened her mouth to answer, a poised smile already on her face. I wondered if she ever got tired of being so polite. She never seemed to hold back her sass with me. I'd have already pistol-whipped the guy, and I found her reaction fascinating.

"She's a botanist. She has a master's in botany from Grayson," I snapped before reminding myself to take the edge off for the sake of this deal. There was no reason to get protective over her. She was nothing to me.

"From Grayson? I have a cousin that got his fine arts degree from Grayson, such a great school," Omar added politely. He'd developed a light sheen of sweat across his bald head that I found myself scowling at as I sat next to him. He was a nice enough guy, even if he was a bit nervous all the time.

"It is a lovely school. I'm envious of your cousin, though. I secretly always wanted to be a painter," Eliza said before clearing her throat with a nervous expression, as if she hadn't meant to say it.

Huh. She seemed so determined to repair the conservatory; it was hard to imagine her having a passion for anything else. What else did Miss Eliza have a passion for?

"Both Omar and John are incredibly savvy and industrious men. They're the owners of JV Plastics, and I am thrilled Blackwood Industries has finally joined forces with them," I said jovially...or at least I tried. Once contracts were signed, I could drop the polite facade.

"Oh..." Eliza's voice dropped as if I'd just told her to cut off her hand. "JV Plastics."

There was something interesting in the way she said it that made my head tilt. There was no way she had heard of JV Plastics before this moment.

"You've heard of us," Omar said, sounding very proud, obviously not picking up on the way her voice had dropped.

Leah and Katya brought out our first course, and as they fluttered around the table, I was careful to keep my ears pinned and ready, needing to hear the answer from Eliza as to how she knew JV Plastics. I had asked her to this dinner to help entertain my guests but found myself wanting to force them to leave so I could talk to her.

Eliza looked down at her plate with a squint and inspected the tiny piece of smoked salmon as if she'd never seen a plate of food before. "Oh, yes, I'm unfortunately quite familiar with your company."

I felt like I was watching her reveal herself to be a spy as she sat across from me, which didn't seem that far-fetched when my eyes dragged over her toned arms and her body in that tight black dress. I don't know why; I obviously didn't know everything there was to know about her, or really anything past what her background checks had shown, but for some reason, it felt like I had come to know Eliza the botanist, and this new version pulled at my intrigue in a dangerously enticing way.

"And how is it that you've heard of our company?" asked John with his brows raised so high that they almost touched his hairline.

"It's smoked salmon. Do you not like smoked salmon? If

not, I can get you something else," I said, cutting off John's question as I watched the peculiar way she looked at her food.

She looked up, and her cheeks were pink. Immediately I wondered if she wore that same pretty shade of pink on any other parts of her.

"It's just... Well, I've never actually had fish," she said, still looking at the little square of salmon, not with disgust, I realized now, but curiosity.

I leaned back in my chair and peered through the doorway, catching Leah's gaze, nodding for her to come to the table.

"Leah will get you something else," I said to her. I'd invited her to this bore-fest; the least I could do was feed her something she would eat.

"Oh, no, no, no, this is fine," she replied enthusiastically, smiling at Leah conspiratorially and politely shooing her away.

"So—" John tried again.

"Eliza, do not eat that fish for the convenience of this meal unless it is something that you want. Whatever you choose, choose it for you and no one else," I stated more harshly than intended. For some reason, it thoroughly irritated me to think of her doing something she didn't want to do. I liked when she perked up and talked back to me with fire in her eyes. This whole time I'd thought she might be a fun toy to break, but every once in a while, when she pulled down the mask, I realized she'd be a hell of a lot harder to break than I'd initially thought. I wondered what she was like in bed—if she kept the controlled exterior, rigid and quiet, or if she let her demons come out to play. Behind closed doors was when the demons had the most fun in my experience...

For a moment, she looked at me as if my words had startled her or sparked something truly thought-provoking in her mind, and I silently begged to know what it was. She thanked Leah and sent her on her way.

"I have always wanted to try fish, thank you," she replied

with a warm smile as she carefully pressed her fork into the small piece of salmon.

I didn't take my eyes off her mouth for a long time after she smiled. The rosy-pink hue made my mind go to places that were giving me a very inconvenient reaction under the table.

"Do it, then," I said as I leaned back in my chair. "Put it in your mouth, Eliza."

The room fell silent except for a small sound Eliza made as she cleared her throat and looked back at me nervously. A playful, lazy grin passed over my face. I liked telling her what to do—I'd known that already—but what I didn't know was how much she'd take before she pushed back, especially in front of an audience.

Her pretty mouth fell open in surprise, but only for a split second, before she recovered. Her eyes sparked with their own flare of heat, and I had to bite my lower lip to stop from commanding her to crawl across the table to me. That vision certainly wasn't helping my situation under the table. I was almost fully hard just from telling her to stuff a bit of salmon in her mouth. I definitely needed to stay far away from her...after this dinner.

She gave a polite smile as she put the piece of fish on her fork.

You'd have thought she was about to be poisoned by the way the three of us men stared at her, waiting to see what would happen next. She lifted the large bite of salmon to her mouth, smiling at the other men for a beat, before her smile dropped and her eyes locked on mine.

"Slower," I commanded, still pushing her. She stilled the fork and gave me a small, curious look. "I don't want to miss anything," I drawled cooly.

"It's just a bite of fish. I'm sure it's not all that interesting," she returned politely before raising the fork back up to her mouth.

"You really think you can handle all of that?" I added just as it went past her lips.

She nodded with a grin and quickly glanced at the others and then back to me with cheeks puffed out slightly from the large bite. Honestly, I was impressed with the size of the bite. It was easy to see this was something she had clearly wanted to try for a long time. How curious.

Just before the fork passed her lips, she realized all of the eyes were on her and blushed with a small laugh, setting the fork back onto her plate with a *tink*.

"Well, what do you think?" John pressed.

"It most definitely was too big of a bite." She grinned. "It was pretty good, but I almost choked." She and John chuckled.

I didn't smile. I didn't laugh. I just watched her—slow, deliberate as my eyes tracked the delicate curve of her throat and imagined her swallowing something else entirely.

I spoke quiet and low, only for her, even though the whole room could hear.

"Shame," I murmured. "I bet you're beautiful when you choke." My gaze lingered at the base of her neck. "Some women are." She would be. I let loose a cheeky grin, lifting the right corner of my mouth before turning my focus to the uptight man beside me. This dinner was most definitely turning out to be more entertaining than I had expected. Realizing that we were behaving like a bunch of prehistoric humans, Omar picked back up where the conversation had left off. "I'm dying to know how a botanist from…" He waited for her to answer.

"Pinehurst," she answered, covering her mouth from view as she continued to eat, doing a phenomenal job of not unraveling for as much as I was trying.

I found myself unable to focus on anything else in the room but her as I sat back, trying to dissect what exactly it was that was so interesting about this woman. Why was she getting to me in such a way?

"I'm dying to know how a botanist from Pinehurst has heard of JV Plastics."

"Me too," I added, catching a stray look from her.

She picked up her wineglass with an odd expression and took a big drink before scrunching her face together, obviously disliking the wine, which made me snort out a laugh before regaining control.

Her eyes opened with an embarrassed look, then she grinned discreetly after realizing I wasn't taking a shot at her. "It's salty," she said to me quietly before turning her focus back to John and Omar.

I raised a cocky eyebrow at her, and she shifted her eyes away from me with a small grin. It was stupid, and only for a second, but I felt like I was in on some sort of joke, that I was a part of something secretive with just her, like we were a team at the table that the other two bozos weren't a part of. It was silly but...nice.

"Yes, both of my parents work for EcoSphere," she said somewhat timidly.

Interesting. I noticed she talked softer anytime she spoke about her family. It seemed so different from the nervous, fiery, challenging woman I had come to know. I found myself wanting to dissect her like a bug, needing to see which parts made her push back and which made her tremble with fear. I liked how she looked trembling.

I remembered the way she had flinched from my gestures when I'd moved too quickly that first day in my office. I felt my brows pinch together, unable to hide my dislike of the resurfaced memory. I enjoyed provoking her fear, but there was something in the thought of someone else hurting her that felt a bit like acid shooting through my bloodstream. I made a mental note to take her out back to the shooting range before she left the manor. Next time someone tried to hurt her, she'd be able to protect herself.

Silence filled the dining room, except for the clack and clatter of plates and silverware. It was like she had just dropped a bomb in the room.

"Ah," Omar said, suddenly looking uncomfortable.

I knew I had heard of EcoSphere but couldn't quite remember what it was.

"EcoSphere?" I asked, breaking the quiet.

"Yes, EcoSphere Conservation Alliance. My mother is a conservation biologist, and my father is a campaign strategist for them. It's why I've never eaten fish in my life or had a glass of wine," she said with a charming smile but with that same timid voice. Was it her family that had hurt her and caused her to flinch?

"You've never had fish *or* wine? Ever? Why on earth not?" I asked, internally on the edge of my seat even though outwardly I was reclined and relaxed.

"Microplastics," John said in mock shame. "You're dining with the enemy. I think I preferred you as a landscaper." He chuckled.

Eliza stabbed her fork into a piece of the fish and lifted it. All eyes were on her. I bet she was used to that, though.

"Did you know that over 90 percent of seafood worldwide is estimated to contain microplastics? Fish and shellfish ingest the tiny plastic particles from polluted waters, and then when humans consume seafood, they can unintentionally ingest microplastics as well." She placed the bite of fish in her mouth nonchalantly with a quick look at me as if she were gauging if I was upset. I wasn't and gave a small nod as I felt the corner of my mouth lift slightly, silently giving her encouragement to go on. Would she? Somehow, I knew her polite persona would take back over. Shame. She was something when she held her own power.

Omar and John shifted in their seats uncomfortably while I sat back and watched with fascination. I wasn't sure I'd ever been more entertained at a business dinner in my life.

"Did you know that it takes an average of eighteen hundred liters of water to produce just one bottle of wine with irrigation and vineyard maintenance being accounted for? And don't get me started on large-scale mono-cropping, which depletes the soil quality and biodiversity." She grinned at me and drained the rest of her wine as the two men squirmed awkwardly. She held herself like a rose surrounded by bees, completely in control.

I was quite certain I'd never wanted a woman more in my life than I wanted Eliza Arnold suddenly. I cleared my throat and threw back the rest of my scotch, nodding quickly for Leah to refill my glass.

Though highly entertaining, this dinner was going all types of sideways, none of which boded well for my business deal or my personal endeavors. Things were getting out of hand, and if there was one thing I hated, it was not being in complete control.

"But don't worry," she said with a bright, perky tone. "As Bo Burnham once said, you say the ocean's rising like I give a shit." She held her wineglass up, and a beaming Leah rushed over to fill her glass like a proud mother. Eliza thanked her and then moved the glass up to her lips. Her eyes snagged mine, and I caught a soft murmur of her finishing the song, "You say the whole world's ending, honey, it already did." She took another drink and looked at me as if we had just plotted a bank heist together. Good Lord.

"Then you forgive us?" John said with a laugh as he rested his hand on the back of her chair.

She answered something in her polite, charming tone. I don't know what it was; I was too focused on his hand to hear what she said.

A little later in the conversation, he moved it to her arm for a beat. Something I learned I didn't like. A prickle of annoyance sparked through me.

"So when do you expect products to roll out?" Omar asked at my side.

I leaned back in my chair and continued to watch *Jonathan* try to get laid. When Eliza started giggling and touching his arm back, I felt obligated to make sure nothing stupid happened. If she'd never drank before, how was she to know it would make her flirty with the peevish businessman? A foreign pulse of protectiveness made me tense—I'd be sure he kept his plastic-loving hands to him-fucking-self.

I'd have done the same if it were Katya or Leah. I was sure of it. I checked the time on my watch, ready for this dinner to be over with.

"April of next year," I replied flatly, not taking my hard eyes off the pair giggling across the table from me.

Without warning, they both stood from the table. I realized coffee had already been served and dinner was over.

I was standing immediately, ready to push these two men out of the door before I did or said something idiotic to make them pull out of the contract. I could feel my loss of control sparking like a fuse trying to stay away from a bomb.

"Well, boys, it's been a pleas—" I started, but *Johnathan* cut me off.

"Actually, Eliza was going to show me her progress on the conservatory and where you've been hiding her. If that's all right?" he said with a mischievous glint to his deep-set blue eyes.

When I said nothing and ground my jaw from side to side with a flat stare, he added, "I'm so glad you brought Eliza to dinner tonight; things would have been so dull without her by my side. I'm not sure I'd have stayed awake long enough to sign the contracts without her." It was a veiled threat and soft claim on Eliza.

This. Fucking. Prick.

I turned my head and cracked my neck, needing some of

the tension in my body to leave. This was stupid. Let him have her; she was an adult.

I needed this deal, and I didn't care about Eliza. *I didn't*. She was interesting and comfortable, and that was it.

"Speaking of, you haven't signed the contract yet," I replied flatly as I reached for the forgotten papers at the head of the table and slid them in front of where he stood, clicking the pen and making a clear statement.

He took me in for a moment, and I must've given a read he hadn't expected because a sinister curve took over the side of his mouth.

"I think I'd like a little bit of alone time with Eliza before I sign." His eyes pinned me against the wall, daring me to say something. She had moved out of earshot, a few feet away, and was laughing with Leah.

"I think it's late. Eliza has a lot of work to do tomorrow and is probably exhausted and wanting to go to her bed." Our eyes held in a challenge. "Her bed in *my* house."

John smirked. I'd let too much show with my last statement. He thought he had me by the balls. That's one thing about most CEOs that I'd met—they were all power-hungry. They'd all grown so accustomed to manipulating the buttoned-up corporate world and bending company policies that they'd gotten big heads. They thought they could do whatever they wanted and get away with it—because most of the time they did.

I was as domineering and cocky as the next man, but most were all talk and chose weak targets that couldn't fight back. That was the difference between me and someone like *Johnathan*; I preferred not to talk at all, and I enjoyed the fight. Violence coursed through my veins, and I enjoyed finding ways to blood let.

"Does your cook make a good breakfast?" He turned his head and trailed his hungry eyes up Eliza's body slowly. "Maybe I'll sign the contract in the morning."

"I've already signed. I'm going to go outside to make some phone calls," Omar mumbled, wisely excusing himself from the tension.

I wasn't stupid; I knew how I was looked at, with my scars. And I knew the things I'd done to *earn* my icy reputation. The only room in this whole fucking house I was in more than my office was the gym—to let out my anger, which, believe me, I had a *whole fuckin' lot of*. At six foot three, I was generally perceived as a big, intimidating motherfucker and I relished it. If this fucking gremlin thought he was gonna come in my house and disrespect me, then he would learn quickly what a horrible idea that was.

"I think it would be in your best interest to leave Eliza Arnold alone and sign this contract now, before this whole deal gets soured," I said calmly, letting my eyes do most of the talking.

"Is that a threat?" he pushed back.

"Of course not."

"You and her aren't...?" he asked smugly.

I glared at him and took my time as I imagined how hard I'd actually have to pull to remove his head from his body as I shook my head once.

He grinned again and left me to walk over to Eliza, making certain he glanced back at me as they left the dining room together.

I let out a slow, calculated breath as I watched them. I folded and tucked the unsigned contract into my pocket before leaving the room, nearly running straight into Sowerby as I moved down the hallway.

"Is everything all right? You look murderous. I just got a car for Mr. Omar. Where is the other one? Has the deal fallen through?" he asked with pinched brows.

"Get my twenty-gauge shotgun from the weapons room, would you?"

"Oh, good heavens, Jasper." His mouth fell open.

CHAPTER 13
ELIZA

I FELT THE TINGLES FROM THE WINE I DRANK AT DINNER SETTLE into my arms and legs with a soft, fluid numbness that eased away a large portion of my immediate tension. It was lovely. It was easier to laugh, easier to be social. I said things that felt good, things that I normally wouldn't have ever said. I think my mother could've used few glasses of wine in her life.

John, Jasper's business associate, followed me around the conservatory, listening to me ramble about the different struggles I had with each flower bed. A bit of discomfort began to settle around me when I caught him staring at my boobs. I had thought the others were following behind us. I tried to brush off my sudden unease. I just wasn't ever in social situations and was starting to feel uncomfortable because I didn't ever trust anyone. It wasn't a big deal. John seemed nice enough, and I didn't think Jasper would've left us alone if there had been anything to worry about… Actually that wasn't true; sometimes I couldn't decide if I thought Jasper wanted to choke me or kiss me—probably neither…maybe both.

John was flirting with me, and at first, it had been fun. No one ever flirted with me. If I left right now and went to bed, this would still have been one of the most rebellious and exciting nights of my life, even if, to anyone else, it had been a simple meal of salmon and a glass of wine while listening to people speak about business. For me, it had been a tiny step of rebellion. Absurd, yes, being that I lived alone and could, in theory, make my own choices, but the thing is, it wasn't that easy, and no one understood.

I'd never been disobedient. I'd never done anything wild or that I wasn't supposed to do. It caused too much backlash and too much chaos. Chaos that hurt and was painful to carry long after the scars healed. Chaos was my sister's specialty. I was the one who took it. The one that, at twenty-five, didn't put up a fight when my mom ordered my groceries for delivery—if only so she would stop showing up at my house and throwing away all of the food I bought. I didn't fight when she did much of anything, too numb from all of the other things she'd done when I was younger, while she was training me to be silent and obedient.

But not tonight.

Jasper's deep voice echoed in my head.

Eliza, do not eat that fish for the convenience of this meal unless it is something you want. Whatever you choose, choose it for you and no one else.

It was stupid, but Jasper's words spoke to me about more than just fish.

Of course, I knew it was an easy thought to have when I was miles and miles away, in a manor high up a cliff and removed from my mother's immediate vicinity, but no one had ever given me a choice before—in anything. And for the first time in my life, I chose what I wanted. I wanted the fish and the microplastics and the flirty evening in the conservatory surrounded by the evening sun and the almost-fixed flowers—except I had hoped my flirty evening with wine in my belly would have been with Jasper, not John.

John reminded me of every other guy I'd known in college. He was decent-looking, and I appreciated his success, but that was it. Everything else fell flat. He was a nice guy, with a nice-guy attitude, and someone I would typically be interested in, but for some reason I couldn't seem to stop thinking about what other tattoos were on the canvas of Jasper's body. John was nice, but I wasn't interested. Especially when I got the sense that he was looking for a quick, fun romp this evening, which made me nervous, and the mood turned awkward and uncomfortable.

Several times during the tour of the garden, he had come up behind me and tried to put his arms around my waist or nuzzle my neck, which I quickly stepped away from. There was something slimy about him that made my skin crawl. Admittedly, I wasn't a huge fan of being touched in general, but this was different.

"We should probably get back to the others," I finally said when his hands started to grow more confident.

"Come here," he whispered, trying to pull me closer.

Out of nowhere, the ear-splitting crack of gunshots rang through the air, breaking the silence and causing me to leap and cover my ears. They were so close that both John and I instinctively ducked. There was a rickety creak, and the shadowed figure of Jasper suddenly appeared at the back door of the conservatory, still dressed in his fine black suit but now holding a shotgun, the barrel resting casually on his shoulder. His face somehow looked menacing, even though his features were completely schooled; something completely unhinged and dangerous was dancing in his eyes. The sight of him was terrifying and sexy all at once. His eyes caught mine in a searching glance as though he was checking to see if I was all right. After a second, he threw a cocky wink in my direction.

My stomach twisted again, this time for a much different reason, and I realized just how much my body liked the taste of danger that Jasper fed me. The fear he pushed into my system vibrated until it turned into a sort of sensuous excitement. There was a seductive shimmer between dread and longing that was so strong, it could've curled my toes. The rush of being insanely attracted to him, while knowing he had the ability to harness his anger, to casually fire a gun in his own house, to intimidate... It was a dangerous game my body was playing.

John put both of his hands up as though it were a robbery. "Whoa, whoa, whoa, Jasper, I—"

Jasper cut him off. "I thought you might want to see what it was I wanted to use your plastic for, since I recalled you weren't in that meeting; Omar was," he said, devoid of any emotion. "Get outside. Now."

His words sent a chill over my skin, little goose bumps rising everywhere. I couldn't take my eyes off the hardness of his gaze. In that moment, I was suddenly sure he had killed Hester and Darius.

"Eliza, my friend." He paused for a moment as if trying to read something on my face. "If you'd like to go to bed, please feel free to leave; the choice is yours." Jasper took a step back, holding the door to the outside open and giving John a murderous stare.

I felt the excitement roll through me as Jasper's fresh, aquatic cologne hit me.

"Let's just calm down," John said, walking out the door.

Jasper shut the door behind John and clicked the lock beneath the handle.

My heart slammed against my chest as Jasper prowled toward where I stood, frozen and shaking. The scent of oil and steel was a contrast to the earthy undertone of the space the closer he got to me. I'd never been that close to a gun before—at least one that I could see. I knew Jasper kept a small gun on him. I'd seen him tuck it away in the holster on the inside of his waistband, but I'd never thought about how close

I was to it, not like I was now. Controlled, confident violence poured off him. Was there a time he hadn't been in such control of that violence? As if he could see my thoughts playing out, his mahogany eyes hardened, and the corner of his mouth curled slightly.

"Go on. Ask." His jaw shifted and he swallowed. "I heard you've been asking my staff about me," he said with cool detachment, though his eyes implied anything but.

My breathing sped up, and I was unable to pull my eyes from his thick throat back up to his eyes. Sowerby must have told him I was asking about him. He took a step closer. I had room to back up…but I didn't—at least not until he took another step forward and shifted the gun on his shoulder.

Every one of my well-trained nerves urged me to back away from him. And I did…until my back hit the large boulder in the center-back flower bed near the water feature.

"Did you kill them?" I blurted, my voice hardly louder than a whisper. I was so confused about the letter, the ghost… and Jasper.

Jasper blinked once. No outrage. Just flashed a slow, cruel smile of white teeth before clearing the little space that was between us and towering over me until there was only a few inches between our faces, the hand not balancing the gun on his shoulder moving to the rock by my face as he bracketed me in.

"Does it matter?" His warm breath curled around my ear and neck, and I had to pinch my eyes closed and force my knees to not buckle.

My heart pounded in my chest like angry, rhythmic thunder. This should have terrified me. It did. But in spite of all of that, every inch of my skin tingled with excitement. His powerful thigh pressed against mine, sending an awareness through my lower body that started to ache in sync with my heartbeat. The heat from his body pressed through the fabric of my clothes and into my sensitive skin, causing a shiver that only made me want to press closer to him.

His thumb moved from the rock and ghosted across the corner of my jaw. Down my neck. "You think I'm a monster."

"I think you want me to," I answered. My eyes moved to the gun, then to the tattoos covering his hand.

He licked his lips. I could feel the pressure of his eyes on my own lips. "Then why are you still here?"

I didn't know what to say, so I told him the truth. "Because I want to believe you didn't."

He leaned in, his mouth at my throat. As he spoke, I felt the light touches of his lips against my skin. "But you're still afraid I did. That's what makes this so fucking hot, isn't it?"

I didn't move. I didn't even swallow. My whole body pulsed—with guilt and longing. It was out now, the unspoken bits between us.

Something caught my eye over his shoulder. A stifled gasp ripped from my throat as I grabbed Jasper's arm. In the glass behind him, the ghost stared at me. Jasper snapped his head around, putting off the same vibe of a dog looking for a fight. He looked back at me, and I could tell from the confusion on his face that he hadn't seen anything. When I looked again, she was gone. I was saved from questions by more movement on the other side of us.

There was a bang at the side door. It was John, apparently attempting to be heroic as he shouted something. Jasper turned his head back to me, his eyes alight with humor as he grinned and cocked his head toward the door, took a step backward, and put his hand on the small of my back, urging me to go toward the door.

"Come on. Let's see how good your aim is."

We left the conservatory to find a red-faced, irritated John. There was a haunting eeriness out there, near the edge of the cliff, that seemed to somehow pull at my spirit. I was terrified of heights—I could barely even climb a ladder. I'd hardly been able to look in the cliff's direction while working in the conservatory, despite how beautiful the view probably was, but this was different. This was where Jasper's parents fell off the edge to their deaths—if they were, in fact, dead. Where something awful had happened and he'd walked away covered in blood, a fact that made me wonder what exactly he had done to have so much blood on him.

We continued out to the open grass, closer to the cliff. A few of his male staff had gathered by a large machine; a few loitered in the back, as if there was about to be a show. One, Luke, I think his name was, stepped out and handed us all flat-looking black headphones.

"Ear protection. You'll still be able to talk; it adjusts for voices. It just blocks out the sound of the gunshots," he added before handing John a pair and running back to the other staff. Jasper didn't have a pair, and I was about to say something when I saw him put small black earbuds in. Jasper stepped away from us, toward the drop over the cliff. With a graceful motion, he dropped the barrel of the gun to the ground, pulled a long green cylinder from his pocket, and popped it into the gun.

"Pull," he commanded in a low voice, snapping the barrel of the shotgun closed and raising it quickly into place at his shoulder. He fired into the sky, hitting something with a small clap before opening the gun again and repeating the practiced action. A bit of smoke rolled out of the barrel, and the shell flew out and landed a few feet away. His movements were so practiced and smooth, it was almost like he wasn't even aware of what he was doing, like muscle memory had taken over. He repeated the graceful motion a few more times, hitting a target every time.

Had the excitement of the evening and the alcohol not been so potent at blurring my senses, I couldn't have been so close to where the edge was, but as it was, my eyes were glued to Jasper and my body seemingly hell-bent on reacting to him.

He waved us over after one of the valets moved to stand on a wide, flat pedal of sorts attached by a long cord to some sort of machine. He was still a good forty feet from the edge, but it was horrifying to be even this close. Had that been what happened to Hester and Darius? Did they all shoot? Was there just an accident of sorts while they were all out by the ledge? I couldn't decide as I watched the man in black deftly load the shotgun again.

My thoughts swirled back to the letter I had found from Hester in Jasper's room. She couldn't have written that if she were dead, and I felt sure the ghost was her...so the letter couldn't be real. Was it just some elaborate cover-up by Jasper, or did he really think she was still alive? Was the letter fake? It had to be...right?

John tried to look casual at my side, but you could see how truly rattled he was as well, and understandably so; the calm danger that poured off Jasper was terrifying—and unbelievably attractive. With his dark, dangerous gaze and hand wrapped under the butt of the shotgun as the barrel rested against the fine black fabric of his suited shoulder, he looked like a rugged, masculine hit man fronting as a suited-up CEO...and fucking making it work.

"You see this little part that surrounds the trigger, John?" Jasper asked before lifting the gun back up against his face, only diverting his eyes from the other man at the last second. His movements were smooth and confident as he aimed at something in the sky that had whipped out of a nearby machine flinging discs.

He pulled the trigger and hit his neon orange target effortlessly. It was like the firearm was a part of him, nothing more than an extension of his body, like an arm or leg.

"It's called a trigger guard. It's made of reinforced polymer to improve strength and reduce weight. That's where JV Plastics *would've* been used." Another two shots, each hitting their mark seemingly without effort. He pulled on some piece of the smoking gun, and empty green shells flew onto the ground with a soft sound. I adjusted the headphones on my ears, wondering how they were capable of only blocking out the sound of the gunshot and not the voices. I could hear the valets in the back talking about how precise Jasper's shots had been.

"*Would've* been used?" John asked, looking sweaty and flustered.

"Eliza, darling, can I interest you in shooting something?" His dark eyes glittered wildly against the setting sun. "Let's start with a clay pigeon." He kept his eyes on John for an uncomfortably long moment, only removing his gaze when John shifted nervously.

The two men had been agreeable at dinner; what in god's name happened between the two of them? Was this all really because Jasper had…grown jealous?

A minuscule part of me was relieved and comforted to know that Jasper had obviously been feeling the chemistry too, that it wasn't just some ridiculous notion in my mind. Of course, at dinner, I hadn't missed his broody glares and bitten-off comments, but aside from the barely blanketed innuendos, I had just assumed that was how he behaved around everyone—everyone except those of us at the manor, like Sowerby, Katya, Leah, and…well, me. He seemed to be a bit more comfortable with the people who were around him at the manor all day long. A flush of adrenaline coursed through my veins at the surprising thought that maybe I was more on the inside with him than I had thought.

And he called me "darling."

The wine sizzled in my system, making for an easy decision. I smiled wide, feeling the chill of air hit my teeth. I stepped up to him, ready for instructions. His now smiling eyes locked with mine in silent approval as he placed the heavy shotgun in my hands.

Oh. My. God. I had a fucking gun in my hands. Me, Eliza Arnold. In a Whole Foods somewhere were the grotesque remains of my mother spontaneously combusting.

Jasper moved his hand over mine, to position them correctly, before moving his tall, muscular body close behind me.

Wine, fish, and guns, and all in one night—what an odd thing for freedom to look like.

"You told me not to bring my doves or pigeons to dinner, and here you are shooting them," I teased softly.

I could feel his smile as his chest brushed against my back. His powerful arms wrapped around either side of me, adjusting the shotgun into the correct position.

I should have felt terrified at being the sudden focus of Jasper Blackwood's attention. How many more ghosts needed to come out of the walls for me to get the fucking hint to stay away from him?

Apparently, more than one.

My eyes fluttered shut at the feel of his body against mine. It was protective, safe, and consuming with the tang of danger attached to it.

"There's a decent kickback, so be prepared for the recoil to hit your shoulder harder than you expect, okay? Are you comfortable?" His low, throaty words brushed against the shell of my ear.

"I'm good," I somehow mumbled. I could hardly focus on the weapon in my hands when the one at my back was pressed so firmly against my rear end and felt so delicious. I was a mess.

"Look through here, okay? See that mid-bead? Line all of these up. That's it," he said with a voice deep and rough like cracked velvet. Goose bumps galloped across the slope of my exposed neck, which he had to have seen, given his proximity.

My eyes widened slightly in alarm when his strong hand slowly skimmed down the length of my side to pull my right leg back a few inches, adjusting my stance. He moved the gun back up to the correct position from where it had dropped with my distracted, slackened arms.

"Lift your elbow, just like this. That's it," he cooed. "When you see the orange in the sky, line up and pull this trigger. When you're ready, shout 'pull' or step on the pedal to trigger the disc."

Adrenaline pushed through my veins, drowning me in a feeling I'd never experienced before. For a second, a whisper of fear came over me; I thought about how upset my mother would have been at my defiance—she would have been furious.

I stepped on the pedal and saw the little orange dot sail across the sky. My finger trembled as I pulled the trigger and missed by several yards.

Jasper was by my side repositioning me before I could hand him the gun back.

"Try again," he encouraged.

On my fifth try, I hit the little flying dot, and it satisfyingly exploded high in the blue-and-red evening sky.

"That's it!" he sang out with a contagious smile. He safely took the gun from me and picked me up, twirling me in a little spin before setting me back down.

"What about the contract?" John, who I had totally forgotten about, interrupted angrily with his arms crossed. "You made a deal with JV Plastics."

Jasper took my place with the gun and, as I moved back, replaced his smile with a cold look at John before quickly firing off a few more rounds, expertly hitting each and every clay pigeon as they sailed through the sky at various heights and speeds.

"Unfortunately, you never signed the contract at dinner. You were too distracted." His angled jaw shifted as he ground his teeth together. "I don't like doing business with distracted men, John, and as for the contract, you've been watching your distraction, and I'm about to blow it into about a thousand pieces above the talus," he said as he pulled an orange disc from his pocket and tossed it at John. White paper was taped around the top of it.

"You cannot be serious; you're ruining this deal over *her*?" the man said, throwing the disc hard at the manicured grass and casting a look at me that made me want to shrivel up and disappear.

Jasper's face turned sinister as he watched. With the shotgun in his hands, he stepped into John until he was towering over him.

"You know how this goes. You don't step into my home and try to fuck me or my things over. I wouldn't test me; you should really already know that by now, *Johnathan*." Jasper smirked and looked out over the edge, where his property ended and nothingness began. "Watch your step when you leave. It's a very, *very* steep fall." His brown eyes were little more than unblinking slits as he watched the nervous man take a hard step away from him and the steep drop.

I took a few steps back myself, still unable to look that low to see the ledge. John pulled out his cell phone and held it up with a malicious grin before turning and walking off quickly. One of the security guards was waiting for him a few paces away.

"Are you all right?" Jasper asked, suddenly appearing in front of me as I watched the other men disappear around the side of the manor.

"Yeah, my stomach's still a bit queasy, though. I don't think I've ever had this much excitement," I said with a laugh.

"Sit with me," he said, motioning to a concrete bench that overlooked the drop.

"Sure, but not there. I'm *deathly* afraid of heights, and I can't get that close to the edge. I'm having a hard enough time not looking over there as it is, and I think the wine is wearing off."

A devilishly charming grin took hold of his mouth. "Don't you trust me?"

"No, I don't, but don't take it personally." My eyes were light and filled with humor, but I meant my words as I moved back toward the comforting presence of the conservatory.

"Come on," he said, grabbing hold of my hand and stopping me. At the contact, I felt a jolt of electricity, which, by the startled look on his face, he had felt as well. "The view is immaculate. I promise I'll keep you safe…or at least I'll keep you from falling." He raised a dark brow in challenge, taking a moment to look down at where our hands were clasped as though he held the horn of a unicorn and not my blistered hand.

This was one challenge I was happy not to concede.

I snorted. "You'll have to hold me at gunpoint if you want to get me out on that bench. I can't even look out the balcony windows in my room," I admitted abashedly. "I have it blocked with the settee." I pulled my hand from the gentle grip of his, hoping I would think better without the contact.

His eyes brightened, causing him to look youthful and slightly like a rapscallion. His hand lightly touched the small of my back and he guided me back toward the conservatory, like he was inadvertently letting me know I was stable and safe from falling—or that he was close enough to push me.

"How will you ever see the twinkling city lights at night resting below the blanket of stars? It's the only good thing about this manor. It's worth a look if you're abandoning all of your morals while you're here anyway," he said with calculating eyes. "No salmon ever?"

We stepped into the conservatory and moved leisurely into the main house, completely content in the gentle flow of conversation.

"No, we were a big tofu-and-rice house," I answered. "And I wouldn't say that I really abandoned any of my morals tonight, just my mother's." I should have stopped talking about this with him. I seemed to have a hard time filtering myself around him, and the last thing I wanted to hear was another person scolding me, telling me that I was an adult, that I didn't have to deal with it if I didn't want to. It was one of the reasons I'd stopped bothering to have friends. No one understood. How could they? When you didn't experience it, it was simple to throw out solutions you didn't understand wouldn't work. I felt trapped, and when I reached for help, everyone chastised me for not simply walking away. No one seemed capable of understanding that I couldn't simply walk out of this prison, not when I had built it unknowingly, bar by unbending bar, while the warden had tricked me, telling me I wasn't a prisoner. As Dostoevsky said, the best way to keep a prisoner from escaping is to never let him know he's in prison. Unfortunately, I carried my cell with me.

"Don't you live alone? Are you afraid of disappointing your family? You won't even try fish out alone?" he asked, turning down hallways I'd never been…or at least I didn't think I had. It all got confusing after a while. Especially when I found myself looking more at his face than the route.

"I live alone, but—" I stopped myself. I never spoke this frankly with anyone, ever. Not about my family. It was unnerving and enthralling all at once.

"But what?" he pushed gently.

Fine. I had wanted to keep myself away from Jasper Blackwood. This would do it. Men hated controlling mothers, and I had hit the apotheosis of controlling mothers. "But my mother drives thirty minutes every week to dig through every piece of my trash to see what I've done without her there under the premise that she is helping to recycle the things I didn't correctly." I hated how the words sounded out loud. I felt embarrassed and weak—as always. It was only one of the controlling things she did, and it wasn't even close to the worst.

I looked away from him and took in the beautiful dark

wood of the eleven-foot-high doors and the intricate moldings we passed. The manor was so large, it was impossible to take in every interesting detail, even though I'd been here for a few weeks now. Maybe I needed to do a little exploring on my own, see if I could find any of Hester's or Darius's old things, see if I could learn anything helpful.

He grumbled a little. Was it uncomfortable for him to talk about mothers?

"It sounds like she means well," he said. They always said that. Usually, I told myself it was because they had normal, loving mothers and were inclined to see the positives in a similar way to something they had experienced, though I could guarantee none of it was ever similar to my mother.

"No," I answered. Normally, this would have been far past the point where I would lock up and regret having said anything, but as always happened when I was around Jasper, I found myself unable to stop talking. "I don't think so. I think she has some of her own issues. You wouldn't understand; she has to control every aspect of my life. I'm surprised she hasn't shown up outside the gates here already, honestly."

There was a weird mumble from Jasper that caused me to turn to face him. He was suddenly turned away, avoiding eye contact with me, the oddity of which made me realize just how often he actually had his coffee brown eyes locked on me.

"Oh my god! She has!" I shouted, stopping in my tracks and praying the floor would open up and suck me down into a black pit.

"I didn't know who she was. The security guys are under strict instructions not to let anyone in unless I tell them to," he said. "I'm sorry. I will let her in next time. That is...if you would like." I could feel his eyes tracing my profile.

"No, that's okay," I said abruptly, catching us both off guard. "I'm not very adept at setting boundaries with her. This is the first time I've had any sort of enforced distance, which is likely the only way I can get it, and honestly, the wine, salmon, space, and…guns have been fun. I'm not ready for the real world to find me yet." I glanced at Jasper in time to catch him looking at me with a thoughtful expression.

After walking me to my room, he said a surprisingly polite good night and left me.

As soon as I was in my room, I ran to the locket I had left on my nightstand and opened it. After the dove had flown from it in the kitchen and caused such chaos, I felt it best to leave the unpredictable locket in my room for dinner with Jasper's business associates. It was probably a good thing too; I didn't think tonight could've handled any more chaos. Certainly, Hester would have something to say about everything that had transpired throughout the evening.

My exhale reversed in shock when I opened the piece of jewelry and the coppery scent of blood wafted forth and a dark, reddish-green viscous liquid began to drip onto my lap.

"Oh my god!" I proclaimed as the green liquid poured faster and faster from the locket, continuing even after I closed it. The surprisingly warm liquid covered my hand, dripping down my wrists and arms. Was it blood? But it was such a weird color.

What in god's name was it?

Panicked, I ran to the sink and tried to wipe off the locket, but the green liquid continued to drip until I was forced to leave the necklace in the sink or be drenched in the substance that flowed from it. I gave up on figuring out what the coppery-scented liquid was and nervously got in bed. The taunting sound of the mysterious green-red effusion gurgled down the drainpipe like a lullaby from a nightmare throughout the night.

Sometime in the temporal breadth of night, the gurgling sound turned to sobs. I awoke in alarm to see the beautiful melancholy ghost in the same exact location at the foot of my bed as I had before. The woman I had assumed to be Hester, Jasper's mother, though with the recent findings of the letters, I didn't know what exactly to think. She wore the same billowing crimson gown as before, only this time she stood with a letter in her hand—a letter exactly like the ones from Jasper's chest, the ones with the red wax seal.

She looked up at me with a cold stare that was so similar to Jasper's notoriously glacial expression that I found it impossible to speculate for another second that this woman could be anyone but his mother. Eerily, she shook her head.

"No," I said out loud, trying to understand. "No...no what?" The energy rolling off the ghost turned the peaceful room suddenly terrifying. My heart slammed against my ribs. I was sure that something bad was about to happen.

She looked back at the letter and repeated her actions once more, crying and shaking her head.

"I—I don't understand. What are you trying to tell me? I'll help you; just tell me what to do." I struggled to get the words through my quivering throat.

Her expression turned less sad and became angrier. Panic settled into my bones. I wanted to scream for help—I wanted another living person to see the terrifying spirit, to protect me with the presence of an additional pulse so that I wouldn't feel so goddamned alone and scared.

More than anything, I wanted to help her. The effects of whatever had happened to this once-stunning woman poured from her eyes in a woeful tide that had already pulled me under and was threatening to drown me.

Bathed in the unsettling darkness of the night, I watched as the last shred of hope in her dark eyes flickered and the trembling of her arms and frail shoulders grew stronger, replaced with frustrated rage. An undercurrent of subtle recognition gripped my senses.

I recognized that my blind, unwavering need to help this

woman was because I knew well what it felt like to be broken and trapped, unable to help myself—but I could help her.

Slowly, as though she was suddenly having a difficult time not throttling me, she cryptically flicked off the red wax seal from the letter as if trying to hit me with it before turning and gliding out through the closed door of my bedroom.

Each part of my body fought to tremble more than the others until I shook so hard attempting to get out of bed that I fell to the hard floor in a heap. Too frightened to sit on the floor for fear she would return, I hurriedly grabbed the hard blob of scarlet and moved to the moonlight that poured through the balcony's window sheers.

The design on the wax seal was a fully bloomed rose with lush petals.

I felt the wrinkles between my brows deepen. Rosa gallicas were generally an incredibly sought-after rose, even used in perfume making for their beautiful scent. I could tell from my work in the conservatory that Hester had tried to get rid of the wild roses there, even though the white flower had forced its way in during the garden's time of neglect. In her entire Gothic garden, she had not planted a single rose—a fact that had stood out to me as quite odd initially. When I'd brought it up to Jasper, he seemed to have never noticed the odd detail about his mother.

Hester Blackwood loathed roses, so would she seal her letters with one?

CHAPTER 14
ELIZA

Every nerve in my body seized as I jolted awake with a sharp gasp.

For a second, I had forgotten where I was, not recognizing the empty bed in front of me before the events of the previous night came tumbling back to me.

I stood from the stiff wooden chair, my back suddenly annoyingly itchy with the small circular indentations where the caning had pressed into my skin. I had sat watch in the corner of the room all night. With every step, even now, my aching body waited for something to leap out and frighten me, my peripheral vision playing tricks with shadows. My senses were so taut, every small creak of the floor felt like a whip cracking in the still loneliness of the room.

Last night, after the ghost of Jasper's mother left, I couldn't settle myself enough to fall back asleep. Every creak of the floor, every tickle of hair dancing from a draft, every goose bump that came on, I took as a warning. Over and over and over, my mind circled with the thought of Hester in red. Was it Hester? Why had she been crying over the letter? What did it all mean?

The only other time the ghost had appeared before me, she

had also appeared sad and broken, but last night was different. Her sadness had turned to anger, and whether it was over the letter or my inability to understand what it was she was trying to tell me, I may never know.

I had thought about following the woman into the hallway, but every part of me had been far too afraid to move after she had flashed her anger in my direction.

It was a very different encounter to be in the presence of a melancholy ghost than an angry one.

Incapable of returning to sleep with the locket still oozing green in the sink, I eventually did what every other person in the world does when they can't sleep, be it due to angry ghosts or insomnia—I got on my phone. I needed to find out everything I could about Jasper's family. Initially, my search was mostly filtering through archived news articles from the last two decades, nearly every single one with bold headlines proclaiming Jasper to be the number one suspect in the disappearance of Hester and Darius Blackwood. It gave me chills knowing that the man accused was sleeping close by from where I was reading these details.

My pulse quickened when several pictures of a young and angry Jasper appeared. In the earliest one I found, he couldn't possibly have been older than fifteen. His cheeks were soft and slightly rounder; they had the look of a child morphing into a man, far from the angular profile he wore now, though his eyes had already begun to take on a hint of their hardened glint.

None of the articles seemed empathetic to the newly orphaned child but instead went into details, not only calling Jasper the son of Satan but even going so far as to say things like "at least Darius was gone for good," and various statements proclaiming their relief that the owner of Blackwood Bladecraft was gone and couldn't destroy any more lives. The latter seemed fueled by enraged members of the community who had lost their well-paying jobs at Blackwood Bladecraft.

Several photos were of a fifteen-year-old Jasper in handcuffs being escorted by the police, most with the headlines "Drug-Addicted Son Murders Parents for Inheritance" or "Devil Child Pushes Parents Over Stormcrest Ridge." Apparently, spoiled and wealthy, Jasper was into some pretty bad activity as a teen—including fighting several other kids at his school, putting one in the hospital with a broken jaw, stabbing another boy—yes, with a Blackwood Bladecraft knife—and selling drugs to a large portion of the student body, all of which were scattered throughout the many articles.

I even found a photo from when Jasper was about seventeen, with Sowerby in the background. I stared at that one for a while. They had known each other since he was young. The relationship between the two of them was starting to make more sense as this all unraveled. There was an ease whenever they were around each other, so it made sense that they had known each other a very long time, though I hadn't suspected it had been quite this long.

I also didn't want to believe it was possible for Jasper to have murdered his parents. Would Sowerby still be around and as comfortable around him if he had murdered the elder Blackwoods? Logically, I had no reason to believe he hadn't done it—in fact, deep down I believed him to be more than capable of killing anyone, but for some reason, there was a tug inside of my gut, telling me that he didn't do it.

Then something occurred to me that made more sense: How had it not crossed my mind before that Sowerby could have killed Hester and Darius?

My immediate thought was why no one had suspected Sowerby of the murders. It was just as obscure to imagine him as the murderer as it was a fifteen-year-old child—of course, whatever money Darius and Hester had went to Jasper when he was eighteen. In the eyes of the public, there was no clear motive for anyone else to have done it but Jasper.

It hadn't helped that after maids realized something was wrong and called the police, Jasper was found sitting over the ledge of the cliff, covered in Hester's blood. When they questioned him, he got angry and violent—so much so that they had to put ties on his arms and legs and a bag over his head. I saw the picture of him in the seat of the cop car with blood all over the front of his white T-shirt.

They'd never found any remains, but they said the terrain of the slope made it impossible to send searchers without risking more lives. Choppers had scanned the area, but it was too dense with debris to see. It was awful to think that their bones could be hidden in the rocks on the other side of the cliff. I was tempted to go look at the view from my window, but I couldn't. I could look up at the clouds and that was about it—at least, without having a panic attack. I glanced at the settee still anchored in front of the balcony doors and relaxed a little.

In the end, the case was dismissed because of police misconduct and mishandling of evidence. Apparently, Jasper's high-powered lawyer leaned in on technicalities; the shirt with Hester's blood on it was taken into evidence early, not logged correctly among other things. Jasper walked away a free man. As I looked at the photos of Jasper as he grew older, my chest grew heavy. I could see the light leave his eyes a little more in every photo as he grew older. As I continued to dig, more articles quoted enraged, angry people of the town or nearby cities complaining that he had gotten away with murder. When he was seventeen, I noticed that, in all the pictures thereafter, his eyes looked almost empty, and he held the harsh, unreadable, dangerous expression that he wore now. Then, the articles changed.

In a particularly disturbing magazine piece, a then nineteen-year-old Jasper was interviewed for his ingenious business strategy. The interviewer asked a series of crass questions before teasing that Jasper was so wealthy now that no one cared who he had murdered. Jasper had given a commanding response, putting the interviewer in their place, and from then on, the articles took on a very different tone—they seemed fascinated and enthralled by him, if not afraid.

Photos of him getting into helicopters, at award ceremonies with leggy blonds, even being mentioned in men's fashion columns and *Forbes* features, it was endless.

It was a lot harder to find anything on Hester and Darius, but eventually, I found an old excerpt from a home and garden magazine. The article itself was somewhat useless, as it mostly spoke about the inspiration for the architectural details of Blackwood Manor, but the photo they used proved more than interesting.

Standing next to a heavyset tan man with a knifelike nose and the same sharp jaw as Jasper stood the ghost woman in her living form. There was no mistaking it. She beamed up at the man as he held her tightly, unable to hide his own happy smile.

It was her.

Jasper Blackwood's mother, Hester, was dead and haunting me; there was no getting around it. And if Hester was dead, then she was incapable of writing those letters to Jasper. Which made me wonder where the ghost of Darius was lurking.

The happy young couple stood together amidst a beautiful, abundant garden absolutely brimming with red and deep purple blooms that set off both of their all-black outfits in a beautifully artistic photograph. Hester looked only slightly younger in the photo than she did in my room, but everything else about her felt different and would have been nearly unrecognizable if not for her strikingly beautiful features, which made you stop and stare. Gone were the sad, hollow eyes and sallow skin of the woman who visited me. She was gorgeous, and the glow of life radiated from her as she stood in a sun-drenched outdoor garden, her arms around Darius's waist. She looked like a woman who had never once been touched by sadness—a far cry from the woman whose red-eyed sobs had woken me in the middle of the night.

I nearly leaped from the mattress when my eyes snagged on a shiny gold chain around her neck. She was wearing the locket. A scream sat in my throat, needing to be released with the buzz from my new information. But I couldn't scream; instead, I moved to sit in the chair, alone in my room, and tried to make the puzzle pieces fit.

Several times last night, I'd gone back to the photo of Hester and Darius in the garden. There was something peaceful and happy about it. The couple's happiness and love poured from my phone screen so deeply, I could feel it in my own skin.

What had happened to them?

And that's when I saw it.

The koi pond that they stood next to. The layout was exactly the same as the conservatory—except they weren't in a conservatory. They were outside in the fresh air with the open cliff behind them, in the exact spot where the conservatory now sat, except that was different too.

In the distance, a large stone wall safely blocked the edge of the cliff—a wall I knew for a fact was no longer there.

Eventually, I moved back to the bed and fell asleep with wild theories spinning webs in my head. Had Sowerby done it and was somehow getting money from Jasper? Hester and Darius were not at all what they had seemed in the photo. They let their plant poison half the town—their own neighbors. They were not good people. Quite the contrary. I knew better than anyone that happy family photos showed nothing of what went on behind the scenes. Had Darius gotten rough with Hester, and Jasper tried to stop him? What had happened for Jasper to have Hester's blood on his shirt? They said it was tested and confirmed to be her blood.

Had Darius done it, and that was why only Hester's ghost had shown herself? It seemed Blackwood Bladecraft, Darius's company, had started to expand and, with it, gained a bit of controversy. Several media sources had shamed Blackwood Bladecraft for their expansion into other more secretive medical areas of alloy testing and manufacturing and for supplying weapons to stores that made them easily accessible to children. Though there were sprinklings of talk about money suddenly hemorrhaging from the company, the timeline was all wonky and confusing.

I needed to find out when the stone wall had been removed. Could they have fallen by accident? Was that why Hester's ghost haunted Blackwood Manor? Did proximity matter to spirits? Or did they haunt Blackwood Manor because their killer was still there? As a kid growing up in Pinehurst, I had already heard most of what I had read about Jasper, mostly little bits and pieces of conversations adults had around me. At the time, it hadn't mattered; I'd barely kept the information. I mostly remembered the ghost stories about the knife victims haunting the manor. Looking through the articles, the ghost stories seemed to have originated from a maid who used to work at the manor who stated she saw the ghosts, which was ultimately what made her quit. It had all felt so far away from me then. Now, it felt like one of the most important things in the world.

It felt like Hester's peace was in my hands, that I was the only one who could help set her free. I had to do everything I could to find the answers about what had happened to Hester and Darius. I had been going about this all wrong, trying to keep Jasper away.

I needed to get closer to Jasper.

Something that didn't sound really all that bad until I thought of the very, *very* real possibility that he had killed them—or maybe even just one of them—and the danger that put me in. He was certainly angry and cold enough that it wasn't all that much of a stretch, but I'd seen him talk about money and luxurious things since staying here, and it just didn't seem like he cared that much about the money for that to be his motive, not really. It sounded like he had been a pretty violent kid, so it seemed likely to me that money hadn't been the motive—anger had been. I also got the impression that he wasn't fond of Blackwood Manor, especially considering how often he worked and lived in his other homes across the world, which raised a lot of questions: If he had such horrid memories tied to the manor, why stay at all? Why not sell it? Something kept him from putting the manor behind him, and I was starting to think it wasn't just memories.

When the hell *was* I going to find time to talk to Jasper? And not just talk to him but get him comfortable enough with me that I could pry, subtly, into the private parts of his life—all while finishing the fucking conservatory.

My head was a blender of thoughts as I made my way downstairs for the day. My exhausted, overstimulated body took me straight to the kitchen for coffee. I perked up at the thought immediately, looking forward to seeing Katya. She had very quickly become one of my favorite people, and only a portion of that was because she kept me extremely well fed and caffeinated. The instant we met, she was warm and caring, always leaving snacks or a plate out for me when I didn't make it to dinner or was working late in the garden. Sometimes, I'd bring her a tiny bouquet of the flowers that had gotten pruned and would have been thrown out, and every time, she'd make a huge deal about it, acting as if I'd brought her a thousand dollars instead of wilted, half-dead flowers. Every time I left the kitchen in the morning, she had the most encouraging, uplifting things to say, just something short and quick. Sometimes, I thought her little words in the morning fueled my work well into the evening. She was like the supportive motherly figure I had always wished for. Not that I didn't love my mother, I did—even when it got really, *really* hard to.

"Katya, my queen, do you possibly have a barrel instead of a mere mug this morn—oh, sorry." I stopped as soon as I turned the corner and saw Jasper leaning against the counter, cradling a large mug of coffee as if it were a precious gold ring from Middle-earth.

"Eliza, sorry. Katya and Sowerby had to run out for something; she'll be back this evening," Jasper said as he nursed the steaming coffee. The clean, fruity scent of Fabuloso and warm coffee filled the air in an uplifting mix.

"Ooh shit, that's right. I can't believe I forgot. I meant to talk to you about letting me run into town to get them a card," I said, slapping my palm to my forehead. She had been so excited for today that I had helped her pick out a sweater to wear a week ago. She had chosen a dark-green cashmere argyle sweater that made her hazel eyes pop beautifully.

His thick brows pulled together as his glare darkened. "A card? You couldn't have forgotten; it just happened. Katya had to run out to grab flour, and Sowerby drove her because she hates to drive on the mountain. What would you get her a card for?"

Oh my god. Jasper didn't remember.

"It's their anniversary. I don't have time to run into town now; the koi are getting delivered today." Shit. I didn't want her to think I'd forgotten. "Do you have some markers and some paper or something? It's the thought that counts." I shrugged as I moved to look through the cabinets in search of the biggest cup I could find.

Jasper made a choked sound. "Their anniversary? That's beyond absurd. They're not..." I could see the pieces slowly coming together in his eyes. Had he not known they were together? Maybe he and Sowerby weren't as close as I'd thought.

"What?" I nearly shouted at him. "How could you not think they are together? They are the cutest couple in the entire world."

He stared at me as if I'd just shot him with a freeze ray.

"Oh my god," he muttered, moving to sit down. "How have I never put it together?" A look of hurt lanced across his face but was gone in an instant. "I can't believe they told you and not me. Why?" The newly darkened bags under his eyes seemed to double in size before my eyes.

I shrugged and took a large swallow of my coffee, torn between feeling sorry for him and wondering how he could have missed something so obvious. It occurred to me that they might have been the ones keeping it quiet from their employer. I hoped I hadn't messed anything up for them. "Do you have any card stock? Want to make a card with me?" I laughed.

"I don't know. Come to my office, and I'll check," he said in a daze.

Twenty minutes later, Jasper and I sat next to each other behind his desk, drawing a makeshift anniversary card with printer paper and only red, blue, and black dry-erase markers to choose from.

"You have to draw something, or this is going to seem really stupid," I said to him as I put the finishing touches on the pot my little chef bear was holding.

"It's already really stupid," he mumbled.

We had started the craft on opposite sides of his desk, but he had moved my chair next to his so he could watch. That's what he'd said, but for the last ten minutes, I don't think he looked down to see my drawing one time. I could feel his eyes latched onto the side of my face. I struggled to not make the stupid, open-mouthed faces that I normally did when drawing. It was hard to focus on anything when he was sitting so close and watching so intently.

"Draw something."

"Absolutely not," he stated.

"What?" I said, falling back in my chair. "You promised you would draw something!"

He scowled and I stiffened, immediately feeling exposed and foolish.

"Didn't promise. I never promise anyone anything. I said I would, and now I'm retracting it." He leaned back in the chair. "You can't expect me to follow that type of skill and still feel like a man."

My mouth stretched open a little, unable to believe what I was hearing. I threw my hands up in the air. "Well, fuck, I'm sorry," I said sarcastically. "I had no idea asking you to draw a sweet card for your closest staff members would be a threat to your manhood." I rolled my eyes.

He grinned and I felt it all the way through my body. "That's not what will destroy my manliness; the stick figure or bubble money sign that I draw next to your masterpiece will shame me and detract from your art."

I snorted and rolled my eyes. "If you don't want to draw anything, just say that. You don't have to get weird. It's a bear with a chef's hat. Ten-year-olds can draw better."

"Interesting," he said, leaning back in his chair, examining me.

"What?" I asked defensively.

"Nothing, you're just awful at taking compliments, that's all." His eyes were alive with a playful gleam that felt more dangerous than his stare.

I returned my eyes to the desk and finished up the words on the card. "Sorry, I don't get a lot of compliments, so that's probably true," I said under my breath as I drew.

"Impossible, with the ability to draw bears like that," he deadpanned. "You said at dinner you wished you could have gone to school for art. What made you choose plants over art?"

Needing to steer away from that line of questioning, I slid the card and blue marker over to him and shrugged. I was trying to get into *his* family details, not give him mine. I never spoke about my family to anyone; no one could understand what I went through with them—except what Jasper had gone through made him feel more like a teammate in the family-problem area.

I shrugged. "I didn't really choose one. Botany was the farthest I was able to get away from what my parents wanted while still doing what they wanted. I'm thankful for it; it's mostly just playing in dirt and looking at beautiful flowers. I think even if I were to have been a painter, I would have done nature and landscapes, although I probably only think that because the only thing I've ever painted are plants in my botany journal," I said with a laugh. I felt like a child admitting that they wanted to be a marine biologist.

He looked at me for a long moment. "So why don't you do it, then? Paint?"

I tried to school my exhausted features, but I felt overcome with frustration and discomfort. How had the subject turned to me?

"Because some of us weren't born with an inheritance. I have a degree and a career with people who depend on me, people that I like, and debt. I have a lot of debt, and I'm still paying for that degree. Only like 10 percent of artists are successful enough to make a living off it, and…and it's just the way things are," I bit out, flustered. I didn't want to get on his bad side, but the last thing I could handle right now was hearing Jasper fucking Blackwood, heir to the Blackwood fortune, judging *me* for not pursuing my dreams. He had no idea what it was like not to have options. From the minute he was born, he had been spoiled. I was tired of walking on eggshells for fear of really angering him, but I wanted more information—and didn't want to be let go from this project. For some reason, of all the people in the whole world, this man brought out the wily, outspoken Eliza I had wished to be in a thousand other scenarios and been unable to.

He grabbed a marker and absently began doodling something on the folded paper. I got the feeling he was only doing it so I wouldn't leave. He was perceptive enough to have picked up that I was uncomfortable and wanted to; he was always watching me, taking in details and things I'm sure I didn't want him to see.

"Things change," he said rather gruffly.

I shifted in my chair, feeling my hackles prickle. "Not for me."

"Why not?"

Why was he asking me so many questions? "Because—" Frustrated, I struggled to find words that sounded better than the real reasons. As always seemed to happen when I was speaking with him, the truth slid too easily from my tongue. "Because I hate disappointing the people I love. I don't like making them mad."

When he didn't react or even bother to look up, I calmed a fraction.

"Would *you* be disappointed if someone you loved did something that made them happy?" he asked, still laser-focused on the doodle he was drawing.

I stilled. Only my chest rose and fell with my labored breath as my eyes danced over his profile, struggling to stay on one spot. "No, of course not," I stammered. "But—"

Irritatingly calm, he continued. "An enemy is defined as a person who is actively opposed or hostile to another. Would you listen to an enemy if they told you what to do?" he questioned.

"No, but—" I wanted to leave the room. The manor. The world. My skin felt hot and tight. He had somehow managed to reach in and take the troublesome, uncomfortable thoughts that were too hard to address out of my head and turned them into a passive conversation.

He glanced up and locked his deep mahogany orbs with mine. If he could read secrets from my eyes before, he'd just gotten a whole library full in one look. "Sometimes our saviors are simply enemies cloaked in white robes," he stated, leaning back from the desk. "You cannot depend on anyone but yourself in this world. You must carve your own path or else someone will cut into your flesh, slicing through every part of your soul and leaving nothing behind. You need to have boundaries, or else everyone, including the saintly clad enemies, get in."

His words struck so sharp against the tender parts of me that I wanted to cry. And yell. And hit something. Lash out. So I did.

"I would much rather have no boundaries and allow others in than to have fortress walls so high no one can ever get inside, so I'm all alone like you," I snapped.

He seemed completely unbothered as he looked at me, the most passive expression on his lightly stubbled face, but a soft flare in his intelligent eyes suggested he wasn't as calm as he projected.

A tingle of fear tickled at the base of my neck. What would he do when I angered him? Would he hurt me? I inhaled and the scent of masculine power and leather filled my head, tightening my stomach.

"Socrates says sometimes people put up walls, not to keep others out but to see who cares enough to break them down. What's in your necklace?" he asked, leaning into my space to get a better look.

My smart retort fell into the ether when I noticed he was so suddenly in my personal space. I could make out every one of the faint vertical lines decorating his soft pink lips when he was this close, the tan skin of his face including the taut indent where his skin had been torn open and forcibly reshaped in a jagged, angular way. The scar was bold and asymmetrical, like an unfinished sketch or the markings of a road map, cutting through the smoothness of skin. On anyone else, the scar would have been everyone's first impression, but on Jasper, it was hidden in the shadows of his dark confidence. It only added to his face, balancing his almost too strikingly beautiful looks with a hint of male barbarism and danger.

My hand twitched to reach out and touch that scar. I pulled my hands into fists and pushed them between my thighs to keep from touching him. His minty-toothpaste breath tickled across my lips and chin. He must have been feeling my own breath on his mouth. He was so close, I could almost taste the flavor of his soapy skin.

Suddenly, it occurred to me what he'd asked about: the locket.

I hadn't realized it was outside of my shirt. It had stopped dripping green before I threw it on this morning...had it not? It felt dangerous to have him inspecting it this closely, like a panther deciding if he wanted to strike out at you or not.

"P-pictures," I stuttered. I'd been afraid a lot in my life, and it had never once turned me on, but the alluring flavor of excitement and danger that Jasper emitted had my thighs clenching together. I was so close to his mouth right now that one small move from him and our lips would touch.

I bet he knew how to kiss in a way that made it feel like he was already inside of me—full and commanding. God, I wanted him to dominate me... *No.*

He was hovering to see how much he rattled me—that was all. My teeth sank into my lower lip with sharp pressure. He could tell what he was doing to me. I was sure of it. I couldn't hide it like he could. There was an element of excitement and lust that poured from him straight into me. I was afraid of him only slightly less than I was attracted to him—in an achy, uncomfortably overwhelming way. I knew he wanted me too; I could see it in his face—not in his stoic, unbothered expression, but in the dark restraint glimmering in his brown eyes as they looked at my lips. My eyes. My chest.

His large hand reached out and coiled around the locket, lifting it from where it sat at the top of my cleavage. His fingers brushed the fabric separating our skin. His hand remained, feeling the weight of the locket. The soft thud of hammering echoed through my head, and I wasn't sure if it was the men outside working or my heart pounding with such ferocity.

Fuck, fuck, fuck, fuck, fuck. He must not recognize it yet. Oh god, what's he going to do once he realizes it's his mother's?

His thumb moved over the seam to open it, and god only knew what was going to fly out at him this time. If Hester wanted to communicate anything to her son, now was her time.

I closed my eyes and braced myself as the locket clicked open in his hand, my chest brushing against the knuckles of his hand with every inhale.

"Love heals everything," he read. "Who gave you this, a sister or something?" He continued examining it.

I let out the breath I had been holding long enough to look down and see the cursive inscription inside the locket. Thank fuck she didn't do something wild.

Love heals everything.

"Why do you assume a sister and not a boyfriend?" I said indignantly.

"I know you don't have a boyfriend. I had my security check before you moved in, and—" He looked away, filtering himself.

"And what?" I practically snarled. I couldn't believe he did a deep dive into my life. A criminal background check was one thing, but prodding into my personal life was another. My privacy felt invaded, and I hated it. What business was it of his?

"And it looks like an heirloom, valuable. Any boyfriend worth a shit, bothering to give you jewelry of value, wouldn't sit back and let you get hurt by anyone, even your family." His eyes flickered with his words. He closed the locket and leaned back in his chair, spreading his muscular legs out comfortably. This man didn't give a shit about anything.

I didn't know what to say. I didn't want to talk about me

and my family anymore. "A security check doesn't tell if someone has a boyfriend or not," I snapped, suddenly feeling filleted open, exposed—my worst fear.

In his relaxed, almost reclined position, I felt him slowly appraising me with his dark gaze. "My security checks do."

I felt my face redden under the heat of his stare.

"I meant to tell you: I have a book my mother kept where she made notes of the flowers she wanted and similar. I think there are original designs for the garden in there as well if you would be interested in taking a look. I know you aren't planting anything yet, still prepping, but it might help if you are trying to keep the original feel. Personally, I don't care if you burn it to the ground." He straightened, opened a desk drawer, and pulled out a checkbook. He grabbed a pen and scribbled a few things on the top check before ripping it free and tucking it into the card on the desk—their homemade printer-paper, dry-erase-marker anniversary card.

I shook myself and focused on what was most important. "That notebook would be amazing. I don't want to bother you if you're busy. You can just tell me where it is, and I can get it." Maybe I could look around under the guise of finding the notebook.

"No. I don't like people wandering where they don't belong. I'll get it."

Nervously, my eyes shot away from his, and I inadvertently glanced at the check made out to Katya and choked mid-swallow. "Holy shit." I slapped my palm over my mouth.

"I agree, monetary gifts are classless and unthoughtful. I would have had my butler go out and choose a lovely present for the happy couple. However, my butler is one half of that couple, so hopefully a check will suffice," he said.

"You made it out to Katya? Not Sowerby?" I asked.

"Yes, I thoroughly understand Katya not telling me about their relationship; she is private and doesn't like to share personal details, which I respect, but Evil Alfred should have told me and must be punished by any means necessary for not having done so." The twinkle was back in his eyes. "Unfortunately, it won't faze him; the man has more money than me at this point." He smiled thoughtfully as if he was thinking about a certain moment between the two of them.

Sowerby had more money than him? Even as an exaggeration, that was a lot of money... How had a butler gotten so much money?

This was finally my chance.

"How long have you known Sowerby?" I asked lightly.

His eyes locked with mine, and for a second, I started to panic. Asking Jasper anything personal felt like lying down in front of him and asking him to gut me with a rusty hunting knife. It was like he could sense I was fishing for details about his family, digging where I shouldn't be.

All humor left his face, and I knew he wasn't going to give me anything; his walls were up and formidable.

In the ongoing silence, goose bumps tickled the back of my neck—a feeling of warning. I cleared my throat. "I should get to the conservatory. Would you give the card to them when they return?" I said and stood to leave, dreading going to work. It felt so nice on my tired body to sit for a bit and not be irritating my sore muscles.

"I've always known Sowerby." His words cracked through the silent room like a whip. I felt them on my skin.

I stopped and turned back around to look at him. His brown eyes looked so full of pain and suffering that I wanted to run from the room. It was unsettling to see the broody, cold-hearted man I had come to know a little in this state of visible emotional pain.

"He worked here before I was born. He used to work in the gardens. When my mother was really into collecting rare plants, Sowerby was the only one she trusted enough to care for them. He was the one who convinced my father to enclose the gardens and build the conservatory around them so my mother could do what she loved all year long." His tone was foreign, wistful, and quiet. Almost as if he were a little boy again—except there was a note of bitterness underneath that didn't quite match. But that all explained the picture of Hester and Darius outside and why the layout of the beds was almost exactly the same.

Jasper had cracked open a door in his walls and was timidly letting me in. But inside the walls seemed far more dangerous than where I currently was.

I sat back down with the same trepidation I would've had if I were attempting to make friends with a bear. What was I doing?

"Sowerby worked in the gardens with your mother?" I asked softly, not wanting to push; the fear of being bitten loomed.

"Yeah. I guess they were pretty close. I don't remember him back then, though; I don't know that we ever spoke. To this day, he refuses to utter a bad word about her, only speaks about my father," he grumbled, then shrugged. "It doesn't matter. I say enough disparaging comments for the both of us." He glanced at me, and I could tell he was gauging my response, calculating if he should continue.

I looked back at the man sitting next to me as he pretended to be dismissive and uncaring, but I had seen how much he cared for his staff members and how he was willing to blow a business deal for me. He wasn't as untouchable as he wanted to be.

There was no possible way he killed Hester Blackwood—at least certainly not on purpose. I just couldn't possibly believe it. It was clear he loved deeply and was loyal as could be by the way he and Sowerby acted. There was no way he was a psychotic, unfeeling killer.

Something told me he was as broken inside as Hester's ghost looked on the outside. I scooted my chair closer, removing the inches between us, taking a small, nervous breath as I reached out and set my hand on Jasper's leg in an act of comfort—all while praying the bear wouldn't maul me.

"Why do you hate them?" I whispered it, but it felt like my voice echoed through the intimate moment.

Jasper's eyes shot to mine with the force of a slap to the face.

I recoiled, removing my hand. I leaned back, grabbed the maroon leather padded arm of my chair, and scooted several inches to the left, giving him some space.

His brown gaze remained sharply on me as his head canted slightly, taking in my actions. It was eerie how much attention he paid to small details.

Every instinct in my body urged me to move farther away, to make a joke and leave his space quickly, to get out while I still could. It was foolish to think that of all the people who had ever been in Jasper's life, I would be the one he would talk freely to. A wave of embarrassment seemed to swallow me at my overinflated sense of value in Jasper's world—in everyone's world.

I knew the score—no one really needed me. Hester truly was the only soul in existence to have ever been desperate enough to believe me capable of helping them.

The thought of Hester anchored me to my seat. I pulled my knees up to my chest, winding my arms around them, refusing to leave because of Jasper's intimidation. He, no doubt, scared away everyone who threatened to get too close.

Silence tensed in the air, and I realized how much I actually wanted to be let inside—not just for answers to the questions I had, but because he and I were so much more alike than I had ever realized. Regardless of the causes, we were both broken, and as badly as I wanted to be whole again, I wanted that for him too. If fifteen-year-old Jasper had actually killed his parents, he'd had over two decades to change and live with the regret of it.

His mouth had opened slightly when I removed my hand, but it closed decidedly as he reached out and grabbed the arm of my chair, pulling it back to where it had been, next to him.

Startled, my eyes widened.

"My father's company began to fail," he said, softer than I'd ever heard him speak. A low bass note betrayed his imposing exterior with the rough edge of unvoiced pain.

I felt the empathy quiver inside my chest. It reminded me of my sister when we were young and she got the brunt of the punishments, too stubborn to surrender to my parents' will.

Inside the door of his fortress, I sat in my chair and quietly listened.

"He made some stupid business moves. He leaned into the opportunity to double dip, not just with weapons but with alloy-based medical testing. The company began to hemorrhage money. When the facility got caught leaching toxins into the town's water, he lost almost everything. The entire company nearly went under, and so did half the people employed by Darius Blackwood, which at the time was a pretty good chunk of this town." He clenched his jaw. "He couldn't pick up the pieces quick enough, so he and my mother ran." He shifted in his seat with a small, vulnerable huff of a laugh, and he continued. "My entire world broke into a thousand pieces in one day. We had gotten into it earlier that day. I'd gotten in trouble again. I stole the principal's car and drove it home from my new private school. I got caught on the way home, no license. I was always acting out, trying to get my dad's attention. Never worked—he was still always too busy with the company to pay any attention to me." His throat bobbed as he struggled to swallow. "Anyway, that day I'd really set them off. Mom was furious. Worse than anything I'd ever seen, but this time it felt different. I was an angsty little shit and she was an emotional mess. I don't know what she was so emotional for, she had no problem leaving."

Jasper's jaw tensed so hard, I thought I might hear a cracking sound.

"She said she had to go, that she couldn't stay here any longer. She told me how much she loved me, made me hug her goodbye. When she was hugging me, she cried so hard she got a nosebleed, a bad one, all over my new shirt, which just made me even madder. I stormed out and slept by the wall of the cliff's edge, debating jumping the whole night, thinking that if I never said goodbye to my dad, they'd have to stay. I never thought they'd actually leave. But by the next morning, they were gone. They wouldn't have even known if I'd have jumped to my death that night.

"The next morning, the maids noticed some valuables missing, the house in disarray, and apparently me sitting outside with blood on my shirt. That was the last time I ever saw her." He let out a dark laugh that made my insides curl up. "I didn't even see my father leave. He didn't bother to say anything to me before he left; he just left. They left me alone and abandoned in the manor. I was fifteen. I don't think they cared what happened to me."

"Oh my god," I whispered, incapable of comprehending what he was telling me. In all the scenarios my mind had imagined, *that* hadn't been one of them. "They...just left you? They never even tried to come back? How could they do that to you?"

His eyes stayed pinned to a spot on the floor, like he would find the answers to my questions hidden within the fibers of the rug.

"I wasn't a good kid, but I thought they cared about me. Both my mother and father were always decent enough, especially my mother, at least until they left—I always thought my mother was a patient saint. All she cared about was me and those goddamn flowers. From the day I was born, they gave me anything I wanted; the maids all complained about me when my parents' backs were turned, and rightfully so. But everything changed when the plant went under and the town went crazy. My parents fought, mostly over me or whatever it was I'd gotten into. When they found out the plant had been poisoning everyone, they fought a lot. They grew more distant, staying away from me for longer periods of time; not just my father anymore, but my mom too." He stood from his seat and turned away from me, putting his hands in his pockets. "I don't really think it was all that hard for them to leave me. I think they were done. They had changed; both of them had grown visibly tired."

"Who did they leave you with? Who took care of you?"

He looked at me sharply, his brows angry. "No one. I told you; they didn't care."

I leaped up and moved to his side. "You were a fifteen-year-old child; something must have happened—they must have thought someone was bringing you…" Tears prickled at my eyes at the thought of a young kid left parentless and alone in this giant manor. I racked my brain, trying to come up with any other explanation but couldn't imagine anything that justified abandoning a child like that.

I couldn't believe it.

I had seen the photo of Hester and Jasper in the locket; you could see the love she had for him. I found it impossible to believe that she would just abandon him like that. None of it made any sense.

"They knew what they were doing," he said gruffly. "Sowerby found me at the house just before the cops took me, and he stayed with me. He called the family lawyer and refused to leave me behind…still refuses to leave me." I could hear the sentimentality in his words. "For a long time, I thought they were messing with me, trying to teach me a lesson so I'd behave. Stupid of me to give them that much credit.

"They never came back. Not even when the police investigation started. By that time, everyone was so mad at my father for the chemical leak and causing everyone to lose their jobs, they didn't care what really happened; they just wanted to punish the Blackwoods in any way possible. A few years later, I started getting letters from them." He turned to face me with a solemn expression. "The police thought they were fakes. They're not. I know it's them. In every letter, one of them gives some type of parenting advice as though in substitution for them not being here." He shook his head.

"Jasper, I'm so sorry." I wished I had something better to say, but my mind still couldn't comprehend all that he had gone through. It was no wonder he didn't trust anyone.

He brushed off my sympathies. His jaw was clenched tight, and his eyes had gone back to their usual harsh, lethal stare. "I hate them. I hate them so much, it wouldn't matter to me if they were actually dead."

The power flickered once before complete darkness took over the room.

I yelped, fear gripping my heart like a claw.

Five loud cracks sounded, one right after the other.

Crack, crack, crack, crack, crack!

Each of the five paintings hanging on his office walls fell to the floor, their frames shattering loudly.

"What's happening?" I shouted.

There was a low rumble like distant thunder, and the lights flickered again, coming back on. It felt like the house was exploding in anger.

"Jasper!" I held on to him, afraid of what would happen next.

"It's okay; you're okay," he said, holding on to me tightly. "It must be an earthquake or something."

"I don't think that was an earthquake," I mumbled into his warm chest, my eyes tightened shut as the house seemed to settle.

I knew exactly what it had been, and it most definitely had not been an earthquake.

It was a *very* upset Hester.

CHAPTER 15
JASPER

I SAT AT MY DESK, WASTING YET ANOTHER DAY GOING BACK AND forth between regret and relief that I had been so open with Eliza. Mostly regret. I should have had her sign an NDA. I should have kept my mouth shut.

I should have told her everything.

After she had left to go work in the conservatory yesterday, I sat and stared at my desk, wondering how it all had happened. I dissected every interaction we'd had since she'd stepped into my office that first day, a month ago, desperate and determined, how her eyes glowed with hope when I'd told her she could work on the garden.

I couldn't pinpoint the conversation or even the day it had happened, but I realized that over the course of the last month, I'd started to care for Eliza Arnold. I'd let her weasel her way in, in a way that was and always had been off-limits. I had started to give her little crumbs of myself, something I didn't want to do but hadn't realized I was even doing until the other day. I wanted to take, not give. I'd already given so much of myself; there wasn't that much left.

I'd never dealt with this before. Aside from Sowerby, I had never been comfortable opening up to anyone like I had with her.

It scared me nearly as much as when I'd been left to fend for myself as a kid. Except then, I'd had no idea the hardships that I had been about to face; now I did. She needed to go.

I couldn't be with her. And god, did I want to be with her. She had to leave.

Not only to avoid getting hurt, but also because she was the one who would inevitably be hurt, and I didn't like that thought.

Things were already too far out of my control.

The other night at dinner, it had taken *every single ounce* of my willpower not to crack John's head against a wall when I saw him dragging his eyes over Eliza's body. When she had laughed at his jokes, I'd wanted to stab him in the throat—that was my laugh, the laugh that had brought me the first taste of joy in decades. I felt possessive and primal over her and her beautiful laugh, and I wasn't going to let him take it away from me.

Anyone could tell within the first five minutes of meeting her that she was different, special. It was obvious there were demons in her past—demons that wouldn't set her free. Eliza was innocent and naive but also strong and determined, all in a way that told me she'd been through some really difficult things. It was probably why I felt so comfortable with her. Our traumas had broken us so deeply that we were able to see each other through our cracks.

She was so sheltered; she had never had salmon or wine before. What else hadn't she done? What other food or drinks had she not been allowed to try and wanted to? I liked the idea that I could be the one who let her out of her cage, helped her experience life. I never shied away from a fight in my life; I thought it'd be nice to fight demons other than my own for once.

The deal with JV Plastics falling through had cost Blackwood Industries about four million dollars. I'd have done it all over again just to keep her from laughing with him anymore. Except, if I had to do it all over again after seeing him touching her in the conservatory, I thought I would have done something much worse with the shotgun than just destroy the contract, which I never actually got to do, since we stopped shooting at that point.

My head sat uncomfortably heavy in my hands. I was so tired. I hadn't had a decent night's sleep since Eliza had arrived at the manor. The nightmares had returned, the ones where I saw my mother. I only had them when I stayed at the manor—another reason why I hated it. I wasn't sure why I kept it. I didn't want to, but for whatever reason, I couldn't seem to let it go. It was like there was some outside force keeping me here, something that tied me to the old wood floors that creaked in the night, the maze of familiar hallways and rooms that reminded me of a time before there were so many issues and when everything was okay—when I was okay. It was like a pathetic part of my soul was forever chained to the manor, secretly hoping my parents would finally come back and get me.

There was a knock on the office's heavy wood door. It was Sowerby; I could tell by the double knock. I was relieved to get a few minutes away from my warring thoughts.

"Come forth, Evil Alfred."

The well-dressed man stepped into my office, his brown button-up sweater with leather patches and plaid newsboy hat matching perfectly with the scowl on his antiquated face.

"If you don't stop calling me that, I'm going to start calling you 'Robin.'" He sat down in the chair across from me. His gaze caught on the unusual arrangement of chairs in my office, with the odd guest chair from the opposite side of my desk still placed next to mine, from Eliza sitting there the day before. I had pushed it off to the side yesterday so I could work, but I hadn't returned it to the other side yet. She had been such a comforting presence when I'd opened up to her. I hadn't felt judged or as guilt-stricken as I'd anticipated. What shocked me more than anything was how comfortable it had felt to talk to her. I had been so confused when she moved closer to me and placed her small hand on my thigh. I had expected her to pepper me with questions and accusations, but instead, she had just sat and listened. It was such a foreign experience to feel any amount of support with anything to do with the subject of my parents that I found myself thinking of the soft comforting words and touches every time I looked at the empty chair. I hadn't been ready to move it back and forget about it all quite yet.

"There's a card for you and Katya in the kitchen; we left it for you yesterday." I cleared my throat. "Eliza and I made it." I threw the words out and watched his eyes. They widened and he froze for half a second before relaxing, realizing his secret was out. "Why didn't you tell me?" I asked. God, I sounded so whiny and childish.

A long sigh came from so deep in his chest cavity that he must have been holding it in for years. He met my eyes with a concerned, paternal look.

"Because it just sort of happened that one day we realized we were in love. I didn't change, she didn't change, and neither of us wanted anything else to change. We didn't want you to feel any type of discomfort when you were here. I hope you know that I wasn't concealing it to be secretive. I just know how little you enjoy change…or feelings of any sort." His mouth thinned in a mischievous line. "And you know Katya. She didn't want to make a fuss of it." He gave a low snort. "She would do anything for you, and that likely includes giving me up if you were uncomfortable with it all, so I do hope that you keep a level head about this. I'd hate to have to tell her how rich I really am just to keep her with me." His eyes were full of amusement.

I leaned back in my chair and stretched, swiveling it from side to side restlessly. "I wouldn't have cared, you know."

"Yes, of course, Jasper. You've always been quite forgiving and level-headed with people. By the way, that ball sack with JV Plastics that you pulled a shotgun on went to the media and stirred things up. The news has been starved of entertainment, and this was, as always, exactly what the piranhas wanted. They have photos of you with the shotgun, even got some of Eliza and the conservatory."

My temples throbbed painfully. Why did they always have to do this? My stomach turned. I was used to this game, but sweet, innocent, naive Eliza was not. I should've shot him when I had the chance. I hated that he'd involved her in this. For the rest of her life, she would never be able to get away from the Blackwood name now that they knew she was staying here. "I'll get Gabriel to send out a legal warning to the stations that are including Eliza in their statements."

"All right. Sorry, did you say *you* and Eliza made a card?" His bushy gray brows rose as if he'd just heard what I had told him earlier.

I glanced at the empty chair next to me. "Yes. I fucked around with a pen, but she drew something really thoughtful and she's good…"

"That's very kind of her," he said stiffly. "You've surprised me with Eliza immensely. You enjoy her company."

I opened my mouth to protest. I don't know why; I did enjoy her company. My silent objection fell to the wayside as Sowerby continued.

"I'm pleased as can be that you *finally* agreed to restore the conservatory to your mother's standards. Had I known that all it took was a headstrong young lady to do so, I would have adjusted my plan of action many years ago."

"Yeah, I'm glad you're happy about the conservatory," I said absently. I was thinking about how quickly Eliza had leaped to my side when I was upset. "There's something different about her," I admitted as I turned my eyes to his, searching for the sage advice he always doled out to me, and I usually ignored.

"Yeah..." he said, looking suddenly unsettled by my admission.

"I like being around her. I enjoy her company. But what if—"

"You have to get a different crew in the conservatory," he said, standing quickly.

His sudden change in demeanor caught me off guard. Did he know something about her that I didn't?

"How long have I been telling you to get people in to tend to that garden? Since we fucking moved into the main house and could afford it, haven't I? Oh, for fuck's sake. The one time you agree to it, it's the nicest, sweetest girl, whom you like." He continued to grumble under his breath, but I couldn't understand anything else. He was normally crotchety and grumpy but not like this. This was something different. He was no doubt trying to protect me. But something felt off.

"What's the big deal? I can help her. I know you said you didn't want to be in there anymore; it's fine. I already told you that you don't have to be in the conservatory if it makes you so uncomfortable. I know you were in there when it was new, in its prime. I'll do it. I want to spend some more time with her, get to know her better," I said, standing up, hoping to calm him down and figure out what the fuck he was so riled up about.

"No. The deal was for her to do it alone. You can't help her!" he shouted suddenly. His forehead had become damp with exertion, and his arms had developed a slight tremor.

For a second, my mouth clamped shut in surprise.

Sowerby hadn't shouted at me since I was a kid, and just like back then, when I was a defiant teenager, I felt my irritation bubble up to the surface. He was being ridiculous. I had just told him that I liked her. Now he was trying to keep me away from her?

"Is this because you think she's going to hurt me? Or that I'm going to hurt her?" I questioned, letting my annoyance with him ooze into my words. I knew she had grown to be quite well-liked by all of the staff, and it had dawned on me that maybe he wasn't being protective of me but of her. Of all people, Sowerby knew the destruction I was capable of.

He made a face and rolled his eyes. "Jasper, listen to me. If you like the girl, she shouldn't be employed by you. It's not right to hold that power dynamic over her head; that's all. Stop her work on the conservatory, and we'll bring in—"

"No, you listen," I started but calmed my shout immediately. I wouldn't raise my voice to Sowerby. "All I said was that I like her. If you had let me finish, I would have told you that nothing is going to happen between us. As you *well know*, I'm far too selfish to bother with anything serious and—" My voice faltered.

"And what?" Sowerby nudged, now growing calm. His gray eyes assessed me.

"And I don't think she's a girl I could have anything unserious with. She's special and understanding. She's intelligent and funny and—"

"Jasper—" he began again.

"I know, okay. I know." I cut him off sharply. "I'm going to stay away from her for the next couple of months until she leaves. As of now, there is nothing between us, okay?" I hated the feelings that hit me when I thought of her leaving. They had no right to be as uncomfortable as they were, but it made my following decision feel that much more important.

"You're misunderstanding me, son; it's obvious to everyone who sees the two of you that there's a connection," he said, looking forlorn and frazzled as he tried to recover the conversation.

I walked past him and slapped him on the shoulder, forcing my face and demeanor into something that might convince the man that I was already over the situation. "You and Katya take the rest of the weekend off. I'm flying into New York tonight."

"Tonight? I thought you weren't traveling until after the holidays?" Sowerby said as he followed me into the hallway.

"I need some distance, and no one's been out to check on the vineyard in a while," I mumbled, heading down the hall.

"Jasper," he called out.

"I'll bring Katya back a case of merlot." My jaw steeled, and I continued walking.

"Jasper, distance isn't going to change what you're feeling," he said gently from behind me. I let the words bounce off my back.

Irritated and dejected, I took the long way to my room so as to avoid any chance of running into Eliza in the conservatory or the kitchen. I didn't want to have to deal with her. Me spending a few weeks at the vineyard would be best. Because of that dickhead leaking her photo, she was already tangled up with the Blackwood name more than was good for her, the best thing I could do was to leave for a while, get some space, get things back to normal.

Not wanting to waste any time, I packed a quick bag and headed out immediately. The sooner I got out of here, the better.

My hand stalled on the doorknob to the garage while I debated if I should say goodbye to her or not. It'd be the last time I ever saw her. I wouldn't come back until she was gone and away from the manor. She'd be upset when she found out I'd up and left, especially after our last conversation. It didn't matter; it still had to happen.

"You're taking off?" Her voice pressed through my ear and into my head like a silk bullet.

Shit.

I turned around, our eyes locked for a second, and I knew my stupid face betrayed me, telling her everything I couldn't.

"Some business came up that I need to take care of at our vineyard in New York," I said in a flat voice.

I watched her pretty eyes when it clicked. She knew exactly what I was doing, running away from her.

"Oh." The well-practiced mask on her face remained polite. She pulled the inside of her cheek into her teeth. "That's a shame; I was just getting ready to plant some of the beds this weekend. It's going to look so much better; I'm finally making some real progress. I think we'll—I'll still make the timeline for the blooming of the corpse flower. Leah is sending out invites for the party. It will be in six weeks."

Her eyes held questions I silently begged her not to speak. It was hard to be distant with her when all I wanted to do was explore.

"How long will you be gone for?" Her mask flickered only for a few seconds, but she recovered it gracefully.

I still held on to the doorknob. A rush of somber feelings settled inside of me as I looked at it and not her. "For a while. Sowerby will give you my number if you need me for anything business related." Why did I say it like that? I really was a prick.

"Ah," she said, pulling back into herself.

Good. It was easier if there was less of her to hurt. I opened the door to leave, telling myself to run to the car before she said another word.

"Will you be coming back for the party? Everyone at the botanical gardens would love to meet you." Her voice held a high note filled with hope that may as well have been an arrow lodging into my ribs. Yeah, she had gotten too close already.

Say something mean and insensitive. Cut her so deep she'll be glad you're leaving.

I couldn't think of anything mean to say to her, mostly because I didn't want to be mean to her; I wanted to be really, really nice to her—an odd thing for me.

"No. I don't like parties." I couldn't look at her. Unfortunately, unlike her, my mask didn't hold up around her very well.

She broke first. "Jasper, you don't have to go. I pushed you too far. I'm sorry, I'll back off; if you want me to stop work and leave, I will. I didn't mean to cause any problems."

Fuck.

My hand dropped from the door, and I spun to face her, glad when a flicker of fear pulsed across her face at my pissed-off expression. "You see, Eliza, I don't want you to go, and that's the problem. I want you to stay so I can do horrible, depraved things to you." I pulled myself together before I said too much. "Text me a photo of you standing next to the corpse flower when it blooms; I'm interested in seeing what it looks like." Lies. I was interested in seeing the beaming, proud smile on her face when she completed the project. My head dropped heavily. "I've given Sowerby the go-ahead to let our gardeners into the conservatory. I realize you've put all the work in so far and only have a few more weeks before the corpse flower blooms, so I'll leave it up to you if you'd like to accept their help at this point or finish it strong on your own. I understand either way. My lawyer is working with the media to keep your name out of further press, but it's hard to say if that will work or only incite them further. Goodbye, Eliza."

I slipped out the door and closed it behind me before she had a chance to say anything. I paused a beat. I felt more in control already. I got in my car, left the manor, and refused to look back. It wasn't until I landed in Rochester that I allowed myself to wonder about what could have happened if I hadn't left. I told myself I was paranoid and stupid and that nothing would have happened between us had I stayed. I was in full command of myself. It's not like I even knew her that well.

I shook my head before putting up the partition between the driver and myself. I didn't want to look at another person. I'd made the right decision to leave.

I kept busy at the vineyard. It had been in need of attention from me for a while, mostly minor things I'd let stack up, but I found that even in a completely different state, Eliza still took up most of my thoughts. I caught myself wanting to pull and save various wines for her to try, fighting a grin like a fucking dope when I recalled her scrunched-up face after she had tasted the wine at the business dinner that night. When I was supposed to be speaking to local vendors at a game bar, I thought about how fun it would have been to challenge her to a game of, well…anything. I could only imagine how much fun it would be to push her competitively. I wondered if Sowerby had shown her the game room or if she even enjoyed things like that. She hadn't seemed like she played many games. I should have shown her more of the house. She was as easy as a book to read—I doubted she'd wait a day before she snooped around now that I wasn't there to catch her. I didn't blame her. I'd have wandered the house the first night after someone told me not to. I didn't hate the idea of her looking through my stuff as much as I thought I would. I would have liked to catch her, though. She looked particularly beautiful when she was afraid of me.

Over the next few days, I began to forget *entirely* why it was better that I stay away from Eliza. I didn't like being told no, even when I was doing it to myself. I wanted her, and I was far too accustomed to getting every single thing I wanted. The house I kept while at the winery was average sized. I didn't need much, especially since I kept no staff at any of my other houses. The only people I even remotely trusted were at Blackwood Manor, always waiting for me when I returned. This time, being at the vineyard was different. It was lonely in a way I'd never noticed before. With the bulk of my work completed by evening, I had nothing else to do but sit alone in the quiet house and listen to myself breathe.

The management at the vineyard was a well-oiled machine, and in truth, I was only getting in their way being here after doing the small handful of things required of me. As the owner, it was good to pop in every now and again to maintain order, but this vineyard had been thriving long before I had taken over. They needed my say on a few small changes and additions, but that was easily done. Typically, in truth, I spent most of my time away from Blackwood Manor. It was easy to leave the discomfort behind. But not now. Now I found I wanted to go home—and play.

Still, it was better this way.

If I'd stayed near her any longer, I'd have ruined her. Even if I pursued Eliza for my own selfish reasons, I would be a possessive, controlling monster, and I liked her too much to subject her to that. Besides, it sounded like she'd already had too much of that in her life.

I needed to call Sowerby and check on things at the manor, make sure everything was all right. I picked up my phone from the kitchen island and saw I had missed a text from a number that I didn't recognize.

I realized the chaotic brown and green photo was of a freshly emptied flower bed with Eliza bending over it accompanied by three bug emoji. Then, *First bed to be planted!* Adrenaline surged in my veins. It was from Eliza. I could feel her enthusiasm through the phone. I typed a response, then deleted it. The whole reason I was in New York right now was to put distance between the two of us. To keep away from her.

Three little dots appeared on the screen from her end, and I felt another jolt of adrenaline.

I waited for her words to come through, my chest tight from holding my breath. The dots disappeared. Nothing.

She was waiting for my response.

Nope.

No.

I threw the phone on the couch across from where I sat with more force than I had intended.

No.

No. Do not.

But she put in so much work.

No!

Had she sent me a photo without a bra on purpose?

I jogged across and grabbed the phone to examine her exquisitely perky tits. It was just talking about the garden; it's not like we were sexting or anything stupid. She was doing a job for me, and as a good business professional, I had a duty to speak to her about any concerns she may have about that job.

My heart raced as if I were a teenager texting a girl I had a crush on. I smiled to myself and tried to think of the right thing to say.

Respectfully, you may want to look into painting; it looks empty.

Sent. Fuck. Did that sound mean or funny? I panicked, added a smiley emoji, and then swore.

I held my forehead and strung a line of expletives together. The phone pinged immediately with a picture of her standing in the bed with dirt smeared across the ridge of her pretty nose and a cultivator in one hand. And most definitely no bra on.

I haven't planted the flowers yet! I just finished breaking up the soil, lol. How is your trip going? Katya said it's beautiful there.

She used an emoji after every sentence—classic people-pleaser. I hesitated a minute before walking to the large window spanning nearly the entire side of the second story and taking a photo of the rolling vineyard and sending it to her.

It's been productive, I typed.

Wow, that's beautiful. Sorry, you're probably headed out to dinner. Or not? What DOES Jasper Blackwood do when he's not being reclusive at Blackwood Manor? she asked, adding a thinking emoji.

I began to unfasten the top few buttons of my dress shirt, planning on jumping in the shower after I typed out my last response to her.

I'm not going out tonight; I only go out when I have to. And I'm not reclusive, I'm just an asshole that hates everything and everyone, I answered back. The words stung with truth.

I don't think you hate everyone, and I don't think you're an asshole…at least not all the time.

The three dots appeared again; she was typing more. They disappeared, and I found myself unable to set the phone down and go to the shower.

Do you know my favorite things about the plants I work with? she asked.

That they smell nice…? I guessed. How could she think I wasn't an asshole after how I'd left? Come to think of it, I hadn't sensed a drop of anger from her. Was she that used to being walked all over by assholes that my behavior hadn't registered? I hated that thought.

No, but speaking of smells, remind me to ask you about Chanel No. 5. Hold on, I can't text and dig at the same time, she said.

What was she doing?

A second later, the video call came through. Immediately, Eliza's face popped up on the screen as she set the phone on something, giving me the POV of a plant looking out of the bed at her while she dug and grated through the soil.

She looked really fucking good in those overalls. My mind immediately wondered what she'd looked like in them without the shirt she was wearing. What shade of pink her nipples were. What they'd taste like when I bit them. If she'd scream.

"Hi." She smiled.

I cleared my throat. "You have something to ask me about Chanel No. 5?" I asked, sitting down on the couch and stretching out while I watched her.

"Yeah, but first, I want to tell you, I've been thinking about it, and you're a plant," she said decidedly, adjusting her purple gardening gloves.

I quirked my brow. It was impossible not to be intrigued by this creature. "I'm a plant?"

"Yes. Would you like to know why?" She lifted up a pale green leaf with a blue metallic sheen to it. "Sometimes, because of how they look, you think they're dead and ugly and—"

"You think I look dead and ugly?" I cut her off, not hiding the amusement in my voice.

She grinned from ear to ear. "And what if I say yes?" She lifted her brow in a challenge.

"Then I suppose I'd be able to come back for your corpse flower party," I replied.

"Well, then, you're hideous, inside and out," she teased. A bright, rosy blush pinked her cheeks, either from her laboring or the conversation.

"You're a horrible liar. Never enter politics," I stated, feeling the corners of my eyes wrinkle.

"Stop interrupting me," she demanded. She was playful but still serious.

Something about the confident command in her voice made me sit up slightly. I liked her feeling like she could boss me around. It stirred something in me that wanted more.

She cleared her throat. "You're a plant because all the time, people neglect them and throw them away thinking they are ugly and dead, but it's only what you see on the outside. Underneath the soil, the roots grow stronger, and eventually the foliage returns, and the plant grows back stronger and more beautiful than ever." She stopped what she was doing to look at the camera with a heavy look. "You're a plant."

Something in my chest ached. My mouth opened slightly as I was hit by the sentiment. I stared into the phone, unable to form a cohesive sentence to deliver back. Her words had glided over my skin and curled up in my bones, where I knew they would stay. It was one of the most poetically thoughtful things I'd ever heard. I wasn't used to being treated like this, and I wasn't quick enough to have a response ready.

It was quiet for a few moments while I watched her work before I found words I felt confident speaking.

"Then you're a painting, confined to a frame. With dutiful brushstrokes that conceal your true colors. You are a beautiful masterpiece aching to break free. A work of art, created and kept as a captive to agony." I didn't say it to flatter her. It was an honest observation.

Eliza sat back, putting her hands in her lap at the edge of the flower bed. We both simply marinated in the other's poetic sentiments for a moment.

"Jasper?" Her soft voice curled in my ear with the comforting lilt of a lullaby as she grabbed the phone.

"What?"

"Are you sure—" She stopped herself and then started again. "I'm terrified of heights, mostly of falling to my death, but sometimes I feel like I'm missing out on seeing the view… you know?" she said. "I always wish I could face my fear for a few minutes. I think the sight I'm afraid of would be so beautiful and impactful that it might be worth it even if I fell. But I'll never know because I'm too terrified to look. I wish I could look." Her eyes melted into mine as she kept her expression slightly guarded.

"Well, you're missing out. Your balcony has the best view of the entire manor," I answered, knowing what she spoke about had little to do with the view. The conversation was getting a bit too poetic for my taste. If she wanted someone to talk with her about feelings, I was not going to be it.

The corner of her mouth lifted. "Says you."

"Are you asking for a different room, Eliza?" I asked sarcastically. "Sowerby said the addition's finished, and the men won't start modernizing the inside of the original manor until after your party, so there's plenty of rooms to choose from now."

Her smile brightened, and mischief glittered in her blue eyes. She seemed more comfortable than I'd seen her before. Huh. Maybe she was less afraid of me than I had originally thought. "You look like you're about to cosplay *Miami Vice* with your shirt unbuttoned like that."

I held back a snort of laughter and schooled my features. "If you mean to insult me by comparing me to eighties Don Johnson, you've failed." She laughed, and the sound left the speaker and poured into my body like hot honey. A notification from Blackwood Manor's security system pinged in a gray box over her face. Someone was at the gate.

A rush of irrational anger and protectiveness jolted through me. I only got notifications from security if someone wouldn't take no for an answer and they wanted to double-check with me. I was sure it was nothing. With the latest leak in the news, it was inevitable the media would be back outside, pounding on the gates for a comment, but this time, it felt different. Eliza was involved, and I had left her there alone. I hated that.

"Eliza, someone's giving security issues. Stay where you are, okay? As you're aware, John from JV Plastics leaked photos of you in the conservatory, and it's all over the news. Hang on a second," I said before opening the live footage as fast as my fingers could.

"What a snake. I'm sure it'll blow over. No one cares about me."

Poor naive girl. The media would have a field day with her. She was easy to push around and get the responses you wanted.

The feed opened to show a woman who looked to be in her mid-sixties trying to physically pry the iron gate open while news crews snapped photos of three of my guards blocking her attempts. I sent a quick text to the head of my security team and swiped back to Eliza.

"Your mother is outside, quite literally trying to gnaw through the bars of my enclosure to get to you," I said in disbelief.

I watched as the liveliness left her eyes, and they grew round with surprise and panic. She looked off into the distance, then completely deadpan, said, "She knows I drank wine and ate fish."

I burst out laughing, unable to control myself even though I couldn't tell if she was joking or not. "If you want to see her, I'll get someone to bring her in, but don't go out there; it's not safe with the media waiting. Ask her to stay for dinner; I'll text Katya and she'll serve salmon."

"You would let my mom come in? To the manor?" she asked, sounding surprised.

I shrugged, setting the phone on the kitchen counter to grab an apple from the basket. "Sure, why not? I'm sure she'd love to see all of your work in the conservatory. That is, if you want to see her. If you don't, she will be kept out."

She rubbed her temples. "It sounds crazy, especially with all the stuff that happens here at night and all the exhausting work I'm doing, but this place has been the first place I've ever felt like I could breathe without her trying to move my lungs for me." She looked off into the distance, deep in thought.

Stuff that happens there at night? What was she getting into at night?

I itched to tell her mother to fuck off, but I would keep that to myself. I didn't care for mothers very much, obviously.

"The choice is entirely yours, but I should text Victor so that he knows what to do before she gets too out of hand," I said.

"I feel like such a coward if I say no and such a pushover if I say yes," she said as she nibbled the inside of her lower lip like a little blue-eyed chipmunk.

I poured a glass of water. "If it's helpful, I could draft a ransom note and have it sent out to her."

Eliza smiled. "And what would the ransom be for? You're already a millionaire."

"For you, of course." I had a drink.

The light had come back into her sky-colored eyes. "She already thinks we're fucking, so that might have legs."

I sprayed my mouthful of water across the counter. Hearing Eliza say the words "we're fucking" made my mind go crazy. "Now why would she think that?" I grinned wickedly. Had innocent little Eliza told her mother we were sleeping together?

"Because, silly man, that's the only reason a single millionaire would hire me and force me to move into his mansion, duh," she said, her voice dripping with sarcasm. "Honestly, though, that's the least crazy thought she's had. I kind of get that one."

"Damn. It's a good thing I left when I did, what with you wanting to fuck me so badly," I said with a wink. "That definitely would have gotten messy."

She scrunched her face and forced a laugh. "I do not want you; you're the one who ran to another state the second you let me in," she challenged.

"No? You don't want me?" I lowered my voice. "'Cause it sounds like you might want to fuck me a little bit. I'm not sure you could handle what I like, Eliza." I'm not sure *I* could handle what I liked with Eliza.

She rolled her eyes, ignoring my words even though her pink cheeks brightened a shade. "Tell Victor to keep her out, please. I'm not sure I can mentally handle her right now. It's no wonder why you hide out here and no one sees you. Gates are pretty amazing; I get it now."

I moved the phone to the bathroom counter and propped it up against the mirror and began to unbutton my dress shirt the rest of the way.

"Okay, I'll let him know to keep her out. I'm going to

jump in the shower. Your nipples have antagonized me enough for one phone call," I said as I continued to remove my shirt.

"Oh my god," she said, moving her arm up to cover her perky, hard nipples. I watched her eyes hover over my chest. She didn't hang up.

"Now," I added, stepping back, half naked, to flick on the shower.

She nodded but still didn't hang up. Her eyes trailed down my body like fingernails. My cock pulsed.

"Eliza," I rasped, picking up the phone.

"Yeah?" she said, her own voice a little lower and breathier than normal.

"Quit looking at me like that if you still want us to be friends," I stated.

She feigned shock. "I'm not looking at you any type of way, and I think we are friends, whether you try and fight it or not."

I rolled my eyes and undid my belt buckle. She really had no idea the fucking fire she was playing with. "Go on and say it, Eliza. Say you want me. Or I swear I'll keep teasing you till you're soaking through those pretty little panties. Or are you not wearing those either?"

Her mouth fell open. "Bye, *friend*. Oh, I have to send you a picture of the naked man orchid I found in one of the beds. It's hilarious, and yes, that's its actual name. Okay, geez, bye." She hung up, flustered.

The next morning, I awoke to an obscene flower photo that Eliza had sent at three thirty that morning.

Why were you in the conservatory at three in the morning? Is everything okay? I texted.

Hey, friend. Yeah...my balcony door kept blowing open.

I thought you had a couch in front of it? Don't call me friend, it's weird, I replied before immediately shooting a text to Sowerby to check the latches on her door.

I did, but the...couch keeps moving, she said before adding, *best friend*.

I sent her a very annoyed-looking selfie, hoping my frustrated face would make her stop with the stupid names. I couldn't hide my concern about what was happening in her room. I had a lot of enemies. *Do you sleepwalk?*

She responded a minute later. *No, at least not that I know of? I would call and ask my mom, but she texted me this morning saying that she is so stressed out over not being able to get to me that she wished she'd never had me and that if I don't meet her at my apartment today, she is going to bag up and donate everything I own.*

Jesus.

Do you need someone to drive you back into town? I know you said you hated the drive because of the whole ledges and heights thing. Victor is going with you. She was lucky I wasn't in town, or I would have made certain her mother quit causing problems.

I'm not going. I don't have time before the corpse flower blooms, she answered. *Everything I have is stuff she made me get anyway. After I get these corpse flower corms to the botanical gardens and get a big, fat raise, I'm going to buy some stuff I like for once...extra nylon and polyester clothes.*

You're a wild woman.

By the middle of the week, we were talking for hours a day; I don't even know what we talked about—everything, nothing. It just came naturally and easily. Stupidly, it still seemed like a safer idea that I stayed away; at least that had been the plan until the following week. Before I'd left the manor, I was a little interested in Eliza and really wanted to fuck her—now I was really interested in Eliza and absolutely feral to be inside of her.

My phone had been going crazy, vibrating in my pocket while I finished a meeting with my employees. By the time I checked, I had a swarm of missed calls from Sowerby, Katya, Eliza, Leah, and Victor. Pure panic set in. Something awful had happened. I got the familiar feeling of barbed wire in my gut.

Just as I was about to check the thirty-some texts, Sowerby called. I snatched the phone to my ear. "Sowerby, what the fuck is going on? Are you all right?" My heart raced. I felt doom sinking into my chest as I waited to find out what had happened.

"Jasper, you have to come home this minute—immediately. Get to the airport now." His voice was rattled with fury and panic.

"Is she okay? Is Eliza okay?" My chest tightened. I should never have left. Was it her mother? Had she hurt her? I would destroy them.

"Your father's here, Jasper. He's here, and he's trying to take back the estate."

CHAPTER 16

JASPER

THE SOUND OF DRIED, DEAD LEAVES CRUNCHED BENEATH MY tires, a harsh symphony that accompanied my reluctant approach to Blackwood Manor. The slightly brighter stone edge of the new addition stuck out a little to the left, hidden behind other parts of the main house. The space was for a vault of prototypes, a heavily fortified wing filled with failed, banned, and illegal weapons—things too dangerous or unethical to sell, but there are buyers and collectors for everything. I was one of them.

The few weeks I'd been in New York dissolved away into the dark, misty evening, replaced by the oppressive silhouette of my home. The skeletal trees that lined the driveway had since shed the remainder of their leaves. They reached out like spectral fingers, casting long shadows across the gravel path.

I gripped tightly to the strap of my leather messenger bag, a talisman of the professional world I'd just come from, but more than anything, I needed something in my hands to stop them from constantly curling into fists. Up to this point, I'd been living purely in an existence of anger and numbness, mostly out of spite for my parents. It's no wonder the feelings Eliza brought out in me felt so uncomfortable—they had been a jolt to the system.

I let out a slow breath and got out of the car. With every step, memories flooded back: whispers of my childhood summers, my mother's laughter echoing across the house, the painful silence of my parents' absence. The realization that all the safe moments had been nothing but lies when they chose work and plants over me. Years of wondering what I'd done to have forced them to give up on me and leave.

The door from the garage to the house loomed before me. It seemed to watch my approach with challenge. I knew every inch of this place, yet it felt like a stranger's house I was entering now.

As I reached for the door, the wood groaned under my touch as I opened it; the quiet of the manor was a tangible weight against my chest. I entered the main living room. Even though no one made a sound, the heavy panic in the air led me right to where they were: the two people who had discarded me. What would my mother think of me now? Was she proud? Did they regret having left? Or would they regret returning? Why now?

Sowerby stood by the fireplace, his weathered hands clasped nervously. Beside him, Eliza watched me with eyes that held both curiosity and caution as they found mine. She took a step toward me but stopped herself, instead giving me a slow, apprehensive nod. I wished I could send her away, keep her out of this, but no matter how much I tried, she kept getting tangled in my life. She had been right: I was a plant—a briar bush full of stabbing, painful thorns that dug in and made it hurt to leave…and hurt to stay.

Then, like a wisp of smoke emerging from the shadows, my father came into view.

Darius Blackwood stood by the window, silhouetted against the failing light of the autumn sky. Years of a life I didn't know about had etched into his features—lines of guilt? Regret? Unspoken apologies? Our eyes met, and decades of unresolved tension crackled between us as my eyes took him in.

I glanced around for my mom but didn't find her in the room.

My dad looked so worn and old, nothing like the image I'd held in my head for years now. Even the little crackle of familiarity in his eyes looked different and off. I didn't know this man—I barely knew him when he was here.

"Jasper." Sowerby's voice broke the silence, laden with a mixture of welcome and warning. "Your father... He has apparently come to take back ownership of his estate."

"My estate," I corrected.

Eliza took a subtle step back, her body language speaking volumes—professional yet uncomfortable, caught in the crossfire of a family drama she didn't fully understand. Her botany had brought her here, and her friendship—or whatever it was with me—kept her from leaving, but now she seemed desperate to fade away into the background.

My father took a hesitant step toward me. "I saw the papers with you threatening a business colleague. Your mother saw the state of the conservatory, the addition," he said, his voice rough with emotion. "Are you just going to ignore the legacy of what we built because you're bitter? We'll be damned if we let you ruin what we built because you can't handle it. Has it finally gotten to you? Is that what's happened? What's in the addition? It's illegal, isn't it?"

The legacy? The legacy that you poisoned when you took out half the fucking town? What the fuck was he talking about? A bitter laugh threatened to escape me. Legacy. What a cruel word, considering how easily they had turned away and abandoned it *and* me.

"What do you want?" The words left my mouth sharp-edged and cold, like the blades he used to make. I watched as they struck him. They seemed to slide into his features, carving lines of pain into his already-weathered face.

Sowerby shifted uncomfortably; his loyalty was once to the stranger in front of us. Sowerby had been more of a father to me than this man *ever* was.

Darius Blackwood remained still—watching, waiting, hope and fear dancing in his eyes. I wondered what his next move was going to be. I let him marinate in the discomfort, refusing to offer anything but hate.

Eliza's presence was both a comfort and a constraint. She was a buffer, preventing the full eruption of decades of my carefully suppressed anger. She watched our interaction, her curious mind likely analyzing the emotional landscape as meticulously as she did the beds of the gardens. She knew enough about family conflict, and I both hated and was grateful she was now in this with me.

The presence of the manor and the conservatory—my mother's beloved glass sanctuary. I hadn't even wanted to touch it, but now its renovation wasn't just about restoring a physical space; it was about confronting the fractured pieces of our family's history, about moving on from being forgotten and left to die. Eliza was clearing the slate of desertion my mother had left behind. Of course they would come in and ruin something else.

My father took a step, his hand half extended—a gesture of reconciliation or a plea for understanding, I couldn't tell, and I most definitely didn't care. "Jasper, I—"

"Don't," I interrupted sharply, my voice slicing through the charged atmosphere. "Just...don't." After everything that had happened, he was lucky my hands weren't around his throat right now.

The manor seemed to hold its breath. Dust motes danced in the streams of failing light, witnesses to this fragile moment.

Outside, the weather took a turn, and the wind began to

scream against the windows. Blackwood Manor had always been more than just a house—it was a keeper of stories, of pain, of unresolved tales, and now the authors of the most horrifying ones had returned.

The silence hung thick. Each breath was laden with decades of pain. I watched my father, his frame seemingly diminished by the years, hovering near the window like a stray cat we had cornered. In another situation, I would have felt bad. But I didn't. I was furious.

"Where is she? Where is Mother?" The question escaped my lips before I could stop it. Her absence was as palpable as the tension that surrounded us.

"It's illegal weapons, isn't it? In that addition? I keep tabs on you. I know what you are about," he said with a haunted look.

"Where's Mom?" I repeated.

Darius's hands trembled slightly. "She couldn't come. Not yet." His voice cracked, revealing a vulnerability I wished he hadn't shown. The more I was in his presence, the more I noticed a difference in him—a fragility that suggested something more than just the weight of his past mistakes.

Eliza took a subtle step toward us. It was a welcome distraction. Our connection—electric and unresolved—hummed beneath the surface of family dramatics. I could feel her eyes studying me, watching how I'd navigate this. I wished I knew myself what I was going to do.

"Not yet?" I repeated, my voice dripping with skepticism. "I suppose she'll just send another tear-streaked letter that I won't respond to. Tell her to save her fucking tears and leave me alone."

"She—" my father started.

Sowerby, who had been quietly standing by, suddenly interjected. "Jasper, your father—"

But I cut him off with a sharp gesture. "No, I'd like to hear it from him." My gaze bore into Darius, challenging him.

Darius shifted uncomfortably, his eyes darting between me and the landscape outlined in the window. "The letters...they were attempts to explain. To reconnect."

I laughed, a harsh, mirthless sound. "Sending letters doesn't make up for disappearing when I was fifteen. You didn't even bother leaving me with someone. You just—you just left!" I shouted, having lost all ability to control my temper.

Eliza fidgeted in my peripheral vision. I knew my voice was powerful and intimidating. Her presence seemed to temper my rising anger. I didn't want to yell with her here. I didn't want her to see me lose control.

"I know we made mistakes," Darius said softly. "Unforgivable ones. But we—I couldn't stay. I couldn't." He rubbed his hand over his face and collected himself. "Now, I'm sorry to have to come back in this way, but the estate belongs to me. I don't want it to fall apart too. You must leave it alone. Blackwood Manor is rightfully mine, and I demand it back. I'd hoped to avoid coming back here, but if I am found out then I am found out—if it means Blackwood Manor remains as it should be. You can all leave peacefully, but the house is ours."

Something in his tone—a tremor of desperation, a hint of underlying panic—caught my attention. This wasn't an attempt at reconciliation. The fucker only came back to get the manor back. He came to take the only thing he'd left me with.

Sowerby moved closer to my father, his weathered hands clenched. "Darius," he warned, a protective edge to his voice.

"I mean it," Darius continued. "I've heard rumors—about the restorations and updates to modernize it. I won't stand for it." His eyes were wild, darting nervously around the room.

Eliza stepped forward. "What rumor is it that you've heard, sir? The restoration is proceeding exactly as planned with the highest amount of respect for your wife's plants. I have black roses going in tomorrow," she said with a watchful eye.

But Darius wasn't calming down. If anything, it only riled

him more. "That sounds lovely, but I'm quite certain she'd prefer to plant them herself, my dear." The rest of his words were jumbled and incoherent and his eyes danced about the ceiling. His mental state was becoming increasingly erratic. Dementia possibly?

I exchanged a concerned glance with Eliza. Whatever was happening, it was clear my father was not entirely stable. The man before me was a shadow of the authoritative figure from my childhood—fragmented and nearly broken. I couldn't help wondering if that was new or if it could possibly have had something to do with everything that happened after they left. Either way, I was pissed off.

"You shouldn't have come back. I'm not the helpless child you left behind. I will throw every ounce of my weight and power around, spend every penny I have, to ensure you don't get this place back, and not because I want it, simply for the fact that I know you want it and I want you to hurt. I want you to hurt, and if this is the only way to do it, then I'll be damned if I don't make it as painful as I fucking can."

But Darius had retreated into himself, mumbling about doctors and blood checks.

Sowerby moved closer to me, his voice a concerned low whisper. "Jasper, look at him. Your father…he's not okay. He's not right in the head. Just look at him."

I looked away, angry. He was right. It was easy to see he was unwell, and it took all of the satisfaction out of being mean.

"We aren't stopping the work, and the estate is in my name," I said, my voice low and controlled.

Darius stepped forward, his hands shaking slightly. "This manor was your mother's sanctuary. You don't understand what it means to her—you can't change it."

Sowerby erupted. "You blithering idiot, you abandoned this boy, Darius!" Sowerby's normally calm face contorted with decades of his own suppressed rage. "You have *no* right to dictate anything about this manor! For god's sake, let the boy heal. It's time everything was finally out!"

"No!" my father shouted as he gave a terrified look to Sowerby.

Before anyone could react, Sowerby lunged at Darius, landing a solid punch that sent my father stumbling backward into the wall. The old gardener's strength belied his age.

"Sowerby, stop!" Eliza intervened, positioning herself between the two men. Her hands pushed against Sowerby's chest, restraining him. The sweater vests had caused me to temporarily forget what a rough-around-the-edges hard-ass Sowerby was.

I stood frozen, watching the scene unfold. "What is it you two aren't telling me?" I demanded, looking directly at my father.

Eliza tried to mediate. "We should discuss this calmly. The restoration is nearly complete. Your mother's original design was quite remarkable." She turned to my father. "I think once you see it, you won't feel conflicted about it any longer. Perhaps she could come and give me her input as well." Her eyes searched his.

Darius seemed to deflate, the fight draining out of him. "No, I won't step foot in there without her," he muttered, more to himself than to us.

Sowerby scoffed. "You've made your bed, Darius. All of this was your doing."

The old man's words hung in the air, a sharp accusation that cut through the room's thick atmosphere. I could see the weight of guilt pressing down on my father, his shoulders hunched under an invisible burden.

"You shouldn't live here," he said, looking at me.

I stepped closer, my curiosity piqued. "Why come back now?"

But Darius said nothing more. Instead, he held a blank

stare, lost in some distant memory that seemed to both haunt and consume him.

"Mr. Blackwood," Eliza addressed my father formally. "Is there something specific at Blackwood Manor that concerns you?"

The silence that followed was deafening. It was like he wasn't there any longer.

Sowerby, still bristling from his confrontation, muttered, "Some secrets are better revealed than festering in darkness."

I couldn't have agreed more, but whatever secrets Darius Blackwood held, it seemed he wasn't here to share, just as he wasn't here to reconcile. I stood frozen, my gaze locked with my father's—a man who had been more of a ghost story than a parent.

He took a tentative step forward, his hands trembling slightly. "Jasper, I know you have every right to hate me, but your mother…" he began, his voice a ragged whisper.

"Hate is a strong word," I replied, my tone deliberately measured. "Indifference is perhaps more accurate." The words were a calculated strike, designed to wound precisely where it would hurt most. "You've been gone for so long, I don't care enough about you to hate you."

Sowerby cleared his throat. "This is a lot for one day. Darius, I think you need to go."

"This is my house, damn it! Mine!" he shouted back. "I was at the top when I lived here."

"Is that why you're here?" I challenged, taking a step closer to him. Even if he wasn't in his right mind, I wanted to hit him. Hard. "You need money? What do you want? It will be worth it to get rid of you."

Eliza took an involuntary step forward. "Jasper," she warned softly.

Darius's anger seemed to deflate, the fight draining out of him. "I don't want your money; I want you to leave this house.

Let the earth take it and every spirit that haunts me," he said, his voice breaking. "I'm here because…because I can't outrun her anymore. I'm tired of the distance. Tired of the guilt. This is where I belong, where Hester and I belong, where we were happy. *You* need to leave."

It felt like an errant rock had lodged itself in my throat.

"After the declaration of my death, they were supposed to dissolve the trust. But they never did. Someone kept paying the property taxes, maybe you?" He gave me a look. "Legally the house still belongs to the trust. And I created the trust. Once I reinstate myself, it's mine again."

For a moment, I saw only a broken man. The anger that fueled me for years suddenly felt hollow, replaced by a confusing mixture of pity, anger, and lingering hurt.

Sowerby moved closer, placing a supportive hand on my shoulder. "We will be expecting something from your lawyer," he murmured to my father. I could tell this was causing him a lot of anxiety as well.

"I want to understand," I said finally, the words surprising even myself. "I want to know why. Why—how could you leave me?"

The fire flickered in the fireplace, a silent witness to our confrontation.

He nodded, a single tear tracing a path down his tan cheek. "Because I had to," he whispered. "I had to. Leave before it's too late for you."

Frustrated, I shook my head. I had to turn away to collect myself. He couldn't even give me a real answer after all this time.

The silence that followed my father's hollow demand sat heavily in the air of the manor. His declarations seemed to shake the very foundation of the estate. I watched as Darius's figure grew smaller, his silhouette disappearing through the doorway, leaving behind a wake of unresolved tension and unanswered questions.

Eliza approached me cautiously. "Hey," she said softly, her hand tentatively reaching out to touch my arm. "Are you all right?"

I wasn't. The confrontation with my father had reopened wounds that had been scarred over. "I'm fine," I lied, my voice more brittle than I intended.

Sowerby, who had been quiet as he watched Darius leave, now stepped forward. His hand clapped my arm. "There's a lot more to this than meets the eye, Jasper," he said cryptically. "Are you all right? I'm going to go call the lawyers now."

I nodded and watched as he left.

A crimson shadow flickered at the edges of my vision, a brief, almost imperceptible movement that vanished as soon as I tried to focus on it. The scent of women's perfume permeated the air, the scent snagging on a hook in the recesses of my mind. It smelled like my mother. I jogged to the door to look out the window as the taillights of my father's car disappeared. I had thought seeing my father had hurt. But feeling my mother's presence was like being cut into without sedation. Had she been with him and just didn't want to see me? My teeth ground together until all the muscles in my face were tender and aching.

When Eliza looked at me with a question in her eyes, I just shook my head. "I smelled my mother." I let out a long sigh. "That didn't sound creepy." I winced. "She wore Chanel No. 5, and I just smelled her." Why did Chanel No. 5 feel so fresh in my mind? Had someone recently talked about it? Worn it? Why did this feel like a full-circle moment suddenly? Did one of the maids wear it?

"Trust me, it's not as creepy as you might think," she mumbled, letting out her own long breath. "Well, at least you're back."

Her smile felt like the only thing keeping me from losing my mind right then. I wanted to grab ahold of her and pull her into my arms, so there were no gaps between us, but I didn't. Even though we had somehow managed to get closer since I'd left, seeing her now was all the reminder I needed that I didn't want to ever cause her any more hurt, and I knew I couldn't do that while being with her.

"I'm going to go to bed. I'm exhausted. I can't imagine how you must feel," Eliza said.

"I'll walk with you." Things felt weird between us; it was easier when we knew we weren't within reach of one another.

Each step we took felt weighted, charged with an electricity that pulsed between us, only adding to my onslaught of emotional turmoil. The adrenaline from seeing my father still coursed through my veins, and I knew I'd either spend the rest of the night in the gym or at the shooting range at the back of the property. If I'd have been a little more of a monster and cared a little less about Eliza, I would have put my feral energy into fucking her into oblivion tonight. I knew she wanted it, but I doubted she could handle me on a normal day, so I knew she couldn't handle the way I would ruin her while I was angry. No. I wasn't going to touch Eliza Arnold tonight.

My head swam, replaying everything my father and I had said to one another over and over again.

"Thank you for walking me," Eliza whispered as we approached her room, her voice barely audible. Her hand brushed mine, sending a current of sensations through my body. I could see the stress still lingering in her eyes. Damn it, she needed to stop touching me before she unleashed the monster inside that would chew her up and spit her out. I wanted to kiss her. The desire burned within me, a raw, primal urge that didn't care how awkward things were right now. My history of emotional disconnection had always kept me somewhat distant, but something about Eliza broke through those carefully built walls and nuzzled against me. Her vulnerability, strength, and understanding were unlike anyone I'd ever known. I hadn't wanted to come back while she was still at the manor. I knew how hard it was to keep away from her—it was why I'd left. I felt like a pit bull on a chain trying to keep a barrier between us. I wasn't a good guy, and she was easy to manipulate.

I watched her closely. I knew everything to do and say to get everything I could want from Eliza if I chose to. I knew what she craved—what she wanted to hear. If I wanted to, I could have her ass up on the bed, milking my cock in the next six minutes.

But that wasn't what I wanted. I wanted to hurt someone. Badly.

"Good night," I said, my voice rough. I was acutely aware of how close we were standing and how easy it would be to close the distance between us. God, I wanted to. Not only because I'd been wondering how she would taste for the last few weeks, but because in my current state, I felt reckless. I knew sliding my tongue in her mouth would make me forget everything else in my head. I found myself leaning in.

Realizing what was happening, Eliza hesitated, her breath catching. For a moment, I thought she might say something, might bridge the gap herself as she had stretched up slightly. But then, as if thinking better of it, she stepped back and surprised me by giving me a merciless wink with her hand on the doorknob. "Good night, friend."

I let out a slow, uneven grin and watched her enter her room, forcing myself to turn away and not do something really, really stupid—like pushing her against the wall and wrapping her thighs around my head. The hallway stretched before me, the dark corridor lined with memories and secrets it seemed like I'd never fully know.

I was halfway to my own room when her blood-curdling scream shattered the heavy silence.

In an instant, I was running back, my heart thundering. I burst through her door, scanning the room for a threat. She had told me something was messing with her door and couch, and I had brushed it off. And security had been having issues with the cameras lately. It wouldn't be the first time paparazzi had broken in.

My chest spiked with a thrill. I'd let them get a few seconds' head start, so that I could maximize the chase. If they were smart, they'd throw themselves over the cliff before I got to them. I would hurt them a lot more than the fall if I caught them. As if I'd willed it into existence, a high-pitched tone sounded from my phone. Security.

Eliza was pressed against the wall, all color drained from her face, eyes wide with terror. A chair lay overturned several feet from where she stood as if thrown. "She—she— Something pushed me." She struggled to speak. "The chair—it just...it flew across the room."

The room was empty. I approached her carefully, my protectiveness overwhelming any skepticism. "Are you hurt?" My hands hovered near her, wanting to touch her but afraid of causing more distress.

She was trembling. "I don't understand. One moment, I was standing by the dresser, and then..." Her voice trailed off, eyes darting around the room before grabbing at the locket around her neck.

"You said she. Who's she? Katya? Leah?" I asked, ready to hurl someone off the balcony for scaring her. My staff knew better than to play games, but they were the only shes I could think of.

The room was freezing, electric. Something wasn't right, but I couldn't tell exactly what it was.

I couldn't look at her trembling for another second without trying to help. I pulled her close, feeling how rigid her body was before she slowly relaxed into my embrace. Her warmth, her scent—like soil and lavender, maybe pine, but all in a way that smelled like she'd just stepped in from a forest—her sudden proximity was intoxicating and dangerous, and even though I saw no threat in her room, I couldn't bring myself to step away from her. Feeling her press herself deeper into my chest felt like a key unlocking something inside of me. I had no room to think about not hurting her because I was filled with determination to keep her safe.

The feeling of something weird in the room lingered, making me uneasy. It was like a hundred sets of eyes were on me and on her, waiting…lurking. I ignored the creepy feeling, not wanting to frighten her any more than she already was.

"You're safe," I murmured into her hair, though I wasn't entirely convinced of that myself. Goose bumps lit up across the back of my neck. No matter what, I wouldn't let anything happen to her. I meant what I said: she was safe with me—if not from me.

Our eyes met, a tension between us coiling like a spring ready to be released. I could see every freckle on her face, an eyelash that bent the wrong way, the slight tremble of her swollen lower lip, the fear still lingering in her eyes, the way her breath caught when my thumb grazed her soft cheek. She looked up at me with so much emotion that it caused me to panic. What was I doing? She was leaving in a few weeks. She'd be leaving me, just like everyone left.

I pulled away.

"I can't do this," I muttered, more to myself than to her. The ghosts of my past—my abandoned childhood, my fractured relationships, my own emotional barriers—all stood between us like insurmountable walls, and no matter how much I wanted to, they were barriers I couldn't get over.

I couldn't do a fling with Eliza; I was already too attached. I wouldn't be okay with having her for another month just for her to leave me. Then what? The manor was a two-hour drive from civilization, and I didn't want to always stay here. What if I had stronger feelings than she did? If I sank my hooks into her,

I could never let her go. She'd know too much, be too branded into my flesh. What if I didn't want her anymore and this was just sexual? I shook my head, trying to quiet the thoughts. She was frightened, and all I could think about was trying to claim her. This was not the night to figure any of this out.

"Why don't you sleep in another room tonight? Would you feel better?" I asked her.

"No, I think this is okay," she said, looking a little embarrassed. "I think I let my, um, imagination get the best of me."

I walked through the room, checking the balcony and bathroom one last time before I left her standing there, confusion and hurt evident in her expression. I swear the manor sighed around me as I retreated into the hallway.

Outside her room, the hall felt alive with whispers. For a moment, I could have sworn I smelled Chanel No. 5 again. There was a flash of dark red, but when I turned, there was nothing. Just shadows and paintings.

CHAPTER 17
ELIZA

WITH JASPER'S FATHER RETURNING, EVERYTHING WAS IN chaos. Jasper insisted that I continue in the garden even though Darius had demanded that nothing else be touched. There was an uncomfortable eeriness to the conservatory now as the layers and the puzzle pieces continued to show but not click into place. The fact that Jasper's father had returned after all this time made me prickle with unease. The fact that he had not brought Hester with him obviously hadn't been a surprise to me, though it was obvious that Jasper had expected her to be standing next to his father when, in fact, she stood dead at the foot of my bed. And the more and more time I spent working in the conservatory getting to know the woman Hester had been, the more I knew how wrong this all was.

All of them—Jasper, Sowerby, and Darius—each continued to act as though Hester would walk through the door at any given moment. But I knew the truth.

And I believed at least one if not all of them did too.

Hester Blackwood was dead, and she was clearly not happy about it, not that I blamed her in the slightest.

Which raised the question: Which of them knew she was dead? Each of them continued to act weird in their own way, though Darius, I knew the least, and he seemed the most suspicious in how he talked about her. I had said I was putting roses in the garden, trying to pull more information from him, giving him ample opportunity to say how much she hated them. Knowing she hated roses from her journal but that they were used as a wax stamp on her letters was one of the only clues I had—even if I had no idea what it meant or how, if at all, that information could help.

Sowerby refused to speak ill of Hester if he spoke of her at all. I knew at one point he had been incredibly close to her, working side by side with her in the garden. Had there been something romantic with Hester and Sowerby? Could there have been a scuffle between Sowerby and Hester out near the cliff? Maybe she told him she couldn't see him anymore and he'd pushed her off the cliff. With a tall stone barrier to prevent a fall and the fact that she still haunted the manor, it was an obvious guess. Had both Darius and Hester left like Jasper believed, but something happened to Hester and that's why she chose to haunt the manor? For Jasper? As a sad and shattered mother hoping to right her wrongs? The hair on the back of my neck rose. Perhaps it was my own wild, all-encompassing fears of the cliff, but it seemed like that was the most explainable place that Hester's body would have gone, lost and never to be discovered.

That left another set of questions that I found myself pushing to the back of my head, not wanting to press into them any further.

The moment Darius had stepped foot in the manor, I expected the worry I had about Jasper killing her to dissolve. Right in front of my eyes was evidence that Jasper had not killed his parents, confirmation that he had been telling me the truth about everything. However, that feeling never left, and instead, more questions filled my mind. I *knew* that his mother was dead, so what had happened to her? If Darius had been playing dead this whole time, that also raised a lot of questions, though at the time he left, I suppose I understood why he would let the allegations against Jasper remain and pretend to be dead; everyone hated him. If Darius had murdered Hester, killed her the night that her and Jasper had fought, then why would he have bothered to leave Jasper? Why not take him? What had caused them to snap and suddenly become such horrible parents who left their son if they had, in fact, *both* left? And why hadn't they taken Jasper with them? The questions continued to come with no answers. I was failing her.

Did Hester remain haunting these halls with tears in her eyes and a hand about her throat because the rumors were true and Jasper had killed her? With every shred of my being, I wanted to think that Jasper didn't have the demeanor of a full-blown killer, and that there was no possible way that a fifteen-year-old version of him could have killed her, but unfortunately, I couldn't say that. There was always a mysterious hardness to Jasper that left me feeling a little unsettled. After I got to know him better, I'd just assumed it was how the scars inside him had formed after his trauma. Cold and distant, unable and unwilling to connect with others no matter how much we laughed and talked—there always seemed to be a part of him that remained hidden and secret. Sometimes, he could be the most charming man I'd ever talked to, if not a little filthy, but in others, he was frigid and terrifying, like when he'd surprised us with shotgun in hand. Shotgun or not, his smile seeped into my bones and made me want to smile; I couldn't help it. I found myself forming a connection with him instantly, sharing things about myself that I never shared with anyone.

Was the connection that we had real, or was he simply someone dangerous who was capable of manipulating me? I'd heard several serial killers described as being charming. I'd watched enough crime documentaries and listened to enough podcasts to know the really good killers pulled you into their sticky web, telling you it was a rope to save you, not to strangle you until it was too late.

I couldn't shake my intense feelings for Jasper, but I also couldn't rule out that there was a whole other side to him he didn't let me see, and I wondered if Hester had seen that side before she died.

When Jasper walked in yesterday, I'd wanted to comfort him. I was thrilled he had returned, but something else lingered. It had been so easy over the phone; the wild, crackling tension between us had been moved to the background since we weren't close. But as soon as he returned, so did the electricity and the danger.

Last night, when I entered my room, Hester had been in there. Every time she came to me, it grew more terrifying. It was a shock to see her, like we were in the presence of something we shouldn't be. This time, the normally sad Hester had been in a panic. Her grayish opaque mouth was open as she tried to scream, but no matter how much she tried, nothing would come out. She needed to tell me something urgently, and I had no doubt in my mind it had something to do with her husband, but whether it was anger or sadness, I couldn't tell. Only frustration floated from her, as she was incapable of communicating with me, the only one who could see her.

In a flurry of frustration, she had thrown the chair across the room. She'd gripped my shoulders painfully, desperately, with everything she had, trying to communicate with me when the energy within her body pushed out and slammed me against the wall. I'd never been so afraid in all my life. And then in ran Jasper.

At first, I'd worried that his presence would set her off more, but the scene that played out astonished me. As Jasper held and comforted me—or at least he'd tried—the ghost of his mother stood behind him, watching him before dropping to the floor in a sobbing pile of nearly invisible crimson and gray. It had been heartbreaking. Even though I had been terrified in that moment, it destroyed me to see her so dejected. A minute later, she began to fade, and her body disappeared completely.

The second Jasper left, I checked the locket.

It was completely empty. Nothing. Not even the velvet backing.

Not knowing exactly how the dynamic between Jasper and I would take shape over the next few days made me tense and uncomfortable. We had just gotten close, and now all I could think about was the very real chance that he had murdered his mother and that she was clearly trying to warn me.

It proved not to be such a factor, though, as Jasper and Sowerby spent the next several days mostly absent in an absolute flurry as they busied themselves with lawyers and the state attempting to stop Darius from taking back the manor.

Everything in the house felt tainted and uncomfortable. So much so that, had it not been for the very real prospect of me losing my job—and, of course, my desire to help Hester—I would have left. It didn't feel safe for me to be in the middle of it all anymore.

I kept busy in the conservatory, thankful for the distraction of being able to throw myself into my work. All in all, I had found close to eleven almost-extinct plants in the conservatory. All of them were thriving now with my help. I had been putting off taking cuttings and propagations from them until they had more growth, but with everything happening, I knew I needed to do it today. If there was a chance Darius got an order in place and I couldn't work in the conservatory anymore, I had to make sure I had these plants for Pinehurst. If that alone hadn't been enough, with the days quickly passing, I found myself facing the very real thought that I would be going home soon and would be forced to face everything I had been using Blackwood Manor to hide from.

Even though it was easy in the moment not to see my mother, I knew that behind the scenes, she was creating a war zone for me to return to. My problems were *far* from over. I'd only pushed them away momentarily.

The invitations for the garden party had been sent, and a buzz about the community had already been set in motion. All two hundred people had RSVPed that they would be coming to see the conservatory and all of the work I had done to restore it. Not one single invite had turned down the once-in-a-lifetime opportunity to see the infamous Blackwood Manor conservatory. So much was riding on my shoulders, and knowing the conservatory still wasn't planted weighed on me like cement blocks resting on my tired shoulders.

I had to put in extra time in the gardens now to be sure that it would be finished, but also in fear that Darius Blackwood might soon be halting my momentum.

As if the chaos surrounding Darius's return hadn't been enough, when I entered the garden this morning, the spadix—the tall, fleshy, phallic column in the center of the corpse flower—had lengthened and was now protruding out of the large cabbage-leaf-looking outer covering of the spathe.

The corpse flower was preparing to bloom faster than I had hoped, faster than even Lithgow had thought, and defensive panic set in. Immediately, I sent photos to Professor Lithgow to lean on his expertise. It was nearly impossible to nail down how much time we had before it bloomed, and once it bloomed, the spathe would only remain open for twenty-four to forty-eight hours. If my work in the conservatory was to be done to showcase it at the same time as the bloom, I had to work faster. Faster than I was capable of working.

Jasper had offered his gardeners, but as much as I needed the extra hands right now, it felt wrong to have someone else help me when I was *so* close to having the entire thing completed all by myself. It was stupid not to take the help, but I had already completed the majority of the hard labor I would have used the gardeners for as it was. It would most likely take me longer to explain what they needed to do and how carefully they had to do it.

I knew I could do it; I had to. But how was I going to do it and solve the murder of Hester Blackwood at the same time?

"Wow, I can't believe how different it looks in here," Jasper said.

I leaped out of my skin as I turned. He stood on the paver walkway near the house entrance, admiring the first section of the finished garden. Beautiful coleus bunched together in tufts of dark purple, with green ruffled edges whispering around the leaves, mixed in with the completely white monstera hybrids, while giant golden pothos spilled out onto the freshly tidied path. It was the simplest of beds, more of an edging to the walkway's entrance, but I had been so excited to plant something that I couldn't help myself, even though I still had far more to do to most of the other scapes before I would be ready to plant them. The next week would be spent working on the soil conditions of the other beds after solidifying from Hester's notebook exactly where tropicals and subtropicals would be best planted to get optimal conditions in the multi-temperate space.

Combing through Hester's gardening notebook had proved to be absolutely fascinating as far as the conservatory was concerned but failed to give me much more information about her, though I did find her absolute hatred of daisies and roses to be quite comical. I wish I knew the backstory because, in her obvious love of dark, mysterious, Gothic plants, it was unusual to hate roses, arguably the most stereotypical Gothic flower of them all. For some reason, though, it didn't surprise me. After being in the remnants of her space for so long, I'd started to feel like I knew Hester personally, not just in a ghost form. It was obvious she did things her own way, not because they were the most popular or beautiful. I admired that more than I could put into words. She didn't do it to please everyone else; she had done it for her. A trait I wished I had more of.

The environmental structures of the conservatory were fascinating. There were dedicated sections for cacti and succulents; desert plants like saguaro, prickly pear, and barrel cactus; a section for Mediterranean plants like lavender, oleander, and rosemary; a section for Alpine and mountain plants with Astor's edelweiss and saxifrage, which were not to be outdone by the ornamentals. Hester had even procured a section of carnivorous plants at one time, and I made sure there was a space in the garden tucked away and protected by large fake boulders and plants, almost as if it were a room all in itself, where the pitcher plants, sundew, and Venus flytraps were kept happy until it was their turn to be planted. Beyond sorting through the forgotten decay of everything, I had to restore each of the conservatory's perfect little environments. Typically, because the various plants required such different conditions, they would be housed in different rooms, but again, Hester had been an original genius and had managed to set up large, visually aesthetic blocks in the giant space that acted as walls, allowing for temperature and humidity customization for each subsection. It was brilliant, and something I hadn't seen many botanical gardens try. My colleagues would be thrilled to see the workings of it all.

The Mediterranean plants enjoyed hot, dry temperatures, whereas the tropical plants thrived in warm, humid environments. Sowerby had been unstoppable in helping me with the heating and cooling systems of the conservatory, even if he complained the entire time. It was odd. After a few days of helping me in the garden while Jasper was out of town, Sowerby had grown increasingly irritated and crotchety, even shaking and tearing up, though not in front of me, of course.

Things I could only watch from the corner of my eye for when I would turn and talk to him, his face would turn to annoyed, stiff stone as it always was, as if nothing happened. Seeing how much distress it was causing him to be with the old memories of Hester and the garden, I insisted he work only on the technical side of the conservatory instead of in the beds with the plants, which seemed to please him, though I couldn't help but feel a bit disappointed at the lack of useful help. I imagine being in here brought back painful memories, and even though I was doing all that I could to bring hope back to the space, it still held her memories. Besides, it was just as easy for me to do it alone, as his pace was slow and significantly more careful than mine had become, with the corpse flower threatening to bloom.

"So you like the dark plants," I said to Jasper, a smile lighting up my face. "So did your mom. I couldn't believe some of the cool things she had planted here. It's like a Gothic gardener's dream. Almost everything she has in here is on the darker spectrum. It's going to be beautiful once it's all complete." We obviously hadn't been able to procure all of the exact plants that Hester originally had. When I gave Jasper the list of plants needed, I tried to find substitutes similar in color or impact but less expensive. Jasper hadn't even wanted to fix up the garden, and though I was more than certain he had the money and connections to get the rarest specimens available, I didn't want to push my luck. Besides, the eleven that had managed to live on in the conservatory were enough to showcase on their own. It did work out favorably, though, that several of the plants that Hester had loved were no longer considered rare and were quite easy to get.

As always, Jasper's mood soured at the mention of his mother. That's right, I was still supposed to pretend she wasn't dead and haunting me, but that she was still alive, as all three men supposedly believed.

"Maybe she'll come back and see it," I said, watching his eyes for signs of deception as carefully as a hawk watches a field mouse.

"I hope she doesn't. My father has caused enough trouble returning; I don't need or want her here," he said as he put his hands in his pockets and walked toward me with his relaxed, confident gait.

"James Bond," I said, unable to help myself.

"Excuse me?" he said, suddenly matching my grin.

"You're always in suits. I think James Bond is much more fitting for you than Batman, even if Sowerby is Evil Alfred… friend." I wiped the beads of sweat off my forehead and removed my gloves as I stood, grateful for the break to stretch my aching back.

A devilish smirk came over his face as his dark brown eyes danced with trouble and amusement. My insides sparked and vibrated when he looked so playful, especially after just seeing him appear so frigid and distant. Everyone in the house seemed gloomy and on edge since Darius had returned. If I had thought the manor had been stuffy and burdened before, it felt doubly so now.

Glad to see my *friend* back, I waited for what ridiculousness was about to come out of his mouth.

"Would that make you Moneypenny or Pussy Galore, then?" He managed a straight face that absolutely simmered with playful charm. Seeing him smile that way felt like cinder blocks were lifted from my shoulders.

Laughter bubbled up out of me. "Neither. I would want to be Xenia Onatopp from *Goldeneye*. She was the one who used her strength and seduction to kill, squeezing the men to death with her thighs." I made a show squatting, which I'd been doing 47,000 times daily while working here in the conservatory. "I think my thighs might be stronger than hers at this point." I raised an eyebrow in challenge but was unable to keep a straight face. It was stupid how candid I could be with him, and I loved it.

His eyes darkened and, as slow as dripping molasses, trailed down my body. I felt the blush creep into my cheeks as they heated. He couldn't look at me like that. I was far too lonely and delusional for him to look at me like that.

"So, friend—"

"Don't do that," he stated, his voice low with command as he took a few steps toward me.

"Do what?" I said, even though I knew what he meant. The first few times I'd called him a friend, it had been a loud, showy way of making sure he knew that that's what we were, that he couldn't get rid of me just because he was scared—because, with real friendship, you don't always get to pick it. Sometimes, we find the things and people that we need where they were never supposed to be found. It doesn't make them any less real.

I realized at that moment how much it would devastate me if he had killed Hester. It would mean that everything between us had been a lie, and it made my anxieties spike. My skin suddenly felt hot and too tight.

Now, I found myself calling him a friend out of frustration. It would be easier to be friends after I left Blackwood Manor, and that's how it needed to stay, even if I was having a hard time keeping him in the friend category. I had never really had a lot of friends, or boyfriends for that matter, but I knew I felt differently about him, even if I shouldn't. I had so little experience with men, but I knew the swirling butterflies in my stomach told me this wasn't friend territory, though I didn't really know what else to consider him.

He was so close to me now that our chests were almost brushing up against one another as his masculine presence towered over me. I felt so small and short when he stood this near, and it made my insides tense in a pleasing way. This was an example of why it was so important that he wasn't lying to me, that he really wasn't the man everyone believed him to be. It was the difference between feeling safe and protected next to his large, strong body and feeling like he would overpower me and hurt me...or worse.

The tension crackled between us as it always did when our bodies got this close. When they were, it was hard to think about anything other than wanting him to touch me—wanting to touch him and trying to fight off wondering what it would feel like, if it would be shocking or comforting.

I thought we could hate each other and the electricity between us would still be there, sparking more. But that was the real trouble—I didn't hate him, and he didn't hate me. It was like two magnets were given brains and flesh, and even though we were scared and didn't want to join with the other one, we couldn't help it, and we couldn't stop it. It wasn't up to us; it was a force beyond nature, something predestined the moment we were put in each other's presence. And even if our hearts and our minds couldn't match up or agree, there was no ignoring the fact that we craved each other more intensely with every interaction.

I turned and continued my work, mostly because I didn't want him to see my eyes. It was too easy for him to read me. "You were a lot nicer when you were in New York," I teased, not wanting the lighter conversation to be over yet.

"And you were a lot farther away," he said.

My stomach tightened. What was that supposed to mean?

"Did you hear back from the lawyers?" I decided to change the subject to something safer. "Have you heard any more from your father? I saw a lot of people carrying things into the new addition. Can I get a tour now that it's finished?"

"No. It's a space filled with a bunch of very dangerous, very illegal things that don't concern you and that you don't want to get tangled up with, although it does bring up a good point.

Eliza, after you leave Blackwood Manor, things will forever be different for you. You need to know how to protect yourself."
He glanced at his watch before pulling his phone from his suit jacket and replacing it after an irritated look.

There was a high-pitched tone that filled the space between us. That was the security ping. I'd been hearing it go off in the distance every time I walked through the main house.

"Quarter after six, I want you to meet me in the shooting range out back. I'm going to teach you how to shoot."

He turned and left before I could argue.

CHAPTER 18
ELIZA

I wasn't supposed to meet Jasper at the shooting range for another twenty minutes. It was time I should have used to continue planting in the greenhouse, but I felt dirty and smelly, and if I was going to be in proximity of Jasper at the shooting range, then I needed to shower, so I took off early and headed up to my room.

Or I was going to.

Until I realized that Jasper was probably already out there waiting for me, which meant I had a few minutes to check another room before I quickly showered and hurried out to meet him. I'd been trying to sneak around the manor when no one was paying attention to take a look through some of the older rooms that I didn't think were even used anymore. I had only made my way through three rooms, and it had been a major disappointment. One had been completely empty, not even curtains, and the other two were used as some sort of ammo-making space. Empty shell casings—at least that's what I assumed they were—littered the butcher block countertops. Dark-stained wooden shelves lined the back walls, which were all filled with small boxes. Several large gun safes were in both rooms. It had smelled like sulfur, sharp wood, and metal with a hint of paper, like what a new instruction pamphlet smells like. I had felt weird and out of place and after quickly looking through them for anything that could be useful and finding nothing, I left.

I was too busy, and it was too dangerous to do more than a room here and there. I didn't know what I was looking for. Something of Hester's or Darius's—or even Jasper's—that told me something solid about what had happened. I kept the locket in my pocket or in my palm in the hopes Hester would help guide me. So far nothing.

Before I left the conservatory, I saw movement around the corner going toward the front of the house. Sowerby—and he was moving quickly. The gun range was on the other side of the property. Whatever he was doing, it wasn't in the main house and that was all the go-ahead I needed. Sowerby had grown more friendly with me, but there was always this underlying hardness to him that I never fully trusted. If he caught me snooping, it would be bad. Worse than if Jasper got me…maybe.

My feet moved quickly, the weight on the balls of my feet to keep my steps silent. I didn't have time to make it all the way across the house, so I took a sharp left, away from the more-used spaces and into spaces I hadn't seen before, closer to Jasper's office. I really needed to look through there, but I still wasn't ballsy enough to attempt that, which was a shame, because that was probably my best bet for finding information.

I passed Jasper's office and picked a random door. I pressed my ear against it to listen. Silence. I tested the doorknob, and it opened into a surprisingly small room that reminded me of a mudroom that looked to not be in use. The inside didn't fit the aesthetic of the rest of the house; even the walls looked older and more worn, with dents and scratches. The soles of my shoes tapped the floor, and I realized it was concrete covered in stains. The air was musty and cold with the same scent as an old basement. It was dark with no windows. I pulled my phone out and pulled up the flashlight, so I could close the door behind me and still see inside of the near dark room. The dim spotlight glinted on something, and I froze, the organ in my chest filling my throat and blocking the flow of air. Just a doorknob. I let out a sigh and moved toward the door a few steps down in the back of the room as I glanced at the time on my phone. *This better be worth it.* I was going to have to take the fastest shower of my life and leave my hair wet.

As I got closer to the door, I heard it.

Muffled cries. Thuds. Grunts. Crying. Centipedes of goose bumps skittered across my skin. Someone was in there, behind the door, and they were in pain—a lot of pain by the sounds of it. The blood drained from my face into my toes as I looked back at the dark stains that patterned the cement floor. Blood.

Oh my god.

Someone was being held captive. In Blackwood Manor.

My hand covered my mouth with jerking, shaking movements. I gripped the round knob, feeling my arms and legs vibrate and tremble in near hysteria.

I had to open it.

Thuds shook the door from the other side. More screams. Begging. I couldn't make out the words, but I didn't need to—the pleas were a sound I'd never forget. Every hair on my body stood on end as panic vibrated through me. My breathing was heavy and ragged, ricocheting off the metal door and back into my face, warming it with the scent of the coffee I'd finished before leaving the conservatory. I turned the knob and opened the door.

My scream lodged in my throat as it tried to escape, but my hands clapped over my mouth.

A black-haired man blanketed in a sheen of sweat was on

his knees, hunched over himself on the floor, his clothes soaked in blood and covered in yellow and brown stains.

With Jasper looming over him with a pistol in his hand.

Both their eyes snapped to mine.

"Eliza," Jasper said, surprised.

"Help me! Please! He's going to kill me, please! He's a fucking psycho!" the man on the ground shouted at me desperately.

"Oh my god" was all that came out.

A raw darkness dripped off Jasper. He looked like a monster, but I couldn't figure out why. He was calm and controlled like always. But then I saw: it was his eyes. They looked completely unhinged.

"Help me! Before he—"

I flinched and slapped my hands over my ears as the loud gunshot tore through the room and echoed in my head.

The man crumpled to the floor. His silence was louder than any sound I'd ever heard.

I locked eyes with Jasper and tried to run to the door but not before a strong hand gripped my arm and stopped me.

"Wait, Eliza," Jasper commanded.

I went ballistic, kicking and clawing at him until I freed myself and made it to the door. I pulled it open, and it slammed closed. Jasper moved in front of it, his face cold. It was terrifying. I glanced at the man on the floor. It looked like he was still moving a little.

My arm pulled back to hit Jasper in the balls, the only advantage I thought I might possibly have over him, but his hand gripped my wrist with bruising force, blocking my hit. His light chuckle made my eyes widen.

"Maybe I shouldn't be so worried about you protecting yourself."

Words were somewhere in the back of my head, but they were out of my reach. I tried to shove off him and move myself backward, but it only made him pull me firmer against him.

"This looks pretty bad, huh?" he said, a lightness in his tone.

My eyes bugged out of my head as I trembled.

He took in every detail of my face, reading me. "You're pretty scared of me right now."

His hands fell from my arms before he grabbed my hand, and I felt warm steel in my palm. He'd put the gun in my hand. Instinctively I clutched it and pointed it at his stomach with shaking arms.

"Any better?" he asked.

"What the fuck is happening?" The choppy words tumbled from my lips.

"Security found him crawling through a window. It's more likely that he was trying to get a story than any valuables or"—his eyes turned fiery and slowly raked over my body—"anything else."

"He broke in?"

He nodded.

"The security pings," I mumbled. I glanced back at the man. It was terrifying to think he'd broken into a space so heavily guarded—a space that had felt so safe and private. It rattled me. "So—so you killed him?"

He crinkled his face in disappointment. "I didn't kill him."

"You shot him!" I cried.

"It's a good thing we're headed to the gun range, so you can learn how to properly shoot someone if you think a shot to the knee is going to kill a man. He's just passed out; he'll be back to screaming any minute."

"What? I'm not going to the gun range with you!"

He took a step into me, the gun shifting against his abs, angled at the wall when he pushed hard against it and me. "Of course you are. Look at how you're holding that. You're going to get someone killed," he said as he removed the gun from my hands in one swift motion and took my arm, gently this time as he guided me out the door.

A few minutes later—though I couldn't be sure how many, but I was sure that I was in some kind of shock—I stood in one of the five lanes of the gun range. It was silent save for the distant caw of a few crows. The reinforced wall built into the cliffside in front of me had targets placed at varying distances along the long, sleek lane. It was mostly outside, but the space had modern stone shelters and coverings that matched the main house—only these felt more tactical. Everything smelled like gun oil and leather. It was gritty and clean all at once. The gun—the same gun that Jasper had used on the intruder—was heavy in my hands. Jasper was right behind me being far too quiet.

I didn't hear him move closer, but I felt him there. It was like gravity had shifted and he was pulling my awareness. I believed him about the guy in the room; he was blowing off steam, taking it out on the man. Just as we'd left the room, the man started screaming again. Jasper had let out a low laugh at my look of relief. I'd never thought Jasper was a saint, but it was a sharp reminder of the powerful, dangerous man that he was. I had maintained a healthy fear of him, even if it had blended into lust, but the fear was back in full force. I could hardly keep my knees locked because I was so scared. I had just watched him shoot a man and now we were playing with guns? What if he turned his anger on me?

"Finger off the trigger until you're ready," Jasper said, voice low. "You don't aim until you know what you want to hit." He'd barely spoken since we got to the range. He didn't need to.

He'd set up the targets, loaded the weapon, and handed it to me without a word—like he already knew how this would go.

I adjusted, trying to copy his tone, his stillness. My quivering finger pulled the trigger and fired the gun. I muttered a low curse when I missed. I got the feeling he wouldn't let this go until I hit a couple targets and we both relaxed a little from the earlier events.

"Go on," he said, now standing behind me. His voice was steady and quiet, filled with an authoritative tone. "Show me how brave you are."

I repeated my earlier action. Raised the gun, fired, and missed.

"Grip's too tight," he said, stepping forward. "You're choking it. Let me."

His hand slid over mine, cool and controlled. His chest brushed my back, deliberate. He adjusted my arms, my fingers, my stance. It should've felt instructional.

It didn't. It felt like foreplay. The sensations that danced over my skin fought to blur the wild thoughts in my mind. I'd just watched him shoot someone, and now that same fear was caught in the space between being frightened and completely turned on.

"Again."

I fired. It hit barely left of center. My knees almost gave out.

"You're holding it wrong," Jasper said behind me, his voice low, lethal in its calm.

"I hit the target."

"You brushed it."

He stepped into my space. Not rudely or urgently. Just... unavoidably.

"But if someone's coming for you?" His breath touched my neck. "You don't brush."

He adjusted my arms again, his body closing over mine like a second skin. He didn't rush. He didn't ask. He corrected.

"Hands loose." His palm flattened over my stomach. "And breathe here. Not in your throat. That's fear. I want control."

I did as I was told. Sort of. It was hard to breathe at all with him this close.

"Again."

I fired and the bullet stuck just right of center. My knees wobbled, threatening to drop me to the ground, and I did my best not to show it. Jasper leaned down and his mouth brushed the shell of my ear.

"Pretty good, but you're still aiming like you don't know what you want to hit."

I turned and tried to hand the gun back to him. He didn't take it. Instead, he wrapped his fingers around mine—firm but unhurried—and guided my hand until the barrel pressed into his ribs. It made me rear back a bit and try to pull my hand away.

"Try again," he said softly. "No hesitation this time."

"Jasper…"

"Go on." His eyes danced over mine. Cool, collected, and completely unbothered. "What's the worst that happens? You shoot me?"

"That's not funny."

"I'm not joking." The metal trembled where it rested against him. "You think you're scared of me," he murmured. "But what you're really scared of is this." He tilted his head and leaned in closer. "Wanting me this much and knowing I haven't even touched you yet."

I opened my mouth, but nothing came out.

"You keep pretending you don't want it. At least I don't lie about wanting you. I'm right here. Unarmed. Letting you aim, and your hands are still shaking."

"Because you're insane."

"No. I'm honest."

"Shut up," I bit out.

He lifted my wrist slightly, shifting the angle of the barrel. "You want me to shut up?" His voice dipped low. "Pull the trigger."

I didn't move. Not even a blink for fear I'd accidentally shoot him.

"That's what I thought," he said. "You don't want me to stop. You want to know what I'd do if you gave in." He pressed in, smashing the gun between us. "But if I were you," he added, his voice lower now, almost affectionate, "I'd keep my finger off the trigger."

"Why?" I whispered, looking at the danger glittering in his deep brown eyes.

"Because if you fire, it won't kill me," he said. "And I'll take it as permission."

The breath left my lungs. "Permission for what?"

He tilted his head, just slightly, like he was cataloging the way my lips parted. His eyes dragged over the flush rising up my neck.

"To stop pretending." He stared at me. Calm. Waiting. "And if you give me permission, I won't stop." He paused. "If you fire, I'll put you on your knees and make you say every filthy thing you've been thinking since the second you walked into the manor."

My stomach tightened and twisted with his words. The fear and heat pulsed through me.

"I'll make it hurt," he added, barely above a whisper. "In the ways you like. The ones you can't admit to."

"You're disgusting."

"I know," he said. "And I know you're wet anyway. You could pull the trigger right now. End it all. But you won't. Because you don't want me gone. You want me closer."

The air between us burned. He let go of the gun just to lift a strand of my hair and curl it around two fingers. My skin erupted in goose bumps.

"You want to pretend you're a good girl, but you're not, are you, Eliza? You'd still want to fuck me no matter how many people I killed."

I swallowed hard.

"Say that's not true," he said. "Lie to me."

My mouth fell open, but all my thoughts swirled with the heat between my legs.

He grinned—small, devastating. "Exactly." His voice went lower in a lethal caress. "I'd pin you to the floor right here and you'd take it. You'd beg for it. I'd put you on your back and fuck you until the leaves stuck to your skin. Make you cry my name into the dirt." He leaned close, lips brushing the corner of my jaw—not a kiss…a threat. "But don't worry. I'd still let you shoot me before I let myself fuck you."

I gasped at his words.

"Because I'd break you, Eliza, and not in the sweet way you're hoping for."

I tried to back away, but my feet were frozen in place. His words were pouring through me like electricity. *I should shoot him just to teach him a lesson.*

"I'd make it messy," he said. "Loud. You'd hate yourself for how much you'd love it." His lips closed and I could almost taste the lie in his restraint.

"I don't want this," I said unsteadily, knowing it didn't land.

"No?" he asked. "Then why haven't you moved?" He stepped away. "Again. Relax your shoulders."

I gaped at him. He wasn't serious.

"You need to learn." For as unhinged of a mood as Jasper was in tonight, he seemed determined to actually teach me to be comfortable with defending myself.

"Why are you teaching me this?" I asked.

"Because someone's going to hurt you eventually," he said. He took the pistol and slid the magazine in with a soft click. "And I'd rather it not be me."

The words hit harder than they should have. "You said you'd ruin me."

"I will," he said without even a hint of apology. "If you let me."

My thighs trembled. "You could be lying about everything," I said. "I don't know what you've done."

"You don't." He leaned in closer. "And it turns you on anyway."

I didn't deny it again. There was no use. Not with Jasper. He saw straight through me.

Instead of handing me the gun butt first, he pointed the barrel at my chest, closing in until it grazed my nipple before sliding it slowly up my throat, bringing it beneath my jaw. He tilted my chin up with it. The metal was cool but my blood was hot.

He smirked. "I think you'd let me ruin you. I think you'd let me use this gun to pin your wrists while I made you beg." His voice was deathly calm.

I shook my head haphazardly and ran my tongue over my lips. His eyes tracked the motion.

"Not because you trust me," he continued, eyes locked on my lips. "Because you want to know what it would feel like to finally give in."

My knees finally buckled. He didn't help. I swallowed, feeling the muzzle of the gun still at my throat.

"I'd fuck you so slowly, you'd forget why you ever tried to resist me."

I shivered and pressed my thighs together.

He saw it and his smile darkened. He holstered the weapon like none of it had happened and turned. "Go to bed, Eliza."

CHAPTER 19
ELIZA

JASPER WAS JUST CARRYING IN THE LAST OF THE PLANTS FOR THE bed I was finishing in the conservatory. He'd been in the conservatory when I'd arrived this morning and offered to help. I was nervous about being so close to him again, but I wasn't going to turn down the opportunity to find out more about what might have happened last night.

My phone pinged in my pocket. I saw the text from my mother, and my face fell. I had been doing such a magical job of tucking my problems away and avoiding them. I knew it couldn't go on forever, but it had been such a freeing change.

I cleared the emotion from my throat. "Sorry, it's my mom." I tucked the phone back inside the pocket of my gray hoodie. "She's having another tantrum." It was uncanny the ability she had to tether and drown my spirits with a simple call or text. Jasper had taken the weight of a cement block from my shoulders, and she had just tied it to my ankles. No one should be capable of having such command over another's feelings. Sometimes, it felt like murder.

"Is everything okay?" Jasper looked concerned.

"She actually did it. I didn't think she really would, but

I obviously should have known better. She got rid of all my things and told her friend, my fucking landlord, to re-rent the apartment." Needing anything to distract me, I pulled the hair tie out of my ponytail and ran my fingers through my dirty, tangled hair before piling it back on top of my head in a messy bun. The familiar sting of acid swirled in my stomach. I needed an antacid. I needed to get this conservatory finished and find a way to fucking help Hester and get back before my mother did any more fucking damage.

"She got rid of your apartment?" he said, his eyebrows lifting in shock.

"Yeah," I snapped, resting my hands on my head. I should have let her in the gates when she came the last time. I had never pushed back, ever, and now she was retaliating. I didn't want any of this. I already knew she was stronger than me; there was no competition. "It will be fine; one of my sort of friends at work has a spare room. I'll text them to see if I can stay there for a bit; he always tries to get me to stay anyway when I watch his pets. I'll figure out the rest later. I literally don't have time to worry about this now. If I don't get these plants propagated soon, I will genuinely not have a job to go back to and won't have to worry about finding a new apartment because I'll be left with nothing and forced to move back in with my parents, which is exactly what she wants." A migraine was threatening to come on, which would definitely not help this situation. I shot off a cursory text message to my friend.

The phone rang seconds later.

With a wave of his hand telling me to take the call, Jasper turned and began to wander aimlessly around the garden.

I picked up the call. "Hi, did you get the pictures of the Black Dahlia pinnata?"

Nick's voice came over the line. "I did, but who cares about those when you get to look at black hellebores? Are you a wizard? How is it blooming right now?"

"I know, right? It's definitely not me. It's wild. None of the plants I bring into the conservatory act like they're supposed to," I said with a forced chuckle. He had no idea; sometimes, I convinced myself that the plants inside the conservatory were all sentient. It always felt like they were watching me, and most of the time, I didn't mind—even kind of enjoyed the company. But every now and again, they would move around—and not just in the nursery pots but also in the beds. Stupid, I knew, and more than likely, I was just being forgetful about where I planted or set them, but after everything I'd seen the locket do and just seeing Hester in general, it didn't feel all that far-fetched to think that the plants in the conservatory were... different. I turned to look at the stunning deep purple blooms of the black hellebores. "Hey, do you still have that spare room available? I had...an issue, and in a month, I'll need somewhere to stay for a few weeks while I look for an apartment. I don't have time to look before the party; you saw how fast the corpse flower is progressing. Please don't be afraid to say no. I know it's an awful lot to ask."

"Of course!" Nick shrieked excitedly. "It won't bother you if the cats sleep in your room, right? Tobias and I just got another one. Mrs. Shushu is the reason I had to move all of my aglonemia to the office; she won't stop eating them. Alas, that's the sacrifice a good mother has to make."

"No, I'll be fine," I said. "I'll call you later to work out details, but it won't be until the party. I'll be leaving right after." My migraine worsened at the thought.

"Okay, sounds good. I can't wait to tell Tobias someone will get to sleep in the room he redecorated. Chat soon, Eliza."

"Bye, Nick. I'll call you later." That wasn't so bad. Maybe things really would be okay. There were worse things in the world than moving in with your super-nice coworker and his interior designer husband in their beautiful house, where they collected ragdoll cats like Pokémon.

What if I didn't tell Mom where I was going? Kept some space. It sounded great, but it wouldn't last long before she found me. In the end, I was only making things worse for myself by making her mad.

"Nick?" Jasper appeared behind me. "You're going to move in with a man?" The darkness that he'd shown last night simmered in his eyes but remained leashed.

I almost snorted in his face, hearing the clear, uncamouflaged jealousy in his possessive tone. I would have laughed if it had not been so disarmingly attractive to my ego.

"And?" For all intents and purposes, I most definitely would *not* be letting him in on the fact that Nick was very much not interested in me and my lady bits to the delight of his husband.

"You sleeping with him?" His jaw hardened, and I found myself too hyperfocused on the flutter of his masseter muscle to be offended by his question.

Internally, I was giggling and kicking my feet. I liked that he cared about me enough to get jealous. It made me feel a whole lot less dumb for caring about him when I shouldn't. But externally, I scoffed loudly. "You know, not every woman that lives with a man is fucking them," I scolded, making sure my face was halfway down a terracotta pot before I let myself smile. "Look at you and Leah or you and me."

"I don't think it's a good idea," he stated in the same way one might reference owning a tiger.

I squinted at him, actually getting a little annoyed. "Who are you, my mother?"

He had the decency to flinch. "Don't leave after the party. You can stay at the manor as long as you want, until you find a place. Behind the gate, away from everyone." A surprising tenderness in his voice struck me right in the chest. Whether he would ever admit it or not, he was actually becoming a real friend. A teasing, infuriating, scary, unpredictable friend, but a friend was a friend.

I stood up and looked at him, taking a hold of all the odd sweetness that seemed to emanate from him. "I can't."

"Why not? I want you to stay," he said sharply.

I looked down, caught completely off guard by his vulnerability. There was an edge to his voice that told me this wasn't the first time he'd thought about me leaving. He could hide behind the filthy comments, but the truth was he cared. A feeling that lodged in my ribs. "I can't drive four hours to and from Pinehurst every day." That was the least of the reasons why I couldn't stay. Dreams are only coveted because you have to face reality for a while to *truly* appreciate them. I had to wake up eventually.

He stared, reluctantly admitting that it wouldn't make any sense. His phone rang loudly, and his eyes fell closed as he pulled it out with a burdened sigh. "I'm sorry, I have to take this. It's the estate lawyer," he said before he walked toward the door to the house. "Yeah?" he snapped into the device.

I silently waved a weak goodbye and turned back to my task of potting a few shadow ferns.

I heard the door open.

"Eliza," Jasper called out.

I whipped around to see him holding the door open with the phone to his chest as he watched me with an unusual look in his eye.

"Have dinner with me tomorrow night. If you're interested in trying more wine, I brought back a few from the vineyard I thought you might like. We could set up a tasting in the wine cellar."

Butterflies tried to escape the confines of my stomach. "Okay, that sounds fun."

A devilishly charming smile flashed before dropping back into a stern line as he returned the phone to his ear and left the conservatory.

I shouldn't have dinner with him. I didn't have any extra

time, but the garden was only half my stress. I still needed to find a way to help Hester before I left, and I was completely at a loss on what to do. Maybe I should tell Jasper about Hester. Maybe he would know how to help her.

I turned away from the closed door and stared at the soil in front of me when I got an urge to check the locket. Wondering if it was still empty, I pulled it out of my pocket. I had stopped wearing it when Hester began getting angry—in fear that she would do something scary like choke me with it.

At first glance, I thought it was empty, as it had been for days, but to my surprise, a small dark-green stem had formed and begun to grow now that there was room for it to do so. My mouth fell open in wonder as I watched the small bud of what looked like a rose the same color red as Hester's gown form.

My face scrunched as the deep-red bloom continued to grow and grow until it was ready to unfurl. "You hated roses," I said softly to Hester's locket as I watched the velvet leaves burst open. The sweet herbaceous scent of the fresh rose lingered before the full-bodied floral scent suddenly overpowered my senses, and all I could smell was the rose. I leaned down and pressed my nose against the flower without a second thought—unlike Hester, roses were one of my favorite flowers. As fast as a flash of lightning, its thorned leaf petiole struck out as if it were slapping me, puncturing my lip with its barb.

I gasped, dropping the locket and the rose to the ground.

I watched in horror as the small rose used its two side branches as if they were arms to push itself out of the locket and burrow its loose white roots into a crack in the pavers. To anyone else, it would have looked as if it a rogue rose had grown up from the floor of the conservatory.

I pulled my hand away from my lip, a smear of blood on it. Fear flooded me, as it had already begun to burn and swell. With a weary hand, I reached over and picked up the empty locket, avoiding the small rose that now was indistinguishable from a normal rose, and let out a string of curse words. What the fuck was that all about? What was I supposed to do with the devil rose now? The thought occurred to me that Hester may have given up on trying to communicate with me and was just…well, haunting me now.

With a heavy sigh, I left the conservatory to get my migraine medicine and some ice for my lip.

ELIZA

CHAPTER 20
ELIZA

TENSIONS IN THE MANOR ONLY SEEMED TO INCREASE WITH each meeting that Jasper had with his attorneys. The staff had been with Jasper so long that even if they were unaware of why his father's appearance was so unusual, the estate flowed with their unanimous support for Jasper, but it was impossible to ignore the mysteriousness of the situation.

The media, which had only *just* begun to fizzle out after the pictures of Jasper holding the shotgun had surfaced, were now back in full force, with Darius Blackwood being revealed to be still alive. It seemed to vary daily, but most recently they had spun it that Jasper had hired a man to claim to be his father in the hopes of clearing his name. The media had latched on to the story that would get them the most hits. Even the ones that were close to the truth remained buried in the sea of lies.

Ever since Darius Blackwood had walked out the doors of the manor, the ghost of his wife had been incredibly active and seemed to be in a near panic. My lip was still swollen and burned from whatever type of devil rose had crawled from the locket and lashed out at me. It had swollen so big I had hardly been able to talk for at least an hour; thankfully, my dinner with Jasper was the following night, and the only one I ended up talking to that night was myself, while I tried to tell myself that everything was all right when the creaks and pops filled my room. No real harm had seemed to come from the rose, which I just avoided. I couldn't understand if Hester had sent it to me to tell me some sort of message or if she just wanted to lash out in frustration.

When I'd initially seen the beautiful depressed spirit of Hester, empathy had overridden the majority of my fear. Now, though, I didn't know what to think. Deep down, I believed she was not violent or malicious, only frustrated and lacking the ability to communicate things she so desperately wanted to. I didn't know the rules of being a ghost or why she couldn't spell out in the locket what it was she wanted to tell me, but it seemed, in the afterlife, things weren't allowed to be quite so simple. Even with my generous interpretation of Hester's behavior, I had begun to grow more terrified. Nearly every time I was alone, something eerie or frightening would happen, sending my already taut nerves into overdrive. Sometimes, it was so subtle that I wondered again if I was being paranoid and imagining things, but those thoughts didn't stick around for very long before something far less subtle would take place, reassuring me of its validity and of her frustrated presence.

After yet another long and restless night, I had come to the conclusion that I was going to tell Jasper that she appeared to me. There was a part of me that felt deceptive in keeping such an important fact from him, and in truth, I'd only been keeping it from him in fear that he had murdered Hester and that telling him would put me in serious danger. And yes, I know I still didn't have any *foolproof* evidence that he wasn't the one to murder her, but I knew he wasn't capable of something so horrendous…or at least I really hoped that was the case. If I found out it was all a lie, I didn't know what I'd do. With the way that Hester had gone absolutely feral with the return of her husband, I put my money on Darius as the murderer, though it still didn't make sense why he would have left Jasper in the manor and not taken him... It was almost like Darius was afraid of him, the way he had seemingly left him to rot in the manor alone.

Jasper and I were having dinner tonight, and I found myself getting excited and nervous as the day went on. I had talked myself in and out of the actual dinner at least four times, but as of now, I was looking forward to it. The first time we met, I had felt the spark of something with him, though then it was through challenges and sharp banter—he brought out the Eliza I always wanted to be: bold and witty. Every day that passed in the manor, I found myself hoping I'd bump into him in the hallway or that he'd find me in the conservatory. Initially, I had felt sort of ashamed of it—that wasn't why I was here, and he most definitely was not a good idea, but I couldn't help it. I rarely had dinner outside of the garden, as I usually just grabbed something from the kitchen and brought it back, so sitting down and having company for dinner sounded nice. Would something more happen tonight? Would we finally kiss? Should I try and stop it? I should most definitely not let him touch me.

My looming deadlines grew heavier and heavier with each passing hour, laying pressure on my sore shoulders. If I couldn't get some of these rare propagations back to Pinehurst, then they weren't likely to have enough funding to make it, at least not without cutting their newest staff members, which, unfortunately, included me. Jasper had been kind enough to invite some of a nearby town's well-known philanthropists in the hopes of Pinehurst receiving more donations. Still, I felt the overwhelming, suffocating pressure that it all sat on *my* shoulders. Sometimes, propagations were unsuccessful; I didn't know what I'd do if these didn't take.

The irony of it all was everything landed in the hands of

the corpse flower. I had already been forced to change the date of the party, pushing it up as it became clearer the bloom was going to happen sooner. The phallic-looking specimen was my only solid beacon of hope. I couldn't harvest a propagation from the corpse flower while it was blooming because the corm was in the plant's underground storage organ, which typically takes years to grow and mature. During blooming, the plant expended a lot of energy on its reproduction, so I couldn't dig up the tuber without potentially harming the plant. I had to wait until after it had completed its blooming cycle and started to die back. This was when the corm could be separated carefully from the rest of the plant for replanting and propagation. With the corpse flower's blooming cycle being as rare as it was and only occurring once every three to seven years if you were lucky and had perfect conditions, my nerves were tense.

Even now, as I stood admiring the beautiful plant, it felt like both a blessing and a curse; this one plant had the ability to save an entire botanical garden and all its employees, and they were all counting on me to make it happen. The other rare plants would be very helpful, but none of them were quite as rare and valuable as the corpse flower. People would flock from all around to see the rare, rotting-flesh-scented bloom, and it gave us the rare opportunity to create and sell more corpse flowers, bringing even more money to the gardens.

"It's quite phallic-looking, isn't it?" Jasper said from behind me, causing me to nearly jump out of my skin. Something he seemed to do frequently. Despite his size, he was able to move like a wraith. It was unnerving. You only saw him when he wanted you to.

His eyes widened with a smile, seeing how he had startled me.

"I'm beginning to think you do that on purpose," I said gruffly, trying to calm my racing heart. Hester's feisty escapades and watching Jasper shoot a man had me jumpier than normal, even though Katya had promised me the man had been taken away with only minor injuries. I looked back at the vibrant green corpse flower. "Wait until you see it in a few weeks," I said. "The long green middle part continues to grow up until it blooms, and that cabbage-looking petal right there? It will open up to reveal a beautiful deep-purple interior around that enormous green spike that only lasts for about twenty-four hours, forty-eight if we're lucky."

Jasper inspected the unusual-looking plant. He didn't say anything, but his eyes darted over to me, and I could imagine the vast number of inappropriate sentences that overflowed his mind and he was trying his best to filter. He sat back on the newly restored bench and propped his arms on the back rest, getting comfortable, as if he were about to watch his favorite baseball team.

I laughed, grateful for the company but uncomfortable with being his entertainment. "Don't you have a job or something to do?"

"Yes, but the job is boring and doesn't look as good as you. I've had enough stress for the day, and I'd like to do something fun," he said with a soft smile as he watched me.

I had just finished planting the freshly tilled bed in the corner and, in truth, was ecstatic to have someone look at it—it was almost as if he knew when to come and praise my work. I wondered how often Jasper watched me when I didn't know. That thought caused a tightening in my lower stomach, and not in a bad way. It was utterly intoxicating to be seen for once.

"You're welcome to help me," I said sardonically, waving my hand over the next extremely large bed that I needed to till.

"And get my suit dirty before our dinner? Okay, but then I'll have to take it off," he teased. "We are still on?" A bit of hopefulness in his words made my heart race. Tonight felt special, like it was going to be a defining moment for us. "What happened to your lip?" he said, suddenly sitting up and looking lethal.

Shit. "Oh, it was stupid. I bumped into a stray thorn." I lowered my face from view as my eyes darted to the tiny demon rose that remained growing in the crack in the pavers I'd been avoiding.

"A stray thorn?" he said, not hiding his doubt in my words.

He was up from the bench and in front of me before I could think of what to say. I sucked in a breath, surprised by his sudden closeness as he inspected my lip. The swelling was minimal now, and the small wound from the thorn had already gone away.

"It's nothing, really," I said.

When he stood so close to me, it felt like my body had been struck by lightning, and all my nerves were standing on end, reaching out for him. A commanding protectiveness poured off him and oozed over my skin, making me feel warm and tingly. I'd never had anyone want to protect me, and by the tension coiled and ready to strike in Jasper, he was ready to kill anyone who had hurt me. Something stirred in my chest.

His warm brown eyes roved over me. His hand moved back up to cup my face and tilt it toward the light with a feather-soft touch. My eyes fluttered shut at the heat of his hand and the intimate feel of his thumb gently gliding over my barely swollen lower lip. I was surprised he had even noticed it, and yet now I felt like he would slit someone's throat had it been by a man and not a rose.

"Are you all right, Eliza?" His breathy words skittered across my skin, leaving a trail of goose bumps behind.

My mind was too empty to answer. All I could think about was how good his light cologne smelled and how much I wanted him to touch more of me. "Yes," I whispered with a nod.

For a moment, all we did was look at one another, reading

all of the feelings in the other's eyes. Absently, my hand curled around his forearm. All that did was solidify the waves of electricity that flowed between us. I'd never experienced such an intense physical reaction to someone. It was unnerving. Just the presence of him pushing against my skin was enough to cause the blood to whoosh through my veins and thud heavily between my legs. It was embarrassing, the intensity with which my body zinged and hummed. It was a bodily elixir that would only cause trouble and pain, but I couldn't fight it anymore. I needed to finally scratch the itch, to know how the skin of his lips felt, how they tasted.

Would he kiss me gently and soft? Full of control? Or would it be a blast of power as sparks were unleashed? The deepest parts of me were too needy to be ashamed any longer. I needed to feel it. Kissing him would only lead to problems, but this foolish voice in my head told me that if I didn't kiss him soon, my insides would explode like fireworks.

His face had moved so close to mine that only a breath separated our lips from touching. I tightened my grip on his forearm and closed my eyes, silently urging him to close the space between us and press his mouth to mine.

I felt his warm, lightly minty breath across the top of my lips, and I eagerly braced myself. The ache for it curled my toes with desperate need. His lips parted and I closed my eyes. Butterflies fought against the confines of my stomach lining.

Without warning, the doors to the conservatory flew open. "He's done it! That rat bastard has had a restraining order put in place," Sowerby shouted as he stormed into the garden. Though he didn't touch them, the lush plants seemed to rustle in answer as he passed by them.

I stepped away from Jasper, and the three of us exchanged shocked glances with one another.

"A restraining order? On you?" I asked Jasper, completely taken aback. "For what? Because Sowerby hit him?"

"On the property," Sowerby said with a pained look. "It prohibits any change to the manor—which includes any more changes to the addition…and the conservatory. I'm so sorry, Eliza. I was afraid he would do this."

"Oh my god…" I muttered.

"Fuck that," Jasper growled. "This is my house. If he wanted it so badly, he shouldn't have left."

I could feel the anger steaming off Jasper.

"I'm sure it will only be temporary," added Sowerby, trying to calm him, though he looked furious himself.

"But the corpse flower—the party," I stammered, suddenly feeling as if I were going to have a panic attack. "You don't understand, I *have* to have the party—and the propagation. Oh my god. I haven't even taken the propagations yet!" I felt dizzy and sick. I was going to throw up.

"Fuck him and her. You're not stopping work on the conservatory, Eliza," Jasper stated with a dangerous edge to his voice. "They are *not* going to come back and turn my entire world upside down again. I won't let it happen. I won't. I promise you, Eliza, no harm or legal repercussions will come to you if you continue working on the gardens."

"Now, hold on," Sowerby interjected. "This is the law, Jasper, and you need to think more about what's happening. Do you really want to draw attention to your stash of illegal weapons in the new addition? Don't you wonder why he's come back just because he heard the conservatory was getting worked on? Right before the corpse flower is going to bloom?"

"I don't give a shit. Half the local police force has already seen and admired my collection. They aren't my problem. *He* is, and you know better than all of us how they were," Jasper scolded. "The two of them were inseparable. Either one of them would have done *anything* for the other. They shared so much love but there wasn't ever enough left for me. They put so much of themselves into designing this manor, they are probably tied to it by the devil. If you thought for a second that they wouldn't come back just to keep it the way they designed it, then you don't know them as well as I thought."

Jasper stopped his rant near the small devil rose in the crack of the walkway, and I held my breath.

"Do you want me to pull this or is it staying?" he asked with a sharp look.

"No—uh, it—I don't know. It just popped up, but be careful. It's the one that got my lip," I said as I watched him nervously.

"How did it get your lip from the ground?" His brows pinched together.

I shrugged, then inhaled sharply as he took a heavy step, smashing the small single rose, grinding his foot into the ground until it was nothing but a crimson smear against the gray stone paver, leaving it to look as though it had been stained with blood. I held my breath in the back of my throat, unable to stop myself from looking around for the ghost of Hester to retaliate. Instead of an angry ghost, a breeze swept in, causing the jungle of green leaves in the garden to rustle and shimmy like a roaring crowd at a concert.

The three of us exchanged glances, and I was relieved to note that both of them noticed the odd breeze.

"I thought the windows had all been fixed," Jasper said as he looked around at the Victorian-inspired covering of glass.

"They were," Sowerby mumbled with unease before clearing his throat.

"So, should I keep working?" I asked, feeling the pressure in my head from where yet another headache was forming. They were near daily now.

"No," Sowerby announced.

"Yes," Jasper snapped. "But not tonight. *Please* tell me we are still on for our dinner. We could both use some wine and a few hours away from everything."

I agreed, still looking forward to dinner with Jasper and a distraction away from the garden for a bit.

Sowerby left to help Leah set up the wine cellar, and I left to get cleaned up.

I laid out one of the black dresses that Katya and Leah had brought for the business dinner. I was going to miss those women so much when I had to go back home. I chose the more professional of the dresses, not even attempting to try on the skimpier dress.

In actuality, it probably wasn't really all that immodest, but I'd grown so used to wearing large, baggy clothes that anything without a cardigan or sleeves felt a little scandalous. But tonight was different; I wasn't working, and I wasn't sitting alone in my room scrolling through art feeds. Maybe I would wear the skimpier dress tonight.

I was growing tired of the constant tug and drop of tension between Jasper and me. If he and I had nothing to offer each other past a physical connection, I wanted to at least know before I had to leave and would be left to wonder. No matter what happened with the corpse flower, the party, or Hester, I knew I would be thinking about Jasper for a very long time after I left Blackwood Manor, even if it wasn't reciprocated. Tonight would solidify if we really could be friends after I left, though, to be honest, even as I thought the words, my stomach sank. I wanted more, but it wasn't realistic. He was a millionaire who traveled around the world on a private jet, and I was a botanist who liked to read in my bed when it rained and pretend I was someone else, anywhere else—even only as friends, he and I were so different.

I should have been happy with how things were between us and not want more. Was I even capable of giving him—or anyone—more? When I said I was lonely, I meant it. Embarrassingly, the last relationship I had been in was when I was sixteen, and that had promptly ended when I showed up at the house with him. My mom had been so mean during that hour that he broke up with me before he left. I was heartbroken, and my mother could only say that I should thank her for weeding out the bad ones. That was the last time I had ever really pushed for anything I wanted. From that point forward, I did the wild, absurd things *she* wanted, giving no pushback, no resistance. It was easier for me to go along with it, never having my own say. In my own way, I did this all to myself.

At least until Blackwood Manor came along. When I learned about the lore and the mystery surrounding the supposed hidden menagerie of rare plants at work one day, I couldn't stop thinking about it; it consumed me. Pinehurst Botanical Gardens had always been a grand, beautiful place, but more than just the prospect of saving Pinehurst was the idea of doing something exciting on my own, away from her reach.

As if on cue, my phone rang, and her name popped up in bold letters. I moved the dress from the corner of my bed and sat down.

"Hey," I said, hoping my nonchalant voice would derail any harsh words from her.

"Oh, Jesus Christ, Eliza. Are you still there? At the manor? You gotta get away from there; our name is already in all the papers. This is not the kind of thing you should be getting messed up in; you should be in the papers for helping save fauna and flora, not for fucking a seller of mass weapons. I'm finishing up something for work, and then I'll be over to pick you up. You better—all the emissions I'm using to go up there—"

"Mom." I tried to cut her off. That familiar ebb of adrenaline rushed through my body as it did every single time she was like this. My body prepared for a fight, but my mind would tamp it down eventually, keeping it buried where it wouldn't bother anybody but me.

"Eliza Nicole Arnold, don't *Mom* me. What type of soil have you been using? Is it on our safe list? I saw everything at your apartment that was on the red list. You will have to be punished, Eliza. You can't do that to Mother Earth and not expect to be punished."

Her words crawled across my skin like tiny blades. I could feel the blood rushing to my face, making my cheeks red and splotchy. "I won't be able to take any days off after being at the manor for three months. I know you're upset with me, but it's not really that big of a deal, Mom. People use plastic all the time; I didn't have anything that bad."

I sat on the edge of my bed, the sexy black dress in hand, wondering how I was staying as calm as I was.

That had been the wrong thing to say. I had known it before I said it, but still, I'd said it. It was like the mechanism that warned me, told me when to shut up and stop talking, had been broken.

"This is exactly what I was afraid of with you staying there without me. Your father and I are counting on you, Eliza. Who is going to care for this planet once we're gone? You ungrateful child. It's a good thing you're moving back in with Dad and me. You'll have five days in the cabin."

My body jolted involuntarily. Bile rose up before I swallowed it back down.

"No, Mom, I don't need to go to the cabin. I'm an adult; we don't need that anymore." A shiver latched on to my bones, and I shook for a second.

There was a shed-like hut in the back half of my parents' wooded property. It was small and made entirely of trees from our forest, using no nails or man-made substances—and it was used for only one thing. When I was particularly forgetful or made a bad decision about something, I had to go to the cabin to learn how to reconnect with nature. My dad did, too, occasionally and my sister as well, until she moved.

We sat alone in pitch black with nothing to do and no one to talk to. You could have small amounts of water, and she would bring you a small vegan dinner, usually just a can of beans or a bowl of rice, but that was the only thing you got to eat for the day. You weren't allowed to leave to go to the bathroom, as that was part of the lesson. As a small child, it had been horrifying, as an adult only slightly less. It had been a long time since I'd been in there—and I wasn't ever going to go back in if I could help it.

"What…type of soil have I been using…in the conservatory?" I asked, my brows pinching together almost painfully as I struggled to calculate the best responses—the ones that would keep me safe. Of all the things for her to demand to know…

"Yes, Eliza! What do you think I'm talking about? Sometimes, you can be so stupid for such an intelligent girl. You're using the kind with synthetic fertilizers, aren't you? You are, aren't you? If I get there and see that you're using peat moss, I will lose it, Eliza. I'm serious."

"I—I'm using good soil," I mumbled. Already, my anger had gone away to the familiar space to hide, and the appeasing, easy-to-manage Eliza had taken the reins, doing her best to navigate the conversation to a safe place. Hearing how she talked to me after not being around her the last month or so had felt different.

Her impact was worse, somehow, after not feeling it for a while.

"Peat bogs are sensitive ecosystems that provide unique habitats for wildlife. You know the extraction of peat destroys the habitats and disrupts biodiversity. Do you want that on your hands? I don't believe you; you've never cared about anything but yourself. Send me a picture of the bags—and you better be recycling those," she snapped in her tone that made me shrink to about an inch tall.

"Yeah, I know, Mom. You've told me," I said, hearing my soft voice as if I were listening to it outside my body.

I regretted answering the phone. I wished I weren't so

afraid of my balcony so that I could hurl it over the large stone railing and never see it again. "You don't need to come get me; I have my car. Everything is fine, and I still have a lot of work to do. Besides, it's not like I have an apartment to go home to now anyway." I flinched, immediately pinching my fists together, wishing I hadn't said my last words. My tongue was looser with the small taste of independence, something that would be hard and painful to tamp down later, I feared.

"You ought to be thanking me for that! Thank god you don't have anyone over at your house ever, and you're just poisoning yourself while you destroy all of your father's and my life's work. Palm oil, Eliza, fucking palm oil. Have you forgotten everything you learned from us? You told me your clothes were all sustainably sourced. That's a move I would expect from your lying sister, but not from you. Sometimes, I wish I'd never had either of you, knowing how you both are. I would be so much happier if I didn't have to spend my days following you around like you were a baby. For god's sake, Eliza, you are a grown woman. Act like it."

Warmth bloomed in my eyes, blurring them with tears.

Yeah, the words hit different parts of me after not having heard their harshness for a while. Somewhere over the course of my stay at Blackwood Manor, my numbness about life had faded. Enough so that I felt armorless and soft now. Her strikes hit harder, more painfully.

Something had to change. I couldn't do this anymore. It wasn't normal to treat people this way, especially not the ones you loved. I bristled even though warning bells sounded in my head.

"I'm not a baby. I'm a twenty-five-year-old woman. Why do you say stuff like that? That you wish you'd never had me? That really hurts, Mom." My voice cracked with the unfamiliarity of speaking up.

"Excuse me for being a terrible mother and caring about

you. God forbid I mention how much you hurt me, Eliza. I forgot I can't have any feelings. Everything is about you," she snapped.

"I gotta go, Mom," I said, struggling to keep myself still as my legs trembled. I needed her off the phone before she got really into her rants about how horrible I was. I wasn't equipped to handle it right now.

"I'm coming now to get you. You'll move back in with Dad and me where I can watch you. The three of us could use another trip to the Congo Basin. You need to remember what it is you're doing when you use palm oil and aluminum cans. A few days without anything will remind you how much you should thank Mother Earth," she muttered. I heard a car door close.

My eyes shut, little stars of dizzying glitter dancing on the backs of my eyelids. She couldn't come here. If she did, I would leave with her. "I'm not leaving, so please do not waste a trip coming up here." My voice trembled with anger and sadness.

She let out an abrasive laugh. "Who do you think you are? If I have to, I will come up there and tear you out of that house. I birthed you. You don't get to tell me no. That's not how this works."

I tucked in on myself. Growing up, that was the number-one rule for my sister and me. It had been drilled loudly into our heads from the moment we were born, above all else. It was the foundation upon which I lived and breathed. We were never, ever allowed to utter the word no to her.

I wanted to ask if she had talked to Lucy, but now was the worst imaginable time to bring up my rebellious sister, and it wasn't like they talked very often anyway. I wasn't missing anything by not asking.

"I have a dinner I need to go to. I'll talk to you later," I said with a trained voice that held nothing but polite respect.

"A dinner? With who? Blackwood? Oh, great, so you'll be murdered next, then?" she snarked.

My tongue refused to hold. She was just like everybody else that didn't really know him.

"Jasper didn't murder anybody. You don't even know what happened—" I tried to explain.

"Don't be such an idiot. I've been in this town longer than you've been alive. That man killed his mother, and his father was probably in on it with him. I've seen his interviews; I get it; he's handsome as the devil, but do you think Ted Bundy wasn't a charmer? How do you think they get their victims to trust them? Idiot girl."

"Bye, Mom, I need to go," I said and hung up to the sound of her yelling.

Tears pitter-pattered on the floor as I bent over, holding my head against the edge of the mattress. I don't know why I had tried to get free from her grip; it was impossible; the woman wouldn't stop. She was relentless.

With shaking hands, I tossed the dress on the bed and wiped my eyes as I instinctually moved for the locket on the dresser.

As silly as it was, especially now that she was so chaotic, Hester felt more like a mother to me than my own mom. Even in the moments that I feared her, I didn't think Hester would ever hurt me intentionally just because she wanted me to hurt. Even when she had, I knew she was trying to tell me something that I hadn't figured out yet. Maybe I was delusional or stupid, but I'd even started to find the lingering scent of Chanel No. 5 comforting in a weird way. Hester trusted me to help with her whole life—or death—and that meant something to me. I felt supported when she would linger in the conservatory or hallways with me. My mother didn't even trust me enough to make my own dinner choices.

I palmed the golden locket and prepared to open it, holding it away and bracing myself for whatever might fly out of it and bite me, though, to be honest, I would've welcomed it right then. I clicked it, and the warm gold fell open, showing my own tearstained face squinting back at me, a small mirror on the inside.

There was movement. A small inscription carved itself across the mirror in beautifully elaborate cursive.

Your worth is not held in her words.

I choked on a sob, snapped the locket shut, and slammed the oval pendant on the dresser; the chain slid over the top of my hand and onto the worn wood. It wasn't even a clue to help her; she'd used her energy just to be there for me. I couldn't take the kindness. Didn't deserve it.

Hester's thoughtful words cut through, pressing into my deepest vulnerabilities, cauterizing some of the wounds my own mother had just opened.

This was too much. Everything I'd been carrying began to topple down. All of the frustration, anger, and sadness I'd tamped down came flooding back, buzzing under my skin like a thousand bees waiting to sting. I was angrier than I'd ever been and had nowhere to channel it. My body trembled as the sound of my loud gasps clapped through the silence of the room. I was hyperventilating, and as angry as I was, I still couldn't seem to make the tears stop flowing from my dry, blurry eyes, which only made me angrier.

There was no way I could go to dinner with Jasper now, not like this.

Angrily, I dug through my plastic clothes basket on the floor until I found a white cotton tank top and a pair of shorts. I took off my bathrobe and put the pajamas on while disappointment curled around me. I had wanted to do dinner so bad, but now I couldn't. Everything flowed so easily with Jasper that I couldn't keep myself together around him, and right now, I was so full of barely restrained anger that I would probably end up crying the whole time.

I grabbed my phone and texted Jasper, apologizing and telling him something had come up.

Not even five minutes later, there was a loud knock on my door. I braced myself and realized I was waiting to hear my mother's voice. I stopped my angry pacing to run to the door and try and look through the crack. It wouldn't be her; she couldn't have made it that quickly, but I still panicked.

"Eliza, let me in. Are you okay? What happened?" Jasper called, banging loudly again. Each knock shook the walls, making the old paintings tremble as they hung.

I rolled my eyes. I didn't have the energy to pull myself together enough to deal with him. "I'm fine. I'll see you tomorrow." My voice was low and surprisingly a little threatening. I couldn't help it. Things were impossible to mask with him.

"What happened? Is it your mom?" he said more gently.

I rolled my eyes again and looked down at my outfit. You could see the pigment of my nipples through the fabric. It was so worn and dingy. I opened the door and poked my head out, keeping my body hidden behind it. I needed to get rid of him so I could curl up and cry.

"Nothing happened. I'm fine," I growled at him. Of course, he had on a fresh outfit with black dress pants and a crisp, dark hunter-green dress shirt that made his brown hair and eyes pop against his tanned skin. For some unknown reason, seeing him standing outside my door looking so fucking hot made me even more mad. I glared at him and moved to shove the door closed on him.

A surprised expression blanketed his face before he blocked it, easily pushing the door open and slipping through so fast that I slammed it closed behind him when I shoved at it again.

"You're not fine. What's going on?" His eyes darted over my body, looking for clues. When they found nothing, they returned to my eyes, chaotically dancing as he gathered information and tried to figure out what had happened.

"Sure, come right on in." I waved my hand dramatically.

"Not like I have a say in anything anyway," I snapped. I wasn't angry at him. "Aaagh!" I growled. "I'm sorry. I'm just angry and upset, and if you stay, I will take it out on you. I can't do dinner right now."

He appraised me for another silent minute, as though deciding if he should leave. He let out a sigh and straightened his posture.

"Want to shoot or stab something? I'll let you in the addition," he asked gently.

"No," I snapped. I couldn't believe I was turning down seeing the secret weapons lair, but honestly Katya saw it the other day and told me it was way more boring than what we'd thought—a room with weapons. Shocker.

"Okay," he said, taking a stiff seat on the edge of my bed.

"Okay, what?" I nearly yelled. Having him on my bed did not guide my lonely, upset brain to any smart distractions.

His eyes roamed over my body, snagging on my very visible nipples before landing on my eyes. "You can take it out on me. I'm ready. Give me your best shot—are we talking physical or mental?" he asked, standing back up and suavely removing his jacket before rolling up the cuffs of his shirtsleeves. His large arms rippled against the snug dress shirt with the movement.

I sat back on my heels and gawked, temporarily frozen. "You're going to let me hit you?"

"If it will make you feel better, though I'd rather you just talk to me and tell me what happened," he said.

"I'm not going to hit you; I'm so frustrated and hurt and angry, and damn it, Jasper, I don't want to get into all of this with you. You won't understand, no one ever understands, they think I'm being a sheltered baby," I shouted.

His jaw tightened. "Your mother. What's she done now, sold you off to make mulch for the environment? All right, all right," he said when I glared at him.

"I don't understand it. I don't know why I can't fucking

talk to her like I talk to you. Every time I try, I end up crying. Ugh!" I snarled and returned to pacing the room just to get the angry feeling out of my legs. "I'm so angry, I feel like I'm going to combust."

"Go on the balcony," he said as he walked over and began to push the small Victorian couch away from where it blocked the double doors.

What the fuck was he doing? "I'm not going on the balcony," I said, shaking my head and stepping backward.

"Afraid I'll push you over the ledge?" he asked sarcastically, but his careful words were unable to hide a hint of vulnerability.

Our eyes locked for a long minute. He actually wanted to know if I was afraid of him and that was his way of asking.

"No. I trust you," I said finally—a revelation to myself as well as him.

A thread of relief filled his eyes, and back was the overly confident bad boy. "Now, why would you do something that?" His voice was low and raspy. He slowly walked to me, stopping when he was right in front of me.

For another minute, we remained in the silence of my bedroom with locked eyes. It felt like the space around us should be crackling with fire.

"I don't know why I trust you, but I do," I snapped. "I think you're capable of horrible things—but I don't think you'd hurt me."

"Then come to the balcony with me. Let's face one of your fears together. Release some of that adrenaline. I promise I won't let anything happen to you, Eliza," he said, reaching out and gently covering my vibrating hand with his.

Was I actually thinking about this? It did seem oddly more appealing right now, in my anger. "Okay," I said apprehensively, waiting for him to guide me to the doors.

When he remained still, I looked up at him in silent question.

"Don't look at me. This is your move. You're the one in control of this," he said in a cocky tone but with reassuring eyes.

He squeezed my hand, and for a quarter of a second, it felt like I could do anything, and he would be there to catch me.

Emboldened, I took a few short steps toward the balcony door before my confidence wavered, and my knees began to shake. I whirled back around, trying to drop his hand, but he refused to let go.

"I can't. You don't understand," I stammered, hating how whiny I sounded. My fear gripped my nerves, reminding me that just because I was upset didn't mean I'd grown wings and was suddenly unafraid.

"You can. *You're* the one who doesn't understand, Eliza. Take your time; I'm in no rush."

He took a step closer to me and put his hands on my waist, spinning me around until the balcony doors were right in front of my face. I pinched my eyes closed and grabbed his hands as they remained a firm, steady presence on my waist.

Why was I even thinking about this? This wasn't going to do anything but give me a heart attack. I *knew* if I went out onto that balcony, I would fall off it. I could feel it. I wasn't going to be an idiot and poke fate like that.

"Jasper, I'm not kidding; I can't even open my eyes right now; I'm going to puke." I panicked, realizing who I was talking to. He wasn't afraid of anything. He was seriously going to push for me to do this because, to him, it was stupid, not a valid fear. He didn't know that if I went out there, fate had already deemed I would fall.

His low, breathy voice was suddenly at the back of my neck and ear. "You're not going to puke," he whispered slowly. "We can stay right here like this all night. Open your eyes when you're ready."

My fear was momentarily hidden by the tingle in my lower

abdomen at the sensation of his body pressed behind me, and his whisper lingered on my skin.

"Jasper…" I whispered in a plea.

I felt a low, pleased sound reverberate from his chest. Had I pushed back on him, or had he pushed closer to me?

My eyes opened, and I tried to recoil. Through the glass of the door, there was nothing but sky and tiny specks of houses clustered together far, far below. I had never seen anything from this high up.

With the comforting pressure of Jaspers's protective body at my back and the surge of frustrated adrenaline still coursing through my system, I felt braver than I ever had.

So much was out of my control that I was suddenly overcome with the need not to be afraid of something so passive and trivial as the height of a balcony or a ledge.

But as badly as I wanted to do it, and as much as I trusted Jasper, I *was* afraid.

My shaky hand wiped off the stream of tears still on my cheek and found the gold door handle. I tried to push it down, but my arm was shaking too much to move it.

"You're shaking like a leaf," he whispered into the crook of my neck, the sensation causing my eyes to fall shut again.

His hand left my waist to brush back a rogue piece of hair on the side of my neck. The feel of his fingertips grazing my skin and my heightened senses felt almost euphoric, and I found myself breathing heavily for a multitude of reasons.

"Take your time. The view will be there for you whenever you are ready. We can stay like this forever."

We stayed that way for a while. I was almost able to enjoy the protected view behind the glass with the closeness of Jasper at my back, pressing against me, reminding me he was there.

When the feeling began to dull and thoughts of my mother returned, I suddenly wanted more. I needed to tune her out.

I turned the handle of the door and pulled it open.

A tidal wave of fear doused my momentary bravery as the cool November breeze pushed into the room, moving my hair back from my face and onto Jasper's chest.

It was too much. I spun back to move away, but Jasper's large, muscular body blocked me. I curled into his chest, too afraid to do much else.

A few seconds later, his hands gripped my chin, moving my face up to look at him. "You don't need me, your mother, or anyone, Eliza. You are the one who calls the shots, always. You are stronger than you know, and you can do *anything*. Think of the view. It will be worth it."

"I've always wanted to paint something like this, to cast it in permanence so that I could look at it whenever I wanted in the comforts of my home and not be afraid." I huffed a laugh into his chest. "Except I realized you have to look at it to paint it, and it's impossible to paint with trembling hands." The nervous, rambling words fell flat when I looked up again into his eyes.

He looked at me as if I truly could do anything in the whole world, and for a few moments, while my eyes remained attached to his, I believed him.

My fingertips found the back of his neck. I couldn't look anywhere but at his lips. I couldn't think about anything else. The need to feel them against mine was suddenly overwhelming. His head lowered slowly but stopped just shy of my lips.

It was my move. It was his way of reminding me that I was in control.

I forced myself to move slowly so I could savor every moment as my lips found his and pressed against them delicately.

As soon as our lips touched, it was as if the world began to fall away. A flame had been lit from the sparks of our tension, and now my body was going to incinerate with the heat of it.

He was restrained, and I could feel it—he was kissing me back but keeping himself on a leash, letting me guide it. For a few minutes, it was sweet and gentle, as if we were telling each other tales with our lips, but soon, I craved more. My needy hands moved over his chest, feeling the ridges and hardness that lay underneath his shirt. It was like gasoline had been poured on the flame.

I gripped the collar of his shirt, pulling him closer, demanding more, but he was already as close as he could get.

"Slow down, love," he whispered into my mouth before spinning me around while holding me as tightly against the front of him as he could. He kissed the side of my neck, sending goose bumps across my skin. My body lit up with sensations, sliding from my back down to my thighs. I could feel him everywhere.

I gasped when my eyes opened.

At some point, we had moved completely out onto the balcony. The thick stone rail was only a foot or two in front of me.

My shock and fear were tempered with lust as Jasper kissed and sucked on my neck. The wind bit at my skin, but I didn't care—not with him this close.

"You're in complete control," he said against my neck.

With chaos in my veins and adrenaline to burn, I stared out at the most beautiful sight I'd ever seen. It felt as if I were sitting on a cloud, looking out on the world.

Excitement swirled with danger, and I wanted even more. I reached behind and ran my hand faintly over the bulge in Jasper's pants. God, he was so hard. He let out a low moan that served as gasoline to my already blazing wildfire. I leaned back against him, feeling myself throb almost painfully between my legs as I gripped his stiffness. His restraint was cracking.

He pushed against me, his hand on my waist moved to my thigh, sliding up until his achingly slow fingertips found the gap between the loose fabric of my shorts. His other palm slid up to brush against my breast. A soft moan pushed past my lips, and I wriggled against him, pleading for more of his touch. His hand left my nipple and moved up to lightly grab a handful of my hair and guide my head to the side so that he could kiss me firmly on the mouth. Our lips met in a feral, hungry kiss, and I was gone. I had fallen from the edge in an entirely metaphorical way that I hadn't expected.

Everything felt *so* good. I couldn't remember the last thing that I did that felt so good. So right. I wanted to forget everything else but Jasper. This moment.

I tried to turn back to face him, but he kept my body facing out toward the emptiness and the fog. I ground my backside against his erection. He grabbed my hands and gently placed them wide on the balcony in front of me.

"Are you okay?" His whisper tickled the shell of my ear. His large, wide-spread hand on the right side of my waist slid across the gap of skin on my stomach and under my waistband as his other hand sprawled across my stomach to brace me, his fingertips moving over the sheer fabric of my underwear and sliding under the fabric of those too. The feel of him touching my most throbbing parts nearly buckled my knees, but I gripped the stone railing, looking out at the sky as if I were a bird with wings.

Loud breaths huffed out of me. "Yes, yes."

His hand slid lower, gliding over me. "God, Eliza," he said breathily as his movements became faster.

He removed his hand and slowly ran it up my side, grabbing the fabric of my shirt and pulling it over my head. Crisp air teased my skin, tightening my nipples. He caught the sides of my shorts and panties in his fingers on each side and ever so slowly slid them down to the ground, moving his hands over my skin as I stepped out of them. I was completely naked and exposed on a balcony of Blackwood Manor, staring out at the sky with Jasper at my back.

My hand felt behind me until it found his hardness again. I began to undo his belt but struggled with it at that angle. His hand stilled mine just before it gave up and moved.

"Tell me to stop," he said.

I didn't.

"You don't want this," he breathed. "You think I'm going to be gentle with you?" he asked, voice low.

I heard the jingle of his belt being removed, the whisper of clothing being removed. His hand slid over me again. Needing to touch and see him and not the view, I struggled to turn, but again, he kept me facing the sky.

Clumsily, I reached behind and let out a low sound as I grabbed his warm, bare cock in my hand. Drunk on adrenaline, I asked for more. "Please, Jasper."

Eagerly, his fingers slid into me as I stroked his length behind my back. A shudder of pleasure rippled through my body as his fingers rhythmically slid in and out of me, causing tingles of pleasure to ripple through my body. I was partially bent over the railing; his fingers brushed against my clit, causing me to tremble as I climbed closer and closer to the edge of an orgasm, every touch taking me higher.

"Tell me to stop," he whispered again. I twisted my body around to face him. My eyes took in the sight of his broad shoulders and naked body by the darkening light of the sunset, and all I could do was stare as my hands found his ridged stomach. Then chest. Then his pounding cock.

"Do you trust me?" he asked. I could tell he was holding back. There was a menacing edge of danger to his voice that I hadn't heard before, and it terrified and enticed me at the same time.

I nodded and pulled him down to kiss me. He resisted and pulled back.

"Eliza, do you trust me?" His expression looked almost angry, he was so serious. "I need to hear you say it."

"I trust you, Jasper," I said, pulling him into a kiss, which he finally allowed.

It was as if dynamite had been set off between us. Jasper was not the type of man to easily give up control, but he had. For me. It felt good to give it back. He wasn't the one I needed to take control from anyway.

His restraint snapped. His hands gripped my thighs, lifting me up like I weighed nothing as he sat me down on the cold stone railing. His mouth took mine in a heated, impatient, passionate kiss that bordered on aggression. He *had* been holding back and had been let off his leash.

My arms tightened around his neck. My chest was flush with his. That's when I realized I was teetering on the stone ledge of the balcony's railing with my upper body hanging over nothing but air.

I screamed, clawing to hold on to him. "Jasper! What are you doing? You're going to drop me!"

"Do you trust me?" he repeated.

He moved my hands from his shoulders and placed them around his neck, kissing me and distracting me with his tongue. My nails dug into his skin, completely terrified. My feet were nearly bent in half from trying to hold on to his waist and not fall off the railing to my death. My eyes were wide with terror as they caught ahold of his coldly confident gaze. He leaned down and planted a soft, tender kiss on my mouth; both our eyes remained open, locked on the other's.

A confusing mix of lust and fear took over my system. My mouth opened, and my eyes softened. It was reckless and wild, but I wanted him more than I wanted not to fall.

"Hold on."

"Jasper—"

"No." His mouth brushed my ear. "You don't talk now. You take it."

He pushed me back just enough to tilt me, my spine pressed against the wall, my legs wide around him. Fear and excitement tore through me.

"You'd cry," he whispered, dragging himself against my

heat. "And I'd kiss you harder just to taste what I did to you."

I gasped, accidentally leaning back too far and needing to grab Jasper to stabilize myself. He caught my jaw in one hand, not rough—but firm. Direct.

"If I touch you now, I won't stop until I've fucked you slow enough to make you beg for mercy."

His thumb dragged across my lower lip. I opened for him automatically. He smiled—barely. My hips moved toward him.

"You'd beg me to be gentle," he said, voice flat. "And I'd lie. Tell you I would." He paused. "Then I'd show you what I really mean by slow."

I reached for him and pulled him closer.

That was all it took.

He pulled himself free with a menacing look. Fear-laced anticipation tickled all over my skin.

He shoved himself into me in one smooth, devastating thrust, like his body had been waiting, aching for the permission I had finally given.

My eyes fell closed as the sensations overtook me, not because of the view or because I was only a breath away from dropping to my death, but the cold of the railing, the freeing breeze that danced across my skin, and the feel of his hard cock entering me. I dug my fingernails farther into his skin, needing him, and carefully pushed my body toward his, reveling in the feel as my body adjusted fully around him.

It felt like the clouds had parted and everything was right in the world. This feeling of closeness to him was what I'd been craving every time the tension between us cracked.

I gasped when he thrust into me again—harder this time, deeper. My head fell back, lips parted, and breath gone.

"That's it," he said, voice low, dangerous. "Let me hear it."

I whimpered. He leaned in close, his mouth grazing my jaw.

"No, Eliza. Not that sound." Another thrust. Controlled. Brutal. "I want the one you make when you forget your own name."

"Jasper..." I moaned against his ear as I held him tighter. I tried to grab something but there was nothing. No edge. No wall. No thought. Just him.

"You'll cry so sweet," he murmured. "I'll keep you right here—legs wide, voice shaking—and I'll fuck you through every second of it."

I bit his lip. "Jasper—"

"You don't need to speak," he growled. "Just keep taking it."

My body jolted as he shifted his angle. His hand slid up my stomach, slow and possessive.

"You feel that?" he whispered. "That's me." He pressed his palm flat beneath my ribs. "I'm so deep in you right now, your heartbeat's trying to sync to mine."

I broke. Soft and high, the sound ripped out of my throat like a prayer and a surrender.

"There you are," he said, breath hot against my neck. "That's what I wanted."

I was trembling. Completely wrecked, gone.

"Fuck, Eliza," he moaned, and his chest rumbled. He leaned back as he slid his cock all the way back inside of me until he lifted me up slightly, then pulled halfway out, repeating the action.

We were both open mouthed and panting as we clung desperately to one another.

The cold stone bit into my ass as our pace grew frantic, my moans growing louder the more pleasure my body felt.

"You'll still feel me tomorrow," he whispered. "Between your legs. In your bones. In your fucking spine."

"Jasper...oh, god, Jasper."

"And you'll want it again," he said, slow and cruel and tender. "You'll hate how much." Another thrust.

My back hit the stone again. I gasped, eyes wide, lips parted, completely lost in the sensation of him. Of this. Of the way he refused to let me drift anywhere but under him.

"You think I'm done?" Jasper growled.

"I—no—" I choked out.

"Good."

His hand came to my throat—not squeezing, just resting. Claiming. I knew he could feel my pulse flutter beneath his fingers when he smiled.

"You're not even close."

He dragged himself out slowly, then slammed back in, hard enough to steal my breath. Again. And again. Until my legs trembled and my hips tilted toward him, desperate.

"Look at you," he said. "Fucking begging without a word."

I whimpered and clung to his arms for fear they wouldn't hold me and I would fall.

He kissed me, opened mouthed, hungry, mean. He bit my lower lip, pulled and kissed me again like he hated how good I tasted.

"I'd keep you up here all night," he muttered. "Use you until you forget what it feels like to be empty."

I moaned—sharp and aching.

"You'd cry," he whispered, his lips dragging down my neck. "And I'd fuck you harder—just to see how long you could take it."

Another thrust. My head dropped back. His hand caught it, held me steady.

"You want me to stop?"

I shook my head because I couldn't speak.

"Didn't think so." He brought his hand between us. His fingers slid down, filthy and firm.

I jolted, cried out.

"That's it," he said. "Fall apart for me."

My whole body tightened.

"Right here. Right now. Around me."

He didn't stop. Not when I broke. Not when I gasped his name like it was the only breath that would keep me alive. Not when I went boneless in his arms.

"There's my girl," he breathed. "So fucking sweet when you're ruined." And still he didn't pull out. "One more."

"Jasper—"

"One more," he growled. "You're still mine. You're still open."

"I—I can't—"

"Yes," he whispered. "You can. And you will."

He pulled me tighter, voice thick now. Low and feral in my ear.

"Because I haven't come yet, and I'm not pulling out until I've finished what I fucking started."

I was already coming undone again. My body clenched around him like it didn't want to let go.

"That's it," Jasper groaned, voice low and frayed. "God, you feel so good like this—shaking, soaked, fucking mine."

My nails dug into his back. He thrust harder, deeper—chasing his own undoing now and dragging me down with him.

"You're not done," he whispered. "Not until I say."

"Jasper—please—"

"One more," he breathed. "You can take it. Let me finish inside you. Let me make a mess of you."

Euphoria filled me, and I cried out as he grabbed my hip tighter, holding me still as he drove in to the hilt, once—twice—

"You're gonna feel this for days," he growled, lips at my throat. "Open for me. Let me fucking fill you."

My body jerked. Pleasure like I'd never known took over every part of my body .

"That's it," he hissed. "I'm gonna come inside you. Gonna fuck it into you."

And then he did—deep and hot, hips grinding into mine, breathing staggered and rough as he stayed there, buried.

"Don't move," he rasped. "Not done."

I whimpered as he came. I felt the warmth bloom inside of

me as his thrusts slowed.

He pulled out slowly, a thick, warm smear of slick between my thighs.

"Still mine," he said, catching me by the throat in a light but commanding grip. "Turn around. Grab ahold of the railing and look at what you've been so afraid of," he said.

A cry of pleasure came out of my throat as I gripped the railing and peered out with fear and excitement at the massive drop below.

"Still with me?" Jasper rasped into my ear.

I nodded, barely able to hold myself up.

"Good. Because I'm not fucking finished. Bend over more," he said. "Now."

I eagerly obeyed, breath ragged.

"You feel used?" he murmured, dragging his hand between my legs. "You should. That wasn't for you. That was for me."

I let out a moan, still wrecked and clenching around nothing as I stole a glance over my shoulder at the gorgeous man. A gasp flew from me when he gripped my ass, spreading me with one hand, the other stroking himself, still hard and twitching.

Without warning, he pressed against my back entrance—just the tip, slicked from my orgasms. I stiffened.

"You can take it," he murmured. "You want it. You want me to own every part of you."

I moaned. He was right, I'd always wanted to try this but had been too afraid.

He didn't wait. "Breathe," he said, and pushed in—slow and forceful.

I cried out as he groaned.

"Fuck—that's it," he hissed. "Tight little hole, and you gave it to me without a word."

Pleasure throbbed through every part of me until it felt like I was floating.

He pushed deeper, both hands gripping my hips now,

filling me until I was sobbing his name.

"Gonna finish like this," he rasped. "Buried in your ass while your pussy's still leaking from the last time I came inside you."

I was falling apart, held up only by his hands and body.

"You're mine," he growled. "Say it."

"I'm yours," I sobbed.

"Louder."

"I'm yours—fuck—please—"

He drove in deep, held me there, and came with a brutal, guttural sound, filling me until it spilled out around him, his grip bruising my hips as he thrust through the high.

"There," he groaned. "Now you're ruined in every way that matters."

He pulled himself out of me and smiled as he scooped me up, carrying me inside and laying me on the bed. I wondered if he would leave but felt him crawling in next to me.

The quiet room filled with the sounds of our slowing pants as he tucked his arm around me, and I nestled into his chest and began to drift off to sleep.

"Sleep well...*friend*," he teased as he pulled me closer.

My laugh was muffled against his body as I draped my arm over his stomach and drifted off to sleep.

CHAPTER 21
ELIZA

I AWOKE TO AN ODD FEELING IN THE LATE HOURS OF THE NIGHT while lying next to Jasper. The pale cast of moonlight lay in streams across the room, illuminating his still, handsome face as he slept next to me. Something moved just at the edge of my vision, and my head snapped to see Hester looming at the foot of the bed.

Startled, I slapped my palm over my mouth to stifle my loud gasp as I moved to sit up without waking Jasper.

Hester's round, glistening eyes were filled with something different as they gazed upon her sleeping son.

Fuck. Was she going to be mad? Would she feel betrayed? How could she not? She had trusted me to help her, and I had just slept with her possible murderer. My body hummed, suddenly filled with nervous energy.

"I—"

She cut off my whisper and pressed her pointer finger against her gray, see-through lips, instructing me to be quiet while keeping her eyes on the sleeping man lying next to me.

I sat frozen.

Eventually, her dark, glittering eyes left her son and moved to me before she did the most puzzling thing I'd seen from her yet.

Hester's mouth curved upward a little—she was smiling. I noticed that her coloring brightened the slightest bit, making her not quite as translucent.

Jasper rustled next to me but remained asleep.

When I turned back to Hester, she was gone.

What had just happened? The blood in my veins thrummed. Had she watched us? Oh god, hopefully not. Was she—was she happy that Jasper and I had slept together? Was I missing something? She had looked pleased.

I glanced at the dresser. The locket was still there, and upon seeing it, an odd thought popped into my mind—when the dove had flown from the necklace in the kitchen, it had brought Jasper and me closer. I thought about the spider that led me to the chest of letters, proving he was telling me the truth, then the rose that had made my lip swollen and how much extra attention Jasper had given me that day—even the time she'd thrown the chair and I'd screamed, Jasper had rushed into the room and held me protectively.

Was...was Hester...trying to set me up with her son?

No. There was no way.

She was helping me figure out who had murdered her, not playing wingman for her son, suspect number one.

Still, I couldn't ignore the coincidences and the way she had looked at me tonight. Almost in appreciation. It was the only time I'd seen her look somewhat peaceful.

I turned my attention to Jasper, but my heart wouldn't stop racing.

At first, I reveled in the satiated relaxation that my body felt as I watched him sleep. Even though everything had felt amazing, it was also foreign and unusual. I shouldn't have slept with him even though it had been wholly unavoidable. The chemistry between us had grown so tense that I found myself sweating every time he was near. I had wanted—needed—to feel what it was like when Jasper kissed me. Once he had, I knew I was lost, that I wouldn't be content again until I felt everything that he could give me. He had ruined me, but I think it had happened long before last night. As I lay beside him, still as a stone in fear of waking him, the side of my thigh rested against his, and it was like it had gone home, found the other half of its magnet.

But as with all good things that happen to me, my overanxious mind refused to let me enjoy them.

Maybe it was the comedown of the adrenaline leaving my body or the fact that in the matter of one night, it had become much harder to play make-believe and continue to pretend this was my life. It wasn't my life. None of this was real. Even if the ghost of his dead mother wanted it, it was still too much.

The conversation with my mother replayed over and over in my head. Little segments of past moments leaked in, breaking apart any remaining illusions. As always, I analyzed them, figuring out what words or inflections I'd used that upset her and how I could have avoided making her say the harsh words that she'd fired off like careless missiles.

Deep down, I knew it didn't matter what I did or said; nothing would change how she treated me; even my father, who generally found it easier just to avoid me, got his share of harsh words from my mother. I didn't want that. I didn't ever want to be in a relationship like that.

I watched the smooth, tanned skin of Jasper's chest rise and fall steadily before looking at the balcony. Looking at where I'd come completely undone—given over every part of me to him—made me aware of the pleasant soreness I felt. My eyes focused on the still-dark sky. Could I walk out there right now if I wanted to? Or had it only been last night because of Jasper?

I could. I wouldn't have said the same for the unfenced edge of the cliff behind the conservatory, but as for the balcony…I could—I almost wanted to now, just see if I could by myself. All alone.

I couldn't remember a time that I wasn't deathly afraid of heights; even ladders had always been too much for me, but last night...I had reveled in the feeling of being as high as the birds in the sky. Knowing I could have tipped over the edge at any second and was only held up by a man who had been accused of throwing someone *over* it was...surprisingly freeing. The view was more amazing than anything I could have imagined. It sparked this near-obsessive urge inside of me to preserve it, to paint it or photograph it as an homage to its glory. When Jasper had me on the railing, I felt like I could take over the world—I felt unstoppable. Even after we had laid in bed, my exhausted thoughts filled with excitement at the stupid idea of painting that exact view while I was here. High above the rest of the world in Blackwood Manor, it was easy to forget that this wasn't really my life, no matter how badly I wished that it were.

I had to leave at some point and return to my other life. The world where I wasn't *daring, spoke her mind, and shared her feelings* Eliza, I was just...Eliza. *Capable of making herself small and adjusting* Eliza. Even if I didn't want to be that person anymore, that's just how it had to be.

I was twenty-five years old, far from a child, and yet most children didn't have the restrictions that I did.

I knew what I should have done: leave. I'd thought about it a million times, but it wasn't that simple. I was terrified. What if I couldn't make it on my own? I wasn't as resilient as my sister. I didn't have the funds to up and leave, and everything I had was linked to my mother. I paid for it all, but my cell phone, car, insurance, and everything else of mine was in her name. Always under the ruse of her being helpful, but in the end, they were all just tools for her to control me. She had shut my phone off and reported my car, which I had paid for, as stolen before when I hadn't done something she wanted.

I made fifty thousand a year at the botanical gardens, and what little I had left after living essentials went to paying off my student loans. I didn't have enough to buy a new car and phone and run away to another state or country. It was just another way my mother had trapped me without me realizing it. I felt so stupid. I was to blame for being trapped like this. I was weak and stupid and gullible, and that was why it had happened to me. I couldn't keep letting it happen.

Facing my fears last night—not just the balcony but being intimate with someone and letting them in—made me realize that even when I went back to my real world, I wanted a change. I couldn't go back to being controlled. I wanted to be free and to make my own decisions. I just had to figure out how.

I didn't know what it would look like or how to do it, but I was going to be my own person. Facing my fears and seeing the view from the balcony had proven that things could change. I would *never* again give a single person the power to control me. Ever. Not my mother, not Jasper, not anybody. I wouldn't go from one leash to another, not now. I couldn't—I wouldn't let myself. It didn't matter how pretty the leash was, it was still a leash.

When he held me over the ledge and slid himself into me, I had fully given every part of myself up and trusted him with my life. It felt dangerous and exciting. Already, I'd begun to want things from him that I shouldn't—that I *couldn't*.

My heart sank at the realization.

I had to leave in a few weeks. Was I so willing to give someone else all the control I was fighting tooth and nail to get myself? Did I actually want a relationship? I didn't know.

Of course, I didn't think Jasper would *intentionally* try to control or manipulate me; I knew he was a better person than that…or at least I believed so. But I also knew that somewhere along the line, my mother had found it a delectable treat destroying me, and once she got a taste, her appetite for hurting and controlling me had only increased with time. The same thing would happen if I let another person in…and already, I found myself trying to give everything up to Jasper so he could devour me in every way.

I couldn't.

I wouldn't.

My mouth was sour with the realization of what was happening.

Here, I had been frustrated with Jasper and his fight against lowering his walls and letting me in when, in truth, I was the one who couldn't let anyone in.

I moved to the edge of the bed and watched the sleeping man with wide eyes. I was nearly in a panic.

I was getting too close to Jasper, giving him the tools he could use to control and hurt me.

For god's sake, I didn't even really know yet if he had anything to do with the murder of his mother. Just because he hadn't pushed her off the cliff years ago didn't mean he had nothing to do with the fact that she was now only here as a ghost. What if he had? Would it make a difference? I could be serving myself up on a platter to another narcissist right now. What the fuck was I doing? My heart pounded so fast, there was no way he couldn't hear it. Panic was about to set in; I could feel my face going numb.

Jasper stirred, adjusting positions, and my heart flew into my throat.

Why did I have to go and ruin everything? I had initiated the intimacy last night—I had touched him first. Now, the fun banter and sparks would be replaced with awkwardness and uncomfortable tension.

My hand flew to my mouth to stifle a cry. What if my coworkers found out? What would my boss say if he found out I had sex with Jasper?

My mother's voice rang in my head: *He only hired you because he wants to fuck you.*

Did they all think that?

It made sense. I wasn't qualified enough for that to have swayed him, and the men from the horticultural society had already been denied almost yearly.

What was I doing? I couldn't be in a relationship. Not that I had any notion that he even wanted something more than a fuck buddy. All I knew was that I had let him get too close.

I was spiraling.

The room felt like it was a thousand degrees. Would he want to keep things between us going while I was here? Or would he start to lean into it, knowing that I felt it stronger than he did? Would he use that to manipulate me? It would work. He had touched me in the exact forceful way I have always craved. He felt my fear and excitement and had leaned into it. For weeks, he'd studied me—quietly, obsessively, the way a composer studies a melody. When he touched me, it was deliberate. Precise. He played me like a cello: low, haunting, reverent in his cruelty. Every stroke summoned my soul and its vulnerability. Jasper didn't let anyone inside his walls; he'd told me as much, and yet here I was, being so stupid to believe that me—stupid, quiet, awkward, mousy me—just happened to be so appealing that I was the one to get through and have something special with him.

I was *so* stupid. Why would he want me for anything other than a quick fuck? He was a charming, fun, hot, millionaire playboy. I had practically hurled myself at him; what else was he going to do? It didn't mean he had feelings for me, and even if he did, I couldn't risk having anyone get that close to me. What if he was really controlling? He definitely controlled a lot of things in his life. Why would I do that to myself? I would get trapped. Fuck, if I thought I was financially imprisoned with my mom, I couldn't imagine what sort of titanium cage

Jasper and his millions could build. I could never get away and escape. I was still trying to figure out how to get out of my broke mother's grasp.

I was going to have a panic attack. Was I already?

I grabbed a wad of clothes as quickly as my hands would allow and silently left the room.

I would be the only one in control of me from this day forward.

I just had to figure out what I was going to do to make sure my mother knew that too.

Hours later, after I had changed in a bathroom downstairs and was using my panicked energy to break up the soil of the long flower bed along the back end of the conservatory, I heard the doors open.

"Hey," Jasper said as he walked in. His eyes locked on me with force. I could feel him trying to decipher what was going on in my head after last night with that gaze. "You weren't there when I woke up. Everything okay?"

"Huh? Oh. Yep, everything's fine." I should've left it at that, but when our eyes locked and he looked so masculine and cozy, I suddenly wanted to run over to him and wrap every part of me around him in a hug. *No!* My walls came up, and the firing squad took aim. "You told me I could keep working in here, so I am." I let out a forced, light chuckle. "My life doesn't stop just because we fucked, Jasper." *Fuck*, this was so much worse than I had been imagining how it would go.

His body seemed to tense with my words. "Eliza, what's going—"

I threw my cultivator down and stood up, turning to face him. "Nothing's going on; we got carried away last night, and things got out of hand. That's all that it was." I returned to digging.

He stepped over the stone border and into the dirt.

I wanted to cry. He was going to make this impossible. I wasn't cut out to be mean or to lie, especially not to him. I simply wasn't, no matter how much my self-preservation required it. I could hide, but being so visible was torture.

He grabbed the sides of my arms, forcing me to stop and look up at him.

"That's not all it was," he said softly. "Not to me."

Shit.

His eyes probed me, and I knew I didn't have a chance of being dishonest with him; it was impossible. Whether it was a good thing or not, we still had a connection that should have baffled science.

I pushed his arms off me. If I felt him touch me for one more second, I would lose all of my resolve and turn into a crying heap in his arms. I had already embarrassed myself enough.

My voice was weaker now. "We shouldn't have done that. I'm leaving in a few weeks. I—I—" I turned to face him, unable to stop myself. "Last night was amazing for so many reasons. You really did help me face my fears, and that showed me that I can do things that scare me, like setting boundaries for myself, not letting people walk all over me."

He grabbed my hand firmly before I tried to turn away from him again. "Those all sound like good things, but what else is going on? Why are you so upset?"

"We—I shouldn't have been so careless. You're technically my employer; what if this gets around? My reputation will be ruined," I grumbled.

His hand dropped, and a coldness took over the brown that had temporarily warmed in his eyes. "Because you are in a relationship with me?" His jaw flexed. "Wouldn't want an association with me to ruin your sweet reputation," he said in a low voice before calmly turning to leave.

"We aren't in a relationship. It was a one-time thing," I snapped.

"It's not a one-time thing if I say it's not, Eliza. I don't know what's happening with you right now. Things were good between us last night—very good. Why are you doing this?" I could feel the vulnerability in his voice turning to venom, and it killed me.

He had finally let me in, and now I was the one who couldn't do it. He had warned me. All this time, he had talked about not wanting to hurt me, and only just now, when I realized how strong I felt, did it truly sink in.

He could hurt me, but worse, I would hurt him. I couldn't be in a relationship. I just couldn't do it, not with him or anyone. This was exactly why I didn't have real friends.

I was a mess. My head was everywhere, with little to none of it making sense. The only thing I knew was that I didn't want to get hurt, and I really, really didn't want to hurt Jasper.

That's the thing about having emotional trauma: It doesn't give you a warning or a signal that it's going to affect you in a way that will spin your world upside down; it just hits you when you want it to the least.

I turned my back to him and faced the flower bed, closing my eyes as I struggled to lie.

"I'm only here for a few more weeks, and we are just friends. It was a friends-with-benefits, fuck-buddies situation. That's all that happened…" I was desperately trying to convince him that I felt nothing and that everything that had happened was nonsense, but I was failing miserably. When I was met with silence, I couldn't help it: I turned to look at his face, needing to see the expression on it, to see if he was buying it. "You were right to have gone to New York." I huffed out an exasperated laugh. "It's just not a good idea. I don't want to hurt you, and I don't want to get hurt."

He took a few steps toward me, barely veiled concern pulling his dark brows together. "I'll only hurt you in ways that bring you pleasure, Eliza. You're safe with me. I wouldn't have let anything happen between us if I felt otherwise."

Unable to stop, I began to pace around the conservatory. Another cynical laugh rose up out of me, no doubt making me look like some sort of a cartoon villain. "You don't know that! You can't possibly guarantee that you won't hurt me; I'm easy to hurt. No matter how much I like you, I can't let myself do this. Jasper, for Christ's sake, I was locked in a room for six days once because I refused to eat cauliflower. That's coming from the woman who birthed me—who is supposed to be the one person in the entire world who would keep me safe. You and I can't be anything more than friends." I had to stop, feeling my lip tremble. "If my own mother could hurt me so easily, why wouldn't you? I'm sorry; I know I'm being a little chaotic, but I'm freaking out. I don't think I'm capable of anything more than what we are right now." I stopped back in front of him and tried to catch my breath.

Jasper made a move to grab me, and for one quick second, my arms wrapped around him before pulling back. I craved his closeness—it brought me comfort, even if it wasn't smart. My stupid brain deceived me, told me he was big and strong and powerful and could protect me, but he couldn't if he was who I needed protection from.

"Stop, we can't do this."

"Your mother deserves to have a rope wrapped around her throat, Eliza," he growled out.

My body stilled in horror.

Hester always grabbed her throat. Always. Was that what he had done to his mother?

No. There was no way.

Sensing my sudden tension, he let me go. "I wouldn't hurt you. I care about you."

I shook my head. "Staying friends is better. Right now, the last thing either one of us needs is more stress."

He let out a long, frustrated sigh and turned around, looking like he wanted to punch something. For a few moments, the only sound in the conservatory was the rustling of plants and the soft wind scratching on the windows.

"Fine," he said in an oddly light tone. He stepped back onto the path and turned to me with a challenging expression I had grown to know far too well.

Something was off. I was completely baffled at how he could be taking this news so well—I certainly wasn't. I stared at him in shock. Had he genuinely gotten over me that quickly? It had been three minutes.

"Fine." I repeated after him, still not understanding how he could be so nonchalant suddenly.

His handsome face didn't show a thread of sadness and instead was cloaked in dark mischief. "Fine. I'll see you tonight."

"What?" I asked, confused and flabbergasted.

"Dinner tonight. Friends have dinner together—or so I hear." The corner of his mouth lifted slightly as if he couldn't keep it down.

"Yes, friends can have dinner, but were you not listening to anything I just said?" I mumbled, feeling completely frustrated.

"Oh, absolutely. Every word. Especially the parts where you said we were friends with benefits." His brown eyes glittered wildly. Dangerously. "I'm not sure if you've noticed, but I'm not the type of man that gets pushed around and manipulated. I get what I want, Eliza, and I want you. If friends with benefits is all you can offer me right now, then I'm going to take it." He winked. "Or should I say you'll be taking it."

My mouth fell open. "That's not—" I began, seeing exactly what he was doing.

"I'll see you tonight for dinner." He turned and walked to the door before turning back around. "Oh…and, *friend*? Wear something lacy I can tear off you. Plan on it being unwearable after tonight."

By the time I picked my mouth up off the floor, he was gone.

He was serious. He really wasn't going to dismiss the idea of us that easily. I hated to admit it, but deep, deep down, I was glad he wasn't ready to give up just because I was panicking. For some reason, it reassured the sick, fucked-up part of my mind that worried I was just a quick fuck to him. It made me feel wanted and special—things I never felt.

My steps stuttered as I spun back to the flower bed, trying to reconnect the wires that had blown in my brain and remember what I was supposed to do now.

A breath pushed from my chest as I tried to stifle a laugh. Even amid my frantic meltdown, he still managed to somehow make everything feel better. Everything was better when he was around, and that's what was so scary.

I grinned. If he thought for a second that I was going to be the one to back down from the friends-with-benefits ruse, he had another thing coming. He knew just as well as I did that he and I couldn't be friends with benefits. We were just prolonging the inevitable. He was doing this so I would admit that I felt more for him than…friendly. So I'd say it out loud instead—we both knew I felt more for him; he wasn't stupid. Still, more than that, I was set on my decision to keep my independence, and I couldn't do that if I gave it to him.

I knew it was a bad idea, a horrible one, and I would go to dinner tonight just to tell him that wasn't what I had meant and that there really was nothing between us but friendship—a *non-fucking* friendship.

My pleasantly sore body pulsed as a reminder of last night. I supposed independent women could have friends with benefits and not give themselves fully away, right? Maybe it wasn't the worst idea.

CHAPTER 22
JASPER

I MOVED THROUGH THE MANOR WITH A MISSION.

I have *always* been a man who got what he wanted. Always. The problem was: The only things I'd ever really wanted were usually just to spite another person. The only reason I had a single dollar to my name was because spite flowed so heavily through my veins. It was all in an effort to cause my father pain whenever he saw his name attached to an article about Blackwood Industries, after he had left me because he couldn't take the backlash that his name was getting after poisoning half the town. This was different.

Want and need burned inside of me. I had known it was there—I wasn't a fool. A man couldn't look at Eliza Arnold and not be filled with desire. But every other woman I'd ever been with had been uncomplicated. It was easy and careless. I had girls I could call who didn't need anything extra from me but a quick fuck or a dinner. I didn't want anyone to be close to me. Until now. Somewhere along the line, Eliza had gotten inside of me—and now that I'd gotten inside of her, I didn't like the thought of letting her go. So I wouldn't. At least not yet.

I stalked through the kitchen and into the garage.

"Are you leaving? Will you be gone for dinner?" Katya asked as she pulled a tray of something that smelled like apples and cinnamon from the oven.

"I'll be back for dinner. I need to run into town. Do you have any extra aprons?"

She canted her head. "Aprons? I think I have some old ones I was going to give to my nieces. Why? Do you need them?"

"Two of them." My hand hovered over the keys hanging on the hook as I decided which car to take before ultimately settling on the Jeep. "Katya, have you painted? What do I need to get for it?"

Her sharp face lit up. "For Eliza?"

"You say a word, I'll fire you," I threatened.

She grinned, looking at me thoughtfully for a minute.

"What are you staring at?" I asked as I grabbed one of the insanely hot apple muffin things.

"Nothing," she said, looking down, the smile still there.

"Katya, don't fucking toy with me," I demanded. Had this been anyone but her or Leah, I really would have fired them, or worse.

"You deserve it, you know?" she said in a surprisingly soft voice. I was used to her gruff, curt tone. "To be happy."

I took a bite of the pastry and scowled at her. "Calm your tits. She's leaving in a few weeks. We're just having fun."

She nodded sarcastically and rolled her eyes. "Well, I think she's the best thing that's ever happened to you and this manor. Even with your father doing what he's doing, I haven't seen you smile or be this happy in…ever."

I rolled my eyes and scowled again, uncomfortable with the attention to my personal life. I leaned in and gave the older woman a kiss on the cheek. "You're lucky you're such a good chef. I'll be back soon."

As I got into my car and left the manor, I realized how true Katya's words had been.

I had tried to run from the storm that brewed between Eliza and me. When I left for New York, I had every intention of never speaking to or seeing Eliza Arnold again. I couldn't imagine letting anyone get so close to me and seeing the parts of me that weren't sharp and defensive. To be honest, it had never even been a thought I'd had to entertain. There was no struggle to keep people out. It was an easy, thoughtless way of life.

Until the brown-haired, blue-eyed botanist entered my life.

She had already weaseled her way in before I left in an effort to keep her out.

Before I had come home from New York, I knew I needed her. At that point, I hadn't thought about the logistics or the details—all I knew was that I needed her in my life. I didn't care in what capacity; I wouldn't spend another day trying to push her away.

Then last night happened.

I had to shift my position in the driver's seat because my dick was stiffening at the thought of how fucking well she took me last night, how needy her tight little body had been—like she had been waiting for me to ruin her. She shouldn't have come apart so deliciously if she wanted it to be a one-time thing—which she didn't.

She was mine, whether she liked it or not. If you summon the devil, it's pointless to flinch when he shows up. I'd never really seen a girl cry before, maybe my mother once or twice, but not in the way Eliza had cried last night before I got to her room. She wasn't crying when I was in there; she was all anger and adrenaline, but I could tell she had cried really, really hard before I showed up. A strange feeling had consumed me as I watched her red-rimmed eyes glare at me in pain-soaked anger. It hit hard—in the emotional parts of me that shouldn't have even still been functioning. Gagging on my cock would be the only thing that made her eyes red and her mascara run, nothing else.

Now that I was in her life, no one was going to make her hurt. I was unexpectedly invested in Eliza Arnold, and I protected my investments. At some point, since being in this house, she had single-handedly reached in and defrosted my cold, unfeeling heart, and she didn't even know it. She was special. I never liked anyone—and I really, really liked her.

Not that I was one to throw stones, but her family had really done a number on her. I knew she kept the darker details to herself, but I also knew she needed to get away from her mother. Apparently, even if they didn't abandon you, they could still be shitty, awful parents. It was ironic: my parents didn't want anything to do with me, and hers couldn't leave her alone.

If Eliza couldn't see her own worth, I would happily make it my job to teach her. Her mother had beaten her down until she was left with nothing. That was why she just took it—every awful thing her mother did or said to her was done under the lie that it all stemmed from love, but it wasn't love. She got rid of her goddamn apartment, for fuck's sake, and now she was ruining things for me with Eliza.

I let out a slow breath and tried to focus on the road. Getting fired up about her mother wasn't going to do anything.

Last night, I wanted Eliza to see how strong she was—that she could do anything and I would be there for her, no matter what happened. Even if things didn't work out between us, she would never, ever have to fight alone again. Ever. Not many people earned my loyalty, but she had it.

When I had suggested that she use her adrenaline to face her fear and her knees had trembled, I'd felt like I was protecting a fragile little egg, keeping my hands on either side of it as it rolled clumsily to its destination, hoping I wasn't going to break it. When she opened her eyes and saw the view, I had no idea that from that fragile little egg, a fire-breathing dragon would emerge, ready to light the world on fire. She was mine.

She was fucking mine.

I was quickly learning that one of the things about having this sort of wildly electric connection with someone was that even without words, one look could give everything that each of us tried to hide away.

Eliza was spiraling, and rightfully so. I had already had my turn when I went to New York; now it was her turn to panic. Neither one of us had had good experiences with the ones who were supposed to be there for you, and because of that, neither of us could trust or love easily—if we could at all. I guess only time would tell if either of us were capable of doing justice to our deeper, stronger feelings.

She could say there was nothing between us all she wanted. But when we first kissed last night, it felt like a Mac truck full of lightning bolts had hit me, and I knew she felt it too. I was an idiot when it came to emotions, but even I knew that type of thing didn't happen to everybody.

Nothing between us.

After last night, there was no fucking way I was letting that woman get away from me. I couldn't even think about her leaving the manor—I needed more time with her. It was perfect; with her apartment gone, she could stay at the manor while she looked for someplace closer, and I would have more time with her. Nick from her work could get fucked; she wasn't moving in with him. She was staying with me.

The fact that she was trying to play off one of the hottest, most soul-connecting moments in history with the term *fuck buddies* was hilarious. I loved her sense of humor; it was one of the first things that drew me to her, but this wasn't going to fly.

I knew what made her tick. If she wanted to pretend that this was nothing, then I would fucking push and prod her until she was so head over heels in love with me that she had no choice but to admit it…and to stay.

I would be patient with her—as patient as I could be. But

I was going to win. She was going to admit that this was far from *nothing*.

I didn't know what exactly it was, but it was something.

I left the craft store with no less than seven bags full of bright-colored shit. I had no idea what it was or what you did with it, but the sales associates had pointed out what I needed, and I had bought it all.

On the way home, I saw that I had missed a call from my attorney. Things were heating up, legally speaking. My father's shithead lawyer had found some type of loophole, and they were running with it. When I had taken over the property, the whole world had assumed they were dead, and I had let them, even the lawyers, which was biting me in the ass now.

I was grateful to have Eliza in the house with me while all this was happening. Aside from Sowerby, I had done everything on my own up until now, but after having Eliza for even a short time, I couldn't imagine ever going without her again.

I would do everything in my power to stop Eliza from leaving me and the manor behind. That meant I only had a few weeks left—until the corpse flower bloomed—to convince her that she should stay.

When I arrived home, Katya was buzzing by the door, eager to help me set up for the night. After that was all done, I went to my room and changed, surprised by how difficult it was to find a pair of jeans and a T-shirt. I hadn't realized how much of my life I spent in suits.

My eyes snagged on the chest with all of my parents' letters. How many times had I thought about burning that chest? Unable to peel my eyes away from it, I walked over and reluctantly pulled a letter out.

My father coming back had been a shock, perhaps more shocking than when he left; I had assumed he would be gone forever. After what had happened, I never thought either one of them would show their faces here again. I knew he was afraid, and he should be. He was delusional thinking that I would ever give up this property without a fight. I didn't even want it, but I sure as shit wasn't going to let them have it. I'd burn the place down before I let them take something from me again.

I ran my fingertips over the letter and my mom's signature and felt something familiar sting in my chest. It didn't matter how much time had passed, I still couldn't get rid of how much it hurt that she'd left. I hated her. I hated her more than anyone in the whole world. She had been the only one on my side. How she could go from such a caring, compassionate mother to abandoning me? No matter how many times I tried to understand, I couldn't.

Heat blurred my eyes and my teeth ground together painfully. My father shouldn't have come back. If he knew what was really good for him, he would have stayed away from me and Blackwood Manor forever, like her.

I resisted the urge to crumple up the letter, instead carefully smoothing it out and placing it back inside the chest full of lies. I slammed the chest closed and took a step before I unholstered my gun and imagined shooting a thousand holes in it. The more my eyes blurred, the more furious I became. After pulling my pistol, just to feel the comforting steel in my hand, I turned to the mirror, watched three tears fall from my eyes before lifting my gun and wiping them away. I placed the tearstained gun on the dresser and pulled my favorite Blackwood Bladecraft knife from the drawer, adjusted it to its place hidden beneath my shirt, and took a long breath. Then, I checked my reflection in the mirror and left to get Eliza.

CHAPTER 23
ELIZA

I STOOD WAITING IN THE GRAND ENTRANCE OF BLACKWOOD Manor, where Jasper had asked me to meet him for dinner.

In an act of defiance and a way of further proving that there was, in fact, nothing romantic between us, I had opted out of wearing anything particularly fancy, an easy choice considering that the only nice dresses I had were the ones Leah and Katya had gotten for me. Even though some part of me wanted to dress up and show Jasper that I could be pretty and put together, I fought it away.

I waited, knowing I would sense when he approached. We couldn't be in the same space without it feeling supercharged with electricity. I'd never felt anything like it, and in the deep, hidden parts of my soul, I knew I wouldn't again. But it didn't matter. No matter how much we might want to come together, to melt into the other, we had both been through far too much to be able to do that; it would never work out. One relationship could only hold so much trauma.

Not to mention, as the ghost of his dead mother reminded me, I still had some pretty important questions that needed answers. There were too many holes in everyone's story, and as much as I really, really, really didn't want to believe Jasper had murdered Hester, I still had an odd feeling in my gut that I couldn't ignore when it came to Jasper and his innocence. I trusted him, but something felt off that I couldn't quite put my finger on.

I had been obsessively checking my—Hester's—locket, wishing and hoping that she would give me something, anything, that would help me. I was running out of time to help her...despite my best efforts, the corpse flower's growth was not slowing down.

Last night with Jasper, I had been reckless. I was *never* reckless. Every move I made was meticulously planned and thought out. It had to be. That's how I'd survived. I wasn't very beautiful or intelligent. I wasn't charming. In fact, I *never* knew the right thing to say or when to say it. I wasn't passionate about anything but trying to get my parents to like me, as pitiful as that sounded. I wasn't an academic environmental juggernaut hellbent on saving the earth as my mother and father had wanted; I preferred smutty fantasy books to ethics and orange Fanta to green juice. I was *never* the person I was supposed to be, but still, I read *The End of Nature* by Bill McKibben, *Silent Spring* by Rachel Carson and could quote *A Sand County Almanac* by Aldo Leopold and all the other things I was told to—not because I enjoyed it, but because it was what I was good at.

Doing what I was told to.

Even at Pinehurst, I was barely cutting it. Don't get me wrong, I enjoyed working in nature with the plants immensely; they were safe and predictable...relatable even, but if I could have done what I'd wanted, I wouldn't have been in these clothes, manor, or garden. Essentially, I was doing what I was told to do, though I was grateful I ended up here with Jasper and Hester and the rest of the friends I'd made at the Blackwood Manor. It felt weird to think of my life without them now. It was nice to feel welcome.

My sister, Lucy, barely spoke to me. She hardly spoke to any of us anymore, and I never blamed her. In fact, I envied her ability to break away. It was really bad at home when she left and moved to the UK, and after she was gone, everything got worse. My mother viewed Lucy's rebellious move as a personal failure and, in turn, was twice as strict with me. My sister had always hated me for being the goody-goody daughter, but she never knew that I had done all of it for her, stupidly believing that if I could take the brunt of it, they would leave her alone. They hadn't.

I'd thought about calling Lucy several times since I'd been at Blackwood Manor. The peace of mind I'd experienced staying at Blackwood made me miss her even more than normal. She was younger than me by a few years, and I couldn't help but feel my soul reaching for her, wanting to ask her advice about what to do about Mom. Lucy was the only other person who knew what I was going through. Mom had gotten so much worse these last few years.

Maybe I would call Lucy tomorrow.

A crackle of awareness drew my attention from my thoughts.

I turned to see Jasper striding toward me, holding a small green nursery pot with a burlap sleeve over the top, with a smile on his face that should be illegal. My stomach flip-flopped when his eyes traced over my body and his smile grew even wider.

Smile, you idiot.

Smile!

Instead of smiling, I just gaped at the sight of his tall, powerful-looking body filling out a pair of worn blue jeans and a white T-shirt. He was always in a suit or insanely luxurious business attire. It was usually a darker color, which only lent to his dark, broody atmosphere. But now, in his jeans—he was devastatingly attractive. Like, *Fuck it! So you murdered your mother two decades ago. Who cares, handsome?* Like, *Oh, you have a couple of felonies and are serving jailtime? It's fine; here's some money on your books. When can we get a conjugal visit?* type of handsome.

I closed my gaping mouth and tried to make my eyes not so bulgy. They felt bulgy.

It was going to be a lot harder to convince him I had no romantic feelings while I was drooling. Were those Wranglers? *Look at how muscly his thighs are…*

Eliza, get it together!

I focused on the newly independent feelings stirring away in my gut, the ones in the very back, just past the horny ones that wanted to touch every centimeter of his skin, and tried to use them as a reminder of how easily this man could hurt me if he ever wanted to, if I ever gave him the power to—which I wouldn't. I swallowed, forcing my butterfly-infested stomach back down where it belonged.

"Jasper, hello." God, I sounded like a news reporter. It didn't matter; I didn't even have time to cringe before he hugged me. I stiffened so that I wouldn't melt into a puddle on his—

"Nikes. You're wearing Nikes," I said out loud.

He released me but didn't let me move too far away from him, keeping a possessive hand on my arm. The skin of said appendage burned under his firm touch, making my whole body sweat.

"If you're going to stare at my mouth like that"—he stepped in close, calm but electric. I could feel the heat bleeding from his body—"don't act surprised if I start thinking about what else you'd let me use it for."

A blush heated my cheeks, and I had to clench my thighs as the barely there soreness throbbed at the thought of letting him use my mouth.

"You look good, maybe too good." His gaze dragged over me, slow and heavy. "It's a good thing I like being tested sometimes."

"You've quite literally seen me in this exact outfit almost

every day for two months," I argued. I did *not* look great. *He* looked great. I looked like a toad.

His brown eyes burrowed into mine. "And you've looked beautiful every one of those times, Eliza. Here, I got you something."

A flush crept so hotly over the back of my neck that it itched as I took the six-inch nursery pot, realizing it had holes punctured all around it, almost dropping it with shaking hands. What was going on with me? I needed to stop being so nervous and get my shit together. My head hadn't been right ever since I woke up to him in my bed—no. Ever since I tasted the softly metallic edge of his lips and tongue.

"What is this for?" I asked as I started to untie the top of the white cloth.

He bit his lower lip as something like excitement danced in his eyes. "I saw you admiring it on the computer a while ago. I knew you wanted it."

His eyes pressed into mine, invading my thoughts.

"When you want something, Eliza..." He paused as his eyes turned frighteningly serious, roving over my face. "I'll be the one who gives it to you. By the way, this one is for you, not the conservatory."

He'd seen me admiring it on the computer? When had he watched me on the computer? I laughed as I undid the last tie and carefully let the covering fall from the small plant.

My smile dropped. "Jasper—" I double-checked that it was actually what I thought it was before I made a fool of myself. It was a healthy, mature ghost orchid, or Dendrophylax lindenii, one of the rarest and most sought-after orchids, and he was right: I had been admiring it, along with every other orchid lover in the world. "Are you insane? I can't take this." The ghost orchid was even more rare than the corpse flower.

"You can; in fact, I insist." He winked at me with dark confidence.

I gawked. "I can't keep this. It's like a three-thousand-dollar plant."

"Consider it a bonus since I'm not paying you to work on the conservatory," he said lazily.

I almost choked. "A bonus? I could quit working on the conservatory right now, and this could sustain the botanical gardens," I said cautiously.

"I know." The amusement in his eyes dimmed slightly. "I want you to stay here and finish the conservatory because you want to, not because you have to."

He was giving me a ticket to leave if I wanted to. A ticket that, no matter what happened—even if I couldn't finish the garden in time—meant that I still had a job if I wanted to at the end of all of this.

It was a gesture beyond anything I could comprehend.

"Thank you," I mumbled, unable to find any other words that could tell him how much it meant to me.

He watched as I carefully, with shaking hands, wrapped up the beautiful white orchid, replacing the covering. I ran back up to my room before returning to where I had left Jasper and throwing my arms tightly around his neck. I couldn't stop myself. No one had ever done something like that for me, and it shook me to my core.

"Thank you. You don't know what that means to me," I mumbled against the cotton of his white T-shirt.

He wrapped his arms around me and firmly held me against him as if we were bracing for a storm, anchoring and safe. He was all hard lines and dense muscle and only a whisper of tenderness, but I felt it. Under the solid wall of unyielding muscle, there was the slow rise and fall of someone who cared.

I dropped my arms, needing to step away from the feel of him so close before I did something really stupid—like climb up his chest and straddle his face. Or worse, tell him how much I was starting to care about him. I walked past him toward the kitchen, hoping I would stumble across a large plastic bag that I could suffocate my libido with on the way.

"Where are you going?" he said, grabbing my hand until it was nestled in his palm safely. "Dinner is upstairs in my bedroom tonight—*friend.*" His eyes darkened for a second before a challenging, lopsided smirk appeared.

It had been two minutes, and he was already calling my bluff.

"Perfect," I muttered.

This was not going to work. I should never have agreed to more time with him, especially not alone in a room when he looked like that. I couldn't have sex with him again, even though I *really* wanted to. My brain was trying to override that decision, but the newly awakened beast between my thighs was currently staging a hostile takeover of my body. We had already blurred the line, and I really needed him to stay far away so I didn't get suckered into handing him over the keys that would take me out of my mom's prison and into his. I was protecting myself.

He paused, waiting for me to surrender. But he should have known better. I wouldn't have sex with him again, but he didn't have to know that. If the man did nothing else, he brought out an absolute competitive demon that I'd never known possessed me. He had since day one. It was empowering and thrilling—and dangerous. Three things I'd recently started to crave.

He smirked as he gently pulled my hand to his side and guided me up the grand staircase to his room. The entire way, my head spun, torn between wanting to cannonball onto his mattress and have the time of my life and wanting to lock myself in the conservatory and finish it as fast as I humanly could, so I didn't make any more dumb mistakes.

"Are you hungry? I had an activity for us first, but if you're hungry, we can eat first," he said as we approached the door to his bedroom. His thumb absently slid back and forth over the inside of my wrist.

Wait, what did he just say?

"The activity is *in* your room?" I asked. Son of a bitch, was he not actually bluffing and really thought we were going to have sex?

"Is that a problem? When you said we were just fuck buddies..." He trailed off. Challenge was in his eyes and voice, daring me to admit defeat. There was a hint of amusement that let me believe he was still messing with me. At least, I hoped.

I spun on him; he was as fucked up as me about this, and I knew it.

"Is it a problem for you? What else would we be? I leave in three weeks," I reminded him sharply.

The humor fell from his eyes and was replaced with something that looked a lot like determination—and something a little menacing that I didn't quite want to name.

"It's not a problem for me, Eliza. I know exactly what I want."

He was not going to make this easy for me.

Goose bumps prickled up the skin of my back as I tore my eyes from his and pushed open the door to his bedroom, moving in and away from his words as quickly as possible. The soapy-clean smell of him doused my senses as I walked into his room. He had no idea I'd been in here not that long ago, following a little gold spider.

Here goes nothing.

I let out a breath of excitement and anticipation and peeled my T-shirt off over my head. Even thinking about having his firm grip all over my skin was enough to make me throb and salivate.

I supposed, if necessary, I could fall on my sword—or, I guess, his sword—one more time and be intimate with Jasper. All in the name of letting him believe we were only fuck buddies, of course. Especially if it meant I won the challenge because I had, in fact, worn a lacy bra like he'd asked me to. I left my pants on but bent over the end of his bed provocatively, sticking my ass up. I would not be the first one to break.

"You can eat now if you want," I said with my ass up in the air as I spoke to the black duvet cover on his bed.

"That eager, huh?" Jasper stood at the door with his arms crossed. His gaze dropped, slow and heavy. "One taste and you're crawling into my bed, ass up, like you're waiting for me to take what's already mine." He clicked his tongue, the sound soft and cutting. "I said we were going upstairs. You're the one who got naked hoping I'd eat." He smirked—a lethal, dismissive look. "We're painting."

I looked around with wide eyes, not understanding.

He took a small step forward as he devoured me with his eyes. "We were..." He swallowed loudly. "Painting." His eyes roamed over my bra as if memorizing it as he absently nodded toward his balcony.

Realization hit me when I looked through the glass doors and saw a small table between two easels set up with canvases facing the sky where the sun would soon be setting.

The activity in his room was painting. Not fucking.

My cheeks burned with embarrassment. "Our activity," I mumbled with wide eyes.

"Last night, you mentioned painting the sky, but I think your activity might be better. Much better." He leaned against his dresser and crossed his arms again, unabashedly checking out my body slowly, leaving goose bumps where his eyes trailed.

I stared back at him in awe. "You set up a painting date?" This was easily one of the most thoughtful things anyone had ever done for me. "For me? I've always wanted to paint a sunset."

"You're lucky I brought paintbrushes." He stepped in, gaze sharp, heat coiled just beneath the surface. "Because if I'd grabbed rope instead"—a slow smirk covered his face as his eyes dragged down my body—"you wouldn't be standing, and you damn sure wouldn't be thanking me."

I swallowed down the small bit of saliva in my suddenly dry mouth. I pulled my shirt back on over my head.

As we moved over toward the balcony doors, he paused. "Are you all right to be out there?" His eyes searched my face.

Needing the serious tone in the room to change, I gave him a wink. "Why? If I'm not, are you going to help me like last time?"

His face remained serious, completely humorless. I hated how he could look straight through me for the truth. "Eliza, do you feel comfortable going out on my balcony?"

I nodded. I had made a point of going out on my balcony a few times alone since he had taken me out on it yesterday, and each time, it somehow felt more freeing—though I had spent most of the day in the conservatory, hiding from him. I nervously toyed with the locket in my pocket, feeling the chain clink around against my fingertips.

"Good. Otherwise, we would have to paint nude portraits of each other, and I am certain my lack of skills would insult you by the end of the evening." He pulled open the glass doors and stepped onto the large balcony.

"Whoa," I breathed.

The sky had started to turn the lightest shade of orange. Unlike my room, which if you looked down over the edge, you could see the yard and conservatory, this view showed nothing but the other far-off cliffs and sky. It looked like a postcard or a screensaver, and suddenly, the architectural structure of the Gothic manor made all the sense in the world. The view was otherworldly—this view was why the manor had been built the way it was.

I sat in front of my canvas and suddenly felt so silly, like I had just put scrubs on and walked into a hospital pretending to be a surgeon. "I don't know what I'm doing. I've only ever painted in my field books," I muttered, feeling like an impostor.

"Me either. I watched a few YouTube videos, though, so I'm probably going to be pretty good." He smiled, confidently pouring a bottle of water into each of our paintbrush holders.

"How do you have all of this stuff?" I asked as I looked in amazement at the plethora of paintbrushes and acrylic paints on the small table between our seats.

He shrugged. "I grabbed it when I was out today. The ladies at the craft store told me what all to get."

My expression fell for a moment—not from sadness, but from the shock at his words. I had no experience with this feeling and couldn't find a facial expression fast enough that matched my delight and awe. This man had driven two hours into town to pick out all of this. For me.

Heaviness pulled at my chest. Under his callous, unapproachable exterior, he was one of the kindest, most thoughtful men ever to exist. His eyes were predatory as they watched me, but I knew there was softness behind them. He cared just as much about me as I cared about him. It was going to be so hard to leave this place and this man and move on. A wave of emotions hit me at the thought of leaving.

No doubt sensing that I was about thirty seconds away from bawling my eyes out, Jasper spoke again. "My actions aren't entirely innocent; I plan on auctioning off that painting when you're done with it," he said, nodding at my empty canvas. "I have a feeling you're a natural."

I snorted, getting embarrassed. "I seriously doubt that."

"Don't do that," he corrected. "Not with me. You left your notebook with all the little paintings in it open in the garden the other day, and I saw it. It's obvious you love it," he countered as he handed me a bright white oblong palette to put my paint on. I felt so official. "I also saw the chef bear you drew for Katya and Sowerby. I tried to sell that too, but Katya won't budge." He smiled playfully at me as he turned toward his own canvas and began confidently dipping his paintbrush in paint and then wiping it on the canvas as if he'd done this a thousand times. I knew he was starting first to make me feel less self-conscious, which was why I couldn't stop staring at him. Just the fact that he knew enough about me to know to do that was baffling. He paid so much attention to my little, unsaid details, it was almost unnerving. And also, he looked absolutely adorable doing things. I was thrilled to be able to paint freely, but I could've enjoyed myself just as much had I only sat there and watched him.

We continued this way in comfortable silence. Occasionally, one of us would remark about the color we were using or joke about something like the names of the paint colors, but it was mostly just me talking as he let me get lost in the task. It was meditative. Every so often, one of us would adjust to acquire more paint, and our arms would brush lightly.

I lost myself to the canvas and the scene in front of me. I didn't know what I was doing, but as soon as I started, it was as though another force took over for me. I was possessed. A wizard in complete control over which world my blank canvas saw. Each stroke of my brush became an exploration. There could be no mistakes in the painting because whatever it became was entirely me. My spirit bled in bright, sunset-hued colors, from my brush onto my painting as if a divine force had commanded it. So much of me went into it that I felt nothing might be left inside my body but a happy, sated soul when I was finished.

After an hour or so, I looked over to find Jasper no longer painting but turned in his chair, fixated on me, fascination filling his eyes, his own painting having been completely abandoned. I don't think I could have pulled myself away from my ministrations for all the money in the world. As I whisked color onto the canvas, my anxieties faded away until it was only me and the remainder of the sunset that was now gone, and I was left working with the photo I had snapped on my phone.

It was as if my cage door had opened and I had been released after a lifetime locked inside. I could do anything. If I wanted the pinks to pop, I added more pink. No one could stop me if I wanted to add something completely from my imagination, like a glint of light or a sparkle. No one was telling me how it should be done or all that I was doing wrong. Even Jasper offered no suggestions or thoughts.

Time slipped away from me and only came back when I found myself fixing details and I decided to stop before I ended up ruining it. Jasper's voice was suddenly behind me.

"It's unbelievable," he whispered softly.

I turned to see him standing, staring at the canvas over my shoulder.

I stood and moved back beside him, stretching my legs and back. It had been hours, and he had been patient, letting me continue until I was ready to stop.

"Yours is great," I said kindly, though only half of his canvas had been painted before he had abandoned it to watch me. "This was so much fun. Thank you so much for all of this." I wrapped my arms around his waist in a hug, unable to help myself.

The second our bodies pressed together, the remainder of my worries flew from me. Like our first hug, when everything else disappeared after he had helped me with the koi pond. There was nothing sexual in the hug. Instead, it was supercharged with something deeper and, unfortunately, far, far more dangerous.

I tipped my head up to look at him. For a full minute, we just locked eyes and savored the comforts of the hug. When it grew too serious, he broke the silence.

"I'll share the proceeds with you once I auction it off."

A grin pulled at my mouth. "You think it's okay?" I asked earnestly.

"It's the second-most exquisite thing I've ever seen in my life," he said, never removing his dark, haunting eyes from mine.

"Thank you again. For everything." Gratitude made my voice tremble.

"Thank *you*. That's going to make me a lot of money," he teased. "Are you hungry? Let's eat. There's pizza in the kitchen."

"Oh, I love pizza!" I exclaimed excitedly, realizing how hungry I was.

"I know," he muttered with a serious face and eyes tethered to mine.

After cleaning up and moving our paintings inside to dry against the wall in Jaspers's giant bathroom, we went to the kitchen and enjoyed the rest of the night in easy, comfortable companionship, laughing and thriving in each other's company until he said good night with a kiss on my forehead. It had been the perfect night, one that I would never forget.

It took me another hour or so to fall asleep after that, unable and unwilling to allow myself to go to another dream world when this one suddenly felt so good.

Tonight, Jasper had shown me kindness, generosity, respect, patience, and encouragement—things I wasn't used to experiencing but would now demand.

He was amazing, and I was forced to finally admit that I was falling in love with him.

It wasn't only the thoughtfulness of the date, but the way he had paid attention, listened to me talk about what I loved, and then sat back in full enjoyment and watched as I did something that brought me joy. It was the encouragement, the acceptance.

Suddenly, I knew: I wasn't going to let my fear stop me from being with Jasper. I knew that there was still a reasonable amount of doubt and questions around what happened with him and his mother, but I couldn't believe he had anything to do with that.

I trusted him.

CHAPTER 24
ELIZA

THE HALLWAY WAS QUIET.

Too quiet.

My hand hovered over the doorknob to Jasper's office; my pulse hammered behind my ribs. I didn't even know why I was shaking. I just had to look around. Yes, I was snooping. Yes, I'd stolen a key from one of the maids to get in.

But this was more than guilt. It was instinct. The locket burned against my chest. It was the last place for me to look before I had to leave, and I knew I wouldn't get another chance.

Something was in there.

Something she wanted me to see.

I pulled the locket away from my chest, afraid it would leave a mark it was so hot. I let out a breath. I was betraying Jasper. If he caught me snooping, I was fucked.

The key slid into the lock with a soft metallic click.

I stepped inside, eager to get out of the hallway's unprotected view.

The air was cooler, sterile with a hint of leather and wood. Everything in here was Jasper: dark wood, iron hardware, sharp lines. No windows. I quickly flicked on the light switch, disappointed when no light came on overhead. Before the door closed and the light from the hallway disappeared, I ran to the corner and turned on a small table lamp that barely did anything more than cast a deep amber glow across the space, adding to the eerie feel. The door whispered shut behind me. I returned to it and turned the lock.

Ten minutes. In and out.

My eyes scanned the room. Cabinets, shelves, files. I moved fast to the desk.

Top drawer. Locked. Of course it was.

I slid open the one beneath it. More files. Financial records, some land deeds. Dull, and nothing that would help Hester.

Then my breath caught as I sat slowly in the desk chair, heart pounding. I opened the file and tilted it toward the low glow of the lamp.

Oh my god.

A witness statement.

"Female matching description seen by employee near the cliffs morning after disappearance. Pale coat. Disoriented."

My fingers trembled across the pages. There was a map with the cliffs circled in red with a bold X.

A police report caught my eye as the locket heated to a painful temperature.

"Blood recovered from Jasper Blackwood's shirt. Matched to Hester Blackwood. No remains found. Presumed voluntary departure or accident."

Then at the bottom:

"Estate searched. Garden grounds cleared. Cadaver dogs negative."

I read it again. Then again. It didn't make sense.

My hands were trembling so fiercely it was hard to read. The locket at my chest suddenly flared cold. I dropped the file in my lap and snapped the locket open—pale limbs beneath a red rose.

The door clicked open in the darkness in front of me.

I froze, unable to see anything. Every nerve in my body screamed to run. The file was still on my lap. The door I'd come through was still shut. I'd locked it.

Run.

But I couldn't move. Could hardly breathe.

Jasper's voice was soft: "Find what you're looking for?"

I turned slowly. Caught like an animal in a trap, about to beg for my life. Of course he had a key to his own office.

He stood in the shadows, watching me with unreadable eyes, his hands at his sides. No rage. No shock. Just calm, terrifying stillness.

"Breaking into my office?" he asked. "Looking for what? Proof I'm dangerous?" His voice moved closer. I could barely see him cloaked in darkness. "Or hoping I'd catch you? Punish you?"

I opened my mouth but only strangled, breathy sounds came out.

He reached me, coming into the soft amber glow of light. His hand removed the file from my lap with cold, casual precision. He set it on the desk and turned his gaze on me. My legs were trembling. I couldn't have run even if I'd tried. Was he going to hurt me?

He stepped between my legs, pushing them open, hands still at his sides. No threat, but his body filled the space like one.

"You think I killed her?" he asked, voice so low the hair on the back of my neck rose.

I shook my head.

"Liar." His tone darkened. "You read that file and panicked. Thought maybe you were next."

I swallowed, eyes wide. Something about him screamed danger, like a thread was about to snap in him.

He smiled. Slowly. Filthily. And then his hand was between my legs.

Oh god.

I gasped. His hand brushed the skin under my shorts, and

he pressed through my underwear. He dragged two fingers over the heat of me and paused. Smirked.

"You're soaked." He pushed inside of me without warning—deep, sure, and deliberate.

I whimpered, legs parting instinctively at his touch. The fear and lust swirled together, fueling my reaction in a terrifying, thrilling mix.

"Worried I'm a killer," he murmured, "and still letting me inside you." He moved his fingers slow and hard, curling against me just right. "You like it, don't you? The not knowing."

I bucked into his hand, my breath ragged.

"Makes you come harder." He leaned in, towering over me. "Makes you wetter."

I came with a muffled cry, biting my lip until I tasted blood. What was wrong with me?

He didn't stop until I was shaking. Then he pulled his fingers out, wiped them slowly, deliberately on the hem of my shorts, looked me dead in the eyes.

"If I ever wanted to hurt you, Eliza..." He paused.

All I heard was the heaviness of both of our breathing.

"...you wouldn't get a warning."

My stomach dropped as he stepped back and turned his back to me dismissively.

"Go. Before I remind you why you really should be afraid of me."

I stood on shaking legs, unable to think. At the door, he stopped me.

"Eliza?"

I looked over my shoulder.

His voice was quieter now, still dark but with something softer threaded through. "Put the file back where you found it. And don't ever lie to me about what you're looking for." Then he added, without turning around, "You're mine. You want to know something? You can just ask me next time."

My head spun. That night we ate dinner together again, but we were quiet. He didn't bring it up, just left me to unravel in my thoughts—thoughts that were about to get much, much worse.

CHAPTER 25

ELIZA

"I DON'T KNOW WHAT TO DO," I SHRIEKED. "I'VE ALREADY LOWered the temperature, shielded its light, and reduced its water; I don't know what else to do. I still have one bed left to plant before the conservatory is done."

"Well, looks like you better get to planting, then," Nick sang into the receiver.

"Oh my god," I breathed, trying but failing to get a grip.

"Yeah, Eliza, can you hear me?" my boss shouted loudly over the speakerphone. "Press your nose against the spathe and tell me what you smell."

It was a carrion flower, so that only meant one thing. If it had a scent, it wouldn't smell good. Their blooms smelled like rotting animals to attract pollinators and scavengers.

Struggling to make my limbs move in my panicked state, I stepped over the freshly swept stone walkway and border, and into the central flower bed. It took up the center of the conservatory, wrapping itself around the towering rock waterfall and koi pond that splashed happily, cascading down to the left of the corpse flower's bed. There had ended up being three corpse flowers in total, but only one was healthy and in a blooming cycle, the others in their leaf stages. Dark-red-and-black orchids peeked out from behind the towering structure of the large eight-foot *Amorphophallus titanum*. The other two were small, and I had to carefully sidestep the rippling bird's-nest ferns and balance between the various clumps of rabbit's foot ferns before reaching the bare perimeter surrounding the corpse flower.

I moved close, grazing my nose against the pleated-looking furls that pressed against the long spadix, and took a giant inhale. My stomach lurched over more than just the smell as my heart sank into the dirt beneath my feet.

"Well?" both Nick and Lithgow asked, prompting me.

"It's horrible. Decaying flesh and rotting meat mixed with urine and a musty basement," I answered. It was the signature scent of the corpse flower when in bloom.

"Well, it looks like we're having a party in two days, Eliza. I'll tell everyone here and pass it on to the philanthropists I've been in contact with," Lithgow said with a bit of excitement in his voice.

"Email me the list, and I'll call the other people coming," Nick added helpfully.

"Are you sure?" I asked.

"Yeah," he answered. "You don't have time. Finish the last bed. I can't wait to see it all. If you want, I can take some of your stuff back to our house after the party, so you don't have to stay at Blackwood Manor."

It suddenly felt like my world was caving in around me.

"And, Eliza?" Lithgow's voice grew clearer as if he'd grabbed the phone from Nick.

"Yes?"

"We'll see you the day after tomorrow. Do you have the propagations ready for Pinehurst? Really, Eliza—I have to admit, I never really thought you'd be able to pull this off. In all transparency, after speaking to your mother so many times while you've been gone, I started to wonder if a job with us was the right fit for you. I figured it would sort itself out if you took all that time away from work and came up empty-handed," he said in a chipper voice. "Okay, get to planting. See you soon. I can't wait to snoop around that place; I've always wanted to see the inside. So mysterious."

I hung up and sank to the ground in front of the corpse flower, careful not to squish anything, pulling my knees up and resting my pounding head on them.

There was no way I could be finished in two days. I still had an entire bed to plant, and I needed to move the last few rabbit's foot ferns from around the corpse flower and mulch everything.

Seeking any sort of comfort I could find, I stuck my hand out and ran my finger over the furry silver-brown rhizomes that crept out from under the green foliage of the rabbit's foot ferns in front of me.

This would all work out. It had to. I was so close now.

I looked around and took in the months of work I had put into the conservatory. It was unrecognizable from the ruinous, wild garden I had first walked into. This garden had my blood, sweat, and tears in it. I had given it my all, and I was so close to success, I could taste it. I would be given a substantial raise at the botanical garden, and we would be able to stay open. I might make enough to start saving and get my finances in order. Things were looking up. This was all good. I needed to focus on the good.

Jasper—

I'd have to leave him in a few days. I wasn't entirely sure where we stood since he'd caught me snooping in his office and then angry finger-banged me. Were we anything? Would he miss me?

The locket, back in my pocket, began to vibrate. I pinched my eyes closed and ignored it, unable to look at it, knowing I'd probably have to leave Blackwood Manor having failed Hester. I wanted to throw myself down on the soil and cry thinking about it. It wasn't fair. She didn't deserve this. She deserved to be free and happy. Whoever did this to her had gone unpunished long enough.

I swallowed the emotion away. I still had a few days.

Petting the furry rhizome under the dark-green fern, I noticed one of the three-inch-long offshoots felt weirdly smooth, unlike the others. I stroked it a few times, absently wondering why that was.

Warmth hit the bottom of my chin and the side of my face, and I looked down to realize the locket inside of my overalls was now glowing gold and heating up.

Lately, I carried the locket everywhere, ready and waiting for Hester to give me another clue. Now that my time at the manor was nearly up, I had grown obsessive over checking it, sometimes opening the locket every few minutes. Nothing had changed, it remained completely empty and blank, with one side a dark scarlet-colored velvet and the other shiny gold without so much as a scratch.

I pulled it from my pocket.

"Agh!" I sucked in air through my teeth, dropping the hot necklace to the ground as soon as my fingers touched the burning metal.

It landed in the dirt, trembling as it glowed brighter and brighter until several inches of the surrounding soil was illuminated almost blindingly. The delicate fern leaves and the other plants around us shivered and swayed. Something had changed in the energy of the conservatory; it was like the space itself was preparing for a cataclysm.

The locket in the dirt snapped open with a sharp click.

I didn't have a chance to look at it before something to my left moved, startling me.

Hester stood a few feet behind me. Her deep-red dress

moved softly, like seaweed underwater, but everything else about her remained eerily still. She wasn't crying, but she looked sad, though in a much different way than I had seen before. She kept her dark eyes on me, waiting and still with one of her pale arms across her chest, gripping her throat as she frequently did.

"I don't know how to help you," I murmured, feeling the heat of tears prickle behind my eyes. "Help me! Tell me what to do!" I shouted. My frustration boiled over. "Who did this to you? Was it Jasper? Darius? Help me!" I scrambled to stand, intending to walk over to her, but as soon as I stood, my nerves failed me, and I remained frozen where I was.

Her eyes were not full of tears but something else—something softly hopeful.

Help me, her cracked lips mouthed, slowly removing the hand from her throat to reach out, slowly flaring her fingers wide before folding them down. I stared curiously.

What was she doing?

The light from the locket grew much brighter before dimming again, momentarily drawing my attention away from Hester. When I snapped my head back to her, she was gone.

I wanted to scream. I was only one person, and the pressures from everything were breaking me. What would I do if I was unable to find out who had murdered Hester? And with the corpse flower about to bloom and the last of the garden needing to be worked on, there was no time to dedicate to digging around the manor looking for clues.

Nearly at a breaking point, I dropped to my knees on the ground in front of the glowing locket to see if there were any clues inside.

I realized that this was almost exactly where I had found the locket buried initially.

Abruptly, the long, furry feet of the rabbit's foot fern nearest the illuminated locket moved and stretched up from the ground as if trying to push through the soil. With a gasp, I froze before I moved closer—there was something tucked under the overhanging fronds of the fern. And it was moving—or trying to.

The soil cracked, and the chain of the locket fell in, ready to fully disappear. I grabbed ahold of it without thinking. The brilliant glow dimmed instantly. I pulled at the locket to remove the chain from the crack, but it wouldn't budge. It was as if something had snagged it and refused to let it go.

Growing panicked at the thought of losing the locket, I pulled the necklace out from the crack under the ferns and moved to close it, catching the inscription on the shiny gold interior right before it clicked shut.

Digging deeper, we uncover both secrets and soil.

She wanted me to dig? Literally dig?

The blood pounded in my ears and through my heart so powerfully that my vision pulsed with the movement. I tucked the necklace back in the safety of my pocket, reached behind, and grabbed my trowel. Fear rushed like a river through my system as I carefully moved closer to the fern.

A crack of thunder made me scream and heave in a lungful of earthy air laced with Chanel No. 5, my tense body stiffened until I was sure it would snap. Light rain tapped against glass overwhelming my senses as it came at me from all directions, echoing in the expansive space. A hum of terror thrummed low. Too loud and too quiet all at once.

I held my breath, pressing my trowel into the crack, and wedged up a decent-sized clump of dirt. On my next push into the crack, the point of the shovel hit something hard, and I froze.

I feverishly dug at the dirt, deciding to remove the fern altogether. Something light in color remained where the furry rhizomes had stretched and crept out mischievously.

Carefully, I used my fingertips and brushed the dirt from it. I threw my trowel to the side, and it clanged behind me as a scream tore out of me.

The bones of a hand lay barely under the soil, with two bent fingers stretched out, mimicking the way the rhizomes of the rabbit's foot ferns crawled out onto the ground.

Bones.

A hand.

Frantic, I slid my body backward, screaming until Sowerby burst through the conservatory doors.

"What in god's name?" Sowerby's words slowed as his mouth fell open, registering me on the ground. His eyes sparked with knowing as he looked carefully at the disturbed patch of soil across from me. "Oh my—Jasper," he gasped before covering his mouth.

"It's a hand. There's a hand!" I shouted, feeling the blood drain from my face. "It's—there're bones buried next to the corpse flower!"

This whole time, Hester's body had been buried in the conservatory. Right where I spent every waking hour. Jasper had done it after all. Killed Hester and buried her in the garden to be forgotten. He must've thought I wouldn't dig that deep, that I wouldn't find her bones.

I turned and vomited on the black bat flowers.

The old man's eyes flickered closed before he calmly spoke again. "You need to call the police, dear."

The doors slammed open again, and this time, Jasper barged through. "What's going on? Eliza, are you okay?" He ran toward me, stopping when Sowerby stopped him from moving any closer to me.

"Stay away from me, you fucking psycho!" I screamed at the top of my lungs, sliding my body back across the stone path, frantically smashing and cracking stems and leaves as I pushed myself as far away from both men as possible. Small wheezing pants came as I struggled to tap the three numbers on my phone and call the police.

"Eliza, what's going on? What happened?" Jasper rumbled, looking between me and Sowerby, confused.

"It *was* you. It was you this whole time!" I screamed, causing my voice to vibrate and scratch my throat. "That's why she's stayed in the manor. You did it—you fucking killed her. Who's ever going to look in a dilapidated old garden?" I shook, covering my mouth with my trembling hand as I struggled not to get sick again. "That's why you let the conservatory fall to ruin. That's why you made the deal with me, you didn't think I'd last long enough to find her!"

This whole time.

The color drained from Jasper's face as he glanced at the disturbed soil.

Sowerby gently grabbed his arm and guided him from me and the conservatory while I called the police.

I watched from outside of the garden, fogging up the square pane of glass with my breath in silence as I watched all of my hopes and dreams die just as poor Hester had. I adjusted my bag, my car keys jangling in my hand, my bag cutting a dent into my shoulder with the weight of my belongings; the rest of what I'd brought with me was in another bag on the ground at my feet. My cheeks felt tight with the raw sting of tears that stained them.

"Ma'am, I'm sorry, but we really do need to cordon off the area," the young officer said as he tried to move me away from the glass.

"What will happen to all of the plants? There are incredibly rare, expensive plants in there. You can't just let everyone trample over them like that." I watched as months of hard work were stomped and smashed as the police swarmed through the conservatory like fire ants.

"That's not really my call, miss. I'm sorry, but you need to leave," he repeated.

"The corpse flower, that big one—you have to be careful. It's almost extinct. It's going to bloom—tomorrow and… there's supposed to be a big party—" I couldn't say the words out loud without my voice cracking and streams of tears cascading down my cheeks.

"Ma'am," he said, ushering me toward the driveway, where my car was packed and waiting with the rest my things.

"But—"

He let out a huff, opening my car door and angling me so I had nowhere to go but into it. "Listen, I will make some calls and do what I can about your plants, but I'll tell you right now, there's nothing that can be done about that big, tall one. It's directly over the remains. The bulldozer has to get in and—" Realizing he was saying too much, he suddenly shut up and tried to get me to sit down in the driver's seat.

"Where are Jasper and Sowerby?" I asked.

"Ma'am," he nearly whined in frustration.

"Tell me where they are, and I'll go."

Another long huff before he finally caved. "Jasper Blackwood is in custody getting processed at the local jail."

"And Sowerby? The older one?" I pressed, needing to know his involvement. When he had looked at the broken soil, he had known. I was sure of it.

"The older gentleman is currently speaking to their attorneys. Miss, I can't tell you any more."

The car door closed, and I placed my hands on the steering wheel and tried to catch my breath.

The phone rang twice. Numbly, I held it to my ear.

Nick told me to hurry over and fill him in on everything.

He was devastated hearing everyone would miss the blooming of the corpse flower. I hadn't been allowed to take the propagations from the conservatory with me. The only plant I was allowed to take was the ghost orchid that Jasper had given me from my room. I glared at the perfect white flowers wrapped in the cupholder beside me.

After hanging up with Nick, I immediately phoned Dr. Lithgow, who flew into an absolute tirade, cursing me for not having smuggled out anything and promising to rain a fiery hell on the police department if they didn't adhere to the legal protection for rare plants before he hung up on me to make some phone calls. It didn't sound like I still had a job, even if he hadn't said it in so many words.

Shifting in my seat, I realized I still had Hester's locket in my pocket. I had meant to leave it in my room when the cops had me go up to collect my belongings. It felt wrong to leave it at the manor where Jasper could get it but wrong to take it. I took it. I needed strength more than ever, and every time I looked at the worn locket, I was reminded of Hester's resilience, how, even in her death, she refused to give up until her murderer was caught.

Admittedly, there were still things that didn't make sense to me, like why she seemed to want Jasper and me to be together— the happy look on her face when he was in my bed. She never acted like she was upset or afraid of him, though maybe she just wasn't anymore.

I couldn't believe she had been in the conservatory the whole time. Why hadn't I ever thought of that? It made perfect sense why Jasper never let anyone touch it, saying it was too painful. Yeah, it probably was painful for him to remember how he'd murdered his mother and buried her in her own goddamned garden to decompose with her own plants.

At least, in the end, I'd been able to help her.

Once they exhumed her body, hopefully they would

be able to finally put all of the missing pieces together and charge Jasper. Part of me never wanted anything to do with Blackwood Manor again, but a more curious—and admittedly broken-hearted—part of me needed to know why Jasper had done it. Idiotically, I found myself holding on to a tendril of hope that maybe it had been some sort of an accident, that he hadn't killed his own mother on purpose. Though at fifteen years old, even had it been an accident, there's no possible way he could have buried that body by himself. It was obvious Sowerby had helped him.

When the old man had stormed into the conservatory at the sound of my screams, he had glanced at where I had been digging and then settled his face with a look of resignation. I should have known something was odd about that space. Sowerby refused to be near it whenever he was in the garden. It made sense why he got so jittery and weird when he had been helping me in there.

Looking back, it was obvious he had wanted me to be the one to find her body. That's why he had been nagging Jasper to get a crew in to fix it up…but why? Was it possible he had known about it and wanted justice for Hester, too?

All I knew was that Sowerby had known that body was there the entire time, and the two of them had been covering up Hester's death together.

CHAPTER 26

JASPER

"You'll be out soon; Leon said they can't immediately arrest you without direct, irrefutable evidence such as a weapon or forensic analysis, which they won't get until an autopsy is performed." Sowerby attempted to calm me with his tense, fatherly voice.

"Where is Eliza?" I struggled to relax my jaw enough to speak.

Heaviness loomed in his eyes. "Security confirmed she left the manor."

I focused on a small spot of black on the speckled floor of the police station as I struggled not to come apart at the seams. I was on autopilot. Breathing in and out. Swallowing. Blinking.

I wanted to throw the stiff metal chair I sat in against the wall. I wanted to curl into a ball on the floor and never get up. I wanted to stab something—someone. But more than anything, I wanted to take back the last twenty years and redo them. This whole time she'd been feet away from me. Dead. I wanted to kill my father.

"The girl will be fine; it was a shock. I'm more concerned about how you are, Jasper." Sowerby sat in the chair at the end of the metal desk, wisely bypassing the one nearest me. It was amazing to me that, even now, he could remain calm and poised. I wondered if that was something that came with age or if he had always been this way.

"How do you *think* I'm doing?" I snapped. "I—I thought she was alive the last twenty years of my life, and every second of *every* one of those days, I've hated her for leaving me behind—but she never left." I clenched my fist to stop myself from punching the wall—or sobbing like a baby.

Sowerby remained silent.

"He did this; my father is the one that did this; he killed my mother." I stood, the surge of emotion too strong to remain sitting. "They must've gotten into it that night too. He must've killed her that night, buried her while I was off pouting by the cliff. I could have saved her had I stayed inside. I'll decapitate him, Sowerby," I stated.

Sowerby's eyes were rimmed with sadness as he let out a long exhale. "Why don't you refrain from making any more threats of murder while we are in the police station, barely staying out of a cell as it is? Leon's a good attorney, but he's not that good. Besides, we should wait until the autopsy report before we go blaming Darius."

I turned. My eyes combed over the man's face. "What do you know?"

"Enough," he answered. "We need to find your father immediately."

CHAPTER 27
ELIZA

"You're *not* staying over at that house, Eliza." My mother's tone was sharp. Dominant. Familiar. It was a warning voice before it turned darker.

Don't back down. You back down one time, and you're done.

"I am. Someone sold my apartment and got rid of most of my things." My body felt tired and anxiously buzzed with too much caffeine. I hadn't had a decent night's sleep since I'd left the manor last week.

"Watch your tone, Eliza," she snapped.

I hated my name. I hated hearing her say it like that. I hated that she had chosen it for me. I hated it.

Normally, that would've been all it took. I would have given up, no matter how badly I wanted or needed whatever it might have been. Her words sounded like words to others, but to me, they felt like chains thrashing across the soft spots of my insides. Her cold eyes homed in on mine like a pissed-off viper as she sat across from me at the concrete-topped table in her small kitchen.

I shrank in on myself reflexively, only to press out again, reminding myself why I was here. If my time at Blackwood

Manor had taught me anything, it was that if I could handle shit—like falling in love with a charming, lying murderer while working twelve-hour days next to the buried bones of a ghost who had asked me to help solve her murder—I could set limits with my own mother.

She pushed on. "I sent your flight information over last night. You need to spend some time in nature. I've volunteered you for a trip to the rainforest with EcoSphere. It'll be good for you." My mother's thin lips pressed together, forming a straight line. "What is that shirt? Let me read the label," she said, standing up to tug at my clothes.

I lightly and very carefully swatted her away. "Enough, Mom. I'm twenty-five years old and can wear whatever I want." I tried to sound strong. I'd spent the last two nights researching how to speak with command and authority, but my voice trembled regardless.

Her gaze darkened, the muscles of her mouth pursing together in irritation. "You've been talking to Lucy. There's no one else you'd have gotten this backtalk from but that sister of yours."

She was right. Since I left the manor, I had been speaking with Lucy. I had reached out, feeling lost and alone and needing someone who knew what my mother was like. She had been receptive and even happy to reconnect. There were lots of tears and regrets shared. Talking to her gave me the backbone of support necessary to set these boundaries.

"I actually have."

Her tired-looking eyes widened for a second. "Great, so you're going to turn away from me?" she shouted suddenly. "Go to another country to get away?" Her worn, veiny hands grabbed the back of the kitchen chair for balance.

"Mom, you have to know that not everything is *that* big of a deal. The fertilizer or soil I use is not a reason to get mad at me and freak out," I tried to reason.

Her chair screeched loudly against the kitchen floor. She turned her back to me, nothing new; I frequently made her so angry she "couldn't look at me." I noticed a small shake to her shoulder. She was crying. Again, nothing new, except for the fact that for seemingly the first time ever, it seemed like she didn't want me to see it.

"Mom?" I prepared for her to whip around and start screaming at me like normal.

She left the kitchen slowly and silently.

I didn't know what to do. Nothing like this had *ever* happened—nothing like this entire interaction had ever happened between us. This was different.

Apprehensively, I moved down the hallway to her bedroom. The door was open.

"Mom, I—" My words fell flat when I realized she was sitting on the edge of her bed with a small wooden box open, a photo in one hand. Silent tears streamed down her face.

She wasn't faking. Something out of the ordinary was happening.

"Fertilizer doesn't matter," she mumbled almost to herself with a blubbering sob.

I took a step into her room. It felt like I was in a stranger's room, a place I wasn't normally welcome to go.

"Mom, I—"

"What is Lucy doing? Did you see any pictures of her? Is she healthy?"

I realized with surprise how hurt my mother was over my sister leaving. Her pain had always been covered with anger. Her actions had always led me to believe that she didn't really care—even that she was happy my rebellious sister had left. But now I saw another side to my mother that I had never paid attention to. She was hurt. I'd only ever seen her weaponize her feelings to get what she wanted.

"I didn't get any pictures, but she is healthy as far as I know,"

I answered with renewed confidence. "And no, I'm not going anywhere, not if you can respect my boundaries."

She scoffed before the words had fully left my mouth. "Eliza Arnold, I am *nothing* but respectful of your boundaries. Sorry for loving you so much that I want what's best for you—"

"I love you too, Mom," I cut her off. "But you need to understand that I am my own person. You can't protect me from everything. You have held me so carefully that you've crushed me. From this day on, you will have no input on what I eat, wear, or think; do you understand that?"

"I most—" She couldn't stop herself.

I held up my hand and continued before I chickened out. I was trying, but it was still all incredibly new to me to not just fold at her sharp glare and threatening tone. "You have no say over anything I do from this point on, so you might as well save your breath." I grabbed the pale purple shirt I wore and lifted the fabric. "This is polyester. I've bought five more like it in different colors, mostly because you threw a tantrum and gave away the vast majority of my clothes." My voice was sharp and confident as things I'd only dreamed of saying to her began pushing their way out, eager to be released. I didn't want to hurt her, but I might not get another chance to talk to her while she was slightly more sedate like this again.

"Young lady—"

"I am not a young lady; I am a woman, and if you cannot treat me as such, then I will be forced to cut you out of my life like Lucy did. The choice is yours, Mom. Be respectful of my decisions, or you are out," I said sternly. "And also, I want to get you some help."

Anxiety thrummed in my veins, unsure of what she would do. I'd never, ever confronted or spoken like this to her, and I didn't know how she would react. Thankfully, I was in a direct line to the front door if I needed to run.

Still tense, I waited, knowing this fight between us would

not end so easily and that she would most likely need several reminders—just as many reminders as I would need to keep those boundaries in place.

"I don't need help. I just don't want to lose you, too," she said as she looked at the dresser in front of her. "I only want what's best for you." Her voice was softer, the words spoken from a place within her and not out of manipulation. For the first time in my life, I actually believed her.

"Well, then stop trying to control me." I cleared my throat. "Lucy said she'd be open to talking to you again if we all went to group therapy. We can do it online. She doesn't want to go in circles fighting, and I don't either."

"I don't need therapy," she growled. "You two are the ones who don't know about the world. You think you can do so great out there alone, Eliza, then go ahead. I don't need either one of you. If my only two daughters think I'm just such a horrible mother, then maybe you should leave for good."

Refusing to take the bait, I grabbed my stuff and moved to the door before she really got recharged. I had known she wouldn't change in a day, but it still hurt.

"Think about what I said, Mom. If you don't think that you can respect my boundaries, then we won't have a relationship. I'll call you next week." I let the storm door swing closed behind me as my trembling body got in my car and drove away, barely able to believe I'd just spoken to her that way.

Flying high on adrenaline, my phone ringing startled me, and my stomach dropped. She was calling to scream at me. A hurt animal could still attack.

I pulled the phone from my purse but didn't recognize the number. Most likely, more people from the party were trying to get more information on what had happened.

"Hello?"

"Mrs. Eliza Arnold?"

My face scrunched. "It's Ms., and this is she."

Something about the way the man spoke felt clinical. "This is Deputy Harkin from the Pinehurst Police Department. I was told you were the botanist who was restoring the Blackwood Manor conservatory when the body was found. Is that correct?" he asked with a slight edge of irritation.

I took a sharp turn and pulled into an empty bank parking lot. Oh my god, they knew I took the locket. The same locket that had probably been around Hester's neck when she had been buried, a detail I only recently had thought about.

I gulped. "Yes, that was me."

"Someone at the local botanical gardens, a Dr. Lithgow, has been raising hell, excuse my language. The chief is requesting you come to the crime scene and identify any plants on the conservation list that haven't already gotten destroyed or whatever since you've already been at the scene," he said.

"You want me to go back to Blackwood Manor?" I asked as my chest tightened.

"Yeah, if you don't mind. Any chance you can make it over today? Chief's getting frustrated, and we'll finish soon."

"Uh, yeah. I'm in the car now. I can be there in two hours," I said.

"Okay, thanks, Mrs. Eliza."

"It's Miss—" But he'd hung up.

When I arrived, my nerves were worse than they'd been during the confrontation with my mother. I'd been keeping tabs on the news and knew that Jasper hadn't been charged with anything yet, but I didn't know where he was. I couldn't handle running into him; I *couldn't*. I hadn't been able to stop thinking about him. I had a thousand questions for him, but I didn't think I really wanted the answers to any of them.

A heavyset cop with a pointy, reddish-brown beard met me in the driveway and introduced himself as some deputy something-or-other. I was too worried and filled with nerves to listen very closely.

He guided me around the back of the house to the conservatory. Heavy mud tracks from machinery had destroyed the manicured grass that led to the outside door of the garden.

"Just point to whatever is on the endangered list that you think is still alive, ma'am," he instructed, opening the door for me.

"Still alive," I muttered, my mouth dropping wide in horror as I stepped inside the large glass structure.

"Sorry about everything. The machines had to dig up pretty much all of it to see if there was any more evidence," he added.

My hands covered my mouth as I stepped inside, and the sights and smells hit me like a two-by-four to the head.

"I should have warned you. It reeks in here. They aren't sure what's causing it," he said, squinting his eyes as the scent of decay lingered thick in the air.

"It's the corpse flower. It smells like rotting flesh when it blooms," I mumbled, moving farther into the mess.

A gasp filled my lungs. The corpse flower had been dug up and tossed to the side, where bits and pieces of the already expired purple-red bloom lay torn and limp in a pile of discarded dirt and rocks.

I moved to climb the messy dirt bed to go to it, but the officer stopped me, gripping ahold of my arm.

"I'm sorry, you can't touch anything until we're finished here. Just point, please. Should be at least another few days," he said.

The rare, spectacular bloom of the corpse flower, which only showed every seven to ten years, had gone unappreciated and unseen, and was now lying forgotten in a heap of dirt. It was the most devastating, tragic symbolism of life I'd ever seen; next to it was a large, deep hole where Hester's body had been hidden.

I spun slowly, the images blurring in my head, as I tried to take in the view of trampled, smashed dirt. Nothing was salvageable. Nothing. Even the pavers on the paths had been dug up and tossed in a pile—on top of the shadow ferns and thousand-dollar black-and-white tuxedo pothos.

Every bed had been dug up and discarded, destroyed and murdered, the plants broken, smashed, and dead. When I first came into the conservatory, it had been wild with life. Though forgotten and untamed, it had thrived in its dormancy. It was salvageable.

This was a wasteland.

My months of excruciating back and body pain had been for nothing. The pots of propagations against the wall were all brown and dead with a lack of care for their barely established new roots. My eyes stung. Everything was dead or destroyed.

I had just lost my job at Pinehurst Botanical Gardens.

I struggled to breathe, even though I was panting and heaving. The tears began to fall. The last thing I wanted to do was lose control of myself inside of this manor, but the more I tried to stop them, the more my throat made a loud gasping noise.

"You okay? Mrs....?"

Everything blurred and spun, and worst of all, I was going to cry in front of these men.

The cop pushed open the doors to the manor and sat me down against the wall of the hallway, letting the lightly perfumed air of the hallway calm me.

"Mrs...., uh, just try to breathe. I'm going to get you some water, okay? Wait right here," he said, hurrying off down the hallway as I hyperventilated.

When my breathing finally began to calm, I looked inside the conservatory's glass doors again, unable to believe the state of it. Suddenly my heart leaped into my throat.

Staring back at me from the other side of the glass was the beautiful, moon-colored face of Hester, standing in all her ethereal grace. Wet lines of silvery tears streamed down her own face; she looked sadder than ever.

I scrambled to my feet. Why was she still here? I'd found her body. She was supposed to be happy and resting in peace now. I didn't understand. Why was she *not* resting in peace?

Her dark, flowing waves of midnight hair moved as she shook her head *no* as if in answer to my question.

"No," I answered out loud. "I helped you." My voice fell. I couldn't bear the thought that not only had all those weeks and weeks of labor in the conservatory been destroyed, leaving me without a job, but it had all been destroyed for nothing; I hadn't even helped Hester when I thought that I had.

I hurriedly backed away from her, needing to separate myself from her haunting presence and another glimpse at the wreckage of the conservatory. I needed to get away from here.

"Elaina," a familiar voice spoke.

Shaken, I looked up to see Jasper's father, Darius, looking lost and disheveled in front of me. His shirt was buttoned at an odd angle, and something about him seemed more off than usual.

"Eliza," I corrected.

"Yes, forgive me. Have you seen Jasper? I lost something." An odd absence in his eyes as he spoke made me uneasy. Why was he here? Had he managed to get ownership of the manor? All of the furnishings I could see looked to be the same.

Something uneasy prickled me about his presence, telling me he wasn't supposed to be there.

"Is Jasper home?" I asked, looking around absently and wondering where the cop helping me had gone.

"Help me look for him, will you? I have to tell him something," he asked earnestly, still looking a little out of it.

I agreed with hesitation and followed as he took the steps up to the second level.

"Does anyone know you're here?" I asked gently.

"Yes, I think," he answered absently as he walked down the hall, peeking his head in each door before moving on to the next.

An uneasy feeling pulled at me as I continued to walk farther into the depths of the mansion with him. Something in my chest urged me to not leave him alone. As we turned the corner, taking the stairs to the third floor, something red caught in my vision, moving behind me.

Hester.

I knew it was her. I could feel her presence behind me as I followed her husband up the stairs, the faint, soapy aldehyde scent of Chanel No. 5 following along with us.

I couldn't take it anymore in the hallway and looked back at her, needing to see which expression she held.

Frozen in fear by her sudden closeness, her sad, apologetic eyes met with mine. She reached out, moving as if she didn't really want to, gripped my face, and used her fingers to pry my mouth open until it hurt. I tried to turn and run, but my legs didn't work. Terror gripped me as the ghost roughly pressed her cold, slender fingers into my mouth and down my throat before removing them and fading to nothing before my eyes.

I keeled over, hacking a deep, low intense cough. With my legs suddenly working, I kicked myself away from where she had been, even though she was already gone. What the fuck? Did she just try to choke me?

"That cough," Darius said as he poked his head out of a door and was suddenly at my side helping me up. "Come sit down." He ushered me into a seat inside the room he had stepped out from. "I haven't heard a cough like that since Hester," he said with faraway eyes as he moved to open the balcony doors, letting in a cool and welcome breeze.

As the cool air hit my clammy forehead, my eyes landed on him with curiosity. My voice rasped painfully as I spoke. "Hester used to cough?"

He nodded, looking off at a spot on the wall. "Before we knew she was sick."

My breath caught in my chest. "Hester was sick?"

Darius nodded again. "Do you know where my son is? I need to tell him something before it's too late."

I glanced at the door, wishing desperately that anyone else would be in this room with me. But I plowed on regardless. "Why did you write fake letters to Jasper from Hester?" My chest rose and fell with shallow breaths as our eyes locked. Concern deepened as I saw things were missing from his eyes that should be there.

"You know about the letters?" he asked, though he didn't actually sound surprised.

I nodded apprehensively. "Hester hated roses. It was in all her gardening notes. She even went so far as to write little poems about her dislike of them. I thought it was odd that a Gothic garden wouldn't have a single rose. It was because she hated them, vehemently."

I waited for him to connect the dots, but instead, he squinted at me.

"The wax seal on every letter from you and Hester was a rose. She never would have used a flower she hated to send her love to Jasper."

He smiled, though it didn't hit his eyes, and looked down at his feet. "I should've paid more attention to her and Jasper, instead of working as much as I did. I suppose then I would've listened enough to know the flowers she hated."

"Why did you fake the letters?" I asked nervously.

There was movement outside the door, but I didn't dare look in case Darius turned and saw it too. I needed him to keep talking. Tension crackled across the tops of my arms, causing the hairs to stand tall.

He let out a sigh. "My biggest regret in life was leaving Jasper and being unable to be here for him. The letters were my only way of making sure his mother and I were still parents to him," he said softly. "As much as we could be."

My eyes shifted to the door, but I didn't move my head.

Jasper held a finger to his mouth and disappeared on the side of the doorway, letting me know he was out there but keeping his distance.

"Why didn't you come back?" I asked after making certain Darius hadn't seen Jasper.

Everything about the man was instantly lit with frantic energy. "I couldn't come back. I can't be here, not with her here. They have to put her back; that was her only wish." Tears filled his droopy-looking eyes.

"Hester? What was her only wish?" I asked, trying to keep my voice gentle and steady.

"To be buried in her garden. After we found out how sick she was, that was her only request. To be put to rest among the beauty and flowers of her garden. Of course I agreed. I'd have given her anything she wanted. I—I didn't know what it would do to me." Tears poured down his red cheeks.

"Hester was sick?" I probed.

He nodded. "She had kidney disease, but we didn't know it. She—" His sobbing gasps broke his sentence in half. "She kept getting UTIs, and the doctor prescribed her sulfonamides. We didn't know there was renal impairment, and the drug built up in her system."

"The sulfonamides?" I encouraged him, needing him to keep talking.

He nodded, wiping his wet face with his shirtsleeve. "She developed sulfhemoglobinemia. It leads to oxygen deprivation. She—she suffocated in her own body." His voice cracked with cries that tore into my chest, hollowing it out. "They told us the news after they took her blood, and it was tinted green. It was too late." He crumbled in on himself, covering his face with his hands.

She suffocated in her own body. Her hand around her neck.

Green blood.

The green, coppery-scented liquid that had leaked from her locket.

"I'm so sorry," I whispered, moving to rub his back gently.

The words flowed out of him like a river now. "She had been doing pretty bad and knew the day she was dying. She told Jasper goodbye. We hadn't had enough time to warn him. He was just a kid, and his mother died. She was the love of my life; I didn't know what to do without her. I was supposed to tell Jasper and soften it, but I couldn't do anything. I couldn't stay with her gone. All I wanted to do was make her last wish happen and bury her in the garden," he whimpered. "I panicked that if anyone found out, they'd move her."

Oh my god.

"Jasper didn't know she died."

"Hester and I agreed: Jasper was a loose cannon and was having a hard enough time with other issues. She didn't think he could handle it—thought it'd push him over the edge. I was going to tell him after she passed, but I—I fell apart. I thought I could handle her body being in the conservatory; I thought it would be comforting to have her still with me, but I couldn't. I lost a part of my soul that day. Everywhere I turned, the grief of her being gone was too much. I saw her at my bed, in the halls, in the same red dress I buried her in—her favorite one. I couldn't take it. The next thing I knew, I woke up and was on the other side of the country."

"Oh my god."

"If her death had done that to me, I knew the kid didn't have a chance—he didn't even know she was sick. No one did. I'd built the plant in town to test some new medical advancements, and we were hopeful that they would work. Instead the plant leaked and ruined everything. Caused her so much stress and worry. All our money went into testing for a cure. I decided it was easier that Jasper hate us for leaving than grieving like I was. It was all too much. I just couldn't bring myself to tell him she was gone forever. I still don't believe it myself some days. I was too cowardly to return until I heard about the renovations to the conservatory. I had to come back and make sure she was left in peace." He began to pace erratically. "You don't understand; she's my entire world. The only thing I promised her is broken now. She's not in her garden; they took her." He had moved out to the balcony and was frantically pacing near the edge.

Jasper entered the room, just out of Darius's view.

"You need to tell the police what happened, so no one gets in trouble. They think Jasper killed her. Talk to them; they'll understand," I said, trying to calm him as he continued to freak out. His words became so jumbled and erratic that I couldn't understand him anymore. I was worried he was going to jump.

I looked at Jasper with wide, panicked eyes.

"It's no good now. They moved her. They moved her from her resting place. I came to tell Jasper that I was sorry and that I loved him. I need to go with her. I can't do life any more without either of them in it. I can't do it," he rasped through tears. He stopped and turned, pressing his body against the railing.

"You don't have to; come back this way," Jasper said, suddenly standing in the open doorframe just inside the room.

"Jasper," his father whispered, crying harder.

"Come inside," Jasper said, and I felt the emotions ripple through his deceptively calm voice.

"I didn't know what to do…" Darius trailed off, looking completely broken.

Movement passed behind me. Two deputies stood at the door.

"I know you didn't," Jasper's voice cracked. "Come over here; let's talk about it."

Darius didn't budge; instead, he sat on the railing with a devastated expression. He was going to jump—he'd decided.

I moved toward him. Jasper held his hand up to stop me from moving and startling him.

Hester was suddenly on the balcony, more visible now than before but still faint. I glanced around the room and quickly realized I was the only one who could see her ghost. With a calm expression, she lifted herself to sit on the balcony's wide railing next to her husband. She moved across the railing behind Darius's back and put one hand on his bicep and the other on his shoulder. He jumped a little at the contact, looking to where she had touched him, but seeing nothing, returned his focus to Jasper.

She wasn't going to let him jump; she was blocking him.

"I already lost her; don't make me lose you too." Jasper widened his arms, urging the lost man into them.

Darius broke down completely. In a quick movement, Hester shoved him, and he stumbled across the balcony and into Jasper's arms.

I hurried over and shut the doors behind them, pausing for a second to let Hester in; she strolled through and moved to stand next to her husband and son. I hated that they didn't know she was there with them. I wondered how many times that happened, that our loved ones were standing right with us, and we didn't realize it.

"Mr. Blackwood, how are you doing, sir? Would you mind coming with me? I want to get you somewhere that will make you feel better and ask you some questions if that's all right," a kind officer said, grabbing Darius's arm in a way that appeared nothing but friendly.

"Can my son come?"

"I'm going with you. Let's get you some help, okay?" Jasper said softly, turning back to me with an appreciative nod before turning out of the room and down the hallway with the other men—followed by me and a beautiful, faintly corporeal ghost.

CHAPTER 28
ELIZA

Jasper remained stationed next to Darius as he talked to the police and repeated to them what had happened to Hester.

It was heartbreaking to watch Darius relive the nightmare when he spoke about his company going under after spending every spare penny to their name trying to find a cure for Hester and failing. His eyes grew distant, as if he was unable to cope when he recounted the process of burying the love of his life himself and then the horrific night that followed, eventually unable to stay with her and the guilt he felt when he had left both her and Jasper behind.

Though everyone seemed to feel for the mentally troubled man, Sowerby remained stiff and cold with Darius throughout, understandably still angry with him for leaving Jasper. When asked about it, Sowerby had his own heartbreaking tale of secrets.

"You knew?" Darius asked his old gardener.

Sowerby nodded. "As you're aware, Hester and I were great friends and spent a lot of time together working in the conservatory."

Darius clung to every word, almost as if hearing Hester's name gave him strength.

"She told me when she realized she wasn't going to make it. Confided that she wanted to become one of her plants and be buried beneath the soil. She asked me to check in on Darius and Jasper to ensure they were doing okay. She had managed to get me another live-in job at another large estate." Sowerby cleared his throat, pulling off his dark newsboy hat to run his hands through his short gray hair. "By then, the majority of the other staff had left, with only a few still remaining, and my quarters were empty. I wasn't supposed to stay, but I couldn't leave her quite yet, knowing she was so sick. Whenever I couldn't sleep, I would go to the conservatory and do the upkeep, set up Hester's area so it was all ready for the next day, mostly just filling bottles with neem spray as that's all she had strength for by then. One night, I couldn't sleep again and went to the conservatory. You were already inside. I watched as you refilled the hole. I knew she was really gone. You were burying her where we had just cleared everything and planted the corpse flowers. It was her most prized plant of all of them." He breathed out a sad laugh. "She always had a sense of humor. She'd known the whole time I planted them that that's where she had chosen to be buried. You didn't even understand the irony of her resting under the corpse flowers. It was perfectly her."

He wiped his wet eyes before continuing. "I left. That night I had a dream that Hester was frantic and upset, but none of it made any sense. I came back in the morning to find them arresting Jasper." He was so choked up that he had to collect himself for a few moments before speaking again. He looked at Jasper with loving eyes. "Good thing I did too." He rubbed his eyes. "I could've killed you, Darius. I would have, had I seen you. I still want to," he admitted.

"You knew all along, and you never told me." Jasper's face

was lined with hurt. "You let me believe she was still alive this whole time," he said angrily.

Sowerby's head dropped, unable to look directly at Jasper. "I didn't want the same thing to happen to you that happened to him." He pointed accusingly at Darius. "There wasn't much left of you when I found you; I couldn't bring myself to do another thing that would bring you pain; you should've seen yourself. What if you lost it like your father? You refused to leave the manor, and I couldn't afford anything else. I did the best I could."

"You should have told me she was dead—and in my house," Jasper bit out.

"I cared about you, Jasper; that was all I knew. I was a gardener, not a psychiatrist; I didn't know what the hell I was doing." He raised his voice. "And you know what? I'd do it all over again in a second if it meant I kept you sane. At first, I didn't tell you about your mother because I assumed Darius would come back for you. But after a few weeks, he sent a letter from both of them, and I didn't know what to do but wait it out. I'm sorry."

"I'll never be able to thank you enough for what you've done," Darius said softly to Sowerby, who glared at him.

Jasper took Darius to the hospital with the police. After matching DNA from the bones to the blood found on Jasper's shirt the night of the incident, they confirmed that the autopsy of Hester did reveal her to have sulfhemoglobinemia, an incredibly rare condition that, because of her diagnosed kidney disease, was diagnosed so late it had caused her death. In a morbid way, Hester belonged among her rare plants; she was one of them.

Jasper and I hadn't spoken other than him quickly asking me to stay at the manor until he returned, to which I agreed.

I woke up to the feeling of arms sliding under me, lifting me. Apparently, I had fallen asleep on the couch in the main room. The clean scent of men's soap and sterile hospital lingered in my nostrils as I looked around. Everything was dark; it was late.

"Shhh, it's okay, I've got you," Jasper cooed, lifting me. "I'm sorry. It took longer than I thought."

Feeling the firm warmth of his body holding me as I looked up and took the man in, it felt surreal. I couldn't believe everything he'd been through, and still, he remained so strong.

I moved my legs, trying to stand. "It's late. You've got to be exhausted." I knew I was.

He didn't let me out of his arms and continued holding me against him. I moved away. The poor man had been through enough; the last thing he needed was to take care of me. I wanted to talk to him and clear the air between us so badly, but it could wait.

"Don't go, Eliza." His rough whisper brushed the skin of my forehead. Not one of his stern commands but a plea. "I don't want to be alone tonight." His mahogany eyes suddenly made him look so fragile, so breakable, and I realized that he was struggling even though he wasn't showing it.

I needed no further encouragement. I wrapped my arms tightly around his warm neck, pulling myself up until my chest was smashed against his, my chin resting on his hard shoulder, not letting a wisp of air get between us. I was home.

He easily lifted me then and carried me up the stairs, pausing in the hallway outside of his room. He needed me tonight, and even if we didn't have *us* figured out, I needed him too. We needed each other.

He walked into the room and moved to the right side of his bed, gently setting me down and pulling the cool, thick cotton sheets over me. "Thank you. For everything," he whispered, bending down. He pressed his lips to my forehead, threading his fingers into my hairline before stepping away.

Still, in a cloudy, exhausted daze, I jumped when he tossed a pair of boxers and a T-shirt on top of my legs. "Close your eyes," I whispered.

He glared at me but didn't say a word. I waited until his back was to me, pausing to be a hypocrite and staring for a second when he pulled the shirt over his head and revealed his broad, muscular back.

"Okay," I said with a small smile once I was changed and had thrown my clothes off my side of the bed in a pile. The locket clanked against the floor from inside my pocket. *Shit*. I needed to return that to Hester somehow. After a moment's thought, I decided that I would just leave it in Jasper's room. It wouldn't make any sense to him, and he probably wouldn't realize it was his mother's…

Maybe I should just tell him and risk him being upset that I took it from her. He'd probably think I was an idiot for not realizing her body was buried there after I pulled her locket from the soil—something I had been struggling with feeling myself lately, though I supposed I could cut myself a break for not assuming a garden was the resting place for a corpse.

Jasper lay down, wearing only plaid boxers, causing the bed to dip slightly.

He slid under the covers, pulling the white, airy comforter up to tuck us both in. The room was dark, causing everything to be painted a dark blue where the lights from the night sky illuminated it. Jasper tucked his hand under the side of his face, mirroring me. For a while, we simply soaked in the closeness of the other, the comfort of knowing we were together in the same space again.

"I'm sorry." I broke the comfortable silence, my words barely a whisper.

His brows pulled together. "You don't have anything to be sorry for." Little flecks of light were reflected in his eyes.

He was being kind. I had a lot to be sorry for.

"I thought you did it," I confessed with a heavy heart.

"A lot of people did." He rolled onto his back.

I pushed up on my elbows and leaned over him, forcing him to look at me. "It's not okay. I know you. I know it's not been a very long time, but I know you, Jasper. You'd never hurt anybody you care about even though you want people to think you're tough and uncaring; I know that's not true. I let the rumors sway what I knew. I'm sorry."

His eyes turned on me. "That's not true at all; I would hurt anybody who ever made you sad."

I blushed at his words and the serious look on his face. "Thankfully, that's not true, or you would be very busy, I'm afraid."

He leaned up to get closer to me. "Yes, it is true, Eliza. I meant what I said before. I will *never* let anyone hurt you ever again, and if by some minuscule chance I *can't* prevent it, I promise you, I will hurt them far worse—by any means necessary."

His threat whispered across my lips. Somehow, we had gotten so close that I could see the little dots of stubble beginning to form on his cheek and chin.

His dark eyes locked on my lips.

I wanted to kiss him so badly, but I didn't want it to be while he had a cloud of confusion in his mind from such a chaotic night. It wouldn't be wise to complicate things before we knew where each of us stood.

"You're probably exhausted," I breathed, feeling my own breath ricochet off him in warm puffs.

"I've been tired for a long time." He laid back down, facing the ceiling.

My head pressed against the pillow, I faced him, taking in his handsome features, the flexed muscles of his arms behind his head.

"For twenty years, I've held nothing but hate for my mother, and this whole time—" He closed his eyes tightly, and his jaw hardened. "She didn't want to leave me. She never wanted to leave me. She told me goodbye and that she was going somewhere I couldn't go." His voice broke, and a tear fell from the outer corner of his eye down onto the bed.

"I'm so sorry." I moved closer to him, stroking his hair, unable to keep myself from touching him. My heart ached for what they all had gone through. To see the powerful man so vulnerable and hurt was shattering me.

He moved his arm up to wipe his eyes and grabbed my hand, pulling it against his warm, smooth chest.

"She brought you to me. I know it." His dark eyes poured into me, heavy and full of emotion. "Without you fighting me to work on the conservatory, none of this would have happened, and I'd still hate her. I'd never know the truth about what really happened."

My eyes began to water, and I was instantly grateful for the darkness of the room. "And you don't hate Darius anymore?"

He was quiet for a second. "I don't hate either one of them. I'm still upset. My father did so many things wrong, but I've always considered Sowerby to be my dad and I think that softens the blow for me. He gave up so much for me. I know now that it wasn't my mother's choice to leave me. She did the best she could."

"What are they going to do about Darius? Do you think you'll have anything to do with him now?" I asked.

"On the way to the hospital, he really came unraveled. He's not doing well. It doesn't change anything that I went through or make it any better, but I don't think he's been okay for a long time. In a way, I think things potentially could have been worse for both of us if he'd stayed. I don't know what's going to happen between him and me but knowing everything that I do now…I don't think I can hate him anymore."

He shifted again, turning back to me and reaching his hand out to graze my arm.

"I'm sorry about the corpse flower, the garden, and all your hard work," he murmured.

"Yeah." I sank in on myself, torn with sadness and anger at what had happened to the beautiful plants. "Everyone at Pinehurst is pretty upset. I'm still going to see if I can salvage some seeds or corms from the corpse flowers, but it doesn't really matter. I sold them the ghost orchid you gave me and quit."

He stilled. "Eliza, I know how important your independence is to you, but you don't need the plants; I'll buy the whole fucking botanical garden and fire every single one of their asses. Better yet, I'll put you in charge and you can fire them. Say the word, and it's done. You don't need them."

My heart flipped, and a small, odd-sounding giggle released out of me. Never had I felt so protected and…loved. I knew he would do the same thing for Katya or Leah because that was just the type of man he was, but still, I was part of something special, a family, and in a way, that meant more to me than anything else.

"I'm not sure why you're laughing," he said with a wide, gorgeous smile. "I will destroy them."

"Don't do that."

When he didn't say anything, I turned to look at him.

He lay on his side, staring at me hard, deep in thoughts I wish I could know.

I scooted myself closer and tucked myself against him, my head under his chin, wishing I could pause time and stay here forever.

"Eliza, there's one more thing you need to know."

I moved my head up on his pillow so I could easily look at him.

Slowly, he bent his head and softly brushed his lips against mine before pressing them harder against me. Sparks shot through my body, and I pressed into the kiss, melting us together. I felt his hand brush my hair away from my face, his actions so different from the possessive, rough touches like before. Our lips pressed with need as though our lives depended on it. Like if we separated, one of us would vanish forever.

The emotions deepened with every passing second until they swelled inside my chest. My hands moved and held his face, needing every inch of my skin to touch his and the safety of him.

He broke the kiss, pulling back just enough to pour his gaze into mine.

"I'm in love with you," he whispered with a low voice.

If this is a dream, let me sleep forever.

He kissed me again with what felt like every feeling the world couldn't hold.

"And I love you," I breathed. It felt like someone had opened the cage door and I'd been set free.

When we kissed again, it was unrestrained.

Jasper's hands slid up the skin of my back under my shirt, sparking a match and igniting my blood. My skin hummed where his hands had touched me—like his fingerprints had pressed permanently into me. His gaze dragged over my body like he was relearning every inch.

There was a calm in him now, but not stillness. Never stillness. Even now, in the quiet, his presence vibrated with intensity. He continued to touch me without a word, tracing the dip of my waist, the soft underside of my thigh. His fingers stopped between my legs, and he dragged them over me.

My breath caught.

He didn't smile. Didn't tease. Just watched me. Possessive and quiet.

"I want you like this," he said, his voice low and even, like it was a simple fact. "Open. Soft. Mine."

I trembled, but this time it wasn't fear. It was the weight of everything unspoken between us. What we'd survived. What we'd become.

His hand slid higher, flattening against my sternum. He pressed down—not to hold me there, but like he needed my heart under his palm, like proof I was there.

"Lie still," he said.

I froze, unmoving. I couldn't—not when his tone sounded like a command and a promise all at once.

Jasper moved to sit back on his heels, his eyes devouring me. I still wore his T-shirt. He still had his boxers on. It felt almost obscene, the intimacy threading between us through cotton. The electricity between us was too much and not enough all at once.

He tugged the shirt up over my hips, slow and deliberate, revealing the skin of my stomach, the tightening nipples of my breasts, inch by slow, aching inch. I tried to sit up to help, but he pressed me down again with a single firm hand.

"No," he said, his gaze pinned to mine. "Let me."

He stripped me bare slowly, like he was unwrapping something sacred. When he looked at me, naked and breathing hard, something flickered behind his expression. Not softness, not exactly—more a deep, violent kind of need.

"Do you have any idea what you do to me?" he asked, dragging his hand down my ribs, between my legs, spreading me open with his thumbs like I was something he was about to dismantle.

I whimpered as cool air hit my slick skin. Jasper leaned in, letting his breath ghost over me without touching, his lips so close to my clit it hurt.

"I'll give you what you need," he said, voice now ragged and hoarse. "But you'll take it how I give it."

He didn't wait for me to answer before he ducked his head and devoured me. Slow, precise, and relentless. His tongue moved up my center with devastating control. He didn't moan, didn't praise me, didn't break his focus once. He consumed me like I was the only thing keeping him alive.

My thighs trembled as my fingers clutched at the sheets. I gasped his name, and he only stopped when I came with a cry so desperate it fractured the air between us.

He looked up at me, mouth glistening, eyes dark. "Don't move."

He stood, removing his boxers with the same slow, deliberate restraint that made me ache. His cock sprang free, hard, heavy, and flushed dark at the tip. He stroked it once, watching me watch him. "Hands above your head."

I obeyed. Chest heaving, my body slick with sweat.

"Good girl."

He knelt between my thighs and pressed the blunt head of his cock against my entrance—just barely. My whole body arched for more.

But he didn't give it to me.

Not yet.

Instead, he leaned down, kissed my throat, soft and slow, so fucking slow, and whispered against my skin. "I want you to feel me tomorrow and remember this wasn't just fucking." Then he drove into me in one sharp thrust with a force that knocked the air from my lungs. Thick and deep and claiming. His cock split me open as my body took him with a desperate, wet sound that made his jaw clench.

He didn't say a word at first. Just fucked me—slow and brutal, his rhythm calculated to destroy. He kept one hand on my wrists, pinning them above my head, the other gripping my thigh hard enough to bruise.

Every thrust hit deep, angling upward, designed to make me unravel, and I was close—so fucking close, already dizzy from the stretch, the pressure, the look on his face, like he was worshipping and destroying me in the same breath.

"I'm going to ruin this pussy," he growled against my neck. "You understand me?"

I whimpered something unintelligible.

He pulled back and slapped his cock against my clit once, hard, then shoved it back inside, making me sob.

"You'll think about this every time you fuck yourself," he bit out, dragging his mouth along my cheek. "Every time you come, you'll wish it was me. You'll need it to be me."

His hand slid down lower on my stomach while he kept fucking up into me.

"You feel how well your cunt takes me?" he murmured, voice breaking with raw heat.

I nodded frantically, tears slipping from the corners of my eyes. He moved, licking one off my skin. Just enough to break me open a little more.

"I want to see you fall apart," he said roughly. "Right fucking now."

Then he shifted, hooked both my legs over his shoulders and snapped his hips forward—harder, deeper. Every thrust a perfect, punishing drag along my most sensitive spot.

A scream tore out of my throat.

"That's it," he snarled. "Come on my cock. Let me feel it."

I shattered into a million pieces. My orgasm ripped through me like a live wire, and Jasper didn't stop. He fucked me through it—kept pounding into me, the wet slap of skin against skin echoing in the room, my cunt clenching so hard around him, I could tell he was about to lose it.

He yanked out suddenly and flipped me over. Pressed my face into the sheets, dragged my hips up, and slammed back in.

"Stay right there," he growled, his hand fisting my hair. "I want to watch your back arch when I come inside you."

I was a mess. Trembling and wrecked, panting his name. He thrust twice more, hard and deep, and then he groaned my name like it gutted him. His hips stuttered as he spilled inside me, his cock twitching with every pulse.

We stayed like that, both of us shaking, his chest pressed to my back, his breath hot against my shoulder. Still joined. Still one.

Jasper kissed the dip of my spine, then the back of my neck.

He whispered possessively, "You'll never belong to anyone else." His voice was low and destroyed, like it came from the deepest part of him.

I didn't speak. I couldn't. I just lay there—ruined and trembling, my thighs sticky, my breath still catching in little, helpless stutters.

Jasper pulled out, slow and thick, and watched the way his cum spilled from me, wet and glistening as it trailed down my thighs in lazy rivulets. A muscle in his jaw ticked.

"Fuck," he growled. "Look at that. Still gaping. Still dripping for me." He pressed his palm to the curve of my ass, spreading me wider, watching me pulse around nothing. "That pretty little cunt's trying to find me." Then—without warning—he shoved two fingers back inside of me.

My whole body jolted with pleasure.

I whined, high and overstimulated, but he didn't stop, just held my hips steady, grinding his fingers deep like he could brand me from the inside.

"Breathe," he commanded.

His fingers slid back between my thighs, dragging through the slick mess he'd left inside of me, then pushed deep again, two fingers sinking in slow. My hips twitched, still trembling from the aftershocks.

"You're still open for me," he said, his tone wrecked but controlled. "Still warm. Still mine."

I gasped, arching as his fingers curled, working his release back into me with dark precision. It was obscene with quiet, focused intensity that made it feel like worship.

"Let me stay in you," he whispered, dragging his mouth along my neck. "You let me in. Now you keep me there."

My whole body clenched around his fingers, and he groaned softly, slowly fucking it deeper into me. When he finally pulled out, slick and shining, he lifted me effortlessly into his arms.

I didn't protest, just curled into him, limp and spent as my cheek pressed to his chest and he settled us back against the pillows. He tucked one hand beneath my thighs, the other cradling my head, his grip possessive even in rest. His lips found my hair.

Just before my breath evened out, before my lashes fluttered shut, I felt the word against my skin.

"Mine."

Soft. Final.

And this time, it didn't feel like a threat.

It felt like home.

CHAPTER 29

JASPER

It was unique to wake up the following day and not feel the firm grip of hatred crushing my chest. Instead, a small, perfect woman lay with her mouth open on my chest, making small, raspy huffs that were something between a snore and a breath. Strands of frizzy brown hair fell over her face; some had gotten sucked into the wetness of her mouth, and other strands flapped like a flag following her inhales and exhales, tickling her lips. My hand moved to brush the hair away. I wanted to see her beautiful face, but I didn't want her to move and wake up, so I put my hand back on the bed.

I thought about everything that had happened yesterday, all of the information that came out. It was overwhelming. In a matter of a few sentences, my whole life had changed.

I think I'd had every emotion filter through me: shock, devastation, horror, disgust, guilt...but mostly relief. Then the guilt and devastation circled back around.

Mom hadn't left me—not really.

For all these years, I'd hated her so much. I'd hated them both for leaving me to die and not giving a shit what happened to me, but somehow her leaving had always hurt a little worse, maybe because she left first, even if it was only a few hours before my father. I was just a kid and that was my mother, the most caring, wonderful person in my life. I never understood what I'd done to make her stop loving me. It had been so easy for me to believe that they had left because of what a shit kid I was. I was angry and hurt. They should have told me she was sick. I could have helped somehow. I wished more than anything she were still around so that I could tell her how sorry I was for hating her all of these years. I wished I could hug her just one last time and tell her everything would be fine.

Eliza made a soft gagging sound and rolled her face into my armpit, clinging tighter to me.

Everything *would* be fine. Had Eliza not come into my life, I would have never known about my mom. I probably would never have seen my father again—or been able to get him the help he needed. I let out a heavy breath and felt a little different. Had Eliza not pushed her way into my office and desperately demanded that I let her fix the conservatory, none of this would have happened.

I shifted her head carefully onto my shoulder and pulled her tighter against me.

I would never let her get away from me. We would go pick up her stuff after she woke up and bring it back here. I couldn't stand to not have her with me; we'd technically already lived together. I would be slow and cautious with her; both of us had our own set of problems from our pasts, but even though I wanted her to feel comfortable and do things at her pace, I couldn't help the way I was around her. I needed her. I already knew she's the only one I wanted to be with, and I'd do anything it took to keep her safe and happy forever. But I wouldn't pressure her. She'd had enough of that from her mother. This needed to be done carefully. I wanted her happy.

She'd need a job, because I didn't want her to feel trapped ever again—like she was reliant on someone else. I'd lived a whole life of doing whatever the fuck I wanted. I wanted that for her, and I would go to any means necessary to make certain I delivered.

An idea sparked in my mind, and I grabbed my phone from my nightstand to fire off a text, telling Sowerby to set up some things with the media. My teeth ground together out of habit. I fucking hated the media, but if Eliza gave the green light, then I was going to use them to my advantage.

"Hey, friend," Eliza teased sleepily.

I tossed my phone back on the nightstand and pulled her closer, kissing her softly.

She pushed me away and covered her mouth with her hand. "You can't kiss me. I have morning breath."

I grabbed her hand and moved it, kissing her again, forcing my tongue inside her mouth. Savoring the taste of her. She giggled happily and it surged up into her sky-blue eyes.

I'm going to make her my wife one day.

I knew it like I knew leaves would fall in autumn or that rain falls from the sky. It wasn't a question but a fact. I'd never let her get away from me.

"What are your plans for the day?" I asked. I didn't want to rush things and scare her away. I knew her. I knew what would make her start to overthink. She couldn't help it.

She let out a long exhale. "I need to go back to Nick's and change. I have an interview at Bernard's, that plant store in Johnstown. Other than that, nothing. Why? You need some help here?" She peered at me, hopeful.

"Do you want to work with plants still? I thought you hated it?" I prodded.

"I don't hate it. I love looking at the plants; it's just not my passion. It's my parents' passion. But it's the only thing I'm qualified to do that will earn me any money, so I don't really have a choice," she said, looking a little defeated.

"Fuck your interview."

She snorted. "Says the millionaire."

I smiled, resisting the urge to grab her and kiss her senseless, morning breath and all.

"Let's go get your stuff from Nick's. I've got an idea that I'll tell you about on the way there." I wanted to demand it, and it would happen regardless, but I needed this to be her decision.

"All my stuff?" Her eyes grew worried. "Jasper, as much as I would want to, I can't move in here and mooch off you, and the nearest job is at least two hours away."

"Come on. Let's get some breakfast, and I'll tell you my idea. If you aren't into it, we'll figure something else out. But I need to call my landscapers really quick."

CHAPTER 30

ELIZA

THREE MONTHS AFTER JASPER HAD MOVED ME INTO BLACKWOOD Manor, he pitched his brilliant idea to me—an idea that at the time had seemed like a dream. Now, it was making my stomach tighten with nerves. "Okay, but can you bend your waist back more and look at me?" I was struggling. The paintbrush kept slipping and adjusting in my sweaty, nervous hand and messing the whole thing up. I adjusted in my seat, trying to get a better look at Hester's nose. Painting noses sucked.

My foot bumped into the A-frame easel, nearly knocking down the whole thing. I jumped to grab it, kicking my brush washer and splashing dirty water all over my foot.

"Fuck!" I tossed the brush in my hand on the grass and ran my hands over my face. Thankfully it had only spilled in the backyard.

What was I doing? I didn't know what I was doing. This was going to be the most embarrassing night of my entire life. If it weren't for Jasper's obnoxiously enthusiastic support, I doubt I would have even attempted to pursue painting. Not because I didn't love it—from now on, I would always paint, but I never would have had the sheer audacity to try and make a career out of it, especially not until I was good. Don't get me wrong, I knew I wasn't awful by the reactions of others, but I couldn't help but feel I was tricking them somehow and that if they looked too closely, they would see what a fucking fraud I was.

For the last month and a half, Jasper had been the most supportive, encouraging boyfriend on the planet. He was ambitious and caring, and I wasn't going to fault him for wanting to help me; the problem was that he was blinded by love, and no one else at the party tonight was in love with me. It was okay; I had agreed to try it, and he had agreed that if it didn't work out, I could sell and ship propagations and starters from the conservatory.

Plants are amazing. You can plow them over, cut them down, and dig them up, and if they are strong enough and want to be there, they pull through—kind of like people. The number of plants we were able to save after the police had left the conservatory was shocking. We found a forty-pound root ball still intact from the discarded corpse flower bloom and were able to save one of the others. Jasper's landscapers had the entire garden back together and looking incredible in two weeks. Had I not been so grateful that I hadn't had to do it all—again—I would have been quite upset since it had taken me over two months. It was fun to go in and enjoy the plants for their beauty and not have to take care of them.

Instead, I started painting them.

The locket in my pocket warmed.

"No. Stop doing this, or I'll start painting you without a nose," I grumbled into my hands. "You don't have to pose anymore; I got what I needed. Ow!" The locket burned.

I glared at the smiling, nearly fifty percent transparent ghost woman and pulled the locket from my pocket. I opened it up, expecting Hester's usual words of encouragement—she was worse than her son—and looked back up, unable to hold back my laughter.

My nose isn't that big.

I returned the locket to my pocket and smiled at the ghost.

Hester still hadn't left yet; I was still the only one who could see her.

Selfishly, I didn't want her to leave. She was happy and wonderful and in an ironic turn of events...my muse.

It started when I grabbed a black calla lily before it got planted and set up to paint it. Most of the painting I had ever done was of flowers, and I was happy with how it had turned out, though it felt a bit boring. I wanted to learn how to paint things other than plants. Hester had appeared as she often did now, and I got the idea to practice painting people with her. When I asked if I could paint her, she was thrilled. She literally lit up the whole room, her whole body brightening. Besides that, she could stand in the same position for hours, and sometimes I couldn't get it right, and it took a really long time. If that hadn't been enough of a reason to keep painting her with the flowers, Jasper's reaction was. Of course, I had to lie and say I'd used one of the pictures in her old notebook, which Hester was kind enough to supply, but the painting had brought Jasper to tears—stiff, angry tears, but tears—which then brought his mom to tears, which then of course brought me to tears.

He hung the picture in the hallway outside of our room, and every time he walked past it, he talked to her as if she could hear him—which she could, but he didn't know that.

Seeing the way something I created has helped him heal even a little bit has done more for me than I could ever explain.

The paintings we were—*I was* showcasing tonight were all of the flowers from the garden with a beautiful woman in a red dress growing out of them. The showcase was Jasper's brilliant idea.

Tonight, art agents, dealers, collectors, wealthy patrons, and some influential figures in the art world were all coming to a private showing of some unknown artist that the media apparently had been buzzing about.

Me.

Utterly ridiculous, but seeing how Hester and Jasper had reacted to the painting made me agree to it. I loved doing it, so it had been fun and easy to make more. I had five paintings in total that would be shown tonight. Jasper, being the businessman that he was, made sure it was okay if he sold them tonight, to which I agreed and laughed.

No one was going to buy them; I didn't have a single raised hope for any of this. To be honest, I had been dreading tonight after the first week passed, and I realized Jasper was one of those types who followed through with the wild things they said they would do.

"What are you doing out here still? People are arriving, and you need to get dressed," a feminine voice called out as they came up behind me.

The best part of it all was that my sister, Lucy, had flown in and was staying with us for a week.

"Eeek! This is all so exciting and proper!" She laughed. "They have classical music playing and champagne set up on that big round table in the entryway."

We went inside, and Lucy helped get me into my dress. She was a hairstylist and couldn't help herself from styling my hair and doing my makeup. It felt like we were kids again—or at least how it should have been when we were kids.

My mom and dad weren't coming; they hadn't been invited. Mom and I didn't talk. And that was okay. I still held out hope that one day she would change and be able to have a conversation with me that didn't leave me in tears, but for now, we couldn't, and that was okay too. Some days, it was harder than others, but reconnecting with Lucy had made it easier. I was going to miss her so much when she left, but apparently, Jasper had a house in London, not too far from where Lucy and her husband lived.

CHAPTER 31

ELIZA

Inside the manor, it had finally quieted. The buzz of excitement and celebration left, and in its wake was the rosy exhaustion of happiness. I was vibrating in pure disbelief from the success of the night.

It had been an intimate event, and apparently, the fact that no one was ever invited to the manor significantly increased the prestige. It was almost comical. Of course, Jasper was an absolute genius at saying the right thing at the right time to the right people. It was magical to watch how he handled some of these wealthy, stuffy people—though not all were stuffy. I met possibly the coolest human on earth—Emily, who wore cool, flowing pants and had a sharp black bob with bangs. She wanted to be my agent. She was really persistent after a rich friend of Jasper's bought one of my paintings for fifty thousand dollars.

FIFTY THOUSAND DOLLARS!

I think Jasper may have put him up to it, but I honestly was too floored to care. That was what I made in a year at the botanical gardens! It was enough that I would have time to figure out what I wanted to do. I couldn't believe it.

I stood at the threshold of the conservatory, the door slightly ajar, letting in the chill of the night. The moon cast long silver shadows across the manicured lawn outside, while the faint scent of fresh earth lingered in the air. Inside the conservatory, the quiet hum of life filled the space with the faint rustle of leaves. It was the kind of stillness that invited reflection. It was perfect.

I had come to love this time of night, the moment when the world seemed to settle. It was definitely one of my favorite times to be in the conservatory, to take notice of the beauty that had bloomed not only in the soil, but in me.

I looked over the smattering of plants and flowers, the sprawling vines and ivy, and I marveled at how it had all come together, how, even after devastation, it had been put back together. The garden was an ever-changing landscape, but more than that, it was a symbol of my journey, a reflection of everything that had grown and changed in my life.

When I had first arrived here, broken and lost, this space had been nothing more than a collection of neglected soil and wild growth, abandoned and forgotten. I had come to the manor unsure of who I was or what I wanted. My family and my struggles had seemed so consuming and definitive within me that I had no idea how to heal the parts of me that had been shattered—no idea that I could.

But somehow, this garden—this strange, beautiful, wild place—had taken me in. It taught me in ways I hadn't understood at first. Something wild grew from the wreckage, and it was me.

When I took on the conservatory as a project, I had no idea it would teach me so much that had nothing to do with plants. I learned that the weeds were part of the process—they came with the blooms, but with careful attention, I could pull them out and make space for new growth. I learned that plants, like people, sometimes needed time to heal and that it didn't always happen as quickly as I wanted. They needed the right environment, care, and space to stretch toward the light, like Jasper and me.

I smiled softly to myself, remembering the first thing I had planted: a tuxedo pothos. The soil had been hard and dry, terrible to work with. The air of the conservatory had still been thick with a sense of abandonment. But I had dug into it, loosening the earth, giving it room to breathe. It was a simple act—planting a starter plant—but it felt monumental to me. It almost felt like I was planting something within myself that had long been buried and neglected. It was an act of hope, a belief that I, too, could finish the conservatory and grow again.

The garden transformed one flower at a time, one plant after another. And so did I. I started to let go of the things that weighed me down, and in doing so, I inadvertently made room for new things to take root.

I walked along the winding path that led deeper into the middle of the garden, taking note of all the plants I had managed to salvage. I looked at where the corpse flowers were; to the untrained eye, they didn't look like anything special right now. The corpse flower had served as my beacon of hope. When I thought that I couldn't keep going and thought I had nothing left to give, they reminded me of resilience. They grew in imperfect conditions with minimal care. And yet, they thrived in the chaos.

Through all of this, I learned that growth wasn't always linear. It wasn't about constant progress or perfection. Sometimes, growth came in fits and starts, in quiet moments of reflection, in gentle self-compassion. I had learned to forgive myself, to recognize that because I was broken, it didn't mean I couldn't heal. This garden had taught me that. Just as the plants grew in their own way, at their own pace, I had learned to trust my own rhythm.

I remained standing where the giant corpse flower had

once bloomed. It had been a difficult moment when I'd seen it destroyed—a symbol of loss and grief that had overshadowed everything else. But even that had its place in my story. The flower had been torn apart by forces beyond my control, yet something remained—something vital that could still be saved.

The garden was alive, not just with plants, but with memories and love and growth.

I looked around as I inhaled the comforting scent of soil and hard work and noticed the familiar fragrance of Chanel No. 5.

I let my eyes mist over with gratitude for all that had come from Hester and this adventure. I looked at the empty patch of soil where her body had been, so bare and lonely amidst the green sea of vines and life inside the revived conservatory, and a wave of happiness hit my heart. Even though the soil looked empty, this part of the garden had grown and healed more than any other plant in the conservatory. It had healed people, and Jasper was one of them.

I had struggled tirelessly, deciding what to plant in the place where we had found Jasper's mother, but nothing felt important or special enough to go there, so it remained an empty plot.

"There you are," said Jasper as he stepped into the conservatory. "Have you started without me?"

I smiled, something I found myself doing a lot more often now. It was amazing what could come from being loved.

I met him in the middle of the garden and wrapped my arms around his neck, kissing him tenderly. A mysterious light breeze drifted through the conservatory, causing the leaves and branches to flutter as if in applause. Our kiss deepened instantly, as it always did. A train could've passed through the glass, and neither of us would've noticed as long as we were in each other's embrace. Time seemed to stand still.

Flushed now, I pulled back. Tonight was special for so many reasons. We had received Hester's ashes back, and it seemed like the time to tell him about seeing her and the locket. I was tired of being worried he would find the locket and get upset with me, and I wanted him to know that Hester was still with him—literally. She followed him around almost constantly.

True fear had wriggled into my chest. I hadn't kept it from him to hurt him, but what if it did? The thought made my stomach flip and twist. I didn't want any secrets between us.

"I have to tell you something, and I should've told you sooner, but—" My voice trailed off as I dug around in the pockets of my jacket. The locket was gone. Where was the locket? I had just had it.

"I have to tell you something too," he said, still a little dazed from our kiss, completely oblivious to the fact that my face had paled as I furiously searched my outfit.

How could the locket have slipped from my pocket? I had just had my hand wrapped around it a second ago. There was no way that it had come out in the quiet of the garden. I would have noticed.

I suddenly noticed the wispy blur of Hester moving to stand in the middle of the conservatory. The leaves all gave another happy shake as a cool breeze rushed through the garden.

Hester Blackwood glowed like a beacon, emotion dancing in her eyes. She gave a slow nod, and then she winked at me before a smile broke out on her face like I'd never seen. She was as solid and lifelike as I was, no longer transparent, her eyes shifting to the ground in front of me where her son was.

"What's this?" Jasper's voice was filled with wonder as he lifted the gold locket from the soil of the empty flower bed.

Seeing what he pulled from the dirt, my head snapped back to look at Hester—but she was gone.

"Look," Jasper said. "It looks like a locket—your locket."

"I have to be honest with you. I found it in here when I first started… It was your mother's."

Jasper pried open the piece of jewelry and, with a thoughtful expression, tilted his head to the side. "Huh…"

"What does it say?" I asked, my eyes unable to move from where they'd latched onto Jasper's face.

"My heart can finally dance in stillness." He glanced up.

She was telling us it was time for her to go. Hester had finally found peace. This whole time she had stayed until Jasper knew the truth and was happy.

"I think it means she's at peace."

He handed me the locket, eager for me to see. "What should we do with it? Would you like it?"

I looked thoughtfully at the locket. "I think we should bury it where it belongs, with her ashes, if you're okay with that."

To me, there was no other place for Hester than back in the garden she loved so dearly. She deserved to be at peace among the moss and vines like she'd always wanted.

"I am, but are you comfortable with her being here?" he asked.

I felt the creases tighten around my eyes as I smiled at his thoughtfulness. "Why would it matter if I'm comfortable with it? It's your home."

"Because it matters." Jasper's voice tickled across the back of my neck and shoulders. "This is your garden now."

When I turned to face him, he was pulling a small velvet ring box from the inside pocket of his jacket and bending down on one knee—the position he had been in when he found the locket. It was why Hester had looked down and winked at me.

"Eliza, will you marry me?"

I froze, my breath catching in my throat as I stared at Jasper. His words, the meaning of them, settling slowly into my heart like the quiet stillness after a storm. For a moment, I couldn't speak. I couldn't move. All I could do was look at him—at the man who had given me love when I didn't know how much I needed it.

His eyes were soft with vulnerability, his hand still holding the ring box, trembling ever so slightly as if he, too, was unsure of my answer. But I could see the hope in his eyes, the same hope that had carried us both through the most challenging times.

I took a slow step toward him, my pulse thrumming in my ears. The conservatory was still warm with the fragrance of Chanel No. 5 and earth. It felt like the world was holding its breath. Then, I lowered myself to one knee just as he had done.

"Yes," I whispered, the word breaking free from the tightness in my chest. "Yes, I'll happily marry you."

The smile that spread across his face was more beautiful than I had ever seen from him, and in that moment, I knew I was home—not just in the manor, not just in the garden, but in his arms. He slid the ring onto my finger with a tenderness that made my heart swell. Then, he pulled me into his arms, kissing me deeply as though we had both waited lifetimes for this moment. Because we had.

When we finally pulled apart, we stood there for a long moment, and the wind picked up again, the leaves fluttering around us in a joyful, gentle applause.

"I think she's happy now," I said softly, glancing down at the empty patch of soil, still tender with the memory of Hester.

Jasper squeezed my hand, his voice thick with emotion. "I know she is." He smiled, but there was a bittersweetness in his eyes, the kind that only love, loss, and healing can bring.

We looked down at the patch of soil again. It was time.

Together, we dug a small hole in the earth, the soil warm under our hands, the scent of the garden thick in the air. The sounds of the conservatory seemed to fade as if the world itself was returning her with us.

When the ground was ready, he handed me the urn. I took it from him, my hands trembling. I looked at him, a question in my eyes.

"It's where she belongs," he said, his voice a quiet certainty.

Together, we carefully poured her ashes into the earth of the garden, the delicate dust mingling with the soil. I hesitated for a moment, holding the locket in my hand, then slowly, reverently, I placed it in her ashes.

As I did, the locket clicked open.

Inside, nestled in the delicate folds of the locket, was a small round seed—one I hadn't seen before. It was a deep shade of green, almost translucent, with a faint shimmer to it, like it held some kind of hidden magic. My heart raced. Jasper looked at the seed in wonder, and together, we gently placed it into the soil, covering it up carefully. The moment was sacred—we were part of something bigger, something mysterious.

"She's...she's still with us," I said, my voice trembling.

Jasper's hand found mine again, and he squeezed it tightly. "I think it's her way of giving us something new. Something beautiful one last time."

Months passed, and the memory of that quiet moment in the conservatory stayed with me. The garden continued to thrive, growing more lush and vibrant with each passing day, but the empty plot held our attention the most. We kept an eye on it, watching the soil, waiting.

And then, one day, we saw it.

A small shoot had sprouted. At first, it seemed like any other plant, but we noticed something extraordinary as it grew. The leaves were delicate and heart-shaped, soft to the touch, their edges curling inward as if cradling a secret.

Then the flowers bloomed.

They were unlike anything I could identify—tiny heart-shaped petals in a warm blush of dark red, veined with black, and the unmistakable scent of Chanel No. 5. It was as if the essence of Hester's love and spirit had taken root in the earth, blooming in a form that was both beautiful and unexpected.

Jasper stood beside me, his hand in mine, as we looked at the new life that had sprung from the soil, the plant blooming with such delicate grace. He leaned in and whispered, "She's here, isn't she?"

My voice was thick with emotion. "She's always here."

EXPLORE JENEANE O'RILEY'S INFATUATED FAE SERIES

HOW DOES IT FEEL?

PROLOGUE

CALLIE

THE DAMP FLOOR OF THE DUNGEON MADE IT HARD TO KEEP the tiny cuts of cheese on my mini charcuterie board. I suppose it was less of a board and more of a loose brick from the back wall, but the rat that visited this cell wouldn't mind.

I laughed out loud at how cute it looked with the little bits of cracker and honey saved from my meal yesterday. My muscles froze. I immediately berated myself for the laughter that had slipped out.

It didn't like when I made noises. When I made noises, it woke up. It had told me they would hurt me again if I made any more noise. I pressed my body into the faulty shelter of the dungeon's shadows.

My fingers poked the open, bloodied wound on my head as a firm reminder of its horrible capabilities.

A deep inhale stretched my sinewy ribs as I imprinted my fingernail sharply into the wound. I bit the iron cuff around my wrist to muffle my cries as the metal tang of blood swirled with the bite of iron in my mouth.

Good; I still felt something. My taut muscles relaxed the faintest amount.

The iron chain between my cuffs clanged loudly against itself with my slight movement.

Blackness immediately consumed me as my eyes shut so tightly that tiny flecks of light speckled the back of my eyelids. The hard stone wall dug into my flesh. I pressed harder, willing it to swallow me up so I would no longer be inside the fear-laced cell of this dungeon.

Had I caused him to wake?

A few stray tears escaped my eyes as my body trembled.

Fuck. Fuck.

I shook so hard, I threatened to wake him simply with the rattle of my bones.

Be quiet or it will wake and hurt you again.

ACKNOWLEDGMENTS

Murphy, I love you endlessly. Grammy, every book I write is because of you.

I want to thank my husband; I would be incapable of any of this if it were not for your help, love, and patience. My kids for dealing with the chaos and being so wonderful. My amazing publisher and everyone that has helped to make these books come to life. My incredible editors, you deserve swords and medals for the work you do. A HUGE thank-you to my readers, I am forever grateful for you. Thank you for loving these stories as much as I do.

—J

ABOUT THE AUTHOR

Jeneane O'Riley is a #1 bestselling author of whimsically dark and romantic fantasy books. Her love of storytelling began as a small child, dreaming up glorious fantasies to fall asleep to. As she has grown older, her love of storytelling remained, but the tales have grown more dangerous and full of toe-curling tension.

She is a hobby mycologist and nature enthusiast who resides in Ohio, at least until she can locate a proper bridge to troll, or perhaps a large tree spacious enough to hold her smoke show of a husband, her Irish wolfhound, pet dove, and of course, her three children.